Hell Blade
The Trilogy of the Void Book Three
Peter Meredith

Peter Meredith

ISBN-13: 978-0983707295

Fictional works by Peter Meredith:

A Perfect America
The Sacrificial Daughter
The Horror of the Shade Trilogy of the Void 1
An Illusion of Hell Trilogy of the Void 2
Hell Blade Trilogy of the Void 3
The Punished
Sprite
The Feylands: A Hidden Lands Novel
The Sun King: A Hidden Lands Novel
The Sun Queen: A Hidden Lands Novel
The Apocalypse: The Undead World Novel 1
The Apocalypse Survivors: The Undead World Novel 2
The Apocalypse Outcasts: The Undead World Novel 3
The Apocalypse Fugitives: The Undead World Novel 4
Pen(Novella)
A Sliver of Perfection (Novella)
The Haunting At Red Feathers(Short Story)
The Haunting On Colonel's Row(Short Story)
The Drawer(Short Story)
The Eyes in the Storm(Short Story)

Hell Blade

Prologue

As her father had once done, the blonde was out of the house by six in the morning, putting the road through its paces. The black top was cool that early and it was some time before the sweat started to work its way from the pores of her wonderfully tanned skin. After eight years in the desert, she sported an Arizona bronze throughout even the deepest days of winter.

Not that they ever had real winter in that state. More like a few weeks where she switched out her ever-present shorts for a comfortable pair of loose jeans. Always loose—so she could move. Nothing bothered her more than being constricted, or bound.

A stray breeze left over from the cool of the night tickled her calves just as the sun peeked out from behind a far hill. It would be a fine day, a hot one, an exact replica of the previous. Change was slow coming to the desert and that was just fine with her. If she had a wish, it was for summer never to fade; the cold was just something she didn't miss. The autumn trees changing to gold—that she missed. Rivers of leaves flowing at the whim of the wind, the pumpkins lit on a brisk all hallows eve, a tall fire on Christmas morning—these she missed.

But never the cold. She had felt cold that even the rawest New York winter paled in comparison too. The memory brought with it a shiver and she involuntarily picked up the pace, as if she were running from a ghost, instead of a memory.

Blowing hard, she crested the worst hill of the lot, the one her father had called, *The Ole Bitch* back when he used to run. It was aptly named. Long and steep. It was only the year before, when the blonde was thirteen that she first conquered it; the pain of that made her question why she ran at all. In truth, she didn't know why she pushed herself along that road every morning.

It certainly wasn't the view. That was the problem with the desert not having anything resembling seasons, the view never changed. The scenic panorama afforded her at the top of *The Ole Bitch* was the same on the fourth of July as it was on New Year's day.

Only it had changed that day.

Two hundred yards down the slope, sat a rusted out four door Chevrolet. It was half off the road, idling crooked, looking as if it held in its dark chamber any number of sinister possibilities. Without missing a stride, the girl crossed to the other side of the road, keeping her blue eyes sharp on the car. She began to lope, working her breathing into an easy rhythm, half conscience of the fact that she was preparing to flee. It was only half conscience because she was always preparing to flee.

Now, a hundred yards closer, a man climbed out of the Chevrolet. His outfit: jeans and blue work shirt was almost the state uniform of Arizona and seemed ordinary enough. His tan however didn't. He was too light. Had he been blonde, or even Mexican, she would've kept going along the road. But he was too light. Black hair and white skin.

In a flash, she dodged off the road and dug in her toes, clawing up the half-sand embankment. At the top, the rugged hard scrabble of the desert lay out, going on forever in front of her. She didn't hesitate. For her the desert held no fear, after all it was only sand and stone. She ran. Despite the terrain, she ran surprisingly light, keeping away from the loose dirt and holding to the bare rocks when she could. The running shoes she wore made barely a mark as she passed over low bushes or leapt the maze of shallow gullies and now she began working up a good lather. In seven minutes, the road was a mile behind and was a barely visible black line.

The man looked after the skinny blonde, but didn't follow.

Chapter 1

Will

The phone in Will's hand rang and rang.

Like a dentist's drill, each of those shrill sounds bored into mind, painfully, and he thought that if the torture were to go on much longer, his head would split open, right down the middle. Yet he waited with patience, despite the pulsating agony of his hangover and the pain of his beating. Lisa would pick up any second. Now, the fifth ring, and on to the sixth; they didn't own an answering machine.

His pulse beat into his brain and he closed his eyes, running his good right hand across his battered and swollen face. The scene in front of him, a jumbled mess of a motel room; knocked over chairs and lamps, an over turned desk, brought with it the sad memories of a dead man. He had been a good man. The ninth ring, she should have picked up by then. That little fear, the tiny squiggle he had tried to ignore when he first pulled himself out of his soot-covered bed, was no longer so little. Eleven rings.

"Hello, Will."

"Hel..." he stopped in the middle of his greeting. The voice on the other end of the connection wasn't Lisa's.

Like magic, the hangover was gone, as was the dull ache from his many injuries. The fingers of his left hand, so recently dislocated in his fight with the evil Talitha, went numb. His sternum, deeply bruised from a bullet, no longer throbbed with each breath and unaware, he rubbed the spot where he had been shot point-blank by the good Talitha. He had been saved only by the heavy pewter cross that he once wore and now he felt naked and vulnerable without it.

"Who is this?" Will whispered into the phone.

"What? You don't know remember me? I'm so hurt."

The voice was light, airy, as if the owner of it was in the best of moods. It was a woman's voice and it wasn't the least bit familiar. It certainly wasn't a friend of his wife's. Lisa had no real friends. A few acquaintances perhaps, but in all the time they had lived in Bangor, she had made no lasting friendships.

And it was no one Will knew.

"I suppose it has been a while," the woman said vaguely, leaving the question of her name up in the air.

"I'm sorry, but I don't know you...can you put Lisa on?" He didn't know why he bothered asking. He *knew* it wasn't going to happen. The woman's insincere laughter was about to come through the cheap piece of motel plastic next to his ear and she was going to add...

"Ha, ha, ha, ha. No, I don't think so. She's...indisposed at the moment. And really, it's you and me that need to talk some things over."

That fake laugh. That obnoxious sound. That was familiar. But with his mind being pulled between fear and confusion, he still couldn't place it. "Indisposed? I really should talk to...who is this?"

To Will's left, a silent movement. His sister, Talitha, the good one...the only one now, walked in from the adjoining motel room. Her entire aspect was blackened and it looked as if she had just been pulled from a burning building. Beneath the soot, her normally tan face was white.

"That's Amy Harris," Talitha whispered with a nod to the phone.

"How do you...?" Will bit back the question.

But he knew how. Talitha, from thirty feet away, through the thin motel room walls had heard and recognized the tinny sounding voice coming through the phone. Her hearing was amazing, beyond human, beyond anything.

"Amy?" The word croaked from his throat.

"Very good," she gushed. "It's been so long...tell me, how long has it been?"

Her tone was still light, but her words were great blocks of stone that she hurled at him with the intent to cause pain. She knew how long it had been since they'd seen each other last. They both knew. It was two days after he'd stabbed her mother to death. That had been eight years previous, but it could've been a thousand years and he still wouldn't forget that day.

How Amy had been able to connect her mother's disappearance with him, he hadn't a clue. However, two days after the corpse of Henny Harris had been burnt down to ashes; Will had run into Amy, an accident he had taken pains to avoid.

Her eyes, red with sorrow, had locked onto his without the pretence of disguising her unspoken accusation. She knew. Somehow, she knew. After mumbling something to her, he couldn't remember what, he had practically run away, as if the ghost of her mother was at his heels.

"It's been...a while," Will mouthed the words into the receiver, not knowing if actual sound had come from his moving lips. He had no strength in his lungs, or in his body for that matter and he sat down upon the room's only bed.

Amy Harris was in his home.

At any time that thought would've left him weak from guilt, but now, not even seven hours after confronting a demon, the same demon Amy's mother had unleashed so many years ago, Will lacked the strength to stand. This wasn't a coincidence.

After a second, he added, "What are you doing there? And what do you mean, Lisa's indisposed?" Just asking the question aloud caused his fear to double and it made his insides tremble.

"I think you know why I'm here, Will," she replied and now her voice lost the gaiety of a few moments before.

"I don't..."

"The sword! I want the sword, you idiot." Amy had lost control for a second and had practically screamed the words into the phone, but now she pulled herself together. "You do know what sword I'm talking about, right?"

He knew. "Yes." So breathless was his response that Amy didn't hear it.

"You're going to pretend you don't remember?" she asked and now her tone was cruel. "It's the same sword you killed my mother with. How bout I describe it for you: it's broken, all black looking, really cold..."

"I know the sword," he interrupted, sharper now. "What do you want it for?"

There was a snort of laughter from the phone. "The same thing that Luke wanted with it. Oh, and thanks for taking care of that little problem for me."

"Problem? I don't..." he trailed off feeling as if the room around him was dissolving. How did she know about Luke? Or the sword for that matter? He looked at his sister, but she didn't make eye contact, she just stepped a little closer concentrating on the phone.

"Yes, Luke was an issue that I was going to have to deal with, and you took care of it. But you didn't use the sword last night." Amy paused as if thinking. "Tell me, how did you manage to send Ba'al back this time?"

"Let me speak to Lisa first, and then I'll tell you everything you want to know." Again, he *knew* this wasn't going to fly, but he couldn't stop himself, he only hoped she didn't hear the whine in his voice as much as he did.

"Oh, Willy J, that's not the way this is going to happen," Amy's voice came across very calm and she seemed far more mature, not to mention more intelligent than he remembered. "Unlike that fool Luke, I haven't come all this way, to this forgotten state, empty handed and without back-up. I'm the one who'll be telling you, not the other way around."

Talitha leaned in closer and whispered, "She's not lying. I hear at least three people in the room with her. Lisa isn't one of them."

"What was that, Will?" Amy asked sharply. "Is there

someone with you? If there is, it'd be really smart of you to tell them to..."

"Don't worry," Will cut across her. His headache had begun to thump again mildly and he knew more was coming. It added to his bad mood; fear always made him cranky. "It's just Talitha."

"Talitha?" For a few seconds Amy seemed at a loss. "I thought..." Another longer pause followed those two words and then Amy said with evident disbelief, "Let me speak to her."

"Sure." Will's blue eyes darted over to look questioningly into his sister's brown ones. Perplexed, she only shrugged slightly.

"Hello Amy, this is Talitha," she said apprehensively into the phone, her brow furrowed showing three little lines between her eyebrows.

Those little lines in the soot suddenly gave Talitha the appearance of age, or rather, she suddenly looked her age, twenty-five. Normally, she looked so amazingly young, that if she wished to, she could pass for a sophomore in high school. And despite everything that she had gone through in her rather horrible life, she had an innocent quality to her that on occasion made her look even younger, almost child-like.

"Who did we have for science in the tenth grade?" Talitha repeated the question for Will's sake, his hearing was altogether normal and he hadn't heard Amy's question. "It was a biology class specifically and the teacher's name was Dwayne Sanders. Yes...yes. Certainly, but first...ok."

Talitha shrugged again to her brother and handed back the phone. "Are you satisfied that was Talitha? It's just her and me, there's no one else here, ok? Do you believe me?" For a few moments, there was silence. "Amy?"

"Right...right, of course I believe you," Amy replied slowly. "All you Jern's are all so honest that it's annoying really. It's just...I had it on good authority that Talitha was dead, yet there she is." Will began to worry who this authority could be. Was there someone here in Boston, spying on them? And for what purpose? The sword?

"Amy, if you want the sword, I don't have it here with me, but I can help get it for you..." Will started, but his sister dug a sharp elbow into him, shaking her head. He glared at her before continuing, "If...if you don't hurt Lisa."

Talitha snaked out her hand in a flash and covering the mouthpiece of the phone, she hissed, "You can't do this! You know what she'll do with..." Will pulled the phone away from her and their eyes locked in a silent heated debate. The sword, an eighteen inch chunk of charred broken metal had somewhere upon its frozen length a pinpoint sized opening. It opened onto the Void.

As far as Will knew, there were only two reasons to want the sword; to destroy it or to make that opening larger. Perhaps large enough to bring something from the Void into this world. It was patently obvious to both brother and sister, that this was what Amy wanted and Will understood Talitha's anger. But Lisa was in danger and so was his unborn child. That beautiful little girl that he had seen so often in his dreams, that little girl he was already madly in love with.

There was no argument in his mind. "Do we have a deal?" he asked Amy.

"Hmmm, nope. You see Willy J, I don't really need your help getting the sword. Lisa knows where it is. Sure, she's been reluctant to tell me where she's stashed it, but I have ways of getting information."

"Like how you got the information that Talitha was dead?" Will threw that out there, hoping to jar her. He sounded far more in control than he actually was. "I think you need me."

"No, what I need is a sharper knife," Amy scoffed. Will's heart froze at this, and though he wanted to beg Amy, just then his throat locked up tight and no sound came out.

"The sword is around here someplace and I know for a fact that she'll tell me where in a few minutes. Here's what I want from you, Will. The incantations Luke stole from me; I want them back. They're very important to me. Can you get them?"

"Yeah, but..."

"No buts. Get them and be back up here to No-where's-ville, by...let's say five. And of course don't call the police or your wife and baby die, blah, blah, blah. I will *know* if you do. Do you understand what I'm saying?"

"Yeah." He knew, or at least had a guess that Amy, perhaps through her gypsy mother had more spells at her disposal. However, she wasn't the only one. "Amy, I'll get the spells, but you should know that if you hurt her in the least way, I will know even before you even try, and..."

"Right, you can see the future. I know," Amy sounded bored, which sent a separate distinct feeling of alarm running through him. How could she know? And if she did, why was she so calm about it? She continued, only now her tone turned braggadocios, "I have knowledge concerning all sorts of things. I know about the witch, Adrina and Father Alba...I know what he did to my mother, and everything that happened that night eight years ago. What I don't know just yet is what occurred last night. I know Luke is dead, perhaps worse than dead in fact. And I know that Ba'al Zubel crossed over from the Void, but was sent back. I just don't know how."

She left the last sentence sort of hanging out there, clearly hoping that he'd answer. Will didn't know exactly what to say. Would it be wise to tell her? The only thing that seemed smart to hold back was the role Talitha played.

"I'm not saying anything until I know that Lisa's safe."

"Well that's going to be tough to do," Amy replied with a bit of a sigh. "You see, I've already threatened her. Not me of course, some of my men. They waved their guns and held knives up to her and told her how they were going to cut her baby out of her and hold it up for her to see..."

"No!" Talitha interrupted with a scream. Will would've screamed as well, but he had been struck dumb by Amy's words.

"Yeah, awful right?" Amy continued casually, seeming to enjoy her role as storyteller. "Pedro had this really big knife, he's just silly about knives sometimes, you know, and he's got this razor sharp blade right up to her little bulge and still she doesn't talk. You gotta hand it to her, she can be a pretty tough cookie. But I can see in her eyes also that she's scared, so you know what I tell Pedro?" She paused dramatically.

Will found his tongue and his fear had him yelling, "What! Amy what did you do? Let me talk to Lisa right now!"

"Chill-out, Will," she said still relaxed. "I'll finish telling you what happened to your wife, don't worry. But you have to tell me what happened last night, first."

"It...it...I, uh," Will spluttered in a rush to get his story out. Suddenly the events of the previous night seemed like they'd been a long time in the past and he had trouble remembering everything, and what he did recall came to him like a puzzle fresh from the box. "I, uh, I saw where Luke was going to be and there were these boys and this girl...Terry. She died and then Jim died, but first we..."

"Maybe Talitha should tell the story," Amy interjected.

Talitha heard this and gently took the phone from Will's numb fingers, "I'll tell you what happened, I promise, but only after I know what's going on with Lisa." She had regained her composure and her tone was neutral. When after a few seconds Amy hadn't responded, Talitha added, "As you alluded to a few minutes ago, subterfuge isn't a fundamental aspect of our personalities."

Amy paused now longer than before. "I suppose you're right, you guys aren't the lying types. So, I'll go first. I haven't hurt Lisa...yet. But I'm on a bit of a time crunch and when Lisa didn't immediately spill where she'd hid the sword, even with Pedro and his knife, I couldn't afford to waste time on torture. I mean people say all sorts of things when their being sliced into, right? She could've told me she threw it in a lake or some such and then I'd be all day trying to find the thing. You know what I mean?"

"Certainly, torture is an ineffective tool when trying to ascertain information," Talitha replied. She shared a silent look of relief with her brother, whose ear was inches from the phone.

"Ineffective?" Amy grunted out the word, disdainfully. "Wrong. It's only ineffective when you don't have a lot of time. Give me a few hours and Lisa will be telling me everything...but like I said, I have places to be, so I had just started this little incantation..."

"A spell?" Will broke in, fear causing his voice to crack. "What's it going to do? Will it hurt her?"

"Damn it, Will. Stop interrupting, jeeze!" Amy cried, put out. "Not every spell is designed to hurt someone. This one will just allow me to browse her memory of the last day or so. There'll be no lasting damage at all, but like I said, I had just started it when you called, so she's out like a light and can't talk. That's it, that's the truth. Now, I told you about Lisa. It's your turn."

Will took the phone from his sister, but waited to proceed. Could he really trust a woman like Amy Harris? She had been a nasty piece of work as a teenager and clearly she'd only become more so. The answer was obviously no; nevertheless, with Lisa as her hostage he saw no alternative and began his narrative. He told her everything concerning the painful day and the terrifying night confronting the demon, with only one exception. Talitha. The very casual way in which Amy had spoke to Talitha, made Will think she didn't know as much as she thought she did. After all, it wasn't too long ago that her attitude might have put his sister in a killing mood. Her role, he left extremely vague and in the telling she came off more as an advisor than the central figure she really had been.

The reason for this was simple. The Talitha that Amy had known years before, though smart and pretty, had been unexceptional physically. Now however, despite not looking to have changed a whit in eight years, she possessed herculean strength. This, coupled with her cheetah like speed made her easily the most formidable person on earth. And if Amy knew none of this the element of surprise could make his sister all but unstoppable.

Amy took a long time in replying, "You two and some big guy, took on Luke, a gypsy witch and the demon?" She sounded skeptical.

"I told you I had a gun and I shot Luke...and it wasn't easy, if that's what you think. And..." Talitha sent him a little frown and put a finger to his lips to keep him from saying anymore.

Amy took her time, pausing for a minute considering. "Did you find out the witch's name?"

Unexpectedly, Will felt a heavy weight of guilt over this. "It was late...I mean it was like two in the morning." He didn't know what else to say, the battle had left them barely able to stand.

"I suppose, but before you come up, find out the name of that gypsy," Amy commanded. She sounded as if she was well used to her orders being carried out without question, and so authoritative was her voice that Will found himself nodding in acceptance.

"Okay, sure."

"And be here by five. It's getting dark so early and I don't want any surprises. You and your sister, come alone, come unarmed and know that any hero shit will just get your wife and baby killed, understood?"

Chapter 2

Amy

The woman set the phone in its cradle and stood thinking, her dark brown eyes staring at the ivory colored carpet. The Amy Harris that Will had known in high school had never once been accused of thinking. She hadn't been considered smart by anyone's standards, but this was a fiction that she had cultivated, purposely. Boys weren't interested in smart girls. She didn't have to look further than Talitha Jern for proof of that. Talitha had been pretty despite herself, and yet had never gone out with a boy of any merit. While raven-haired Amy, who acted the ditz to perfection could have any boy she chose.

Almost any boy. Not Will Jern. For some reason he had turned up his nose at her advances, and instead, went after the dull twig of a girl that was currently lying upon the floor at her feet. To be passed up that way had been quite a slap in the face for Amy and she had hated him for as long as she could remember, though she had hid that fact as well. Even when she was coming on to him, throwing herself at him, Amy had hated Will. She had so wanted to humiliate him, to hurt him, and it hadn't been an easy thing to do to keep up that fake smile.

But then her mother had disappeared.

Back then, she didn't blame Will as he suspected. That last time they'd seen each other, it was the pure hate for him that had finally shown through that he saw. No, she didn't blame Will back then, but she did now.

"Pedro! Get your ass in here," she demanded in a harsh voice that carried throughout the house. It was loud enough to wake the dead, but the blonde girl stretched out on the floor didn't stir. Perhaps it was because she wasn't quite dead, yet.

Pedro was there in seconds, huffing as quietly as he could and Amy smirked at the sight.

Only two people ever called him Pedro, his grandmother, and Amy Harris. Anyone else who dared would have been bleeding in seconds. Amy knew this about the big man and more. Early on she had decided that she wouldn't make the same mistake as she did with Luke and extensively explored his background. Using the dead, and there were many, many dead souls who had known Pedro, the witch discovered far more about the Mexican than he would've ever dreamt about.

She knew that Pedro was not a man to take lightly. At six foot three inches and two-hundred and forty pounds, he was big for a Mexican and he enjoyed the intimidation factor that his size allowed. He enjoyed doling out pain as well and had no qualms about killing in any manner. These attributes were highly sought after and not just by her and it was during his first stay as a guest of the California Department of Corrections that he'd been recruited into Emeros.

Emeros was a Mexican prison gang and though they liked to throw around the term Mafia in relation to the name, they were really nothing of the sort, and did little besides use drugs, sell drugs, and kill people over drugs. Since he was exceptional at all three, Pedro quickly progressed to the level of lieutenant in the hierarchy of the gang.

However, the *White Witch* as he called Amy Harris behind her back, with a small show of her power had ended his connection to the gang in a single afternoon. This was the only thing that could've won him over, since power was the single authority he respected. Amy had great power.

"Yes, Ms Harris?" he asked, keeping his eyes low, but all the same not looking at the blonde girl splayed on the floor. He seemed nervous at her unnatural sleep.

"How many of your boys do we have in Boston? And how many still in L.A?" the witch asked, running her hands through her thick black hair. As a habit, she would tease her hair or stretch provocatively and Pedro as always, forced his yearning eyes from her stunning figure. He'd been trained well; to ogle her was to invite trouble.

"Six in Boston and och..." Amy's eyes narrowed and Pedro quickly bit his tongue. She always demanded that he speak only English. "I mean eight in L.A."

"Have the boys in Boston get to Logan airport and make sure they're ready to fly," Amy ordered and then began pacing, her mind whirling. "Who do you trust down stairs? As soon as I'm done with her," she nodded to the blonde. "We're out of here, but I need to leave a few men behind. Later today I'm expecting two people a man and a woman. Now the girl is nothing special, but the man, may be tough..." she left off thinking.

Will was far tougher than she had first realized. Three times he'd been in the presence of the demon, Ba'al Zubel back on Governor's Island, yet he lived. And last night, she knew that he had taken on Ba'al again, as well as Luke, something that should've been far beyond him. Somehow he came out of it alive. And so did Talitha. That was an even bigger surprise.

Yet, did it really matter?

Amy was there for the sword, not some petty revenge. That she could indulge in at any time once her obligations were fulfilled that is. She hadn't been lying, when she told Will she was on a time crunch. Promises had been made in blood and she had received much for them, but the time of her payment was coming fast upon her.

"Ramon is good," Pedro answered the earlier question. "I'd leave him and Tre."

"No, make it four men." Amy nodded her head as she spoke. Will's ability to see the future would be quite easy to overcome. A simple charm would do the trick; something Luke had disregarded when he had made off with half her incantations. And without the capacity to see the future, Will was as good as dead...but she was done taking chances. There was Talitha to consider after all. The only thing Amy really knew about her was that she had gone insane the night Amy's mother had died.

Was there more to her than just brains? The insane were notoriously unpredictable after all, capable of anything. The witch began to pace, thinking, worrying, biting her lip, but after a minute she realized she was wasting her time. Worrying about Talitha would have to wait, since if she didn't find the sword nothing else mattered.

"I have some *work* to do in here and while I'm at it I'm going to need absolute silence. Set men around the house. No one comes in, no matter what. No mailman, no police, no nothing. You got it?"

"Yes, Ms Harris," Pedro backed away in haste, shutting the door behind him.

Amy looked down at Lisa once more and shook her head. The girl was so plain. Where was the attraction? She gave the body a quick shrug, not really caring much anymore.

Three years ago she'd cared a great deal. Her hate had been burning like a fire in her belly since her mother's disappearance. Then by accident she'd stumbled across some of her mother's belongings including a diary that at first made no sense. In fact, it seemed to purposely not make sense, as if an imbecile had written it. *3 days running out plays sometimes, off for picnic, including grapes. Bugs, little owls, otters, dams*. It turned out to be a code and a very simple one at that, however, Amy wasn't a genius. Fortunately for her, Henny Harris was even less of one and as Amy read the diary it became increasingly clear that the first letter of each word had been stressed slightly.

Once Amy saw this, the code became easy to read- *3 drops of pig blood*. It was so obvious that Amy became embarrassed for her mother, but that embarrassment became worse as she realized what her mother was up to.

Spells? Incantations? It seemed her mother had been into all sorts of foolish things...rites, virgin sacrifices, Ouija boards. Wondering if this had anything to do with her disappearance, Amy delved into the diary and in four very long days had written out the entire thing in English. There was some scary stuff there, but nothing personal that gave a hint to where she'd gone.

Late on the fourth night, when she had finished with the diary, Amy took up her mother's Ouija board and thinking that it worked more like a Magic Eight Ball, asked, "Where's my mother?" She then spun the little wooden heart that came with it. The arrow pointed squarely at the "W." Another spin had it pointing at the "G."

"Wug... wig... wag?" Amy said, turning her head this way and that. "This fuckin thing's broken."

Tired and stressed she went to sleep. In the morning the little wooden heart shaped planchette pointed squarely at one of the four words on the board, *hello*. For a very long time Amy had sat on her bed with her feet drawn up off the floor as if she thought that something could be laying in wait under it. The pointer had moved, there was no doubt in her mind that it had, but how?

Eventually, she came to terms that the Ouija board was the real deal and from then on, she was hooked, far deeper than her mother ever was. Amy delved into the underworld with a passion, but also with care.

Her caution was fully justified, since it wasn't long before she came to discover what a tremendous fool her mother had been. Henny had been timid at first, afraid to use even a single spell. But then, as if rolling the dice at Vegas, she turned full bore in the opposite direction by trying to open a *Gate* to a hell dimension. No simple love potion for her. She went for the big money and paid for it with her life.

Learning from her mother's mistake, Amy started small and it was weeks before she attempted even the simplest things. And for a time, she also steered clear of the Ouija board since she had no clue, who or even what would be answering her questions. However, eventually she made the attempt and one thing became crystal-clear to her. The creatures that were out there trying to communicate with her were desperate; they needed her far more than she needed them. They were utterly powerless on earth and craved even the smallest touch of life. More and more she saw this and soon she began forcing heavily favored bargains upon them.

Yet despite the lopsided arrangements they were eager for more.

At length with the help of the board, she discovered a spell that would allow her to commune with the dead. It was a massive break through. The dead were a vault of information and demanded nothing in return but to be listened to. When at last Amy discovered her mother's soul, the truth of her disappearance came out.

At that point, Amy's hate for Will became a current of fire that had her raging for days. In due course, as she kept learning and growing as a witch, and as time stretched out, the hate faded. It never left, but she had more important things to consider.

Demons for instance.

Dealing with the demons and fiends of the Void was the most fearfully difficult thing to master. Always they were trying to trip her up, to gain control of her soul and she was perpetually on guard against their schemes and plots. She traded with them, blood and souls were her currency, and power was their commodity and always in these dealings her soul was put up as bond. Yet not once did she make a deal where she couldn't hold up her end of the bargain and continuously she prevailed and as she did her capabilities increased.

Her ego grew in proportion to her power, so that she was blind to the smallest thing that lay at her feet: Luke Sheldon.

During those early days he worked in a very curious

curio shop in New York City. It sold the most outlandish items legally and illegally available. Amy Harris frequented it so much that Luke quickly figured out what she was up to. He worshipped her. He went out of his way for anything that she needed and became almost a slave to her. She allowed this and slowly he wormed and groveled his way into her confidence.

It turned out that he was a liar and a conniver of great ability. He was not a gypsy nor any sort of witch, but nonetheless he learned things and became powerful in his own right. But Amy was oblivious to what her underling was up to and remained that way until she woke three months ago to find most of her spells missing and all four of the virgins she had planned on sacrificing, dead. Dead virgins were useless virgins.

Luke had left her with almost nothing but the Ouija board, yet despite that she'd worked around the clock to re-build her spell list, taking chances that previously she would've scoffed at. So that now she was almost as strong as she had been. Along with her strength she built up a thirst for vengeance. Even as she attempted to regain what she'd lost, she searched for Luke with a fiery determination, and had been getting steadily closer.

He knew she was closing in on him and this was probably why he'd gone for the sword, prematurely. It was premature since clearly he had not yet discovered Will's talent and had botched the attempt to lay hands on the blade, as a consequence. Stupid mistake. But for Amy, a timely one.

She'd known about the sword, her mother had mentioned it in passing long before, but unfortunately Henny had groused and complained so much over her body being burned by the priest that Amy had missed the supernatural aspects concerning the artifact. To her it had only been the weapon that had killed her mother.

But as a result of Luke staking everything on acquiring

it, Amy had become intrigued by the idea that there was more to the blade than she knew. A quick investigation conducted only the night before, possibly at the very moment that Luke was opening his gate, revealed the wonderful secret that the sword possessed. And the knowledge couldn't have come at a more opportune moment.

To get her power back in so short a time, she had gambled and very nearly lost. All of her excessively imbalanced bargains came back to haunt her and she began to mortgage her soul six ways from Sunday. Still, she knew that once she recovered all of her spells, she'd be able to turn the tides back again. But then children began to disappear in Boston.

This struck a cold fear into her. The children were being used as a conduit to gain knowledge. A knowledge of powerful evils and she feared what Luke was up to and she feared also what he would do to her when he was done. She was his only real rival and had the tables been turned, she would've destroyed him in a second. And so feeling terribly vulnerable, she had gone to Ba'al Zubel.

Ba'al was the ultimate power broker in the Void. It had been the first time she was forced to commune with that awful entity and worse, she went hat in hand, in the weakest of positions. The demon gave her the power that she wished for, putting her on par with Luke, and in return Amy was to open a gate just as her mother had done. She was given a month to accomplish this and the days had ticked by with an amazing alacrity.

Her problem was in finding a virgin. Virginity was a difficult thing.

It was all a matter of perfection. A physical lack of penetration wasn't even all that important; what mattered was the purity of the soul and the rightness of one's mind.

Her first attempt had been so dismal that she disliked to even think she'd been a part of it. The girl had been a fraud and had been no more a virgin than Amy was at her age and it was only just in time did she figure it out. Had Amy tried to open a gate with an impure soul, her own would've been forfeit, and whenever she thought about it, shivers ran across her back. People were just such liars these days.

Amy smiled at this.

The Jerns weren't liars. And Lisa Jern especially wasn't going to lie in the state she was in. It would be an impossibility. Though impossible or not, it was going to take time. Memories were like that. Amy would have to start at the point under which Lisa had been ensorcelled and work her way backwards. She was going to find out what Lisa had for breakfast, whether she did the laundry that morning and if her favorite squirrel had come out to beg for a piece of bread. Tedium. Suburban tedium at its worst.

Amy got comfortable and worked herself into a positive mindset. Perhaps Lisa had hidden the sword moments before they arrived, somewhere around the home, or maybe out in the forest under a rock or a log or some such. Either way she would have the sword soon.

Despite her attempt at positivity, that last thought dampened her spirits somewhat. She needed the sword, but in her heart, she was afraid of it as well. Who knew precisely what happen when it was used?

Chapter 3

Will

Talitha stood in the dim hotel room; her eyes cast down to the carpet and Will waited for her to speak, knowing that his little sister would know what to do. She always knew what to do. She was a hundred times smarter than he was, so he sat on the bed waiting, purposefully not thinking.

To think would only bring about pain. Mental pain. Physical pain he already had by the truckloads. Almost every part of his body nagged in a dull aching way, but not his mind. He had left off the conversation with Amy, dropping a foolish sounding *good-bye,* and as he did, terrible thoughts of the frightful misery his wife was going through came to him. Therefore he immediately switched off his brain.

With near religious faith, he sat looking at Talitha and minutes snuck by unnoticed by either of them.

Finally she spoke, "What're we going to do?"

It was then Will noticed that she seemed bewildered or perhaps overcome with everything that had happened to them in the last few days. The look wasn't acceptable. And neither was her question; she was the super smart one.

"What do you mean?" he asked feeling a flush of anger. "I'm counting on you here. Lisa's counting on you."

"I guess we go get the incantations then?"

"Tal, what's wrong?" Her eyes were brimming with tears and when he tugged her down beside him on the bed, they began to spill over.

"We're going to have to do it all over again," she said in a staccato, the syllables bouncing up and down to the rhythmic hitching of her chest. "I thought...I thought that after last night, I could just go home. Back to the cabin. But now, if I stay or go, it doesn't matter. It'll mean more death and blood and it just never ends. How much killing can I be a part of...before I'm...I'm..." Her tears came heavier and for a few moments, she sat mute with the force of her emotion.

"Before what?" Despite the renewed pounding in his head and his growing sense of desperation, he kept his tone calm.

"Before I'm like her, the other Talitha."

"Listen Tal, there is no other Talitha. That girl is gone. She's a demon now and whatever she did, it has nothing to do with you. Her evil is not your evil."

"I created her!" she cried out unexpectedly in vicious anger. The change from the fearful sadness was so abrupt that Will leaned back, startled. Talitha seemed not to notice. "I'm responsible for everything she did. All those people she killed, their blood is on my hands, both literally and figuratively." With that she brought her blackened fingers to her face. Sniffing at them she cringed in disgust. "I need a shower."

Ignoring her brother, she was up, heading for the shower in the trashed out room, but suddenly she thought better of it. The night before she'd sat in that shower after being raped. Her shoulders slumped at the sight of the door and she turned to the adjoining room.

"Tal?" Will called out. She turned her face, beautiful despite the soot and the emotion clouding it, toward him and he asked her, "You're coming to Maine with me right?" He knew that she would, but on a gut level he had to hear it.

"I have to. I'd never let anything happen to Lisa...or the baby," she replied, and barely looked back before she slipped through the doorway. In that instant, he saw there was a hardness to her face, a nastiness that would've given her demon twin a shock to see.

Talitha knew that more death was coming and the look suggested she was steeling herself against it. He would have to as well. In eight years he'd barely ever thought of Amy Harris. Her mother yes. You don't kill a person and then go about your life without reflecting on it frequently. Clearly, Amy had given Will a lot of thought and sadly, her thoughts had now turned to vengeance. He should've seen this coming.

Really, he should have, since he had the power to see into the future. Regrettably, that power wasn't always exact, nor was it timely; the visions came and went, almost unpredictably. *Almost*, since if he wished he could purposefully look into the future for something specific, but even that was fraught with danger and uncertainty.

Uncalled for his mind flashed to an image of a corpse; a boy tied over the back of a chair. The body was that of 11-year-old Rick Brabec, his head had been practically sawed off with a steak knife. Clutching his own throat, Will shook the picture from his mind and got up from the bed, feeling a pain inside him that wasn't physical. There had been too much death already. The death of innocents like Rick, and his mother, his sister Terry. And so many others.

Because of Luke there were eleven innocent people dead, but none stood out so keenly as that of Jim. Will saw in his mind the homely face of big Jim. The gap-toothed giant of a man. Sweet and shy, quiet by nature, he had become more than just a friend in the two days that Will knew him. He had been a brother in arms and had died like a hero, but now his soul was burning in hell, trapped in the endless Void.

And strangely Will couldn't remember his full name. Big Jim, Jimbo, White Jim, these were all the names that Talitha had called him, yet his last name wouldn't come to him.

"Jim..." he said to himself, hoping to spark a memory. Nothing. He went to the phone and dialed Saint Thomas Catholic Church. Other than his sister and himself, no one knew about the death of Jim, or of the battle beneath the factory where the demon Ba'al Zubel had been defeated.

"Saint Thomas?" The words were rich and warm,

coming from the voice of a practiced speaker, but the tone wasn't honest. There was just a touch of apprehension beneath it and Will had a brief flash. The man on the phone was a priest, decked out in his working black attire; alone he sat at the desk in Father Alba's office. He was middle-aged, with the regular features of an Italian; grey at the temple, brown eyes with growing bags beneath them. Though the room wasn't in any way warm, there was sweat in his hair and down his back. He had a nagging fear to him and Will *knew* that his name was Father Alfano.

"Hello Father, may I please speak to Sean Shay?"

There was a pause on the other end of the phone, perhaps because Will had unwittingly called him Father, and when he spoke again, that nervousness in the priest's voice was more pronounced. "He's not available; would you like to leave a message?"

A message was out of the question: *Will called. Your best friend is dead.* That would be horrible.

"Do you know when he'll be in? This is kind of important," Will replied. But just then he saw clearly where Sean was. The picture bloomed in his mind like it was a memory: Standing in a hospital room, Sean, his large pumpkin sized face looking whiter than usual, held out a sheaf of thick papers to a small tidy looking man. A priest. Neat and trim the man appeared with his short grey haircut and his perfectly trimmed goatee. Confidently, the priest had his hand out about to receive the yellowed and ink scrawled vellum, his eyes were on them and he seemed equally curious and skeptical.

Another person sat in a chair near to the single hospital bed that stood in the center of the room. Will could only see a part of the person and knew not whether it was a male or female. He guessed male and guessed as well that it was another clergy member; the person wore all black but unlike the priest, this man's clothes were lined with a deep red and about his waist, he wore a red sash.

The vision was like a single frame of a movie. It was there in his mind, pure but not complete, the edges faded to black and only a portion of the hospital bed was visible, its occupant unseen. But, he didn't have to be seen and Will didn't need a supernatural power to know that it was Father Alba. His arms flared in goose bumps at the thought of the priest and all the man had gone through.

"Never mind," Will interjected just as the Father Alfano began to answer the question. "I'll...I'll just talk to him later, thank you."

"Who is..." Father Alfano started, but by that time Will had hung up the phone. He didn't mean to be rude, but his mind was whirling over the idea of losing the incantations that Sean had and there was no time for pleasantries. Running about the two motel rooms, he gathered their meager belongings and was just about to shout to Talitha to hurry, when he caught sight of his image in the bathroom mirror.

"Jeeze..."

Below the layers of soot and splattered blood, his face was unrecognizable. The swelling on the left side seemed to unbalance his entire head and for the first time he realized that he could barely see out of his left eye. The right side was only marginally better. He touched himself tenderly, but winced all the same.

"I'm so sorry about that," Talitha said poking her head out from behind the shower curtain.

The day before, when Talitha's body was under control of an evil being, a creature of her own making that resided inside her body, she and Will had fought. And now he was a complete wreck while she was unhurt, and save for her sad frown at the sight of his misshapen face, completely unblemished. One would never know by looking at him that he'd won the fight. She healed quickly.

"It's not your fault," he replied around the fingers of his right hand, which were currently testing the extent of the wiggle in one of his loose teeth. The wiggle wasn't bad, and if he lived through the day, the tooth might just be saved. The thought did little to cheer him. "We gotta hurry, ok? I think Sean Shay is on his way to hand over some incantations to some Catholic bigwig and I don't know how much time we have."

"You better clean up too," Talitha spluttered from under the water.

"You're right about that," he mumbled with a final glance at the horrible looking person in the mirror.

His shower was done in minutes and he pulled on the spare set of clothes that he'd brought with him: jeans and thankfully a hooded sweatshirt. This, he tugged up, yanking it as far over his forehead as he could. Talitha didn't have an extra set and was forced to wear the disheveled black dress she'd worn the day before. Luckily, it was jet black and hid most of the soot stains on it, but it still smelled heavily of smoke.

After dropping a much larger than normal tip for the motel cleaning staff, the brother and sister ducked into the steady cold rain that blanketed Boston and jumped into the old paneled station wagon that belonged to Father Alba. As he started the car, Will cast a quick glance at his sister but she didn't return the look. She only had eyes for what lay in front of her and kept her face steadily forward. In the back seat, the dried blood of the priest was a painful reminder of the day's previous adventures.

Having been to the city on a number of occasions, Will knew a quick route to Faulkner hospital and by the time the clock on the dashboard switched over to read 10 am they were pulling into a parking spot.

"Father...uh...Father Alba's room please," Will didn't know the man's first name. "He's a Catholic priest and had some eye damage." This he said to the thousand-year-old volunteer at the information desk. Even with her inch thick glasses, she squinted up at him. What she saw appeared to sour her look and her face crawled into a frown.

"Albert?" she asked loudly.

Feeling as if all the eyes in the room were upon him and his battered appearance, he leaned in closer and spoke even louder, "His last name is Alba."

"A...L...B...A," she spelled the word slow and steady as her eyes searched for the letters on her computer keyboard. "Room 306...but it says no visitors. Sorry you can't go up."

To get to the elevators, they had to bypass the lady. Will smiled, turning on the charm, but where once his handsome features might have turned the trick, his face was now too much of a wreck for that to work and the volunteer only looked a little disgusted. In defeat, he wandered over to Talitha, who had hung back due to the fact that a police officer was sitting behind nearby desk.

Talitha headed his way and all but ignored him. She strode past, keeping her face turned from the policeman and went to the information desk. "Hello, Elizabeth Johnson's room please," she said with a clear voice.

"Let me check," the old lady began and then peered down at her keyboard. "J...O...H...N..."

Talitha stepped back calmly and then with a little nod toward the elevators she proceeded to head in their direction.

"S...O...N. And Elizabeth...E..."

Will got the hint and they were in the nearest one, heading up before the lady could locate the "Z". Pushing the three button, Talitha grinned at her own cleverness, Will was right there with her.

"Whatever you're doing to your face, I would stop it," she said after seeing his look.

"What? I was smiling," Will couldn't tell if she was joking or not. She wasn't, judging by the fact that her brows shot up at his words. Thankfully, they were alone in the elevator and he turned to look into the mirror, which took up most of its rear wall. He gave it a small smile.

"Crap," he muttered. It wasn't a pretty picture.

"It doesn't look..." Talitha began, but she trailed off in an odd manner.

Will barely noticed; he only had eyes for his poor face. "It doesn't look that bad? Whose face are you looking at?" The door opened behind him and a man strode in, not bothering to wait to see if anyone was thinking to exit and hit the one button and only then did Will recognize the man. It was Eric Milner. *Detective* Eric Milner.

Talitha stood only a step from the door, but she froze in place as her nostrils dilated—she knew his smell. It was an awkward moment filled with an awkward silence and it was perhaps this that clued the detective that something was amiss. Milner glanced at Will and his eyes came to squints as he tried to place the man beneath the bruises.

"This is our floor," Will said in a hoarse whisper to his sister, hoping to get her to move, but she only stood as if glued in place. Now Milner turned toward Talitha, it was a slow motion turn, almost like a dream. His eyes shot wide as he recognized the slim young girl that had only two days before thrown him around like he was nothing and had threatened to cut off all his moving parts if she ever saw him again. Clearly, Milner had taken that threat to heart, because in the space of a half second, as the doors closed on the third floor, he pulled his pistol and aimed it square into the girl's face.

Chapter 4

Will

Eric Milner had been very fast on the draw, but not that fast. Yet still the gun had come out like a black streak, cutting a line across Will's vision and surprisingly nothing stopped it. There it was pointed straight into Talitha's face. And a second later, it was still there.

Perplexed that after all this time Milner still held the gun, Will pulled his eyes from the barrel and looked at his sister. Her face registered little more than a mild surprise.

"You were at the church," she told the man, trying to peer around the gun. "It's ok, you don't have to be afraid. I'm the good..."

"Shut the hell up!" Milner's voice was very loud in the small elevator. "Don't move."

"Detective Milner," Will began. "This is the good Talitha. We were just on our way to see Father Alba..."

The gun swung in his direction and Will leaned far back away from it striking his head with a small thump on the mirror behind him. The cop's eyes were wild. "I saw what she did to Father Alba. I don't care anymore about this good Talitha, bad Talitha crap. She's a danger to everyone who comes close to her and she's going to jail."

"Officer Mil..." Talitha began, but now the gun swung back towards her. Milner had it around in a flash, however, just then Talitha used her speed.

A second later, Will punched the emergency stop button and the elevator came to a halt with a little bouncing jolt. "Is he going to be ok?" he asked his sister.

"Oh sure. Here take this thing," she held out the gun that she had taken from the officer. As the gun had swung at her, she snapped out with a quick light punch that hit the detective in the inner part of the wrist. The muscles and the tendons in his hand had immediately flared and his hand had sprung open, releasing the gun. She followed this up a tenth of a second later with an accurate strike to his solar plexus and as she had caught the gun, she lowered the cop gently to the floor.

He was now red as a beet and making on odd hitching sound in his throat. Tucking the gun into the waist of his jeans, Will sighed and waited. It felt like a long wait.

"Whatever happened to his other gun?" Will asked as the cop continued to struggle to find an opening in his lungs that would allow in air. After seeing that bright flash the night before, Will couldn't recall what happened to it.

"It's back at the factory. I think I dropped it sometime after Ba'al...you know." Talitha dipped to one knee then and looked into the cop's face. "Are you ok? I didn't want to have to do that, but you were being very unreasonable."

Milner began to breathe easier and massaged his right wrist, however his face held a wild fearful look as if he would run screaming the second the elevator doors were to open. They waited in silence until the police officer recovered enough to speak.

"Why are you here?" Milner asked, still from the floor.

"A couple of reasons," Will answered slowly, hoping not to spook the cop. "We wanted to be able to tell Father Alba and Sean Shay what happened last night. And we need some help."

"Help? What kind of help? Not from me I hope. I could be facing a jail term already," Milner said scrutinizing Will's injuries. "Man you're all messed up. Did she do that to you?"

"Yeah, but I'm going to tell the story only once so if you want to hear it, you gotta promise us that you aren't going to go all crazy, deal?"

Milner nodded and Will got the elevator moving again. The ride was very uncomfortable in its silence. At length they came to the third floor and the cop walked them to

Father Alba's room. Outside it stood a young priest dressed in the normal black garb with the hard white clerical collar. He seemed about Will's age and was fresh faced and handsome with dirty blonde hair and bright blue eyes. Those eyes widened slightly at Will's appearance.

"I'm sorry, but no visitors," the priest moved between them and the door as they approached.

Milner's face, which was already set in lines of stress, formed into an angry frown at being told where he could and couldn't go. "They're with me." He didn't bother to wait for the young man to move, instead he brusquely reached for the handle and pushed him out of the way with the door.

"Excuse us," Talitha added in a quiet voice, embarrassed by the cop's actions. There was a pretty pink to her cheeks. She slipped past the man and moved into the hospital room as silent as a ghost.

The room was just as Will's vision. In fact, at their entrance everyone froze in place so it had the same picture quality as well. Father Alba sat in the bed, his face was thankfully, heavily bandaged. The image of the man's torn and bleeding eye sockets had lain just under Will's conscious since they had entered the hospital and the bandages, though he knew they'd be there, were a relief.

Sitting in the chair next to the bed was an elderly priest...*Bishop Keenan*, Will suddenly *knew*. This was the man in Will's vision that wore the red sash and his clothes were trimmed with the same color red. He didn't wear the usual neat black outfit, instead he wore a cassock, which was a close fitting robe of sorts that reached down to his black shoes. Despite his age, seventy or so, the man had an open, almost cherubic face. He had unlined round cheeks that held a touch of Irish red and he smiled at them in the most pleasant way.

The immense form of Sean Shay leaned against the wall to their left. He wore a grey sweat suit that would have to be retired soon since it appeared to be stretching to its limit across his great gut. That he had only just got there in the last few minutes was evidenced by his damp black hair, which clung to his head like a helmet. His face was wet with a mixture of sweat and rain and it was completely unreadable. It held far too many emotions: nervousness at being so close to a bishop, shock at the sight of Will's bruised face, fear of Talitha, and a deflating hope when Jim Anderson didn't come into the room after them.

Quickly, Will looked away, feeling oddly guilty that he had lived, while Jim hadn't.

The last man in the room, the dapper looking priest with the finely trimmed grey goatee, stood by the window and as they entered, he looked up from a stack of yellowed papers. This man held Will with a steady grey-eyed gaze for a second before he turned his face toward Talitha. She stared back and her eyes were wide open as if declaring herself fit to be judged. She even lifted her chin slightly, exposing her slim neck, one of her most vulnerable points. It was an odd moment.

Will broke it. "Hello Father Alba. It's me Will Jern, and Talitha is here as well."

"Talitha?" The priest's voice sounded hoarse and worn to a whisper. "And Jim?" The siblings shared a look.

"No...he didn't make it," Will said with even less life in his words than the priest had used. Sean Shay hung his head, his emotions hidden behind the curtain of black hair that obscured his face. "I'm sorry, Sean."

"Another death?" The bishop let out a long slow sigh. Turning slowly he eyed the new comers, especially Talitha. His bright blue eyes seemed to penetrate with their intensity. "And are you the girl that did this to the good father?"

"In a manner of speaking, your Excellency." Talitha faced the bishop and matched the look that he had given.

"Really? This little girl did this?" The old man no longer appeared cherubic, instead he glared scornfully at the assembled group of men, all of whom stood at least a head taller than she. "And no one could stop her?"

"It does add credence to Father Alba's claim." This was from the dapper priest. He strode over from the window and gave Talitha a closer look, staring into her eyes.

"Rubbish, Carl." The bishop shifted in his seat to face the girl better. "Alba has already said that he didn't fight back. Anyone could have the power to do this terrible thing, when the victim doesn't fight back."

"Credence?" Will asked, putting himself between his sister and the two clergymen. He didn't care for how they were speaking as if she wasn't in the room. "May I ask who you are?"

The bishop waved to the other priest, who answered in a raspy sounding voice, "My name is Father Carlton Vogel. I am the Exorcist within the See. And this is his Excellency, Bishop Keenan, auxiliary to Cardinal Archbishop Law."

Will, who didn't know what a See was, glanced back and forth between the two men at a loss as to what sort of protocol was expected of him, he had never before met a bishop. For a moment, he considered attempting to kiss the man's heavy gold ring, but it seemed just too silly. After a second, he ended up giving the older man a simple nod. It went unnoticed as Vogel began to speak again.

"Mr. Jern, I used the word *credence* for the simple reason that a claim of possession is not something that we in the Catholic community take lightly. Each case must be proven before an attempt at exorcism is made."

"Which clearly didn't happen here," the bishop interjected. "Oh Alba, we talked about this. When you first came up from New York, remember? You said you were done with this demon talk and now you're trying to spin some tale about magic swords and not one, but two demon possessions. And where's the proof? Eh? Mr. Jern, do you have this magic sword?"

Feeling suddenly stupid, Will answered, "It's more of a cursed sword actually...and I don't have it here with me." His ears felt to grow warm as he spoke.

"I didn't think so," Bishop Keenan responded. "Alba, please...I don't think we should go on with this charade. You screwed up. You were in a terrible position, I understand, I really do. If a psycho told me that he had five children held hostage, I don't know what I'd do. But...but possession? Really? Help me out on this, Carl."

Vogel went the bed and touched Alba's leg. "Father Alba, from what you and Mr. Shay have told me, there really wasn't any possession concerning Luke. It was all a trick of some sort. He probably knew all about your past, and he put on a bit of a show. The only question I have is why?"

"You already know this. He wanted the sword," Talitha stated matter of factly. "Luke could've left at anytime, but he stayed for the promise of the sword."

The priest nodded gravely. "Yes, he risked quite a bit for that sword. Mr. Jern, would you mind if I went up to Maine with you to retrieve it?"

The Bishop cut in as if speaking to a child, "No. Carl, please. I'm trying to nip this exorcism thing in the bud. I know that it's part of your job, but you're like a kid with a hammer; everything looks suddenly like a nail. You've investigated three possible cases of possession already this year and where has it got you?"

"Closer to God, is always my hope, your Excellence. If I am to take my position as exorcist seriously, I will investigate every possibility out there. But if it will make the Cardinal happier, I'll fly up to Maine on my own dime."

Father Vogel gave Will a nod as if the matter was settled. Will could only shrug, feeling a growing desperation about him. "I don't know if I can get it. My wife Lisa hid it, but it's probably being stolen right this second. That's why..."

"See Carl? Father Alba?" The bishop jumped in. "No sword, no proof. All you have is a bunch of wild stories that no one is going to believe, certainly not the cardinal. Alba, he's going to see this as you trying to get out of all the trouble you have caused. Why didn't you come to me right away when this Luke first showed up?"

"You would've sent for the police and I couldn't risk the lives of those children by calling his bluff," Father Alba replied dejectedly.

"So in order to deal with a serial killer, you bring in someone worse... an escapee from an asylum for the criminally insane? And of course she ends up freeing the killer and now we have *another* death on our hands!" The bishop rubbed his hands across his smooth face. Just then, Will feared to correct the man's mistake, seeing as it would only hurt Father Alba even more; they had a total of six more deaths; four innocent, two guilty.

Just then, the bishop glanced toward Talitha. "Miss Jern, I'm sorry if I'm being offensive, but you don't look much in the way of being possessed to me."

Will gave his sister a look of warning, not to say anything, but seemingly on purpose she turned from her brother, uncharacteristically rebelling.

"Would you really know what a possessed girl looks like?" Talitha asked; her words, cold and cutting, quieted the room in a heartbeat. All eyes went to her and those who knew her capabilities felt sweat cool their backs suddenly. "Possession is far more prevalent than you realize. There are hundreds of demons on earth even now. The smart ones lay low, burrowing into their hosts, feeding off them, turning their souls black and only when there is nothing left, do they show themselves. And even then, most people are all but unaware how close to a demon they had been living."

She paused to let the idea sink in. "Tell me your Excellency, if I was possessed would you really want me to show proof right here in this room?"

Milner's eyes were huge and he and Will shared a look, the cop was growing nervous, as Talitha appeared to be getting more and more agitated. Will tried a smile of reassurance, but it failed, and the cop only swallowed hard at the distortion in Will's ruined face and turned away.

"Are you saying that you aren't possessed?" the bishop asked in a calm fashion. Will had to credit the old man. Despite sitting next to a priest who had his eyes torn out only the day before by the very girl who stood in front of him, the bishop was playing it cool.

"No, I'm saying be careful what you wish for." The two stared at each other for a moment.

He smiled as if the tension in the room hadn't jumped. "Perhaps you're right; maybe it wouldn't be such a good idea. However, I've been told that your brother possesses a talent that would be harmless to demonstrate. It would go a long way to convincing me that all this talk of the super-natural is true. And believe me, if I don't get convinced, the cardinal will never be."

All eyes went to Will. Even Father Alba swung his bandaged head in his direction and despite the coverings, there was a hopeful look to him. There was only one problem; Will wasn't getting a spontaneous vision. And he wasn't going to purposely look; he had done that twice before and both times had been horrendous. It was something he would never do just to satisfy someone's curiosity.

As always, Talitha seemed to read his mind and knew the reason for his hesitation. "You want to see him do some tricks? Is he a trained monkey?" she demanded of the bishop in a strident tone.

"I suppose not," the bishop replied evenly. "But I have three dead bodies to account for, as well as a priest who has aided and abetted two known criminals." He pointed a finger at her as he said this. "The way things have been going for the Church lately, the cardinal is likely going to want to wash his hands of Father Alba and without his help..." he left off with a sad shake of his head.

The room went silent at this and Will shared a guilty look with Talitha. It'd be the height of injustice to the blind priest to blame him for any of what had happened. His actions had been heroic in the face of great evil and because of this Will decided to help the man. Still, it was such a terrible thing to purposely look into the future that it was a minute before he spoke, "Maybe I can do something. Maybe..."

"No you won't, Will! This is such crap!" Talitha cried. "You should be giving Father Alba a fucking medal." Her volcanic anger and her use of profanity in front of a bishop stunned Will. It was so much like her demon plagued self that his heart began to bang against the insides of his bruised chest.

"Whoa, Tal, hey are you ok?" he asked this, turning his sister so he could look into her eyes. He feared that he would see her normal soft brown eyes looking jet black, as they sometimes did when her evil self was in control, but her eyes hadn't changed and he had to remind himself that part of her was gone. "Are you all right? You're not acting normal."

At this, she registered sudden guilt and a touch of remorse. "Oh...oh you're right. I'm sorry, your Excellency, but what you're asking of my brother is obscene and what you're doing to Father Alba is criminal."

"I think it's rather hypocritical for *you* to be throwing around the term criminal," the red in Keenan's cheeks was pronounced. "But I can do so without any qualms. The five of you," he waved his hands at the siblings, Milner, Sean Shay, and Father Alba. "You have all engaged in criminal activity that is guaranteed to besmirch the good name of the Church. Yet you expect the cardinal to jump through hoops on the basis of wild claims and dead bodies?"

Along with the other four who had been pronounced criminal, Will dropped his head to his chest feeling a heavy guilt. The room was silent for a time and then Talitha spoke up.

"Since this is all my fault, I will show you something if it'll help Father Alba." After a quick glance around the room, she went to a cabinet that stood near to the bed. It was filled with medical supplies, but instead of opening any of the glass-fronted drawers, she simply punched one of the little windows. Shards went everywhere and after they finished bouncing and skittering about, she picked up the largest piece and went to stand before the bishop.

She drew up the sleeve of her raggedy black dress and then with dreadful slowness, she sliced deeply into the muscle of her left forearm. Blood drained from the wound, but she didn't wince or cry out, but only dragged the sharp glass further along.

"Oh my!" exclaimed the bishop, leaning away from the wound. Talitha only smiled and tossed the stained glass onto father Alba's breakfast tray where it plopped ugly in his uneaten scrambled eggs.

"A high tolerance for pain. Very interesting," Father Vogel murmured. "Unfortunately that's not enough. There are certain sects..."

"I'm not done, but since you are such a doubting Thomas, would you like to put your fingers in the wound?" She held out her arm to him and instead of shying away, he did indeed touch the outer edges of it. Blood ran from it like water from a faucet, but even as he probed it, the blood stopped completely and not another drop oozed out. The priest's mouth came open, and his eyes widened.

Talitha paused to see if this was enough, but when the two clergymen only glanced at each other and nothing more, she continued, "Father Vogel, look at me please." Despite the please she threw in, it was more of a command. "Are you familiar with any of the tongues of the Void?"

"Do you mean Hell?"

"There is no Hell. There is only the illusion of Hell. Hell is a place with walls and dungeons and chains and demons. That place doesn't exist except in the minds of the damned, but the Void does exist. It's vast and horrible, endless. The Void is filled with pain and lies, and everything in it is an illusion, including the way out. There is no way out, but...but...but I digress. Do you have knowledge of any of the 'Hell' languages?"

"No, how could I?"

Talitha sighed in exasperation and turned to the bishop. "How can I demonstrate a knowledge of tongues if your exorcist doesn't know any?"

"Well..."

"Never mind." Talitha, again was agitated and surly. This was so unlike her that Will would have asked her to stop her demonstration if it wasn't for the fact that Father Alba needed it. She continued with a note of superiority, "Do you know any language besides English? Sprechen sie deutsche? How about... govorite li bosanski? Or... an bhfuil gaeilge agat? That last one is Gaelic and it's quite a mouthful let me tell you." Talitha then began to yammer away in different and odd sounding languages until Father Vogel put out a hand.

"I would like to tape record this, if you don't mind."

"I would say go right ahead, but you don't have a tape recorder on you."

He cocked his head curiously. "How do you know? *Sony* makes a very small recorder. I could have one in my back pocket."

"But you don't. Intimate knowledge of a person one has never met is a sign of possession, correct?" she asked the priest. He nodded with a slight smile. To Will it looked as if he were enjoying their little encounter. Everyone one else in the room only stared with varying levels of uncertainty.

"I know things about you, Father," she stated baldly.

"Such as?" Father Vogel hadn't blinked at her statement.

She studied him for close to a minute before answering, "You enjoy Italian food and have red wine with dinner, almost without exception. When you were younger, you played the violin, but now not so much maybe once or twice a year, instead you sing and not just at church. When you're alone... in the shower or in the car. How am I doing?"

He had lost his smile and said faintly, "Very good."

"Hmmm. You smoke cheap cigarettes, Camels I believe, but oddly, you don't use a cheap lighter. Instead you use something that has meaning to you...a Zippo adorned with an emblem."

"Yes...how did you know?"

"It's in your left front pocket. And you have a pen in your back right."

He dug these out and held them up for the others to see. "Amazing."

"Not really," she said with a shrug. "I could go on if you wish." She turned to the older clergyman and gave him once over. The bishop did little save raise an eyebrow, but his attitude was one of growing wariness. "You drink only single malt scotch at night, but during the day you drink vodka, because of the lack of an observable odor. As a child, you were poor and you suffered from rickettes, and now you sleep on a bed with Egyptian cotton sheets and you eat at the finest restaurants. You had salmon this morning for breakfast and steak last night for dinner."

"How do you know all this?" The bishop demanded. The pink in his cheeks had turned to grey that had him looking very old. "Are you...are you possessed? For real?"

"I was," Talitha replied, with her shoulders slumping. In fact, all of her sagged. "It's a long story."

"They have to hear it, Tal," her brother murmured. He knew they were now well satisfied that something supernatural had occurred.

"I know, but do I have to be here for it?"

He understood completely. Although he would do his best to skim over the worst of it for her, in the re-telling she would come away looking horrible. Like a monster, merciless and beyond redemption.

"No, but don't wander too far please. And, if you don't mind, book us on the next flight into Bangor." She gave him a glum smile and a quick head bob, before leaving. He watched her head out the door feeling wrong for some reason, but then his ability kicked in and he *knew*. She was deathly afraid of being hated.

"Talitha," he called down the hall. She turned back in apprehension, her hand going to the neck of her dress. "I forgot to tell you that I love you."

She smiled shy at the unexpected words.

Chapter 5

Will

The telling of their ordeal went by relatively quickly with Will staring at the white tiled floor and speaking in a dull monotone, but the question and answer session that he hadn't been counting on, following just after, did not. It was a slow painful torture. Every action by all involved was second-guessed to such a ridiculous degree that Will quickly grew angry. The worst of the lot was Eric Milner.

"Why didn't you arrange the bodies when you were done? You could've made it look like they had killed each other."

"Did she have to use my gun? She could've killed that guy with her bare hands."

"Why didn't you wipe down Terry's apartment? Now you'll have left fingerprints everywhere!"

"Why didn't you just shoot your sister in the church?"

This last roiled Will to no end, especially since the cop asked it more than once. Eventually, Will simply began to ignore the cop. This sped things up somewhat, yet it was still awhile before they were satisfied with the details of the story. Then came endless questions concerning the powers demonstrated by the brother and sister. The extent of them, their limits, their uses. The bishop stayed quiet through most of this, letting Father Vogel probe here and there for information, while he sat back studying Will.

During this part of the questioning, Sean Shay excused himself with a quiet mumble and left the room. He had been silent throughout and his sad face was ashen by the time he left. Will felt for the man, not only sadness but guilt as well. Survivor's guilt. It was an odd feeling and one that he would have a hard time putting into words if ever asked.

Sean didn't say good-bye and too late Will realized that he didn't either. But he wished he had since within minutes of the door closing behind him, Will *knew* he would never see the man again.

"I'm sorry for all of this," the bishop said, indeed sounding quite sorry, as if he'd been a part of what had happened. When he wished to the bishop could sound incredibly emotional. His voice had a quality to it. It made everything he said more true or perhaps more real. When he was sad, nobody seemed sadder. When he was angry, people cowered. When he spoke, people listened. He turned to Milner. "Tell me Officer, what can you do about all of this?"

Milner seemed to shrink in front of the bishop and he took two small steps back as he spoke, "Well...the crime scene with the boy, the one Will dreamed about, we don't have to do anything about that. It's clean as far as we're concerned. Mainly, it's just the one crime scene we have to worry about over at the factory. I'm guessing that the fire burned up all those little boys pretty good and since they're buried beneath tons of rubble, I don't think I can do much about that. But the rest? Seeing as Jim killed that girl, I could maybe put a gun in his hands and make it look like he shot Luke too."

"I was hoping that you could just make it all disappear, if you know what I mean." The bishop's Irish blue eyes smiled, but the cold words weren't really a suggestion and Milner nodded to the bishop while his eyes darted around.

"I might need some help. A van and maybe some boys to..."

"Whatever you need. Please speak to my assistant Father Charles, he'll be glad to aid you in any way he can." The bishop nodded to the door as a way of dismissal and Milner was up in a hurry to obey, but he paused at the door.

"Uh, Will? I'm going to need my gun back."

Will hesitated. He didn't trust Milner. "I need to go back to the factory as well. When we're done there, you'll get your gun back."

Milner looked to pout, however the bishop shooed him away simply by lifting his chin. "What do you need at the factory?" Keenan looked only casually inquisitive, yet there was sharp intelligence behind his eyes.

"The incantation to open the gate onto the Void is there. I need it, and I will need those ones too, Father." Will pointed to the stack of thick vellum in Vogel's hand. "Where did you get them?"

"Mr. Shay found them in a small nap-sack in the storage room beneath the church," Vogel answered. "He thought they were important."

"Sean was right." Will went on to explain about Amy Harris and the fact that his wife was being held hostage. As he spoke, his chest began to throb where the bullet had struck it and unknowingly he rubbed the spot.

"Oh my." The bishop sat back looking tired. "More of this?"

"Mr. Jern, this Amy Harris probably won't give your wife to you," Father Vogel said. "You have to know that once you turn over these...papers you have nothing left to bargain with and if she's anything like how Father Alba described her mother, then she isn't the type to worry too much about killing the both of you."

"I know." Will rubbed his chest some more now that his unspoken fear had been put into words. "But what choice do I have? She'll know if I call the police."

"Maybe the Church can help. We have resources," Bishop Keenan nodded knowingly as he said it.

Will hesitated, wondering exactly what that meant, but then shook his head as if clearing it from a dream. "I can't risk it. I don't know the extent of her abilities."

The bishop sat back giving his exorcist a long look, he then turned to Will. "Mr. Jern, I can't stop you from going to help your wife, nor would I ever want to. That being said, you aren't leaving with these incantations. Just as you made the decision to leave the sword behind..."

Will's sudden laugh stopped the old man's words. "Your Excellency, you don't know who you're dealing with. Even if it was just me you had to worry about, it's doubtful you could stop me from taking those papers and going to Maine. Police or no police. But you're also dealing with Talitha, and she'll leave behind a trail of bodies from here to Bangor if she has to."

"I thought you said your exorcism worked," the bishop replied, his hand going involuntarily to his cross that hung about his neck. "Is the demon Ba'al Fie-ere still in her?"

"No, the demon is gone; back to the Void. It's just Talitha you'd have to deal with...only she thinks she's cursed and that her soul is doomed either way. And after the last eight years, especially the last few days, I think she might be right. But there has been only one thing in all this time that has brought her joy, and that is my coming baby. Right now, this baby might be the only thing she has to live for and I have a feeling that if you were to get between her and Lisa..." Will left the sentence unfinished. For the most part, Will was bluffing about this, yet still he had felt uneasy a couple of times when around his sister that morning. There was an unnamed quality about her that had him a little nervous.

The two clergymen glanced at each other in uncertainty, while Father Alba lifted his chin from his chest. "Give him the incantations, please. We should not be the cause of the suffering of innocents."

Bishop Keenan looked unsure of himself. "Are we talking about a moot point anyway? If the sword can do what the two of you say, then the incantations can't be any worse. Or can they?"

Father Vogel frowned looking down at the papers. "They could be... anything is possible. Perhaps we should bring your sister in to decipher the writings."

This was agreed to and ten minutes later Talitha sat

hunched by the window, pouring over the vellum. Next to her was an ordinary pad of paper and in her right hand she held a pen with which she had already written out a string of notes. She turned the first page sideways and a second later, she had it upside down.

"Can you read that language?" Father Vogel asked from just behind her. Though he was a precise, intelligent man, he was also like a curious boy, hoping to see the secret to a magic trick revealed.

"Yes...and no...and kind of," Talitha answered cryptically. "There's actually a mash of three languages being used and one of them I've never seen before..." She paused, frowning at the text. "But that's not such a big deal. There are thousands of demonic languages, yet they're all somewhat similar, especially written out."

She squinted back down at the papers, turning them as before. Minutes slipped by as she continued to scribble away and the three clergymen and Will only sat around in silence. Waiting.

"Ah!" she exclaimed.

"Have you translated the text?" Bishop Keenan asked in a rush. He had fidgeted more than the rest, clearly unaccustomed to waiting.

"No, I just discovered that the texts are enciphered!" Talitha beamed at them in excitement. Will shook his head in mock sadness at her enthusiasm.

"A code? Great!" The bishop sat back again in exasperation.

"Don't worry your Excellency. Amy Harris could never come up with a code that Talitha couldn't break," Will stated positively, however he did glance at the time 11:40 a.m. He knew that these things could take time.

"It's a cipher actually. And before you ask, there is a difference between a cipher and a code. I just hope it's only a triple-alphabetic substitution cipher. If she used a Caesar shift, this will take a while."

"What's a..." the bishop began, but Will stopped him with a headshake. Given half a chance, Talitha would talk non-stop for hours on a subject such as this and he didn't have the time.

A few minutes later: "Oops." Talitha scribbled at something, scratching over a line of text and rewriting it again. A little bit after that: "What? How did I miss..." She frowned at the paper and rechecked her work. "Darn it!" She exclaimed and then with a sour look she stacked up the papers and handed than back to a flummoxed looking Will. "I can't decipher these. Sorry, but somehow the writing on the pages shifts from language to language. It's magic of some sort. Without a spell, or perhaps a counter-spell, these are useless."

"Magic writing?" Will held them up to the light but the words didn't shift or move as he expected. "Are you sure?"

She nodded. "Yes, there's no doubting it."

The bishop put out his hand to look at the incantations as well. He stared hard for a minute. "Whoa! One of these little squiggles changed. This one right there, it didn't look like that a moment ago. I didn't see it change, I just looked away and when I looked back..." The bishop held his head down for a moment, looking at the polished floor of the hospital room, thinking hard. "I believe we need to burn these...I know what you're going to say Mr. Jern, but if they're so important to warrant this sort of protection, they can't fall back into the witch's hands."

"Your Excellency, it would make little difference," Father Vogel said. "From everything we've heard, the mother, Henny Harris discovered the secret to opening a gate into the Void by using only a simple Ouija board. It was probably quite time consuming, but effective nonetheless. My personal opinion is that we allow Mr. Jern to take the incantations with him in his attempt to rescue his wife. I think we can trust him."

"Your Excellency," Father Alba whispered. His face

had slowly turned as white as his bandages and his voice was that of a man far older that he actually was. "I trust Will Jern to do the right thing."

"And what of his sister? Do you trust her?"

The blind priest's head slumped to his chest as if in defeat and he sat there like that for so long that Will was on the verge of giving him a shake to see if he had passed out, when he spoke, "My head says no, she can't be trusted, but my heart says yes. There is love in her still and deep down she is good."

Bishop Keenan stood and stretched, his back popping. He was surprisingly tall. At six-foot-two, he was able to look Will in the eye and did so for close on a minute before he spoke, "Take the incantations. Do not fail to return without them, and the sword too, bring that back as well. I'll pray for you and your family." Will took the stack of vellum, solemnly.

"I will, your Excellency. And thank you for your prayers."

"I want you to take Father Vogel with you," the bishop turned to the trim priest with iron-grey goatee. "Do you have any qualms about going?"

"Not in the least. I think it..." he broke off as he noticed the look of fear that the siblings shared. "What is it?"

"Priests don't last too long around Ba'al Zubel," Will answered. "Perhaps you should have a look at the basement of the factory before you decide to come along."

Chapter 6

Talitha

A half hour later, when they entered the room beneath the partially destroyed factory, the balance between life and death was equal between the bodies that breathed and those that never would again. But Will didn't stay for long, he cast his eyes about quickly, looking slightly dumbfounded as he did. A second later, his head gave a little wiggle that Talitha recognized as an effect of a minor vision. Will had been searching for the incantation that the gypsy had used to bring Ba'al forth from the Void and now he *saw* that Eric Milner had it stuffed in his right front pocket. Talitha could have told him this, she had known where it was hidden the second they walked in.

"I need to talk to you outside," Will growled at the cop. Milner's mouth came open but he didn't say a word.

When the two left, the dead held sway, they commanded the room and for some reason, the four corpses seemed larger than they had been—as if in death, they had grown more important to her. At first they held her attention, captivating her with the inhuman way their bodies splayed out in odd positions. She wanted to arrange them better, to make them more real looking, but she was afraid.

It was a strange fear, especially since she'd seen many dead bodies in her time. Normally, they only made her sad, but now she was decidedly creeped out by them. Particularly the huge corpse of Jim and the slighter one of Luke. Always as she turned her head, they were just at the edge of her vision and sometimes they seemed to move.

Because of this, she stuck close to the priest. Where he went, she went and she liked that he was alive, his heartbeat was reassuring to her. A steady seventy-eight beats a minute.

"You say you shot Luke twice, where was he when that happened?" Father Vogel asked. His voice was not melodious as the bishop's had been and she would've rather kept listening to the man's heartbeat. She pointed to a spot on the floor.

"Hmm." The sound was unpleasing to her as well, as was the spot on the floor. There was something unrecognizable on the floor; part of a human.

He went to it and studied the ground around it from different angles. Next, the dead came under his scrutiny; he studied them, touching their limbs, moving them back and forth. With Luke he spent a good deal of time on, inspecting his wounds, opening his mouth, and peering in. After this, he undressed the body, and the smell, which had been difficult for her to ignore before, was now impossible. It was the smell of the little boys on his corpse, and also it was the smell that came from the filth-laden box beneath the church. Suddenly that image came to her, the box and the foul, decomposing mysterious creature that it held. Yet she had never seen it before. It had been the other Talitha that had seen it.

Talitha squeezed her eyes shut and stepped blindly away from the priest, silently demanding that her mind ignore the horrific vision and instead she forced it to classify and quantify the various sounds of water dripping into the room. There were sixteen different trickles ranging in intensity from a feeble third of a liter per hour drip that landed on Terry Brabec's exposed arm, to a four liter per hour flow that came down just in front of the doorway.

The night before two drops from that flow had struck her with equal intensity as she dashed to the still form of Jim Anderson. The first struck her left wrist right at the junction of the radius and ulna, the second landed on her right cheek. It mingled with a tear of hers, changing its composition. Was it still then a tear? She wondered.

She forced herself not to care.

Drip, drip. Drip, drip, the water came down all around her. Loud and soft. Some faster. Some were heavy, full drops. She saw one of these and the tear was huge. It reminded her of her little sister's tears. Somehow, Katie could hold together tears well beyond the normal surface tension would allow. This one was oval shaped, or rather it was tear shaped.

Talitha shook her head. Realizing it was a drop of water not a tear that she had seen. It must have fallen from the partially destroyed ceiling of the factory and not from an eye. Her own eyes were meant to be dry. There wasn't a foreign body in either one of them that would elicit the need for any tears. Nor did she have allergies. A tear just then running down her cheek would be illogical.

The wet upon her face was only from the rain.

The priest interrupted her thinking, "After you shot Luke, did he come at you?"

Talitha suddenly remembered something as if it were a dream. She was in the factory and it was dark. In her hand was a very large gun. It was black and when she looked down its barrel, it felt as if she held the night. Her brother had handed it to her and she remembered then thinking what a fool he was and that he would pay for his stupidity. At first, she liked the feel of the gun, but then she had changed.

At that point, she hated and feared the gun. It was clumsy and she recalled how it didn't fit her hand, it was too big, made for someone with longer fingers, but she had compensated and shot her brother in the chest. Her aim had been true. She had accounted for every variable, yet he didn't die.

Instead, he screamed and screamed. That was of course an impossibility. It was illogical for a man so recently shot in the chest to scream like that.

Just then, she heard her voice answer the priest, "Yes. Luke walked toward me and so I shot him a second time."

She had shot the thin blonde man dead center in the

chest. But he didn't scream as her brother did, neither did he die. Another impossibility.

"What happened next?" The priest took a picture of the floor of the room and the flash of the camera caused Talitha to blink. A natural reaction, certainly. She blinked again repeatedly and water, warmed evidently from the recent fire dripped upon her face. The water ran to her lip and she took it in. Her mind, the way she had constructed it, instantly classified the fluid, ninety-nine percent water, with traces of mucin, lipids, lysozyme, lipocalin, immunoglobulins, glucose, urea, sodium, and potassium.

An interesting mix, but altogether illogical and certainly not rain. Even the pH values were off.

"The demon looked at me from the Void." This statement was the antecedent for more of the strange fluid that wasn't rain to fall upon her cheeks.

Scientifically, she tried to tell herself that there was no Void. Such a thing was impossible to measure, to know. How big was it? What were its dimensions in kilometres? Or was it most practical to measure it in millimetres? Where was the Void? What was its longitude?

"And what was that like?" The priest took notes in a black and white composition notebook as he asked. The scritching pen was loud. She tuned it out.

In the dream, it hurt to be looked upon by the demon.

It was indescribable and thus she didn't bother with the attempt, she turned away ignoring the question, ignoring the feeling of that warm rain upon her face. Instead, she listened to the water drip. It was musical. There was a beat and it had rhythm, but it wasn't a symphony. It was all percussion, still it was nice.

Music was illogical—but happily illogical. Music held no use. It had no practical value. What was its function? How did it run concurrent with human emotion? It was essentially inexplicable in evolutionary terms. In fact, it defied evolution and made a mockery of it. It was wonderful.

She managed a smile as she lost herself in the thousands of sounds that played upon her ears, all the while ignoring the words of the priest.

He spoke to her in sentences, but those tiny drips raining from the blackened ceiling above were a thousand times magnified in her head. Illogical. Illogical. Warm rain upon her face was all illogical.

"Talitha, are you ok?" Will's voice was loud, like the voice of God. She had been standing facing a wall that in all her dreams had no memory. This one wall in that horrible room was blameless. The night before it had stood mute and empty, never once framing an image of the demon or that of Will raging in pain or of Jim Anderson dead. This was the good wall. She could face this wall and see only it...nothing.

"Can I leave?" she asked her brother as more of the warm rain found its way down her cheeks. "Can I wait outside?"

"Sure Tal. You don't have..."

There was a sudden roar of a lion filling her ears. Anything else her brother might have said was drowned out in the fury of that sound. The priest was in the process of undressing Jim Anderson, inspecting his many wounds, looking into his eyes. Her first impulse was to dash the priest's head against a wall, instead she walked stiff legged out of the room. Talitha held her decorum together until she was safely out of view of that room that held so much death and then she raced for the stairs. Leaping piles of debris or dodging around the avalanches caused by the fire. She was up the stairs and standing in the rain in seconds.

Her breath came in huge gusts, like billows.

It was forced, she was letting her emotions dictate, not her mind and her emotions wanted her to act...like a girl. Or perhaps like a human. For so long she had fought that impulse, to be human. Always on guard, she had kept herself resolute to the point of being less animated than a machine. The blame for this had always been the demon, the other

Talitha that haunted her, possessing her, who had used her feelings only to bring about more pain.

But that excuse was gone. Like a miracle, the demon had been sent back to the Void and now Talitha was free to cry if she wished. She could rage and scream, or laugh. The entire range of human emotion could be hers, except for love. That simple thing she would deny herself, not as a punishment, but rather as a gift to herself. Love frightened her badly.

In the Void, love was the ultimate instrument of torture. It was the sharpest knife. The cruelest whip. When the acid hand of love plied the lash, it shredded the flesh more deeply and brought pain to its greatest height.

For this reason, she would cast away love...if she could. If not she'd run from it and hope that it never would find her again.

Out into the rain she bolted, not knowing or caring where she was going, letting the elements run down her face. Ahead she recognized the church, St Thomas and she dashed off to her left, not wanting to recall the confusion of memories that swept over her. They came nonetheless; there she was standing in the steeple letting Jim stare at her, pretending she didn't notice. There they were having dinner together, gorging themselves silly on pizza all the while feeling his love for her radiate off of him. There she was pulling Father Alba and Luke along on the leashes that she had formed from the priest's stole.

This last memory was like a thunderbolt and it stopped her dead cold. She replayed it in her mind, not knowing where it came from.

"It was a nightmare, is all," she said aloud to the rain. She had slept the night before and surely that was where it had come. "It's only a nightmare!" she called out loudly. The rain's only response was to come down harder than before. The words felt like both the truth and a lie at once and in confusion, she ran again, even faster than before.

In a minute, she had lost herself in a maze of trash strewn back alleys that ran behind the dirty little hovels that passed as homes in that low rent neighborhood.

She cried. Logical or not, she cried. In truth, she bawled. She remembered another dream, perhaps the same one, and in it Father Alba seemed so resolute as her fingers, hooked like claws came at his face.

"Talitha, please know that you are forgiven for what you are about to do. Yours has been a hard life and I..."

"Shut it, Alba..."

Talitha squeezed her head hard with both hands and cried harder drowning out the memory. It was an alien sensation to cry. Or at least to cry so freely. There had been tears since her return from the Void, but always they had been light and were over with after only a minute or two. Anything close to hysterics would only bring out the demon, who got off on her misery, relishing it. So she had held back, despite the fact that it felt more and more that she was losing herself, becoming someone terribly cold and dead inside.

There had been no mourning the loss of Brian Galt. He had died. Murdered actually. Talitha had come back into her body and looked upon her cabin and knew in a second whose blood it was soaking the walls and making her hands so slippery. She hadn't cried. Even when she had found his body deep in the forest, broken and tumbled, almost unrecognizable, she hadn't cried. Not a tear.

Instead, she threw a wall around her heart that had held firm like steel until Jim Anderson. Falling for him, and so quickly had been completely unexpected, especially from a logical point of view. And perhaps that's how she allowed it happened. Who could have guessed that two people with only the extremes of loneliness in common would have been smitten so quickly. Yet there she was allowing that first kiss, begging for it, in reality. It had been illogically wonderful.

She missed him already.

"You ok?" A black man of forty or so, stood huddled

beneath a tattered and weathered oversized patio umbrella. He had made a home of sorts beneath it and all of his worldly possessions were stacked in green bags around him. The smell alone had Talitha categorizing him immediately as alcoholic and homeless. His tone wasn't polite, it was more his way of announcing himself so that she would notice him and move on. She did, still crying.

Two blocks later: "Hey baby! Come on over here, get out of the rain!" The alleys were more populated than the empty streets. Most of the houses had little more than stoops in the front, but a good number of the backyards had covered porches and under them little throngs were gathered, here and there.

"Come on baby. I got some weed."

Talitha stopped at the word weed. The man had used the word as if it were an enticement. It made no sense. She glanced into the yard and indeed, there seemed to be a veritable bumper crop of commonplace weeds, dandelions, and such, growing in abundance.

Through them, a man of about her own age sauntered toward her. "Watcha doing back here, baby?" He was tall and broad with white teeth and skin the color of mocha. His tone was pleasant, but it ran inharmoniously with an insidious corruption in his eyes. These ran up and down her slim body. It was an unpleasant hungry look and it grated on her.

She remembered a man just like him once. He had come too close, thinking he was only dealing with a tiny slip of a girl, but he didn't realize what a monster she was. He had no idea how much pain she could dish out in a flash.

"I like the way that dress clings to you, very nice." The man with the weeds said and then made a low grumbly moan of desire deep in his throat.

"Go away," she warned soft and dangerous. Talitha marveled at herself suddenly. Her tears had turned to cold rain and a feeling gripped her that she had not thought possible; she wanted to hurt this man. It was a desire like she had felt so many times when the demon had controlled her. She would come alive from the black of her subconscious and it would be there, a need to lash out, a need to hate, a need to make someone pay.

"Go away?" he said with amazement. "Bitch, I live here. You must be on crack. Are you? Is that what your deal is?"

"Crack?" She fought the urge to look down to see what he was talking about, instead she gave in to the hate that roiled inside her chest. Talitha took a step forward and now a smile that wasn't matched by the cold look in her eyes flashed across her face.

The black man's eyes blazed at the smile. "Yeah, you want some hail? You gotta attack, strawberry?" His look was like a wolf's and so was hers.

"First you call me baby, then bitch and now strawberry?" she asked shaking her head. She was going to enjoy this, she always enjoyed the pain. "These are improper ways to greet a young lady such as myself. First of all etiquette would suggest that when addressing an unfamiliar individual you should use..."

"Talitha."

Out of the gloom, further down the alley her brother materialized through the grey of the rain. Even with his hood thrown forward, she could see his eyes. He loved her. She hated him.

Her breath came in heavy and she held it, feeling white-hot anger flash through her arteries. His presence was a catalyst, the spark of a primer that set her world aflame. She gave in to the hate that had no beginning. She should hate. If anyone had cause, it was her.

"Go away!" she cried out and her small slim hands drew themselves in to form rock hard deadly fists.

"This isn't smart, Tal."

"What do you know about smart?" she screamed at him.

Hate! It was a drug that she needed. To be rid of love, she would need to hate and she tried to hate her brother. Will was a goody-two-shoes and a moron and Jim was worse! And stupid little Brian...he was...he was...

Brian was sweet and perfect.

"I know killing this guy won't help," Will said advancing.

"Hey, what the fuck," the black man exclaimed, his head swinging back and forth between the two intruders in his world. A world he thought he ruled. "You two think..."

"Go mind your own business, Will," she called out interrupting the man. "He has a gun. I would be only defending myself." Talitha stepped closer to her victim, as if protecting her soon to be kill from another predator. Her reasoning was flimsy to hear even as she said it and a touch of shame cooled her hate.

"Tal, I know what's going to happen. You'll kill him and then you'll wish you hadn't," Will kept his voice calm. Talitha cast a quick look up at the man. He was a drug dealer and a thug and very likely a pimp, judging by the smells and sounds emanating from his tiny home. She didn't know if he deserved death. "Are you trying to find a reason to hate yourself?" Will asked.

"No, I want to hate you," she said, but her words sounded horribly false to her own ears. She had no clue what she wanted. Her insides were a great pain of chaos.

The black man watched this little encounter with an odd expression on his face as if he were the butt of a practical joke. "What the fuck? I ain't the one gettin killed here," he intoned with confidence as his hands went to the back of his jeans.

Talitha presumed that he was reaching for the pistol that she knew he had tucked into his waistband. Now was her chance to let lose her pent up hate, to become savage. It was a chance to stop her mind from dwelling on its own pain by inflicting some of her own. Her eyes flicked to her brother, who hadn't moved. He hadn't budged, even to reach for the gun that she knew he still carried.

This was peculiar. He must have *seen* or perhaps *knew* that the thug next to her was reaching for his gun, yet he did nothing. Did he actually want her to attack the man? Or was the man not going for his gun at all, as she supposed? The second question answered itself as she saw the black pistol emerge from behind him.

The sight of it was a relief. It was a permission slip from the teacher, a doctor's note excusing her from gym class, a *get out of jail free* card. She could now kill him with no qualms.

Liar!

No qualms? Of course she would have qualms and doubts and misgivings. They would nag at her and always she'd know that she had killed a man who might not have deserved death. That he was a bad man wasn't doubted by her, but what were his crimes that merited the ultimate punishment? There was no way to know.

She sighed, tiredly.

And then with inhuman speed she struck the man three inches below the center of his chest, forcing his diaphragm to contract and contort. For a second the man's eyes were huge white globes in his dark face and then he pitched forward, no longer concerned with his pistol or the crazy white people. All he cared about was his next breath.

For Talitha it was déjà vu. She had seen this once before. She had done this once before.

Chapter 7

Will

In his mind Will saw the alley. It was a muddy bog from the rain, and Talitha would add the dull maroon of a man's blood to it. He saw it all. She wanted to kill; to drown her pain in another man's death. He felt keenly his sister's agony over the loss of Jim Anderson, however beneath that was the wild selfish pain over the loss of her own life. Her past had been horrors piled on horrors and her future—doom. The days she had left on Earth would come and go and then...the Void would have her once again.

It was a strange vision filled with knowledge, but absolutely no understanding and it scared him badly. Bad enough for him to briefly put aside his fears for his wife and child.

He ran out of the factory after his sister, but as he cleared the police tape and the debris he saw her sprinting away. She was a blur. Only an Olympian would have any hope of even keeping her in sight, and he was no Olympian—though he could drive. He *knew* where she was heading and he pushed the station wagon to its top speed. As he came upon the alley of his vision, his mind thought bog once again and fearing that the old pathetic station wagon would only get stuck, he left it and hurried along the one time dirt alley. The sides nearest the haphazard fences were the firmest and he kept to them, until he came to her.

What anger and pain was on display in her eyes!

For his entire life he could count on his Talitha to be emotionally collected where anyone else would've fallen apart. Yet just then, with no provocation, she wanted to kill this stranger.

Emotionally it pained him to see her like this. "Talitha,"

he called out.

His vision, capricious as always, failed him at that point. Nothing came, not even a hint. Will forced himself to rely on his other, lesser abilities and stayed calm and spoke calm. He advanced on her with deliberate slowness and made no sudden movements, even as the man went for his gun.

Will had a gun. It was stuck in the front of his jeans, beneath the grey sweatshirt that he wore. And despite the rain making his clothes cling to him, he could've had it out in a flash, yet he stayed his hand. In this situation, the gun was useless. Yes, he could pull it out and point it at his sister, but he couldn't shoot her. She was too important to him.

Amy Harris had known about his ability to see the future but had passed it off as nothing. That was an insanely stupid thing to do, unless she had some Gypsy trick to counter his ability. Increasingly, he thought this to be the case, which made Talitha even more valuable. He couldn't afford to hurt her. So he watched, sending out silent prayers that his sister would regain some sense of herself as the black man drew his piece.

The gun came around as if in slow motion and Will was struck with a horrid sense of déjà vu. Only the night before he had looked down the midnight black barrel of a pistol that was a twin of the one coming to bear on his chest. It was then that Talitha struck. The move was too fast to see. A blur of a white hand and the man was down, his eyes bugging out in a dreadful manner.

"He'll live," Talitha answered the question that had formed on his tongue. "What's wrong with me, Will? I'm going crazy." Her eyes did indeed sparkle with madness.

Will was no psychologist. "I don't know...stress? Grief? Everything?"

For a long while she didn't reply, but only looked down upon the man with barely tamed ferocity as he slowly recovered. His gun sat in the mud near his right hand and

Will had a feeling that if the man went for it, she would kill him. She radiated hate that rivaled the demon that had possessed her for the last eight years. The man in the mud seemed to sense the same thing and pulled his hand back toward himself timidly.

"I want to kill him so bad," she said turning back to her brother. "Why? Ba'al Fie-ere is gone, yet I want to kill this man."

The young black man nearly had his breath under control, but clearly the talk of his possible death had him too afraid to do anything except lay in the cold rain as still as he could. Unexpectedly Talitha knelt down next to him.

"Look at me," she commanded. With the rain coming down into his face, he had to squint up at her. Even so he had a handsome face. "Are you a killer?" she asked. As she waited for him to answer she drug the pistol from the mud and sniffed at it. Will got the shivers remembering how the demon in her had done the same thing. It was cold in the rain and the shivers didn't leave him. He wrapped his arms about himself, noting the man...the guilty man shivered as well.

He was a killer.

"No...I thought you was looking for some crack," the man lied.

Too late Will turned away and Talitha saw his look of judgment. She knelt down on the man's back, forcing him deeper into the mud. He groaned at the unexpected force. Then there was silence, but for the rain. It came down steadily and loudly, jumping into the puddles all around them. Will continued to shiver.

"What should I do, Will? Should I kill him? Part of me wants to, badly but another part begs that I don't and still a third wonders if I should suffer a murderer to live? That part of me wants justice."

"Can you honestly judge a man?" Will asked, wondering how any of this had come to pass. One moment they were in the factory, the next she was running away as if death were upon her heels and now this.

"I don't have to," she replied. "You have judged him. I saw it in your eyes. You know the truth."

"But we don't do that here..."

"Because, no one has your vision! Wouldn't you kill him if he were threatening your baby?" she asked and pressed the gun into the back of the man's head, thumbing the hammer back. Even with the sound of a million raindrops all about them, that noise was loud. It had such dreadful purpose.

"Talitha, stop! I don't know what he's *going* to do. If I did then yes, I would kill him, but I don't see his future. Maybe he's going to change, make amends..."

"Ha! Yeah right," she exclaimed loudly, manically to the heavy clouds above her. "Are you going to go to church? Are you going to repent?" she asked the man.

"I...I..." he sputtered pathetically.

"Talitha, look at me. Why are you doing this? The demon is gone, you don't have to act like this."

"I don't know why!" she shrieked. The misery in her voice was plain to hear and so was the fear and puzzlement. "I feel so..." she looked around in the mud for the answer. "Strange, I guess. Everything I feel or want or think seems magnified. I don't understand it."

"Maybe you're feeling a delayed reaction to your grief," Will suggested. "Maybe now that you're freed from the demon, your emotions are... I don't know suddenly uncorked and you're overflowing like a bottle of champagne."

"Champagne? It feels just like that. My desires are suddenly uncontainable. I'm hungry like I've never felt before. And I'm angry. It's like a swarm of enraged bees are in my mind, running over everything."

She paused suddenly, her brown eyes going wide. "Wait, I know. It was that damned priest who did this to me!" Abruptly, she sounded savage again. "He kept questioning me, bringing things up and then... he touched

Jim. And his hands weren't gentle like they should have been. Jim saved me! And who knows, maybe he saved us all, and that...that priest! His hands were cold, as if Jim was a science experiment to him. All he cared about were facts and...and..."

Her face went slack with sudden realization and she came off the shivering man beneath her, and knelt in the mud next to him. "That would've been me. I would've done the same things, except I would've been worse. I would've mapped out angles and bone fragment trajectories. All the spatter would have been..." Talitha stopped and began to blink rapidly, but the tears came in spite of that.

"The other Talitha was right. I was so useless before her," she said to her brother. "I think I want to get drunk. I've never had champagne before. Do you have any champagne...uh...mister..." She tried to give him a smile and despite the rain and her misery, she couldn't help but be beautiful.

"Jackson is his first name, but he goes by J-Bird" Will prompted. The man's name was just suddenly there in his mind.

An inch from the mud, Jackson's eyes went wider than they had and he shook his head, no. "I got some forties if you want them. You can have them, ok? They're yours, anything you want." His tone was pleading and the sound of it struck the pretty smile from Talitha's face.

"No, they're not mine. It wouldn't be right. I, uh...I'm sorry Jackson for hitting you so hard." She tried to look contrite and he nodded his head in a tiny way, still afraid.

"We don't have time for that either way. Tal, we have to go." Will held out his hand to his sister. She didn't take it right away.

"What do we do about him?" She nodded Jackson's way. "Do we leave him to continue selling drugs and running his brothel? Or do we threaten him or perhaps beat him or maybe break one of his legs?"

"Hey..." Jackson started to say, but Talitha, as if by magic had him by the collar and yanked him in close.

"I wasn't speaking to you, insect," her voice had changed like the speed of her hands and it was low and dangerous sounding.

"Tal, please stop. We let him go. We can't force a person to be good." Will came down to her level, putting out his hand to touch hers. "God doesn't do that, maybe we shouldn't either."

"You're probably correct," she replied. "But I'm going to warn you Mr. Jackson. If you continue down this road, you'll end up in hell with me, and I will remember you. I'll hurt you badly and you'll scream like a little girl being raped for the first time."

Her words had a slow heavy nightmare quality that was horribly unsettling, at least for Will they were, but not for Jackson. His sister, though so small compared to the man, had her hands hooked into his jacket with such strength that it pulled tight across his throat. Once again, his eyes bugged as his breath was choked out of his lungs. Her eyes, on the other hand held a storm of insane fury, but thankfully the fury died out in a second and she released him, standing in a single fluid motion.

"I'm starving," she proclaimed to the rain. "Mr. Jackson do you know where we can get some good French toast around here? You're welcome to join us of course."

2

Jackson logically declined the offer and they left him still in the mud and the rain.

At breakfast, the brother and sister had a breakthrough in their relationship. They did not eat French toast. It wasn't much of a breakthrough but it was something. Though in truth the meal wasn't exactly breakfast, as it was almost one in the afternoon when they ate.

"Maybe we can find an IHOP, they make good French toast, at least they used to," Talitha suggested as they walked, hand in hand down the muddy alley toward where Will had left the old station wagon. Will tried to smile at the idea, but the wires that would've held that fake smile in place felt oddly broken. In truth it wasn't the idea of eating French toast for the millionth time that did it, it was worry over his wife and the fact that time seemed to be against him. The seconds of each minute were glacial in their slowness. Their flight wasn't for another two and a half hours, and with no bags to check and the airport only fifteen minutes away, they had too much time.

Not only did he have time to fret, there was also time to spare for worry and even anxiety.

She caught his odd look. "You don't want IHOP? I thought you liked it," Talitha said with a slight frown on her wet face.

Will sighed as he climbed into the car. "No I don't, sorry. After French toast for breakfast so many times, I'm kind of sick of it."

"Me too!" she cried, with manic jubilance. "All this time, we've both been eating the same thing because we thought the other person liked it."

"Yeah." The car spluttered into being, kicking out blue smoke. Will turned it toward the factory.

"That's so stupid." Her smile was suddenly gone. "We've been eating crap for so long because neither of had the guts to tell the other..."

Will had to interrupt. Her abrupt mood swings were unsettling, and when she was in her angry phase, she was just as bad as the evil Talitha had ever been. It bothered him nearly as much as how slow time felt to be progressing and he couldn't take it any longer. "Talitha, listen to me. We said nothing because we each didn't want to hurt the other, even in this inconsequential thing. That's love. Maybe stupid love, but love nonetheless."

"I guess so."

Will pulled over, the blackened frame of the factory just visible down the road. "I need you, Tal. And so does Lisa, but not like this. You're out of control and you'll end up getting us all killed. You've been through hell, I know it, but can you pull it together?"

Talitha nodded her head, though she kept her face down, staring as her fingers knotted and unknotted in her lap. "I can't seem to stop myself. I have so many memories and dreams all running together, I sort of don't feel like myself. One second I'm furious, the next I'm sad and then I'm excited."

"Maybe you can start by realizing that you can live now and that you don't have to go to hell when you die. You're a good person and..."

"Shut up!" she screamed. Her fist drove down onto the faded passenger side dashboard, sending an explosion of plastic in the damp air of the car. "As always you don't know what you're talking about. I am going to hell. It's done. My future is set."

He leaned back from her outburst, unsettled not by what she said, or even how she said it, but by the unguarded look of hatred she sent his way.

"Do you think that it's my fault?" he asked in honesty, not trying to dodge blame, or to anger her further, but only trying to understand.

She took a long time to answer, which was answer enough for Will. "No, none of any of this is your fault," Talitha said, now suddenly docile. "Will, you'll never understand, unless you go there yourself. And you...you're the last person that would ever feel that they would have to go. So please, don't ask. It just hurts."

She was correct about his not understanding. "I'm not asking, I'm telling you. The Void is for evil people and you're not evil, at all."

"How can you even say that? Of course I am," she replied with an odd faraway look in her eyes. Talitha fingered the ruined glove compartment, the door hung open reminding Will of a groper's mouth, absently she worked it up and down. It looked to be chewing.

"Tal, you are not ev..." He stopped in mid-sentence. She had said this to him before. He tried to recall the conversation, but it only came to him in bits and pieces and just then he couldn't remember if it had been her or the evil Talitha. "Tal, you had an odd look on your face before. It looked like you hated me, can you tell me why?"

She seemed to feel pain at the question and kept her face down looking at her fingers, which had retreated to the safety of her lap and began meshing themselves nervously together. "No...I can't, I mean I don't. I don't hate you."

"Are you mad that I took you from the Void?" he asked, fearful of the answer. She nodded with a blank look in her eyes. "Because you had value? Because you were worth something?"

She shook her head and replied in a whisper, "No, because I was becoming. Becoming powerful— becoming a demon." The eyes of the brother and sister met and there was fear in both of them. These had been the words of the demon.

"Is Ba'al Fie-ere in there with you? Right now?" Will asked, his eyes straying to the gun Talitha had taken from the man from the alley only a few minutes before. It sat between their two seats.

"I...I don't know. I can't tell. I don't think so. It's just that I'm remembering things that the other Talitha had been doing and saying. It's horrible, it's like I've done these things and I'm only now remembering it."

"Can you stop it?"

Talitha started crying again, hard. "I don't know. We shared the same brain clearly, but our memories were always inaccessible to each other before. Yet now hers are sifting into mine. Pretty soon, I won't know which ones are which. Did I rape you?" She gasped in horror as the memory struck her like a slap.

"No, you tried but I stopped you. Tal, look at me. Look at me." He waited until her eyes were full on him. "What is the square root of, uh one-hundred and sixty-nine?"

Her eyes shifted up for a second, before she answered, "Thirteen. Why?"

Will blew out, exasperated. "Because, that's why. What's the square root of two-thousand and sixty-nine?" Her brows came together and he could tell she was about to ask again why. "I'm trying to occupy your mind, while I try to figure out how to stop these memories from happening."

"Oh." Her eyes went up again and she began calculating, as she did, her lips started to move in time with the math running through her mind.

Will reached out and wiped away the fug that had settled on the windshield. The view was only slightly better, a grey curtain that came steadily down. He drove, and at first he headed toward the factory, thinking about asking Father Vogel what he thought they should do. He seemed like an intelligent man, but Talitha's eyes went wide when she saw the building looming before them.

"Oh, God! What did I do? What did I do to poor Alba?" Her hand went to her mouth.

"Tal! Where are you on that square root?"

"I don't know, uh...fort-five, point four something," she moaned out the words.

"Do you want a new calculation to do?"

"Yes...hurry." She began tapping her cheeks rhythmically. Her eyes hollow spheres of fear.

"Two-thousand three hundred and four," he called out, hoping that it would be a good number. Personally, he could only calculate the simplest square roots in his head. Deciding against the factory, where awful memories abounded, he turned to his right down the next street, but didn't catch its name, the condensation was building in the car rapidly. The street was a twin to the next one. The houses were all unremarkably similar.

"Forty-eight. Will, I'm going to become her! I know it..."

"You aren't!" he cut across her. "Twelve thousand three hundred and six." He turned right again at the next main intersection. He had no clue where he was going or really what to do.

"That one's too hard, give me an easier number. I have to become her, it's a certainty."

"Twelve thousand three hundred and six," he repeated, feeling scared that she was correct. She was so rarely wrong.

"One-hundred and eleven...I think. Right around there," she replied desperately as if the right answer could help her in any way. "Will pull over. See that pizza place? It's the same one that Jim got our dinner from last night. I'm hungry. I want that; it was a good memory."

The place was a hole in the wall. Still, when it came to pizza those were usually the best. Almost as a rule, a fancy pizza joint was a poor pizza joint.

Sliding into the booth closest to the door that had jingled merrily above them, Talitha looked around wide-eyed at the other people in the restaurant.

"Why does their hair look like that?" she asked timidly, running her hands through her own straggling locks.

Will glanced back. For the most part the customers and staff in the restaurant were young and resembled his stereotypical vision of people of Italian decent. The women had great masses of hair and in his opinion too much makeup.

"It's the style I guess, don't worry about it," he replied, but she was quite worried.

"And their clothes?" she whispered.

Their stone washed jeans were worn high up, above the waist and they were pegged or rolled up at the ankles. In eight years, Talitha hadn't been in public save for her weekly trips to a rural podunk church, and popular clothing styles had changed dramatically in that time. Compared to the other women in the place, with her ill-fitting black dress, she looked like an Amish girl who had lost her bonnet.

Before he could answer her concerning clothing, a waitress came over, eyeing their raggedy appearance with distaste, probably sensing little opportunity for a tip. She had a magnificent head of dark brown hair—teased almost to the point of being a mane and Talitha gazed at with wonder.

"Kinda wet out, huh? Didja come in on an awk?" the waitress asked in a friendly manner, expecting at least a smile. However, her Boston accent was terribly thick, with the word *ark* coming out sounding like *awk* and Talitha only opened her eyes wider and looked at her brother, bewildered.

He was used to the dreadful sounding accent and replied easily, "Nope just a station wagon, which is pretty close in size to an ark. Can we get a couple of Cokes and two large pies, please? One a supreme and the other just pepperoni."

Just then Talitha made the mistake of glancing back up at the waitress, who asked her, "Uh cupla lah-ges? Aw ya expectin any maw?" Again, Talitha was forced to look to her brother for interpretation and he thought she was coming across as a retarded Amish girl now.

"No just the two of us. We aren't expecting any more people," he answered for the two of them. Talitha's mouth came open slightly and she nodded gently in understanding.

When the waitress was safely out of ear shot, Talitha smiled, her troubles momentarily put aside. "Wow, that's a thick accent. I think while we're in Boston, I'm just going to pretend I'm deaf."

"Yeah," he agreed absently, checking his watch for the hundredth time that day. Two hours until their flight. Another hour and fifteen minutes in the air and then a twenty-two minute car ride. He had a total of two-hundred and seventeen minutes to help his sister come to grips with her memory and mental issues.

"Tal, we have to fix this thing going on in your head," he started. "Yesterday you told me how you could control aspects of your body, can't you just lock away these memories."

Talitha looked about to speak, but her brows came down and she paused for a moment first. "You know something strange? The other Talitha, she actually liked Jim Anderson too. She thought they had some sort of connection."

"She did? That's a little strange," Will agreed. "You wouldn't have thought so, she treated him pretty poorly. But you're getting off subject. Can't you control memory just as you control your sense of smell?"

"Only when I'm concentrating on something else. Also, I don't know what memories to try to reject until they come to me. You see in order for me to block a memory, I have to know what to block first. I'll give you an example, look around this restaurant." She turned her head scanning objects and people.

Will did as well, not seeing her point. It looked like just a hole in the wall pizza joint, one of many that he had been in. Arranged in a long rectangle there were maybe fifteen booths running down the wall to the right and due to the bar there were half that many on the left. There were Italian themed pictures on the walls; the leaning tower of Pisa, the Roman Coliseum. As well, there were pictures of famous people of Italian heritage; actors and sports figures for the most part.

Joe DiMaggio's relatively ugly face sat large in a frame centered on their booth. He gave it a glance, wondering what in the world Marilyn Monroe saw in the gap-toothed ball player.

"Ok?" he asked after a minute.

"Everything in this place has memory associated with it. See this tablecloth." She held up an edge of the red and white checkered spread. "Remind you of anything?"

"Yeah, Papa Gino's." Papa Gino's was an east coast pizza chain they used to frequent as kids.

"That's what I thought as well. But remember that guy?" She flashed her white smile.

He remembered. Every one of the chain's restaurants had tablecloths of checkered red and white and once when the Jern's were eating at their local Papa Gino's, a man came in wearing pants of the exact same pattern. Every head in the entire place turned in unison and stared. It was terribly comical as the man paused in the doorway not seeing the tablecloths but only seeing fifty pairs of eyes following his every move. It was only when he was shown to his table by a hostess, barely suppressing a laugh, did he notice. The poor man turned on his heel and walked out with fast strides and when he had scampered to the parking lot the entire restaurant burst into laughter.

Even now Will had to smile at the memory. "That was funny. The guy probably went home and burned those pants. I know I would've."

"I agree, but my point is, how could I suppress that memory without experiencing it first? I'm going to have to feel everything that she felt and it isn't going to be like a stranger's memory either. It's going to be me doing those things...I saw what I did to Father Alba. I tore out his eyes, I dug..."

"Tal! Focus on me. Ok?" She had quickly turned white under her tan at the memory of what happened to Father Alba. Will grabbed her hands and squeezed hard. "Let's just deal with the man with the Papa Gino pants, ok? We'll start small, can you suppress that memory?"

"Here go," the waitress seemed to just suddenly appear next to them. She plunked down their cokes with an unreadable look and left as quickly as she could.

"Papa Gino's pants man," he reminded his sister. "Concentrate." He tried to sound smooth and confident in her, but he was in truth nervous.

"I don't think I can," she sounded scared herself. "The memory is so entwined with others. Even this little conversation would have to be hidden away behind a wall in my mind. Remember Foghorn Alley? You would take Lisa and me to picnic there?"

What that had to do with her memory he didn't know, but all the same, he did recall those times. The wind at the southern point of Governors Island was always nice in the summer, making it feel ten degrees cooler. For fun, he had taken the three of them there for picnics a number of times and they had enjoyed the breeze, relaxing, watching the ships plying the wide mouth of the harbor.

"Yeah, I remember. And I remember the old blanket we used as well. It was red and white checkered, but the pattern wasn't the exact same."

"True, but you may recall we told Lisa the story about the Papa Gino's pants guy. In detail. All in all, I think I've told that story a half dozen times and I've heard you tell it as well. You see how impossible this can be? In order to suppress that one memory of that poor guy, I would have to cover up or contain a dozen others and perhaps more. Do you know what song was playing in the restaurant at the time he came in?"

"No. Do you?"

She shook her head. "I don't, but my subconscious does. You see? Even if I were to suppress all the horrible things Tal... I mean Ba'al Fie-ere has done, I would still have to deal with my subconscious mind. That part of me, with its trove of insidious memories would pervert me just as if the memories were all fresh in my mind, only it would be slow and torturous."

"What about destroying the memories outright?"

With a moan, she buried her head in her hands. "I can't. I mean, I don't think I can. Physically, I can control my body to a great extent, but the mind is different. It's far too complex. Aristotle is oft quoted as saying, *The whole is more than the sum of its parts.* He was referring to synergism, the concept that certain agents when combined become far greater. When things are acting with synergism one plus one is greater than two."

"I know the term."

"With regards to the brain, it's so complex that it's like one plus one would equal a million. It can't be done," she sighed as a way of finishing her sentence.

Will was about to speak, when lunch arrived. Their big haired waitress had brought along another girl, whose hair was equally as grand in size and they placed down the pies, ogling the brother and sister with less than secretive glances. Will felt self-conscious about his bruised and swollen face and too late did he recall that smiling only made him look worse.

Their waitress leaned back as if he had leprosy. "Anything else?"

"No thank you, Tracy. I think we have all that we need," he replied. Her name had popped into his head as if they had been introduced. She looked shocked all of a sudden, and her eyes narrowed at him searching his face. Her nametag read *Meg*.

"Do I know you?" she asked quietly.

"I'm an old acquaintance of your mother's." It was all Will could think of and it sounded strange even to him since the waitress looked just a couple of years younger than he.

"Ok...sure. Enjoy," she nodded at their food and turned away still with a skeptical look. He *knew* she was on her way to call her mother.

"Crap," he murmured to his sister. "We might want to eat quick. She's going to call her mother right now." He checked his watch. The slow hand of time was still against him, one-hundred and ninety-six minutes left.

Talitha had her eyes squinted in concentration. "I can hear her..." She paused and suddenly tense lines of hate distorted her pretty face. "That whore-bitch just called you gruesome. I should go..."

"Talitha, hey!" Will hissed at his sister. She had been very loud. "Look at me. Look at me."

"What?" She seemed unsure of herself and looked around in puzzlement. "Did I just use the word whore-bitch? Did I?" She was close to tears again.

"Yes, please quite down." People had turned to look at her.

"That just popped out, I didn't mean it," she explained. "It was like listening to someone else say those words. Will, I'm in trouble. I'm going to be her. I am her! Oh my God...I killed a lady once with a hammer...or did she? I don't know. Did I do that or was it her?"

"Shush, please. It was her. It was her, you'd never do something like that." Clearly, Will wasn't convincing his sister. Talitha's eyes grew wider and wider as memories came to her. He tried a different tact, "Talitha...what is eighty-one squared."

"Uh, uh nine."

"No, I said squared."

"Oh...sixty-four hundred...sixty-five hundred and sixty-one." She looked at him to see if that was the correct figure. He had no idea, but he had her more focused.

"Good job. Now listen to me. You are the good Talitha. Trust me; I can tell the two of you apart, you haven't called me names since last night." He tried to smile as he said this, but her look was too forlorn. "You want memories? I've got some good ones. When you were three years old, you were already practically a lawyer. This one time, mom told you not to play in the street and later, there you were sitting in the street with your dolls. She started to yell, but you calmly pointed out that you were actually playing in the gutter, not the street itself. She gave you that look... you know the one, where she takes a deep breath while shaking her head like she wants to say something but she just doesn't know what.

Eventually she says very clearly, *I want you to stay on the side walk."*

Talitha was looking at him in the most delightful way, just then. He pointed to her food. "Eat your pizza. So, we were playing, I forget what, and once again you were out in the street and mom comes up and she really starts yelling at you." He paused to take a gargantuan bite of his pizza.

"What happened?"

"Mom yells, *what did I tell you about staying on the sidewalk?* And your reply was, *I am on the sidewalk, look*. Although most of you was in the street, you still had one foot on the sidewalk and you said, *I never left it*. After that mom always had to spell out her instructions, just in case."

"I did that?" She smiled and for a few seconds it warmed the brown of her eyes. After the story, Talitha seemed to calm considerably and they ate quietly. This was just fine with Will since he was too famished to tell too many more stories just then.

After he had eaten half the pizza, he asked her, "Tal, can you do me a favor and try to destroy those memories? Isn't it worth a shot?"

She shook her head. "I've been thinking about this and I have to tell you that it's not worth a shot. The brain is far beyond even my abilities. Remember that old saying, if a million monkeys typed for a million years, one would produce the works of Shakespeare?" she asked. He gave her a little noncommittal shrug in return. "The complexity of the brain is such, that what you're suggesting would be like having a single monkey build a typewriter from scratch, learn English and then type out *Hamlet*. It's impossible."

"Not really. If you can find a monkey that can build typewriters, I bet the rest would be a snap."

She didn't smile. "You have to realize that memories aren't exactly named, or color-coded. They're enmeshed in everything we are...our personalities, our thoughts and feeling, are all shaped by our memories. And monkeying around with them is filled with so many hazards that I couldn't even name them all."

He peeked at his watch, they had one hour and twenty minutes until their flight was scheduled to take off. "Then what are we going to do? You know Lisa's predicament. You know what the evil Tal wanted to do to her...and my baby."

A case of the shivers struck her, it was a long roll of her muscles down her back. "I know what she wanted to do. She wanted to...to box up the rest of the pizza." Her face unfurled into a broken looking grin.

"Huh?" Will asked perplexed.

"I'll getchya a box," Tracy/Meg the waitress had come up suddenly, stealthily. She left just as quiet.

Talitha glared at the girl as she walked away. It was a feral look that only became more so when she bared her teeth suddenly. "That little cunt was trying to eavesdrop. Can you believe that shit? Somebody should do her a favor and yank all that stupid hair out by the roots!"

The restaurant went silent.

The word cunt had so startled Will that he had sat speechless as Talitha had gone on in a loud voice that had carried as far back as the kitchen. Quickly he dug into his wallet and dropped three twenties onto the table.

3

"Fuck you, bitch!" Tracy/Meg screamed from the doorway of the pizza place. Behind her was a throng of angry Italians.

Thankfully, just at the moment, Will was peeling away at the station wagon's top speed. For a few precious seconds, just long enough to pull her to the car, Talitha had seemed stunned by her own outburst. Now she seethed.

"I know where she works, Will! When we're done with Amy, I'm coming right back here," her face was marble in its hardness.

"Tal, stop it, please. What's the square root two-thousand..."

"Who gives a fuck about square roots? Do I look like a fuckin calculator to you?" She yanked her hair back into a quick braid. Her hands pulling hard were punishing her scalp.

Will began to feel an awful desperation growing in him. His sister was fast becoming a time bomb and he needed her whole and sane. "You're not trying hard enough, Tal! Please fight this, you've got to be tougher."

Practically since he had woken up, he had been hoping for a vision concerning Lisa, a hint, a clue as to what he should do, but instead he *saw* Talitha reach for the gun between the seats.

Yet even with the vision, he knew he'd be too slow. There had been too little warning. Her hand was a blur and a fraction of a second later he felt the cold steel pressing against his cheek.

"Let me pull over first," he whispered, keeping his hands at the ten and two position on the wheel. They were sweating so badly that he worried that he would slip and drive into one of the parked cars lining the street.

"I remember I used to want to kill you, when you had the impudence to order me about," as she spoke, she drilled the gun into his face. It hurt. His flesh was still terribly sore from his beating at her hands only the day before.

"You don't wish to kill me now?" It was a small spark of hope, but it was all he had.

She laughed cruelly. "I want to kill you now more than ever. You did something to me. I don't really know what. I only know that now there's a demon in the Void wearing my face. Ruling where I should be ruling. Hurting those I want to hurt."

Will again wished for a vision, instead he got the sound of the hammer of the gun drawing back in his ear.

Chapter 8

Talitha

A fury burned a fire within her, blotting out the sound of screaming. The screaming was far away, as if from another time or another mind. She couldn't tell which it was or whether it was both at once. However, it didn't really matter. Of all the beings she hated, and there was quite a list, none deserved death more than Will Jern. And no amount of screaming and begging echoing in her psyche would stay her hand another second.

Except that she did pause. The begging sounded familiar and after a second, she realized that it was Talitha begging for her not to pull the trigger. But...but, she was Talitha, or at least that's what she used to call herself, before. And then she called herself...Ba'al. That's right, she remembered. Her name had been Ba'al Fie-ere, denier of Ba'al. But when was that, she didn't know.

Her mind, rocking and swimming in confusion though it was, was well made up on one thing at least. Her brother would have to die. Simply the fact that he had beaten her twice, once physically in hand to hand combat and once mentally with his deceitful exorcism, meant that he was a living embarrassment to her. She thumbed the hammer back, and as she did, a low trickle of sweat crept meekly from his hairline at his temple.

It made her smile. "Any last words?"

"If you don't mind, I wanted to tell you a final story. It won't take long. When I was five years old and you were four, we used to play that game with the lava monsters, remember?"

Unbelievably, she nodded. She put off his death for another moment as she recalled that time, running and jumping over the sidewalks, which back then seemed so unbelievably wide. Was it always summer when they had been children together, it felt so. Always warm and sunny.

Will had nervous eyes and they slipped toward her, briefly, fearfully. She liked that and let him go on, prolonging the moment, "That day we were playing over by the Davidson's house. I don't know what we were thinking. Timmy Davidson had been grounded and couldn't come out to play and there we were right beneath his window, laughing and screaming, '*Look out! The lava-monster*!' With him sitting looking all mopey. You had pigtails in your hair that day, with yellow yarn tying back each. I remember you had on a yellow turtleneck and brown cords. It's like a picture in my mind. You jumping over the bricks, with the green-green grass behind you, framing everything."

Talitha sat in the car, frozen in place, remembering this moment in the past only as it unfolded from Will's lips. She didn't know what was to come and her curiosity kept her finger a hair's breathe from finishing the pull on the trigger of the gun. It hadn't wavered an inch.

"We were both barefoot you and I. Didn't it seem as if we were always barefoot back then? Perhaps it made the prospect of touching the lava that much more exciting." He shrugged as if that little observation didn't matter. "Either way, you were giggling up a storm all along and your mood must have affected Timmy, because he started playing with us from up in his room. *Right behind you Tal, run!* He'd scream down. We ran and jumped over the sidewalks and Timmy kept directing back and forth until we were all out of breathe and then Mrs. Davidson came. *Timothy Nathaniel Davidson! What are you doing? You're supposed to be grounded.*" Will's voice was way up high and Talitha suddenly remembered Mrs. Davidson, a small woman with a big voice. It carried up and down the block when she was upset with her son, which was frequent.

"His mom scared Timmy so bad he almost fell out of

the window. She yanked him back in and then she turned to glare down at us...do you remember what you said to her?"

"No," she was clueless.

"You suddenly point up at her and scream, *Run Willy J a lava-monster has gotten Timmy*! Oh my God that was the funniest thing! We both took off, laughing our heads off because of the look Mrs. Davidson had on her face."

Talitha smiled at the image. "That's a cute story. Did it have a point past keeping you alive for a few more seconds?"

Will gave her a little shrug. "I wasn't done. So there we were running back home, but we were so weak from laughter and from the lava-monster game that we were practically stumbling and we weren't watching where exactly we were going. You have to remember that German-shepherd that lived between us and the Davidson's."

Talitha did indeed. In her mind, its teeth were four inch long curved sabers and it could open its mouth wide enough to half swallow her. It was a nightmare dog, and the legend of it in her mind was probably pitiful compared to its actual ferocity.

"That day we accidentally walked into its ring of death." He gave her a knowing look around the pistol. Though the rest of the story opened up in her memory only as it went along, she recalled quite clearly the ring of death. It wasn't something she would enter even on a dare.

Will went on, "The dog's name was Nancy. How stupid is that? I couldn't think of a worse name for such a beast as that even if I tried. It ran around on a chain and cut a perfect circle in the grass, a dirt path that meant certain doom to anyone foolish enough to cross its boundary. That day you walked right over it without thinking."

"I don't remember this at all," Talitha murmured shaking her head in slight way. The gun in her hand was now forgotten. It had fallen into her lap and she couldn't even feel her fingers around its grip.

"It's true. We were just laughing away and didn't hear

Nancy charging at us. She was always so silent...but that look in her eyes, yeesh." Will paused as his body became racked with shivers. "She came at you and I swear she could've swallowed you in one giant bite. Her mouth looked to open a foot and a half, but at the last second, I saw her and pulled you back. Those freaking giant teeth came down with this really loud snap an inch from your face." Will puffed out his cheeks and blew long and slow.

"Huh," Talitha nodded a series of small little nods, suddenly remembering that moment with amazing clarity. Nancy's teeth, curved and wickedly sharp were a beautiful white, as if they were polished on a daily basis. They came together with a clicking sound and when they did, a large huff of her breathe struck Talitha in the face. It was hot and wet, and it stank of aged garbage.

"I remember that. I thought my heart had stopped in my chest," she paused a moment feeling that fear from so long ago come back to life. It felt so real, almost as if it had just happened.

"I..." Just then, she looked down, becoming mystified. "Will, what are we doing in the car? And why am I holding this?" She held out the gun, with shaking hands. The last thing she had remembered was hearing someone approach the table at the restaurant and then she was there in the car, listening to the story of Nancy and the lava-monsters feeling extremely confused. Part of her confusion was the low burn of anger that was even then draining away from her. She'd been so monstrously angry just a few moments before, but now she couldn't understand why.

Will reached out and took the gun from her. "You are...how do I put this? The other Talitha, the one I thought I banished, or exorcized I mean, is back. Or maybe it never left."

"No she's gone," Talitha implored. "She has to be gone. I would feel her in me. I would know it!"

Will put the car in drive and sped off into the rain. "I

don't know what to say. I know her better than you do and it was definitely her. I don't think it's a memory issue you're dealing with."

She didn't know what to say either. Odd memories flashed through her mind. In one, she was masturbating in bed expressing her pleasure with embarrassingly loud moans. In another, she was talking to a doctor from the asylum, pretending to be sane, trying to lure him just a little closer so she could get at him with her teeth. A third saw her outside a home, one that was set way back in the woods. A man stood near a fireplace in the living room and she couldn't decide whether to kill him or rape him.

"Talitha come on, I can't leave you here alone," Will said, his voice was a combination of stress and fatigue.

They were parked outside the wreck of the factory. "How did we get here so fast? We were just..." They had just been by the pizza place only a second before.

"What do you mean? It wasn't that fast. But come on, I want to get you some new clothes before we go to the airport. So we got to grab the priest and hustle. Are you still doing ok?" He wiggled his fingers at his own head.

"Yes, it's still me in here," she replied, attempting, but failing at giving him a smile. Talitha climbed out of the car feeling a nervous thrill in her stomach. She had barely blinked and they had been at the factory. Had she been daydreaming, or perhaps concentrating on those old/new memories so much that she missed the entire car ride? She didn't think so. Time had just snapped by in way she couldn't describe.

Before her the entrance to the factory was a black nightmare against the cold grey rain. Portions of its charred walls still stood three stories up into the gloom. She barely gave these a glance, what concerned her was below them. Deep in the black pits of the building were nine corpses.

"Did you hear that?" she asked her brother. He had to have. It had been plenty loud. A scream had come up from the depths of the factory. A man's scream of horrid pain. It was Father Alba's voice.

"No, I didn't hear anything. What was it?" Will had his head cocked to the side listening.

"It's..."

Father Alba sounded like he was being tortured. As if his eyes were being torn from their sockets. One of her new memories came back to her and on impulse, she tentatively gave the air a sniff. The smell of the priest was distant and fading, he wasn't in the building, and hadn't been since the day before. Just like that the scream seemed to die away.

Had it even been there in the first place? The scream had sounded so real when she first heard it, but now only seconds later it was more an echo in her mind.

"It's nothing. Just something settling, I think," she lied. Will's brows came down, he didn't fully believe her, all the same he turned back to the entrance.

Steam or smoke wafted up from it making it look eerie, reminding her of another doorway she had been through once. That one she had to be dragged into. How she screamed so hysterically! That one entered upon the crypt of Jubal and it was the first time Talitha had sent her to be tortured in her place.

"Talitha...sent?" she asked aloud to the building. "Who am I?" Her mind wavered in confusion. Was she the other Talitha? The evil one? She didn't think so, yet her memory was definitely of forcing the good Talitha into the crypt where the teeth came alive? She could picture that girl even now, she looked so innocent, so fearful and so weak.

"Will...I'm having problems. I...I...I don't think I can go down there."

"Tal..." Will had a pained expression. "Time's running out, we got to do this, how about I hold your hand? Will you be able to come down then?"

She didn't want to go down there regardless, the many teeth of Jubal kept flashing anew in her mind, but she had no choice and took his large hand in her small brown one. They descended quietly for a time before she caught the scent of the police officer who had been in Father Alba's room at the hospital. She remembered his name was Milner and she remembered as well throwing him about a small white room. She had made him look weak and pathetic, and he had cringed, practically in tears when she looked his way.

The one thing she couldn't recall was *when* any of that had happened.

She didn't dwell on it, however, the thought of Milner was too distracting. There was something about him that she found terribly annoying. He was irritating like an itch you couldn't scratch and his voice had the quality of nails on a chalkboard. Quickly all thoughts of the crypt of Jubal vanished, they were buried beneath a growing anger. The anger simmered rapidly into hate. It was a warm feeling, one that made her forget her worries and fears. Hate could conquer all of that nonsense; it could conquer anything. Talitha knew this. She remembered now how weak and frail she was without it and she allowed herself to be engulfed in its powerful arms.

Chapter 9

Will

The little room hadn't changed. And neither did Will's reaction to it. When he entered he gave it a quick glance and a familiar depression settled onto him. Other than the remains of the fire the gypsy had built the night before, the room was furnished solely in contemporary American death.

"Father Vogel, I hope that you're just about finished down here," he said, checking his watch, feeling a flight of humming birds swarm for a brief moment in his chest. Their plane would depart in one hour and two minutes.

"Yes, I am. However, I still have some more questions, but they can wait until we're on the plane." The priest answered in an amiable manner. His tone was light and it didn't go with the morbid surroundings.

Will didn't relish the idea of any more questions. He was sure that they would only set Talitha off again and that was something he couldn't afford, at least not yet. His main fear was that if the evil Talitha came out too many more times, she would be impossible to contain.

Eric Milner was in the room as well, weaving a beam of light around. He stood in a long grey coat, bundled against the chill, wearing a glum look on his face, shaking his head at all of the bodies. "Will, I'm really gonna need my gun back now. You aren't going to be able to get them on the airplane you know."

Will shrugged, knowing the man was right, and held out the weapon. "Keep it out of sight will you?" A gun in his hands was another thing that could set his sister off, her other self seemed to hate the cop with a dreadful passion. Will sighed heavily, not knowing how he was going to keep Talitha together long enough to overcome Amy.

"Mr. Jern, where is your sister?" the priest asked, his own flashlight he sent shining past Will. "I have some questions for her as well.

"Huh? Talitha is right..." Will turned around, his sister was nowhere in sight. A burst of fear went through him that he tried to ignore and he put his head out into the dark hall. "Talitha?" he called out to her, hoping that she'd only stepped out for some air. He was getting nothing in the way of a vision and had no idea what was going on in her mind. "Talitha!" This time he yelled louder, but the building felt empty.

"It's ok Mr. Jern, it can wait," Father Vogel said, before heading for the door. Will grabbed him quickly by the arm and spun him around, putting his finger to the older man's lips. Will then pointed to the two men and then pointed to the floor. *Stay here*, he mouthed. The priest looked surprised at the hard look on Will's face, but complied. Milner was another story.

"Oh shit!" The cop, who had just put away his gun, yanked it out again and held it at arm's length, his face looking as grey as his coat. With his free hand, he produced a second gun. It was the one that Talitha had shot Will with the night before. "What's going on? Is that bitch sister of yours going psycho again?"

"She can likely hear you," Will replied quietly. Milner's face went white. "I really don't know what's going on, it could be nothing whatsoever. She could be outside getting some fresh air, or she could be wandering around the building. All I know is that she was right next to me when I came in. But all the same, I'm worried. Talitha has been acting a little odd."

He paused, unsure how much to tell them. If he told them too little, he could be putting them in danger if the evil Talitha was really back. If he told them all that he knew and suspected, the cop would likely shoot first and ask questions later. It would mean putting Talitha in danger and he didn't know if he could risk that, he needed her too much.

"What do you mean by odd?" Milner hissed.

"She has been acting...only for very short periods, mind you, kinda like her other self. You know, a little violent, a little weird."

"Mother fucker, you can't be serious!" Milner reacted just as Will had feared. The guns were trained on the door and he was sure that the cop would shoot at the first sign of movement in the hall.

"Aren't we being a might bit paranoid?" the priest whispered. "Would she really attack us? Three grown men, one of whom is a police officer?"

Milner looked at the priest as if he was an idiot. "No disrespect Father, but we weren't lying about this girl. She's freaking possessed! I told you how strong she was, and you heard Sean's story. There were six men in that room beneath the church and even though she was unarmed and blind, she managed to take two of them hostage. And you saw how big Sean and Jim was! They ain't no tiny guys."

The priest considered for a moment, stroking his grey goatee. He turned to Will. "You were rather certain that you had exorcized the demon in her. What has changed?"

"Honestly I don't know. It started this morning, but it got really bad only an hour or so ago, when we came here. She acted a little distant, kind of spacey you could say, and I figured it was due to seeing Jim. They liked each other quite a bit." Will paused as Milner gave a contemptuous snort. He sent the cop a hard glare before continuing, "So we were all standing here looking at the bodies and the next thing I know she takes off and runs out into the rain. She started talking about having memories from the other Talitha coming into her head, but I think it is way more than that."

"More than that? What the fuck does that mean?" Milner asked. His fear and anger battled to turn his voice into a whine. "And what are we supposed to do? Just sit here and wait to see which freaky girl shows up."

Will didn't know. If the evil Talitha was controlling her as he suspected, then to go out into the dark factory where shadows ruled, would be suicidal. He shrugged.

For a long while, none of the three men budged. They all stood staring at the door, beyond it was only the blackened wall of the corridor. The iron haired priest showed his light in its direction, working the tight beam around the edges of the doorway. Other than soot-covered sludge, it revealed nothing.

Will checked his watch and what he saw made his chest tremble, time was now clicking by in hurry. "We should go back up to the street."

"No way, I'm staying put." Milner stepped further back from the door as if Will was going to drag him upstairs with him. "She could be anywhere out there, waiting to drop a desk on our heads or something."

"Fine. I'm going up. Give me one your guns," Will demanded, holding out his hand. The gun that Talitha had taken from Jackson had been thrown into a dumpster on the way to the factory.

"Hell no!"

The response wasn't unexpected. Milner feared Talitha and for very good reason. "Do you want me to fix this? I can't do it without a gun. You..."

A great crash from somewhere in the building echoed down to them cutting off his words. It was so loud that Will wondered if part of a wall had fallen in.

"Perhaps she tripped?" the priest suggested. He seemed extremely unperturbed, which was quite the opposite of Milner who shined with sweat and backed further away.

"Talitha doesn't trip. Ever," Will replied truthfully. "That sounded like that might have been part of a wall coming down." The three men looked at each other uneasily. "I think we all should go up."

Milner looked unconvinced. "It wasn't that loud. It could have been anything, or maybe she's just trying to get us to think that..." Another crash came, this one closer and to their right. For a few moments the three men stood breathing lightly, trying to listen past the steady monotonous dripping of rainwater seeping down from the ruined roof of the factory.

"I do believe she may be trying to trap us down here," the unflappable priest said calmly.

"Can she do that? Aren't there a number of ways to get out of here?" Milner asked. At one time, the factory had been large, running over a football field in length and stood three stories high. After the fire, however it was hard to judge what percentage was still standing and impossible to know how much of the labyrinth like lower floors were still intact.

"There can't be too many ways out," Will replied searching his memory. "Part of the lower basement, near the center is actually open to the sky and if we can get to that it would only be a matter of climbing out. That being said, I do think we can be trapped and maybe easily since so many of the corridors down here are already blocked. Some of the upper floors have collapsed onto them." Will began to think that the day before, Talitha had done perhaps too good of a job at destroying the factory.

"Crap," Milner muttered. He held out one of the black pistols to Will. "Let's get outta here. Take this... you should go first. Since you can see the future. Father you go next, I'll take the rear."

"What an interesting predicament," Father Vogel announced nodding his head in agreement with his own words. "Mr. Jern, would you like my flashlight?"

"Thanks." With the gun in his right hand, Will took the light in his left and shown it at the empty doorway. "I'm afraid if the demon is back, *interesting* wouldn't be the word I'd use. Now, stay close, both of you."

"Well it's interesting to me," Vogel explained as they began moving toward the door. "The life of a priest can be somewhat routine."

Will paused at the doorway, shining his light back and forth a moment. It was an eerie sight. Fire and water appeared to have warped the building. In places the walls sagged as if they bore far too much weight, in others, great cracks ran up them to the ceiling where large chunks of wood and cement had fallen in. The concrete floor was cracked and buckled as well and everything was blackened and tortured looking. It gave him a nasty thrill to see the place like this, knowing that evil lurked in it just it had the night before. His stomach knotted, but the priest seemed so calm that Will was a little embarrassed. He put a little more bravado in his voice.

"Routine? I would think that as an exorcist you'd lead a pretty exciting life for the most part."

"It can be, but..."

"Will you two stop talking for Pete's sake?" Milner interrupted hissing out the words. "Your freak of a sister could be sneaking up on us right now."

Will glanced back, but the man was barely visible in the odd shadows made by the two flashlights weaving about. "She could be, and if she were I really doubt that we would hear her, but I'll be quiet. You need to stay closer Milner, try not to leave such a gap."

The cop was a good nine or ten feet away. Too far in Will's opinion. After Milner closed the gap, Will started forward again, but hadn't gotten far down the sludge-filled corridor when he came to a great tumble of charred beams blocking the way they had come. It was a new cave in and it forced them to turn around.

For the next ten minutes, the three men moved down different corridors trying to find a way out. Sometimes they ran into natural dead ends, as a number of the halls would suddenly open onto large storage rooms and at other times damage from the fire stopped them. Each time they were forced to turn about retracing their steps in the black muck.

It was after their fourth such turn that Will saw a clear

set of tracks running down another gloomy hall. The shoe prints were quite small. Excitement grew in him and he realized then that in the back of his mind, this is what he'd been after all along. He still needed his sister. Getting out of the building and going to Maine alone had been his last resort.

He set off following along after the tracks, moving slowly and as carefully as possible, shining his light into every room before progressing. Like Milner, he was afraid that his sister would try to collapse a ceiling onto them and thus he paid particularly close attention to the roof above their heads. And more than a few times, he felt a peculiar tingle as he stepped beneath what looked like an avalanche of precariously balanced wreckage.

The others followed, close in the case of the priest, while Milner hung back. The beam of light coming from the cop's shaking hand jittered about. Sometimes it would shine ahead of Will and then at the slightest sound it would disappear into the gloom behind them. This constant motion of the man's light only made seeing into the shadows harder, making them seem to grow or move.

Will knew they were in an impossible situation, his gut told him that Talitha hadn't run away, and that the footprints they were following after wouldn't lead to a way out. She was there in the building, somewhere up ahead, plotting. After a few minutes he began to distrust the tracks they were trailing—she had to know how obvious they were. It was almost as if she wanted him to find them and follow after. Although he didn't have one, he wished he had another choice. The imprints went steadily without deviation except for when they came to a door to a room. At each of these, they turned and Will could picture his sister peering in before moving on.

She was after something. A weapon perhaps. He picked up the pace hoping to find her before she could find what it was she was looking for and soon he made the mistake of barely giving each room a glance as he passed them. The hall they were traversing came to an intersection of another hall and without warning, the tracks disappeared as if Talitha had suddenly grown wings and had flown from then on. Will cast his light down both directions but where there should've been marks in the soot, there was only what looked like black carpet greeting his light.

"Look at this," Father Vogel pointed to the wall at Will's right. There was an odd smearing of the soot on the wall and Talitha's small handprints were clearly visible. It looked as though she had been wiping away the grunge to see beneath it, but there was nothing there to see. It wasn't like her. She wouldn't casually mark up the wall like that, there was a purpose to it. But what that purpose was, he couldn't figure out until a vision came to him a second later.

A second too late.

Chapter 10

Will

With the charring and the coating of dark ash, the room was blacker than night ever could be. Suddenly the wall to the left of the door appeared to grow eyes. They blinked once and then shown steadily with an unhealthy evil light. Around the eyes a face, also blackened by ash seemed to form from the shadows, and then beneath that a body materialized as if from nothing. The creature, all the color of pitch save for those fiery eyes, stepped forward soundlessly, moving toward the door, moving to where beams of light danced about as if in play.

"Milner!" Will snapped his head back and screamed at the cop. "Behind you!"

He was too late and Milner too slow.

The cop's light seemed to leap from his hands, spraying the hall with radiance and shadows. There was a flurry of movement and grunts and then Eric Milner was gone, pulled into a room by what appeared to be a shadow that had come alive. Sluggishly, as if the flashlight weighed many pounds, Will turned his light down the hall and saw little but a jumble of footprints on the floor as if a waltz had been danced there. Shocked by the rapidness of the attack he stood listening, breathing heavily, with Father Vogel a step in front of him doing the same thing.

But then he *saw*.

Will knew what was coming, but for half a moment his mind was too disorganized to act. A bullet was going to come screaming out of the dark straight down the hall, centered dead on the chest of the priest in front of him. The man would fall back into his arms knocking the two of them over and there he would be lying in the dark with a dead priest draped over him, protecting him...just like yesterday... just like yesterday. It was an echo of déjà vu.

And so close was this coming moment to the dreadful one of the day before that Will's mind was nearly paralyzed with confusion. Was that horrible scene going replay itself once again? Was it a bizarre reverberation of a past event haunting him or was this real? Questions flashed through his mind, but his left hand cared nothing for them.

The flashlight fell forgotten from his hand and began a slow motion spin to the ground, casting strobes of light down the hall. That left hand, now free, shot out and raked furrows into the skin on the back of Father Vogel's neck, as Will's nails dug in to gain a purchase on the man's tight collar. With his grip firm, Will's left foot planted and he pistoned outward with the great muscles of his thighs, sending both him and the priest hurtling in a dive toward the junction of the two hallways.

Down the corridor, light blazed for an instant and then a huge flat crack, like sharp lightening, erupted. Will landed in the sludge and slid, not knowing if he or the priest was hit by the bullet. Another flash lit the hall and this one seemed altogether silent save for the hiss of a hot angry bee zipping by his neck.

The two men finished their slide, pitching up against the far wall and instantly Will scrambled up, bringing his gun to bear. He moved to the corner where the halls joined and quick as a wink, dodged his head out and then back again. The two flashlights were still shining bright, but both, unfortunately were sending their light his way. Everything beyond them was impenetrably dark.

"You're getting pretty quick Willy J," his sister called out from the inky black. Will took another peek, barely letting his head show; the corridor was still empty. He then whipped about to see the wide-eyed priest climbing to his feet.

"Are you ok?" he asked the priest in a hushed tone,

ignoring his sister.

"Oh yes. Was that the demon?" the priest asked with some excitement. He attempted to look around the corner as Will had done, but the bigger, younger man held him back.

"Shhhh," Will hushed him, pulling the man in close. "You have to get out of here. Take this hall, go down it, and keep veering to the right and..."

"I wouldn't do that if I were you Father," Talitha called out. "You'll be going out blind in the dark and I can hunt you by sense of smell alone."

"Can she do that?" the priest asked without a hint of nervousness.

Will nodded, and leaned close enough to touch the Vogel's ear. "Go. Follow the corridor." The words held only the strength of a baby's breath.

"You need me." The priest was being obstinate.

"Oh, he needs you, Father," the girl spoke loudly. "He needs you to be a distraction to me so he can run away. Will Jern ain't no hero. Remember Father Alba? I gave Will the chance to trade places with him, but he was too much of a coward."

Involuntarily, Will looked back at Father Vogel. The older man gave him a piercing glance that only stoked Will's guilt. "She's lying about the distraction part, Father. Only I can deal with her, I need you..."

"You can't deal with shit, Will!" Talitha screamed at the top of her lungs. "Vogel, don't you go anywhere. I say who stays and who goes." A weird gasping noise came from her direction, which was followed by the sound of a sharp slap.

"I'm not going anywhere, Miss Jern," the priest said loudly. His firm raspy voice sounded composed, which matched his outwardly calm demeanor. "Miss Jern? Is Officer Milner all right? Is he injured?"

"Oh, I suppose he's ok. He just had a little trip and bashed his face in a bit. He's so clumsy." Another little cry of pain accompanied this.

"Miss Jern..." Vogel began, but Talitha's voice stopped him cold.

"Father, if I hear the words 'Miss Jern' one more time, Officer Milner is going to have another accident."

"Of course," Father Vogel remained unruffled despite the threat. "What would you like to be called then?"

"Ask Will, he knows."

Father Vogel looked at Will. Will looked at his watch.

Forty-four minutes until their flight was scheduled to take off. If he kept his foot stomped on the gas pedal the entire way, he could get to the airport in ten minutes. With ditching the car and running to the ticket counter; he was looking at another ten minutes. A dead sprint could get him anywhere in the airport in five minutes add another five for complications. He had no time for this.

"I don't have time for this Tal. Why don't you tell me what you want?" He called out angrily, earning him an irate headshake from the priest.

"Nothing other than to prove to the world what a coward you are," Talitha answered back just as furious. "Everyone just loves Will. He's so handsome and good that he's practically a saint. He stopped the demon, he saved poor little Talitha. Let's all kiss his ass and worship the ground he walks. But I know you, Will. You ain't shit! In fact..."

Will interrupted heatedly, "Wrap it up Tal. What's your point?"

"My point is, dear brother, you're nothing. And despite what everyone thinks, you're not even a good person. Dad died trying to save you, mom was in the hospital because of you. You killed Henny Harris and Adrina. You let Father John die and you let Father Alba have his eyes torn out. You were too chicken to look into the future at first, so we can add Terry Brabec and her family to the list of deaths that are all your fault. What else...oh yeah, does the name Jim Anderson ring a bell? That poor man is probably being tortured right this very moment all because you lacked the guts to..."

"That's not true," Will said quietly. "I was fighting Luke."

"The whole time? I don't think so. You told me last night that you hit him in the head with a piece of wood. Why didn't you just go kill the gypsy? Wasn't that our plan? Kill the witch as soon as possible?"

That had been the plan. She was right. So why hadn't he followed through with it? Had he been afraid to face the Void again? Will couldn't exactly remember. His memory of those seconds was a terrible blur. He remembered the pain in his chest and the torture by Ba'al Zubel that followed, but then what? He had laid upon the black ice for a few seconds trying to breathe, trying to come to grips with just being alive and then he had heard the gunshots. They were like a needed slap, bringing him back to his horrible reality. He had struggled to his feet and the first thing he'd seen was Luke beating Jim, smashing his elbow into the big man's face repeatedly, blood was everywhere.

"I was trying to save Jim," Will said in a whisper.

"You were trying to save yourself!" Talitha screeched.

Will didn't argue; he hung his head instead. In the shadows of the hallway, Father Vogel patted Will on the arm and tried to give him a warm smile. Will kept his face averted. Was Talitha correct? The absolute truth was that he didn't know. She was spot on with the notion that he was afraid of going into the Void again, but all the same he didn't know if that was the underlying reason why he had attacked Luke instead of the gypsy witch.

After he was silent for a few seconds, Talitha continued, "There is a way to make amends you know. Officer Milner, a fine upstanding man of the law is about to go through a very heinous and long death... you could trade places with him."

Seeming to oblige her words, a strangled cry rolled down the corridor to greet them.

"I can't," Will said, again in a whisper.

"What was that dear brother? We couldn't quite hear you down here."

Father Vogel spoke up, "He said he can't, but I will trade places with..."

"No! I want Will only," Talitha interrupted. "What's your excuse this time, Will?"

"You know what it is. Lisa and the baby. And the sword." Will refused to even glance toward the priest. He felt small.

"Oh sure," Talitha snorted back laughter. "What a champion you are. I can't be a hero now, but I promise I'll do it later. Sorry Milner, it looks like you're out of luck."

"Will please!" Milner screamed out. The man's fear was a knife to Will's guts.

"I...I can't," Will called back with a voice that cracked. He didn't have time to explain things to Milner, and even if he did, would the cop understand? Not likely.

"You're an asshole, Will! An asshole. If..." Another slap silenced the fear driven fury of Eric Milner.

The priest grabbed Will by the shoulders and tried to look up into his face, "You have to stop this. You have the power to end his suffering."

"He won't do it, Father. Will's last real heroic act was rescuing me from a dog named Nancy... a scary little puppy dog. Why don't you tell everyone that story? It's another *look at me, I'm Will. I'm so great* story. Why did you even waste my time on that one?"

"That story wasn't about me," Will replied in a small voice. "It was about you."

"Then you must have told it wrong."

Will checked his watch, he had wasted four minutes already, but this little story of Talitha when she was young was something he felt both the good and the bad side of her should know. It had nothing to do with lava-monsters or scary dogs or even bees or glass. It was the day that he, at five years old, had known that he loved his sister with a greater love than he had thought possible.

"I didn't tell the story wrong, I was interrupted," Will began, ignoring the curious look of the priest standing next to him. "When Nancy charged at you, I actually started to run, but at the last second I saw that you were staring at those gigantic teeth and hadn't budged an inch. Your eyes were huge, but the rest of you looked so small. Anyways, I reached out and grabbed you, and pulled you back, but you went completely mad. It was like touching someone drowning, you threw yourself on me and clambered over me in an effort to get past those teeth."

There was silence from down the hall, but Will only paused a moment before going on, "You tackled me right there, and for a moment we were all arms and legs flying everywhere trying to escape, but eventually we managed to crawl out of the circle of death. We ran like crazy, but this time we weren't laughing. We were both crying. You were practically in hysterics over the dog and I had cut my foot on some glass.

"This is the part that I will always remember, this the part that I wanted to tell you. Because of my cuts, I had to go to the emergency room, and when I got back, I was all mopey having to sit on the porch, unable to walk or play. So...you danced for me."

"I didn't," Talitha said from her end of the hall.

"Oh yeah you did. You were cute as a button and danced like a little ballerina until mom came out to applaud you. After that you became shy and then..."

Talitha interrupted, "I stepped on a bee."

"Yeah, you stepped on a bee. On purpose."

"What?" she asked, skeptical.

"You stepped on a bee so you could be with me."

"That doesn't make any sense. I could've been with you without having to hurt myself." Her point was logical.

"I used to think it was because you loved me so much that you wanted to feel what I felt. You used to be like that when we were young. If I was sick, an hour later you were sick, even if I was faking it to get out of going to school," Will replied. "But who knows? Maybe you were worried I was bored or lonely, either way we spent that afternoon sitting on the porch drinking that super tart lemon aide that mom used to make."

"That stuff was crazy, I don't know if she ever put sugar in it," Talitha said. There was a momentary pause and then she added, "What are we doing here? What's... shouldn't we be going to the airport?"

Pausing only long enough to snatch up one of the flashlights Will dashed down the hall, feeling sick with relief. He knew his Talitha was back, and he found her straddling Milner looking lost with the heavy pistol in her hands. Her face was black and fierce, but her eyes were innocent.

"Will, we were just outside talking." She held out the gun to Will as if it could explode in her hands. "And now...what's going on with me?"

Will pulled her off the cop and went to help the man up but Milner shoved him aside. "Don't touch me! I'm done with this, all of this. Give me those." He grabbed the guns from Will. "If I ever see the two of you again..."

"Officer Milner, I'm sure the Cardinal is deeply in your debt," Father Vogel said in his calming manner. "I'll let him know that you have gone above and beyond."

"You do that," Milner replied backing out of the room and he then dashed off down the hall.

"I think he's going the wrong way," Talitha murmured. "But I don't think he'll listen to me."

"I don't think he'll listen to any of us," Will added, checking his watch. "Thirty-seven minutes till take off; we got to go. We can talk about what's going on with you once we're on the plane. Which way is out?"

Father Vogel took a hold of his arm and attempted to pull Will in close. "Will, your sister can't come with us. She's a danger to everyone around her. She needs psychiatric attention."

With a twist of his large arm, Will pulled away from the smaller man. "She's coming. The only person I question about who may or may not be coming, is you." His words came out quite bit more nasty than he had intended, causing both Talitha and the priest's eyes to widen. He had trouble caring—his head had begun to thump almost as soon as the evil Talitha had departed.

Talitha looked unsteady and a little sick beneath her black camouflage and Will grabbed her arm, steering out into the hallway. "Which way?" he asked again. She pointed back the way they had come. As they walked, he turned to the priest. "I don't mean to be rude, but I need her, I don't really need you."

With his usual serenity Father Vogel responded, "That remains to be seen. Miss...may I call you Miss Jern?"

"Call me Talitha, please. Take the turn to the right, Will. This is weird, I don't really remember coming down here, but at the same time I do, like I dreamed all this."

Will's pace was frantic and in seconds, Father Vogel was panting, but still he managed to say between gasps, "Talitha, do you mind if I ask you a few questions?"

A glance at his sister told Will it wasn't a good idea. Her eyes looked still wild, the whites oddly huge in the black soot. "Not here, Father. Not just now." His tone was much kinder this time.

Chapter 11

Will

Will only allowed a real conversation to occur once they were safely on the plane.

They quick marched with dogged determination through the factory losing two minutes in Will's calculations due to the slowness of Father Vogel. The man was gasping loudly at the pace, but Will pushed them on relentlessly. With his iron-grey hair and web of wrinkles around his face, Will put the older man's age at close to sixty. Yet with the safety of his family on the line Will wasn't going to miss their flight no matter what.

He made those two minutes back up on the drive to the airport. It should have been a white-knuckled ride, only everyone was so covered in black soot that it wasn't obvious. Even if the priest wanted to ask questions, there was no way he could have as Will drove the old station wagon like it had never been driven before. Relying more on luck than on his second sight, he careened through the light traffic like a man possessed and pulled into the airport parking lot with twenty-three minutes left. A minute later, the station wagon was abandoned to its fate and they were dashing to the ticket counter.

A thousand pairs of eyes were upon them.

"You can't board the plane like that. They won't let you," the woman behind the counter said with an embarrassed smile.

The three of them were a sight, with the priest being the least offensive. Talitha's borrowed black dress was in tatters, but worse was her face. The soot that she had applied had been partially smeared by the rain, making her eyes appear creepy and with her bedraggled hair, she looked ready for a starring role in a haunted house. Yet worse than her was Will.

His blue jeans and grey hooded sweatshirt were covered in black muck, as was his hair, which went in every direction. However, it was the spectacular bruising of his face and the burning fierceness of his blue eyes that drew people's attention.

"There's a boutique on the way to our gate," Will tried to sound smooth. "We'll stop and get a change of clothes there."

"Ok, but you only have eighteen minutes," she gave him a smile, but it faltered when he tried to smile back. It only distorted his face more.

"Thanks, I guess we'll have to hurry." Will knew precisely how much time they had and they were wasting precious seconds. He began drumming his fingers impatiently. The counter woman was either terribly uncomfortable with this crazed man in front of her, or finally got the hint that they were in a rush. She began typing at a blazing speed and a minute later, they were racing away with tickets in hand.

As the least disreputable looking, Father Vogel went directly to the gate. "I'll hold the plane until you arrive."

Will didn't bother with a smile. He was feeling far too stressed to make the attempt and every time he had tried people only looked at him as if they were about to be sick. He waved instead and sped off to a little shop that sold purses mostly, but also had a section for clothing.

A sales lady, very tall and blonde saw them approaching through the glass and her eyes went wide at the sight. Will ignored her and strolled in, heading straight for the men's section, which consisted solely of two racks of expensive jackets. On the spot, he stripped off the grey sweatshirt and pulled on a brown leather jacket. It did little to help his appearance. He also grabbed a blanket to cover his seat when he boarded. His shopping time twenty-eight seconds.

"Will, look at these dresses," Talitha's eyes were big for the clothing. Her head wagged this way and that, surprising her brother. She had never been much for shopping. "Can we afford these?" Nothing in the store was priced below two-hundred dollars.

"Yes, just pick something, ok."

There was no hurrying her and Will's agitation soared to new heights. He began pacing back and forth, as Talitha went through every rack, slowly.

"All these outfits are so dark. It's kind of depressing," Talitha said with a shake of her head. To Will, any of the clothes would be an improvement. She currently looked as if she had stepped out of a nightmare.

The sales lady tried to be helpful, "They're dark because it's after Labor Day you know. Will you want new shoes also?" Talitha's black pumps were ugly.

Will groaned. "Nine minutes Tal," he tapped his watch. "We don't have time for shoes."

"Ok, ok. Can you grab me a blanket as well, please?" She went to the rear of the store. In a moment, she giggled oddly and came dashing up to him. "How about this? Can I get it, please? It's on clearance."

It was a flowered sundress. Had she been in the least bit presentable it would have pretty on her. "Of course you can," Will answered. With a quick tug, he pulled the tag off the dress. "There's a bathroom across the concourse, you have eight minutes. Go get changed."

She took all eight minutes. Will ignored the sale lady's explanation of how a sundress wasn't the right choice for that time of year and paid for the clothes. He then went to wait outside the bathroom. There he paced again, feeling a growing anxiety in his chest that ran down into his hands making them shake. With an effort, he tried not to think about Lisa or the baby, or whatever spell Amy had them under. All of that only made him want to throw up, so he paced.

Talitha came out of the bathroom just as he was about to stick his head in to yell at her to get out. It took him a second to recognize her. Her skin was scrubbed clean and her tan fairly glowed, even her hair, though damp, was no longer a straggly filthy mess, and was now its usual deep brown.

"I need some money," she said glancing around nervously. "I made a huge mess in there and I think I should leave a tip or something. Is that what people usually do?"

"Not when they're late," Will answered, grabbing her hand and running. Soon, he had to let go however. He was an athletic man who trained regularly, due in a large part because of his sister, and because of this training, most people would've considered him fast. Yet next to Talitha, he was dead slow. She sped on feet that seemed barely to touch the ground while after thirty seconds of pure sprinting he was beginning to lumber, falling behind.

"I see Father Vogel," she said seconds later as if they were strolling in the park. Will could say nothing. It was all he could do to breathe. He lifted his head and indeed the priest was there, seven or eight gates further on, waving his arms for them to hurry. Talitha increased her speed and all eyes were upon her; she was a sight with her hair streamed out long behind. As she lengthened her stride, her coltish legs looked longer than normal and only then did he notice she wasn't wearing shoes.

"Here they come," Will heard Father Vogel say as he came huffing up, winded. They were escorted aboard the plane by a stewardess in blue who tried her best not to stare at Will's face. He helped by keeping his chin down, popping it up only to glance down the length of the plane. Thankfully, though the plane wasn't a large one, it was only half-filled.

"Let's go to the back," Will gasped. He didn't want to be too near anyone, since he was sure the priest would start in with the questions as soon as they sat down. Always the keeper of the rules, Talitha turned back pointing to her ticket and Will spoke before she could protest. "Talitha, we paid for the seats, we can sit where we please as long as no one's already there. It'll be fine." He gave her a nudge.

"Talitha," Vogel pointed to the window seat and after she slid in, he sat down next to her. "Where are your shoes?"

"Do I have to wear the shoes?" she asked drawing her feet under her and looking around as if the shoe police were on their way. "Is this airline one of those: no shirt, no shoes, no service, deals?"

In truth, Will didn't know, but just then, the plane began backing away. "If it is, then it's too late now, so don't worry." He took a seat just behind his sister and lifted up the window. The view was ugly. Dour rain beat down against the pane steadily, but as they moved toward the runway, the drops turned sideways.

"Will it be ok if I ask you some questions?" Father Vogel inquired of Talitha. Her shoulders slumped and she turned her face to the little square window, she nodded.

The priest paused for a moment in thought and then spoke quietly so as not to be overheard, "I need you to be as honest as you can. Is the demon, the one you called Ba'al Fie-ere, is she still inside you?"

Talitha turned her head from the retreating airport. "I don't know, but you're an exorcist. If she's in there, you can do something about it."

Will put his head between the seats and interrupted, "No. Not while we're on a plane. Tonight, after we make sure Lisa's safe, you can try another exorcism then."

"Maybe not even then," Vogel replied. "I still need to establish that she is indeed possessed. What do you think, Will? Last night you say you exorcized the demon, but here she is today doing all sorts of remarkable things."

"I don't know what's going on. I saw the exorcism work. Ba'al Fie-ere's face was beyond furious at being cheated; I mean it was so real. But now it's like all that never happened." Will paused for a moment as a question of his own came to him. "Before we go too much further down this road, do you believe in any of this, Father? I know you're an exorcist and all, but that doesn't necessarily mean you believe this stuff."

"I believe that possession happens, with all my heart."

"Have you ever had to exorcize a real demon?" Will asked.

"Once for sure and two other times where I couldn't be certain. They were..."

Talitha turned sharp at this and grabbed the priest's arm, interrupting him. "What were the names of the demons?" Her voice was loud and held a manic quality.

With a worried look, Father Vogel leaned back from her. "One wouldn't give its name and the other two...well, I don't think it would be wise to bring up their names just now."

Will concurred, "Please don't. Talitha shouldn't get worked up." The plane had reached the end of the runway and was cleared. It accelerated quickly, pushing them deep into their seats before nosing up into the rain.

Talitha watched the ground dropped away. "I'm not getting worked up. But that 'demon' who wouldn't give you his name was a fake. All a demon really has is its name and they aren't shy to let you hear it."

"Thanks Talitha, I'll keep that in mind for the future."

"If you live to see that future, Father," Talitha kept her face to the glass as she spoke.

The priest gave Will a glance. "Why do you think that I might not live?"

She huffed out a long breath. "Because you don't fully believe our story. If you did, you would've begged to stay back in Boston. There it goes." Just then, the city disappeared below the heavy clouds and she watched it with sad eyes.

"Actually, I believe your story. All that remains to be seen is if you're still possessed and I for one think you are." For a moment, there was an awkward lull in the conversation with only the thrum of the engines running through their ears. Talitha nodded in agreement.

"Are you sure?" Will asked the priest.

"Pretty sure. She's been exhibiting quite a number of signs that point in that direction... the personality changes alone are drastic enough for me to believe that she's possessed. But it's her super-human powers that make this case incontrovertible. I've never seen anything like it."

Will's stomach knotted and unknotted unpleasantly. "I explained that to you already. She doesn't have unnatural powers, she only has magnified abilities. Like those people who walk on coals or lay on beds of nails, or like those people who can lift a car off of a loved one...like that."

Father Vogel shook his head. "She knew things about me that she couldn't have. And look at her arm, it's practically healed."

"She heals fast! Like I said, she can send out chemical *thingies*...markers I mean, to speed up the healing process. And the stuff you ate for dinner, she smelled it on you, I bet."

"What about my Zippo, she knew it had an emblem on it." He pulled it out and there was a cross on the silver finish. "She also knew about my violin playing and...that I like to sing."

Will was at a loss. He didn't know how she knew those things.

Talitha shrugged. "You have a habit of tracing the outline of the cross on the Zippo in your pocket. I knew it wasn't a normal lighter by the smell; due to their construction, Zippos lose their butane at a higher rate." She took the priest lined fingers and held them up. "The tips of your fingers on your left hand still have the calluses of a violinist, as does the pad of your right thumb and tip of the right index finger. You use the Russian bow grip, I presume?"

"Yes," he was surprised. "And my singing?"

"That's easy. You have tears in your vocal chords that are common to...rock singers." She seemed embarrassed, as if she were accusing him of something bad. "My guess is that you are losing your hearing somewhat and are over compensating."

"You see that?" Will cried out in his excitement. "These were only observations and anyone could've seen them."

"But if I'm not possessed, what's wrong with me?" Suddenly she looked a little green as if from airsickness. "I disemboweled a man once. I made sure that he was still alive and I fed his own..."

"Talitha! Stop it." Will growled. "That wasn't you, ok? That was someone else."

"No it was me...I did it with these hands. I can feel the man's blood, hot and sticky... I'm scared, Will," she refused to look from the window but Will could see her tears in the reflection. "I became a demon once before. I think it's happening again."

Will got up and went around to the seat in front of her and leaned over it. "These are only memories. They're not who you are."

At this Vogel's eyebrows shot up meaningfully. "There is a small possibility that you are suffering from dissociative identity disorder."

Will looked to the priest nonplussed. "What's that?"

"It means that he thinks I'm crazy," Talitha answered and her words were suddenly colder than they had been. "Right priest? You think I've gone off the deep end?"

"Tal, don't do this," Will said with menace in his own voice. "He said a small possibility, maybe he's wrong."

"He is wrong, Will. There was a demon in me and now it's coming back. There's no other explanation." She slumped back in her seat, glaring out of the window moodily, the tears on her face now forgotten.

"Why don't you tell me what dissociative disorder means?" Will asked his sister, purposely looking at her, and not the priest, wanting her to talk and definitely not wanting her to change.

She sighed loudly fogging up the window. "It's dissociative identity disorder. It's a fancy way of saying that I have a split personality. But we both know that's just crap."

"Actually I agree with her," Vogel said with a nod. "Generally speaking, dissociative identity disorder is one of the most overused and clichéd diagnosis in America. It's become a fad. We're number one in the world when it comes to this mental disorder. It's diagnosed at ten times the rate compared to countries like Germany or France and four-hundred times the rate of India or China."

Talitha turned back to him. "If it's all such claptrap why did you suggest I may be afflicted by it?"

"Because of everything you and Will have told me. There was a real person residing in your mind for the last eight years. You mentioned that you never knew what she was up to when she had control of your body. This means that though she was using your brain, she was using different neural paths than you, creating memories that you couldn't access. But now there is no guardian of that part of your mind and as you stumble across memories, your brain...and this is only conjecture, your brain travels down the path of least resistance and you become her, at least for a little while."

Will was scared of this possibility, as well as confused. "I don't get what you mean by path of least resistance. Isn't her brain like mine and just kinda flows back and forth?"

"It's not. Think of her mind like a railroad. Running all through her brain, she has two sets of tracks, but of different gauges..."

"Gauges?" Will shrugged not knowing what the priest meant by this.

"The widths of the rails. A train's wheels can only sit on the correct size track. So Talitha is churning along thinking her brilliant thoughts, but suddenly she comes to a memory that is shared between her and her evil twin. Let's take what happened at the factory for instance. They both had traumatic moments there and because of this, her train jumped from one track to another. Suddenly she's on a new track and her thinking is easier as long as she stays on it. You see? Right then she has just become the other Talitha."

"Why would her mind do that? Why doesn't it stop itself?" Will asked looking at his sister thoughtfully.

She kept her face steadily out the window, but even in profile, he could see that she was thinking on this as well.

"Curiosity at where those memories lead? Guilt?" Father Vogel shrugged his shoulders. "Perhaps that is just the way the mind works. It's all a guess, even to those of us with advanced degrees in psychology. It's one of our dirty little secrets. The mind is far more complex than we'll ever likely know. And though we can work out some of the details of the *how* things work up here." He tapped his forehead. "The *why* is frequently beyond us."

"I had a psychologist once...DeBracy," Talitha said with a frown on her face. "One day he was there and the next..." she trailed off.

Will snapped his fingers in front of her face. "Talitha, don't think on that." Seven years ago, the evil Talitha had snapped kicked the man's larynx in and only an emergency tracheotomy by another doctor had saved him.

"Why not? Whatever happened to him? Did I do something to him? If I did he deserved it that rat faced-asshole." Her face clouded into anger, snarling her lip.

"He's in private practice." Actually Will had no idea. "Speaking of doctors, did I tell you that Lisa has been dragging me to Lamaze class?" Talitha nodded vaguely, losing her sudden anger and her eyes wandered around the plane in confusion. She was trying to get her train on the right track. He continued, "Remember, I told you all about that goofy breathing they were making us do?"

"Oh right. I remember." She paused a moment, her brows coming down. "Were we talking about Lamaze before?"

Father Vogel spoke up before Will could say anything, "What's the last thing you can remember before we started talking about child birth?"

"Train tracks? Were we talking about trains... no wait. We were talking about your voice. You have tears in the vertical aspect of the ventricular folds of your vocal chords. Right? From your singing, right?"

Will plastered an imitation of a smile on his face. The conversation about her abilities had been a few minutes ago. "Yep. Tell me, those two stewardesses, can you tell me what they are saying?" Two women in the blue uniform of their profession were all the way at the front of the plane. They seemed to be whispering to each other.

Talitha gazed toward them and shook her head slowly. "No, there is too much ambient noise from the engines. I can read the blonde woman's lips if you want. Actually, they're talking about us, or rather you, Will."

"Tal, it doesn't matter. Look at me. I want you to do some math while I talk to Father Vogel in the front of the plane. What is a good sort of problem for you to work on?"

"You're going to talk about me?" Talitha asked meekly, dropping her gaze down.

"Yes. I need to be able to talk freely about subjects that might get the other Talitha all riled up. But it's only to try to figure out how to help you. Ok?"

She nodded. "Ok. I guess I could figure out the decimal representation of *Pi* past the fifteenth point. I just need some paper and a pencil."

Father Vogel dug through his bag and pulled out both items and they left her scribbling away. To Will, she wasn't working with the enthusiasm that she normally found in math. She was going through the motions, only.

"Do you mind if we talk up here?" Will asked the blonde stewardess.

She gave him a fake plastic smile, that didn't touch the slightly disgusted look in her eyes. "Only for a little bit. Passengers aren't really supposed to be up here, ya know." She left them, pushing the drink cart down the tiny center aisle.

As soon as she was out of earshot, Will hissed in a loud whisper to the priest, "What's happening to Talitha? Why couldn't she remember so much of our conversation just now? She was right there."

Father Vogel leaned in close. "This can happen to a person with split personalities. Likely, the conversation was not transferred from her short-term memory to her long term and thus poof; it just didn't happen for her. Or the conversation is with the other Talitha who was just starting to emerge. If it is she will have a full recollection of it while this Talitha won't."

"Will it always be like this? Earlier today, she was afraid that she was going to become the demon. She acted like she had no choice. Is that really going to happen?"

"Possibly, though I wouldn't find it probable," Vogel responded with a glance back down the plane. "Most likely she will develop an amalgamated personality. A mixture of both the good and bad sides of her, but dominated by her good side. You see she has had now... how old is she, sixteen?"

"She just turned twenty-five."

"Really? That's amazing" He gave another look back, shaking his head. "But back to my point, she's had twenty five years to lay the physical ground work, the actual neural path of her thoughts in her brain. The evil side of her has only had eight years, so in most things, she will use the older, better-worn paths. It will only be when she is confronted with a stark memory of her evil, that her dark side will emerge."

"What about when she gets angry? It seems to be coming out then as well."

Vogel pondered this for a moment and then asked, "Before all of this, was Talitha quick to anger, or was she more the mellow type?"

Will turned his swollen face lopsided with a smile. "She was generally the sweetest girl. Only very rarely did she get angry."

The priest's shoulder's sagged at this. "Then I think you can expect her bad side to come out whenever she would get angry. And really, it will probably come out at many other times as well. As an example, just now her bad side began to emerge when we were discussing psychologists. Death also seems to bring it out...she talks as though she has been associated with more deaths than just the ones from last night." He made it sound less as a statement and more as a question.

Will leaned back against the pilot's door. "Yeah a lot more. I never knew about them until a couple of days ago." His headache began to pound away and he rubbed at his temples. "So what do I do with her? Is there some sort of treatment, some counseling maybe?"

Father Vogel crossed his arms, thinking for a moment. "The usual treatment is to try to consolidate the different personalities into a single working one and then deal with the underlying issues that caused the split in the first place. But with Talitha..."

Will jumped in, "That can't be her treatment! The other Talitha is beyond help. She's a monster; she's more vicious and cunning than humanly possible, she can't be allowed to become a part of Talitha. I have a feeling that if that happens, her evil side will corrupt the good and wear it like a mask." Will looked down the plane at his sister. She wasn't working on the math problem; she was staring out of the window. "That could be the evil girl right now sitting there and we wouldn't know until..." he left the words trailing.

The older man sighed. "I agree, that can't be her treatment. Though I have to say that when personalities collide they generally don't stay so true to form as what you are suggesting. In other words, the evil will be tempered by the good and vice versa, especially now that she is aware of her situation. She will feel shame at her hate, but also angry at her supposedly weak feelings, such as love. But for her the best news is that there's no reason for her to keep the other personality."

"Is there ever a reason?" Will didn't see how there could be.

"Yes, and I have to say that even though I called dissociative identity disorder a fad, it is a real condition. The people afflicted with it develop their extra personalities for actual reasons. Perhaps not entirely sane reasons but they are legitimate to the individual. I knew of an unfortunate young lady whose mother never allowed her to have an opinion of her own. She grew up to be the meekest person and married a man who took over where the mother left off, silencing her whenever the subject wasn't what she was making for dinner. Eventually, she developed a separate personality—that of an actress. She would sign autographs, audition for plays, show up at cast parties, all without being aware of it. I mention her to illustrate the point that there is sometimes an actual need, a reason for the extra personality."

Will shook his head in bewilderment at the weirdness of people. "Talitha doesn't fall into that category, I'm sure she wants to be rid of it even more than we do."

"I agree and it's one of the reasons that I believe she will be a good candidate for hypnotherapy." The priest seemed serious.

"Really? That's an actual thing?"

Father Vogel smiled at this. "Yes. It's been used since before the Civil War, and there have been some notable successes using it to treat mild forms of dissociative identity disorder. The idea is to induce a hypnotic suggestion when the patient is in that in-between state of personalities. That way both personalities accept the suggestion as their own thought, each reinforcing it through the subconscious mind."

Despite an inherent belief that hypnosis was bogus, Will grew excited. "What sort of suggestion would you put into her?"

"In Talitha's case we have to deal with two distinct issues. The first and the one that I feel we should begin working on right away is the rage and anger that's left over from the demon. She can't seem to control it and in fact, she doesn't seem to want to. That's because those neural paths are conditioned to loop, to stay angry. In order to break that loop we must be able to feed the demon's rage into the good Talitha..."

Will held out his hand for the man to stop. "Wait. Hold on, that sounds like it'd hurt more than it would help her. Why on earth would we want to do that?"

"It won't hurt her, trust me," Vogel replied. "Picture, if right now, without warning you became angry. I mean furious. The first thing you would do would be to question its causes. Why am I so angry? What's doing this to me? Just asking those questions would go a long way to calming you and soon you'd understand where the feeling came from. By channeling the emotion into the good Talitha, we bring her personality to the forefront. She will then be aware and in charge of herself and able to deal intellectually with her emotions."

It seemed like a good idea to Will, if it could be done. "I would love for this to work, but Talitha is pretty smart. She's not going to go to sleep with you waving a watch in front of her face."

The priest smiled at this. "In one sense, you don't know how right you are. Talitha appears to be a very concrete thinker, and hypnotherapy works best with fantasizers. Yet she's also dissociative, which is the second best group to work with. And I'll have you know, I won't be waving a watch and I won't try to trick her; any attempt at subterfuge will focus her mind away from our objective. It's important that she will know beforehand everything that I wish to accomplish, and how I wish to accomplish it. This knowledge plants the seed in her mind and as we progress, and I do exactly what I said I would, her expectations are fulfilled, one after another, making each step that much easier."

"I'm probably the most skeptical person, yet you almost have me halfway convinced this'll work," Will said.

"I'm fairly certain that the first part will work, it's the second that has me worried," Father Vogel replied. "The second issue Talitha has to deal with is guilt. The memories are going to feel completely real to her. She'll be able to picture her hands doing all those terrible deeds. She'll second guess every one of her thoughts and actions, and likely yours as well."

"She won't be the only one. I am complicit in every death she's been a part of." Will's mind began to drift toward all of the deaths he had been associated with, but Father Vogel began speaking again and he focused his attention on the priest.

"Because you didn't die eight years ago?" Vogel asked.

Though he wasn't feeling the least bit amused, Will gave a weak rueful chuckle at this. "The flight is only a little over an hour long, Father. You don't have time to shrink me."

"I do have time to start on your sister," Vogel answered back. "You'd be surprised, but a half empty plane is a wonderful place for hypnotherapy. It's that constant thrumming noise from the engines. Take a look, most of the passengers are already asleep, or halfway there."

"Father, no. Really, we don't have time," Will replied as his anxiety came back to him. "When we're finished dealing with Amy, by all means, let's try this hypno-stuff. I'll fly you to Denmark and back if that what it takes to help Talitha, but not right now."

Father Vogel stepped back from Will with a queer look in his eyes that made Will very uncomfortable. "Mr. Jern, we have nearly forty-five minutes, which is very good for a start. The loop within her that I'm suggesting to break will make her much less dangerous."

The priest was of course correct. Will looked down at the worn black linoleum floor and said nothing.

The priest persisted, "We could be done with the first session in half an hour. What I want to do is bring Talitha's...the good Talitha's anger to the..."

"I said no," Will answered, allowing his own anger to show, hiding the self-disgust.

"For the life of me, I don't understand." The priest's grey eyes locked on Will's ice-cold blue ones. "You want your sister to stay like this? She could snap at any second killing who knows how many people. And you're ok with this?"

"Excuse me?" the blonde stewardess broke in. "The girl you're with? She's getting kinda mad. She wants a drink but we can't serve anyone under twenty-one."

"A drink?" A sudden worry came over Will and he dashed down the aisle.

Talitha sat in her seat looking confused and before Will was even halfway to her, she called out in a loud voice, "Will, I'm over twenty-one, right? I swear I am." Feeling embarrassed with all eyes on the plane on him, Will put his fingers to his lips, but this only angered his sister. "Don't shush me! All I did was ask you a question."

"You're right, I'm sorry." Will went and sat on the arm of the chair catty-corner to hers. "You say you want a drink?"

"Yes but these whore-bitches won't serve me one. They say I'm too young, but I'm sure I'm older than twenty-one...only I don't remember any birthdays, or parties."

On her twenty-first birthday, she had alternated between trying to rape him and kill him. "I didn't throw you a party on your twenty-first."

"Why the hell not?"

At the end of word *not*, she hurled the pen at his throat. He *saw* it coming and he knocked the pen aside with a backhand move. His hand stung fiercely, he didn't let it show on his face. Talitha liked seeing pain and it usually made her hungry for more.

"We were still in mourning over Brian's death. I didn't think it would have been appropriate."

"Brian? He screwed me out of a party? Even in death he tried to fuck me over!"

Father Vogel spoke up from behind Will. "Did you kill Brian?"

"Of course I did." Her face was shocked at the question.

"You seem very angry just now...no make that furious. Were you ever this furious before your initial encounter with Ba'al Zubel?" The priest's tone was astonishingly calm. It seemed to jar Talitha.

"Before? Hell no. I was a complete wimp. A fucking pushover."

"Did you ever feel like cursing like this before, back when you were a wimp, but didn't?"

Now it was Will's turn to grow angry. "Don't answer that Talitha. I told you, Father we aren't going to do this right now."

"She needs me, Will," the priest returned.

"Actually what I need is a drink," Talitha said sullenly, sounding more like a barfly than either the innocent girl or the insane killer that she really was.

"What do you want to drink?" Will asked. "I'll get whatever you want."

This question stopped Talitha. Save for a single beer, she had never drunk before as far as Will knew and the question stumped her. With her confusion, her anger seemed to depart.

"I don't know. Remember that Jackson guy from this morning? He mentioned having *forties*. Do you know what those are?"

In spite of everything, Will had to smile. "Trust me, you don't want that. It's malt liquor and it's nasty. But you had wanted champagne before. I bet I can get you a mimosa. That's a mix of champagne and orange juice," he added at her look of puzzlement.

"Oh that sounds nice." Her aspect seemed to calm considerably at the prospect and Will thought that he had headed off a potentially dangerous moment.

The stewardess had been further back behind Father Vogel watching the spectacle play out. She looked as though she had been slapped by what she had heard. "Sir, like I said, I can't serve..."

"Four mimosas please. They're all for me." His stare was like granite and the stewardess decided against pressing the point and hurried off. Father Vogel sighed loudly and meaningfully, but Will ignored him. "You didn't get too far on your calculations." The paper was scribbled on from top to bottom, but it didn't look like there was enough math for what she was trying to accomplish.

Talitha looked sheepish. "I don't know why, but I couldn't concentrate. I also... I couldn't concentrate." She finished lamely, hiding something inexpertly.

"Will, can I talk with you," Vogel asked, sounding very much like a parent wishing to chastise a child.

"Perhaps after I've had my drink. You don't know how my head is just pounding."

A silence, save for the steady drone of the engines befell them as they waited for their drinks to arrive. Will's head did indeed hurt, but no more than it had all day, he had just mentioned it because he didn't want to have to talk to the priest. He didn't want to have to tell him why he was against Talitha being even a little bit cured just at the moment.

"Here ya go, that'll be eighteen dollars. Cash only." The blonde stewardess would have made a horrible actress. Her smile looked sick on her face. Clearly serving them drinks, perhaps getting them drunk, was the last thing in the world she wanted to do. But still it was her job to smile and so she did.

Will gave her a twenty and took two of the drinks handed them to Talitha. "Hold these for me will you." He then grabbed the next two. "Keep the change."

The mimosa was good, as was the second one. Father Vogel refused the drink he was offered and waited patiently until Will had finished both. "Will, if you don't mind." The priest went to the front of the plane.

Reluctant to follow, Will looked to Talitha. "Do you like your drink?"

"Oh, it's so much better than that beer I drank that one time," she said with a smile. She appeared to be relaxing, allowing the alcohol to do its thing rather than biochemically neutering it as she could have.

Will attempted a smile. "I'll be right back. If you have any weird feelings or get angry at nothing, just wave your hand." He left her nodding up at him, very much looking like she was his baby sister from so many years ago.

At the front of the plane, Father Vogel barely waited for him to clear the first two rows of passengers before starting in on Will. "What's wrong with you? She has a real chance here."

Will only stared at the priest, not knowing what to say.

"Will, the longer she stays like this, the greater the chance she'll kill someone! And if she does, she'll no longer be able to blame it on some demon or some evil twin living in her mind. It will be all her. Do you know what that will do to her? *She* will become the killer."

"That's not what you said a little while ago," Will countered. "You said her good side was too ingrained in her psyche and would dominate her evil side."

"I did, however if she happens to kill someone, then truly which side of her is good and which is evil? From her point of view, they will both be bad and as more and more memories of torture and death come to her, she will find it impossible to categorize them. They will all be her. Is that what you want?"

"No."

"Then why won't you let me help her?"

"I need the evil Talitha and I need her whole," Will whispered this. The two of them had been getting loud and Will was afraid at least some of what they were saying was filtering back.

"You can't be serious," Vogel was back to being loud. The second stewardess, a girl with short brown hair came up the aisle.

"Can you two please take your seats? You're starting to make the other passengers nervous." Clearly, she was nervous as well and glanced at Will frequently even though she spoke to Father Vogel.

"Certainly," the priest responded cordially, but Will could tell he was more than peeved. In seconds, they were back to their seats and Will thought he was done having to explain himself when Talitha hopped up.

"I haven't been on a plane since I was six years old and I can't remember, is one of the bathrooms designated as a ladies room?" she asked. Will shook his head and Talitha gave him a slightly disgusted look. "Well they really should have one." She nudged her way out to the aisle and as soon as she was halfway down Father Vogel turned to Will.

"Why on earth do you want her evil? I demand that you tell me why."

"I told you when we were at the hospital what I was up against," Will answered. "My wife and unborn daughter are being held by a vengeful gypsy witch who has at least three men with her. She knows about my ability to see the future and she doesn't care! And that means she has some way to counter act it. I haven't had a vision concerning my wife all day. Just that alone is enough to tell me that I'm right. And that means I'm all but useless."

"But you aren't even giving Talitha a chance to fight as herself," Vogel replied heatedly. "Logically she can fight to protect loved ones. It would be considered noble and set her good side apart."

"Wrong. It'll get us all killed... including you. Talitha can't fight, let alone kill. I know her better than anyone, and I know she'll hesitate to hurt people or to strike to kill—Amy Harris won't. But the other Talitha...she's a living weapon and is all but unstoppable."

"You know you may be dooming her and I just don't mean here on earth."

Talitha had exited the bathroom and came down the aisle smiling at people as she passed. She looked terribly innocent to Will.

"Talitha?" Will began as she sat down. "Father Vogel and I have been discussing what's going to happen when we get to Bangor. It's going to be dangerous, and uh, I don't know how to say this..."

"I'm aware of what you want, Will," she said with a smile so tight that it stretched her lips into little pink lines. "You want to turn the evil side of me lose on Amy Harris. Don't give me that look of surprise. You know that I am blessed with somewhat above average reasoning capabilities."

Father Vogel jumped in, "Talitha, I need to warn you that if you end up killing anyone, you may be setting yourself up where we may not be able to fix your duo personality problem. Do you understand? Your subconscious will have it further ingrained that all you are, is a murderer, both sides of you."

"That is the least of my concerns, Father."

"What about your soul, Talitha? Don't you think you ought to be concerned for that?"

She smiled prettily at the priest, her teeth, straight and very white next to her natural tan looked like something out of a television commercial and to see her like that one would never think she'd gone through so much. With a shrug, she turned to look out of the window.

Vogel was mystified over her reactions and glanced at Will. "What about you? As her brother shouldn't you be concerned with her soul?"

"I am, but I have to be concerned for Lisa's as well. She is innocent in any of this..."

Vogel interrupted slamming his fist down on his armrest, "And your sister isn't! She's as much a victim as any one and right now I would have to say she is being victimized yet again, by you. What do you have to say about that? You're using her and won't even give her a chance at any sort of future."

Will suddenly needed another drink. He stretched his long muscular arm up, hitting the call button and decided, after seeing the stewardess's face contort into a grimace at who it was that rang for her, that he would have two drinks. He turned to look out the window just as his sister was. "You're asking me to blunt my sword right before going into battle."

"No, I'm..."

Will wasn't done speaking and rudely talked over the priest, loudly, angrily, "If I take your advice and we lose this fight, what do you think will happen to our souls then? Amy Harris is a witch! She buys her power with souls. They are the currency of the Void, and mine and Talitha's are almost priceless. Ba'al Zubel would pay dearly for us...as would Ba'al Fie-ere for that matter." He had been loud and he didn't care. The stewardess had an odd look on her face as she tried to figure out what it was she had just heard. Will, still staring out the window asked her, "Do you have Wild Turkey?"

Her mouth came open at the question, "Uh, Wild Turkey? Oh, you mean the whiskey. No, we have Jack

Daniels."

Will shook his head in disappointment yet still dug out a couple of twenties. "Let me have six please and keep the change."

With eyes that were wide in surprise, the stewardess left, her blonde hair swinging back and forth. Will didn't notice. His own eyes were on the great gold and red expanse below him. The clouds over Boston hadn't extended into Maine and he was looking down on her wonderful forests. It gave him a thrill for home, which mingled with his nervousness, making his stomach seem particularly light and empty.

After a few minutes of silence, Will felt he had to finish explaining himself. "There was never going to be any trading of incantations. I didn't need second sight to know that. We're going to Maine simply to save my wife and daughter. *And* there will be a fight, there's no question about that. If we lose, then all our souls may be forfeit, if we win... then maybe just Talitha's. I wish there was another way."

"Will? Are you going to look into the future? Purposely?" Talitha asked timidly. Her tone suggested that she he hoped he would, that maybe it was her only chance not to be a killer.

"Yes, when we land." He got the shivers. "You know I can't do it here." Will was desperately afraid to look into the future, knowing that it was unlikely to show anything but pain. His leg started bouncing up and down nervously and he looked up for the stewardess anxiously. She came down the aisle, parading the tiny bottles about for the other passengers to see and more than one head glanced back in Will's direction. They were quick glances only as Will was in a fierce mood and no one cared to accept the challenge he held in his eyes.

The stewardess gave him the fake plastic smile of hers, which he didn't bother to return, and handed over the Jack Daniels. Even before she turned away, Will had the first small cap unscrewed and guzzled the shot down. The second bottle went just as quick, but the next four he spread out over the remaining time of the flight, which seemed very short.

For a long time, the three companions didn't speak until Will said, "This way, Tal."

Up till that point, their silence seemed unbreakable. They had deboarded the plane and progressed through the small airport without saying a word. They were currently in the parking garage and he pointed to his red jeep, the one with the bullet hole in the passenger door.

"Huh?" Talitha seemed confused and she looked around with a start. "Where are we?"

"Did you lose track of time?" Father Vogel asked with concern.

"Yes. We were just in the plane and you Will, you had just ordered some drinks." Her eyes went wide, "Did I do anything? Anything weird or...mean."

"Try not to be too concerned, losing track of time is a symptom of a dissociative," the priest replied in his soothing tone. "You didn't do anything weird, you were just quiet. We all were. I was praying and your brother was drinking."

If Father Vogel had meant anything by the comment, Will didn't know nor in fact did he care. He was lost in his stomach churning fear. It was two minutes after four in the afternoon and there was no more time to put off what he had to do. Yet he did put it off for another moment. After scanning the near empty garage, he climbed into the hard-topped jeep and fished out a bottle of Wild Turkey from beneath the seat.

The burn of the whiskey was a relief to him. This bottle was his 'Saturday afternoon drive to Talitha's cabin' bottle. It was almost empty. He held it out to the priest, who quite unexpectedly took it and drank. Even more of a shock, Vogel held it out to Talitha.

"Does it taste bad?" she asked looking at the bottle squeamishly. Father Vogel nodded at the same time that Will shook his head. She gave a little laugh at them and then tipped the bottle. It was worth giving up some of his whiskey to see the little jig of revulsion that her body involuntarily went through a second later.

She spluttered for a moment and then smiled. "Does this mean I passed the initiation?"

Will took the bottle and drained it. "Let me stay under for only three minutes...no five minutes. Five minutes only. You may have to hit me to get me out of it, just watch the nose, will you? It still stings from yesterday."

Talitha climbed into the passenger seat and gave Will a nod, but Father Vogel looked confused. "Hit you? Why would she have to do that?"

Ever since Amy Harris had picked up the phone at his house, Will had been battling a fluctuating anxiety. It was now reaching its highest peak and he was too nervous to even try to explain and he gave his sister a jerk of his head.

"Can you explain it to him, please?" While he spoke, his fingers began to mush themselves together. "Crap!" He felt a sharp pain from the fingers on his left hand, and only then did he remember they had been dislocated the day before. He massaged them gently and tried unsuccessfully to tune out Talitha.

"So as to have an accurate picture of what is coming, Will is going to endeavor to look into the future on *purpose*. Normally, visions just come to him out of the blue, and invariably these are disjointed. Now, he's tried this twice before and both were very difficult on him, mainly due to the horrific nature of what he was looking for, but also because the visions wouldn't let him go. Am I describing that correctly?" she asked Will. After a flash came to his mind of the decomposing corpse of a boy, he swallowed loudly and nodded.

"It's like I can't pull away. My mind becomes synced with the vision as if that's my reality and this," he indicated the car with shaking hands, "is all a dream."

Leaning against a shiny black Buick next to the jeep, Vogel nodded trying to understand. "And you are worried about what you might see in your home, I get it now. Good luck Will."

"Thanks. Here we go. Shit, I'm so scared...five minutes only, and then get me out. Five minutes...five minutes," Will took a few deep breaths. And looked.

Chapter 12

Will

There was nothing to see, which gave his nerves a jolt. He tried a second time and again saw nothing save for the black behind his eyelids. His anxiety reached an unhealthy pitch and a pain began developing behind his breastbone. "It's not working," the words escaped out of him in a frightened warble.

"I hate throwing psycho-analytical babble out every few seconds, but your fear of what you may see is probably inhibiting your ability," the priest said, coming to stand next to Will.

"Or maybe...there's nothing *to* see." In the front seat of the jeep, Will went white as he spoke. "Maybe Lisa doesn't have a future. Maybe she's already..."

"Don't jump to conclusions," Vogel advised. There was concern written on his face and gently, with soft cool hands he reached out to grasp Will's wrist and took a measure of his pulse for close to a minute. "Hmmm, a hundred and fourteen beats per minute," he said with a touch of unease.

"For Will, that's tachycardia. His resting pulse hovers around fifty," Talitha took his left wrist.

"My chest hurts too, I think something's wrong with me." With his right hand Will massaged his chest, feeling the pain where he had been shot the night before. Suddenly and quite atypical for him, he felt himself start to hyperventilate, his breath started to blow in and out rapidly. He looked with wild eyes to his sister for help.

"Relax Will, breathe easier. I can feel that it's sinus tachycardia, not ventricular," Talitha said. He had no idea if this was a good thing or a bad thing. Just as he was about to ask her, she reached out and touched his neck. "And your blood pressure is still very good. Panic attack?" she asked the priest.

"I believe so," Vogel agreed. "Will, look at me. I want you to remember your Lamaze training. Give me a signal breath, nice and slow."

"Signal...do you mean a cleansing breath?"

Vogel nodded and smiled, and began to breathe along side of Will. Soon their breathing became matched and Will tried to make a joke of his situation, "I feel so stupid. This is for pregnant ladies." What he really felt was a thrill of fear running all along his nerves like lightening.

"No, it's for anyone who's in a stressful situation and needs to relax," Vogel replied evenly, breathing slightly slower.

"He's correct, Will," Talitha added. "Most people think that the mind controls the body, but they don't seem to realize that it's actually a two way street. A person who doesn't exercise feels mentally torpid as well as physically so, while a person in peak condition feels more alert and cognitively attuned. You see? In your case, calm your body and your mind will follow."

"Or I can listen to you jabber on with your big words until I forget what had me so anxious in the first place." It was only a half-jest since he had to take a pause from his anxiety long enough to interpret a little of what she had said. And that, coupled with the Lamaze breathing had him calming to a degree.

"Well if it ameliorates your apprehension, I could extemporize for a time on a multiplicity of subjects," she replied with insincere sincerity.

"If you were hoping that I'd ask what ameliorates means, I'm not going to do it."

"Good. It'll save me the trouble of telling you to look it up."

The brother and sister looked at each other like they hadn't for some time, as if the years had fallen away and they were young again. After a moment, she smiled and seemed carefree, and he did his best to return it in the same manner, but he was far from carefree. He had many cares and she was not the least of them. Was he going to destroy her mentally by unleashing her on Amy? Would the personality of the evil Talitha take over for good? Would any of this really matter since she thought she was doomed to hell anyway?

It made his chest tighten up again just thinking of those questions. He pushed them aside. "I'm going to try again." Without any fanfare, he closed his eyes just as he had done before. There was nothing. A blank wall. He tried harder, ignoring any fear or anxiety, concentrating on the future, picturing Lisa. But there was only emptiness. "I can't do it. I'm not seeing anything."

"I bet she's blocking you somehow, like you thought," Talitha said.

This was very likely true, but he could only summon the energy to agree halfheartedly, "I guess."

A part of him was relieved that he couldn't see. A million terrible things could've been done to his wife and he didn't want to have to know any of them. Another part of him felt suddenly weak, vulnerable and terribly unsure of himself.

"So where does that leave us?" Father Vogel asked. Will remained quiet. For so long he had relied on his vision that now, without it, the future looked endless and impossibly full of wrong choices. Fear of making one kept him quiet.

"We go on to the house," Talitha replied in a quavering voice, after a long moment. "Will, drop me off just past that little bridge, ok? Wait four minutes and drive slowly on. I'll go through the orchard and approach the house from the rear and hopefully with all eyes on you, I'll be able to enter through the back unseen, and I'll, you know uh...take care of business."

Will nodded, grateful that Talitha had come up with

something. His own mind had frozen up. Father Vogel looked skeptical. "Are you, *Talitha* going to try to do this yourself?"

"It'll be the other Talitha," she answered, not lifting her eyes to meet his gaze.

"You're risking too much," Vogel said with a touch of anger in his voice.

"I'm not. I have nothing to risk," Talitha returned.

Before the priest could reply, Will slid out of the car and pulled the seat forward. "We have to get going, Father. Hop in, if you're coming with us, but if you do, please don't try to stop her."

Looking as if he wanted to say more, Vogel clambered in and Will steered his car toward home—toward certain danger and very likely death. It seemed that this concept was on all their minds and for most of the ride they were silent. It was only when they left the tiny city and were winding their way under the autumn trees did anyone speak.

"I miss my cabin," Talitha murmured. "I miss my books."

"You miss the false sense of security that these afforded you, Talitha," the priest said from his cramped perch in the short back seat.

"Yes, I do miss that." She stared out of the window. Will missed it as well. He felt lost, like a blind man in a strange city. The bridge came up quickly.

He stopped the jeep in the middle of the road and looked out at the view. On all sides, they were surrounded by trees that seemed like nothing more than low flung golden clouds and as they watched, these let loose their dry autumn rain. The leaves flicked and ticked about the street, coming together by the thousands to form a great river of gold that flowed before them.

The breeze was sharp and ran steadily away from behind, and in the distance, a yellow house with a wraparound porch could be seen sitting placidly, as if waiting for an artist to draw it into the idyllic forest scene.

Talitha opened the door letting the fall air, cold yet clean, run into the jeep. "When I see you again, make sure you have a story for me. It helps."

"I will."

"Love you, Willy J."

"Too."

Talitha smiled at this, before sliding from the jeep and running off into the woods. With her floral print dress and her fine brown skin, she looked to be a part of the forest itself, like nymph, a spirit of nature leaping through the grass. She was beautiful, and as long as Will watched her run, he wasn't afraid. However, she was gone too fast and a gloom settled over him.

"She's still barefoot," Vogel said with a shake of his head. "I'm afraid for her. What happens if the other Talitha doesn't come out?"

"Trust me, that's not the worry. It's getting the real Talitha back, that's the worry. Who am I kidding? Actually just living through this is my worry."

"You're worried for yourself? Aren't you going to let Talitha...the other Talitha that is, take on the witch and her men? These words are so weird for me to even say," Vogel said with a half-smile.

"Yeah. Witches and demons it seems so..."

"Unreal," the priest offered.

"No, stupid," Will replied. "But stupid or not, I can't give Talitha free reign in that house. If she takes out all the bad guys that's great, but then who knows what she'll do? Maybe she'll go after Lisa, and if she does, then I'll need to deal with her and that means I'm going to need a gun."

"Oh, I see. Maybe we could come in once..."

Will was quick to interrupt, "There's not going to be any 'we'. This is where you get out, unless you're going to sit there and tell me you're some sort of a ninja priest?"

"No, but there's the witch you have to deal with also,"

Vogel said this with very little enthusiasm. They both knew he would be of little use against her as well.

"Father, I think it'll be best if you stay out of sight. If Talitha and I both fail then I'll need you to alert the police, and the Pope too for that matter."

Vogel rubbed his head as if he was getting a headache. "We should call the police right now. That was where Father Alba made his big mistake."

"And what would we tell them? That Amy Harris is a witch? That she's threatening to conjure a demon from the pits of hell?" Will stared out the window, wishing it would be so easy as to call the police. "Besides, she said she'd know if we did, and I'm not going to call her bluff. No, the way to go is to strike hard and fast while we have any semblance of an upper hand."

There were a few moments of silence and then the priest surprised Will, "Do you have any sins that you would like to confess?"

Will's mind suddenly went blank. "What? Oh, I don't think so. Nothing new since the last time I went to confession."

Vogel got out of the jeep. "I'll pray for you, Will."

They waved to each other as Will put the car in gear. "Thank you. That means a lot." And oddly, it did. The shaking in his hands grew less pronounced as he started down the road.

The scenery was beautiful and he found it odd that he took the time to notice it at all. He thought that he would be freaking out, but for some reason he wasn't. He had been all day, but now he was tooling along at ten miles per hour, slow and steady, like a one car funeral procession, looking out his partially open window at the golden trimmed trees and feeling strangely calm.

Even at the unhurried pace at which he traveled, the house quickly loomed and the jeep rolled into the driveway only minutes after he had waved good-bye to the priest. He pulled behind a long black Cadillac and on impulse, he laid on the horn briefly. That ought to get their attention.

His feeling of calm ended abruptly when he stepped down out of the jeep, still it wasn't replaced with nerve rattling anxiety, but only with loneliness. He felt very alone standing on his white gravel drive. This was his house, yet it didn't feel welcoming, as had always been the case in the past. Though he knew there were people in it, the house had an empty feeling. Perhaps even a dead feeling, but most certainly it had an ominous expectation. It seemed the house was waiting for him.

"Let it wait," he murmured aloud to himself. He hadn't checked the time when Talitha had ran off into the woods, something that he regretted, and he didn't know if he was too early or too late. By the lack of screams and gunshots, he suspected he was running too early.

Movement in a second story window caught his attention. That was to be his daughter's room. Now he felt a cold anger. He had painted the trim of that room in pink, he had spent two hours assembling the crib, and there were stuffed animals lining the wood rails that he had personally chosen. And now there was a strange person in that room. Had it been Lisa she would have smiled down at him as she had done countless times before, perhaps giving him her usual little wave as well.

He glared up into the window, but there was no one to be seen. All the windows were glassy and reflected only the magnificent autumn colors around him. There were no lights on in the house.

With a deep breath, he walked purposely up toward the porch, but stopped after only ten feet. He wasn't afraid. Not for himself at least. He stopped because he was sure the people inside weren't expecting it. They were in there, crouching behind his furniture like a bunch of children playing at hide and go seek. And now this little unexpected thing he hoped would have them wondering what he was up to, perhaps worrying what he was going to do. All but Amy that is.

She would be sitting casually in his living room. This would be her triumphant moment and he pictured her wearing a great big beautiful smile. Right now, it would be frozen in place as she waited.

Purposely he lingered, counting to ten before he started forward again, and when he reached his porch he made sure to tread loudly on each of the three steps running up to it. Slow and deliberate: thud... thud...thud. Again, he paused, hoping that the muscles in her face would begin to tire and that when he finally opened the door her look wouldn't be that of a triumphant witch but rather that of a sour bitch.

He could hope. There wasn't much more he could do. Fishing the incantations from his pocket, he held them up briefly and then gripped them in both hands. These were his only insurance and he would tear them up as a last resort or perhaps as his last act.

Where was Talitha? He could go no further without her. It would be the height of folly to step through his front door too early, as Amy's thugs would likely shoot him at the first sound of a commotion in the back of the house. Yet at the same time, to hang out on the front porch for too long might clue them in that he was only acting as a decoy.

"Amy! I have your spells," his voice was clear and strong. "I'll shred them up if Lisa isn't out here in ten seconds."

Silence greeted this. Will stood there and ten seconds went by quickly, "Amy!"

Still nothing. Not from Amy, or her thugs and worse not from Talitha. Had she been neutralized by some sort of spell? His front door was a thick heavy wood that he had painted a bright white. It was unblemished and he kicked it three times as a way of knocking, marring the paint.

"Amy, stop your hiding." Another twenty seconds ticked by.

He was now out of options. Stepping to the side of the front door, he reached out and tested the knob. It turned easily beneath his hand and he pushed the door open.

"I'll teàr the spells," he cautioned as he stepped just across the threshold of the doorway and scanned the room. Had he not been in such danger, he might have smiled. Two young men of Hispanic dissent were making a childlike attempt at hiding behind his furniture. One crouched behind the long sofa, ten feet in front of him and the other was further back, squatting behind a large high backed chair that Lisa had picked up at Ethan Allen.

As expected, they both held guns in their hands. Yet what wasn't expected was that both of them sprang up at nearly the same instant and leveled their guns in his direction. For the briefest part of a second Will felt as if he were at a surprise party, but then a brilliant light seemed to erupt from the barrel of the gun being held by the man who had been hiding behind the sofa.

The light was followed by the magnified sound of a gun being discharged and this was followed by the sharp sound of a loud crack inches from his left ear. They were shooting at him! Just before light blazed from their pistols a second time, Will realized he was framed as a perfect target in the doorway. At this range, they could hardly miss.

Chapter 13

Talitha

To the average person, the forest in that fading afternoon sun would've been considered quiet, sleepy even. Save for a few birds and a late season fly buzzing past, very few people would have noticed any of the abundant wildlife going about their dangerous lives in the serene way that God had laid out for them.

As she passed, squirrels dodged to the far side of trees. Mice scampered beneath fallen branches. An orange tabby hunkered lower, blending with the gold leaves about her perfectly. A buck in the rut sniffing out a doe tensed and prepared to spring away. Talitha saw and heard and smelled all of this.

She felt wonderful. For the first time in eight long years, she felt wonderful. The air was perfectly crisp and she breathed in all the smells as if she was at a feast. The sweet odor of decaying and fermenting apples, the wet leaves molding below the layer of dry ones, a far way wood stove burning and an even more distant scent of a final barbeque. This last made her hungry.

Normally she didn't allow the feeling of hunger, it was a waste. But that wouldn't be for too much longer. The other Talitha liked the feeling. It drove her. She gave into all her urges no matter how primitive or animalistic. Still she wasn't in control yet. Talitha pushed away all thought of her and ran.

The earthen floor beneath the orchard was clear compared to the forest and she was able to pick up speed, stretching out her legs to their maximum. Already her feet were black from the rich soil and she smiled at them, feeling a touch childish. This would be allowed. She had never had much of a childhood, her mind had matured far too quickly and now it was a regret.

She had never regretted her abbreviated childhood before; she'd been too busy exploring her books, searching for knowledge and understanding. But there, flying along beneath the boughs of the apple trees, she wished she had played more and laughed more and lived more.

Soon, very soon she would lose that opportunity forever. The Void beckoned her. Really, it beckoned the other Talitha, who wanted it badly and wouldn't be put off forever.

Ahead, a ramshackle fence six feet high barred her way. She cleared it with ease, soaring over it, propelled by the great strength hidden in her slim legs. It felt a little like she was flying and though she was sprinting close to world record speed, her breathing was easy. Her heart rate at ninety beats a minute was triple its resting average yet she could've gone faster.

Off to her right on a low branch, an apple hung forgotten by all. It was very red and perfect. Impulsively she ran to it. She wasn't heedless of her mission, Will's jeep still idled by the bridge, even from a mile away she could hear it plain. She had time. The apple was sweeter than expected and very juicy. Feeling a childish need to be a child again, she let juice run down her chin and slurped at her apple. She giggled.

The jeep began to move. With a last sigh, she spun and pegged the apple core at a tree and watched with approval, as the remains seemed to disintegrate. It gave her an idea and she snatched up a fallen apple and sent the worm eaten piece of fruit zipping through the air at the same tree. Her aim was perfect and it struck dead center, exploding outward. The action struck a very satisfactory note within her and she laughed, wishing she had never grown up. Wishing. Wishing on a lot of things. Mostly wishing that time could stand still for her.

Will's jeep moved ever closer.

She took off again, speeding parallel to the road, leaping another fence, scattering a gaggle of blue jays. It was with difficulty that she refrained from chasing them and instead increased her speed, knowing she had to get past the yellow house and then double back. A few hundred yards later, she slipped across the road and blended in with the foliage on the other side.

Now she slowed, ghosting along in the thickest cover she could find. Her run had been easy and carefree; she could feel her breath running in and out, her blood working through the pipes of her arties. It was all good.

The wind, a gentle forty-seven degree breeze that playfully lifted her light summer dress began to bring to her the scent of strange men. At one time, there had been seven men, all Mexican in the house, but now there were only four. A part of her felt disappointed at this and she sighed.

That disappointment was just another symptom that her eight-year vacation was coming to an end. She wouldn't be Talitha much longer. On the plane she had lied to her brother and had overheard their entire conversation. Father Vogel had been right on so many counts, but he was missing facts. Facts that her brother had routinely ignored. Talitha was going to hell and not because of anything that her evil side had done, but what she had done. Knowingly done.

Her soul was stained with the screams of people she had tortured and as soon as the evil Talitha, this new one, this one that wasn't really a separate entity, but only just another personality, when she found out...well, it would be all over at that point. And she would find out.

Just as she was getting her evil twin's horrible memories, it stood to reason that when the other Talitha was in control, she would be getting access to her secret memories as well. And this was where Vogel had it wrong. The good side of her wasn't completely good or pure. Not even close. There were horrors in her that she had buried deep and when they came out, the evil Talitha would destroy her with them.

Perhaps this was the way it was meant to be she reasoned, slipping around one of the last trees on the edge of her brother's finely manicured lawn. Perhaps she should just allow it to happen and be done. She was doomed to the Void either way, perhaps she should go, not kicking and screaming, but go there as a conqueror. That was how Ba'al Fie-ere had gone and after all, they were essentially the same being.

The demon was in truth her real twin. This evil personality that battled for control of her body was simply the remains of the fiend. For a second, Talitha wondered what would happen if she did go into the Void fully evil, as an almost exact match to the demon. It would be interesting.

Her reverie was cut short. The crunching sound of gravel beneath the jeeps tires announced that her brother had arrived. It was time for action and Talitha peered into the dark windows of the house. A man, Mexican, aged nineteen to twenty-three stood just to the side of a window on a second floor. He was nervous and constantly licked his lips. He was an asshole.

Her reaction to the man at first surprised her. "What?" she said aloud. The thought seemed so unlike her, but then she felt familiar anger brewing in her and she knew that it would consume her, devouring everything she thought she was if she didn't do anything about it, but this time she didn't fight it.

2

For a second Talitha was unsure of herself. She had no clue as to what time it was or even what day. She felt as if she had been drunk or perhaps drugged. In her mind, she could picture odd flashes of strangers. A priest, a bishop, a big haired waitress that she had wanted to kill. There was even a snotty stewardess, who looked down her nose at her. It was all so strange.

Her last real clear memory had been standing over that cop Milner back in the factory. She had hoped to kill him too, but just then, out in the cool of autumn Maine, she couldn't remember if she had. Bringing her hands up to her tall slim nose, she took in their scent.

"Mother fucker!" she hissed. There was no blood on her hands. This was Will's fault, she knew it—only she didn't know exactly how she knew it or exactly how he had stopped her.

Though there hadn't been blood, there was the scent of apple on her fingers, it made her feel strange and reminiscent, lifting her head, she took in the air through her nostrils and ignored the extraneous markers of the orchard and the wildlife about her. Now, she knew where she was.

This was Will's *Little House on the Prairie* home, where he liked to pretend he was mister goody-two-shoes Charles Ingalls. Will was such an asshole. Only an asshole would paint his home yellow. Only an ass... the thought stopped abruptly. There had been another asshole she remembered, a very recent one.

Her eyes scanned the windows and saw there was some sort of Spanish boy...no a Mexican peeking from the corner of one them on the second floor. She breathed in, catching the scent of three other Mexicans in the house.

"Bean eatin mother fuckers," she whispered savagely. Her anger over her brother was momentarily forgotten as she took in the smell of their guns. They thought they were so tough sporting their little pistols...

A jeep's horn rang out for the space of three seconds. The sound focused her in a hurry and she cocked an ear. The jeep's door shut loudly and the scent of her brother grew. He was heading for the house. He was walking into a trap! The idea brought a smile to her full lips and she chuckled, but then she wondered what in the hell she was doing outside his home, hiding in the trees. Was he expecting the other Talitha to come rescue him? Or perhaps to attack from the rear?

"But..." But what happened to the other Talitha? This was very vague in her mind. There had been a confrontation with Ba'al Zubel, this she recalled and she had been named. That was very clear to her. She had named herself Ba'al Fie-ere, Denier of Ba'al, but now she was standing out in a forest. What the hell had happened? Everything was such a hodgepodge of images and memories.

Around the front of the house, heavy footsteps sounded on the porch. They went up the stairs and then paused. Will must have used that damned second sight of his and saw the attack coming, she thought.

"What a cheater," she murmured to herself.

"Amy! I have your spells," Will's voice was clear and strong. "I'll shred them up if Lisa isn't out here in ten seconds."

Spells? Amy? Talitha sniffed at the cool air once more. The scent of Lisa was obvious and strong, but she ignored those markers and concentrated on the fainter ones. There had been another woman at the house and three other Mexicans, but they were long gone, hours gone judging by the faintness of their odor. The scent of the woman was unfamiliar, but the only Amy that she knew of was Amy Harris. Interesting.

"Amy!" Will called angrily. There was a few seconds of silence and then he hammered, or maybe kicked at the door. Again, interesting. He must know that he was about to be attacked, was he really expecting them to answer the door?

"Amy, stop your hiding," came the cry from the front of the house.

Talitha's mind suddenly pounced on an unsettling idea. If Will knew he was about to be attacked that meant that he was probably carrying a gun as well. And if that was true, those Mexicans wouldn't stand a chance, ergo, Will would remain in possession of whatever spells that he had been mentioning. Probably the ones that Luke had in his possession beneath the church. It would also mean that since he had a gun and spells, she would be in a weak position relative to him, something she hated more than anything.

On the ground, a foot from her was a smooth rock the size of an egg, she hefted. It would do nicely. Her brother was going to be in hell of a rude surprise.

"I'll tear the spells." This was the last thing she heard from him before she took off at a dead sprint for the back door. The man in the upper floor window had disappeared at some point in the last thirty seconds and she crossed the lawn in moments, unseen.

Just then, gunfire erupted from in the house, but that had been expected and she didn't slow a whit. When she was twelve feet from the door she leapt, sailing through the air with her left foot back and chambered. She struck the door with that left foot and sent it blasting inwards, not knowing or caring whether it had been locked or not. Her momentum carried her into the kitchen where the man that she had seen in the window of the second floor was just rushing in from a separate hallway to her left.

Before he could even think to bring his gun up, Talitha hurled the egg-sized rock across the room directly into the man's forehead. In between the sound of gunshots that came loud to her ears from the living room, she was able to hear a wonderful *thock* sound. The rock shattered the man's skull and like a tennis ball off a wall, it bounced right back to her. She was out of the room before he hit the floor.

Down the hall, she flew towards the sound of guns. There were two guns firing in sporadic manner as if the men who wielded them were unsure exactly what they were shooting at. They were clearly amateurs.

In the living room, she discovered two men both with their backs to her. The one closest stood in a half crouch. A roundhouse to his throat not only crushed his larynx but also drove it into his cervical vertebrae. In a second, he was dead twice over. With her momentum carrying her, she spun, deftly catching up the dead man's pistol with her left hand. At the culmination of the spin she torqued her body much like a pitcher in baseball and hurled the stone faster than the eye could follow at the second man.

Talitha could have fired the gun with her left hand without losing any of her inhuman aim, but the rock was just so much more fun.

"Oh poo!" she pouted with a small stamp of her muddy foot. Her rock had imbedded itself in the back of the man's head. She'd been hoping for another lucky bounce. After all, there was another man coming down the stairs. He thought he was being sneaky.

Talitha took two silent loping steps and then slid across the smooth hardwood floors on her knees. It was something a child might do, but no child had ever worn such an evil gleeful smile. She zipped toward the stairs with only a whisper from her dress, and as she passed them, her angle was perfect and her aim exceptional, she fired twice, shattering both of the man's kneecaps. With a girlish scream, he crumpled, losing his gun, but managing to cling to the railing. She ignored him and his pathetic whimpering. He would keep for now.

"Oh Willy J!" she called out with a happy sing-song. It turned out that he hadn't been armed after all. Otherwise, she was sure he would've killed the two idiots that had been firing at him. Their aim had been atrocious, she counted five bullet holes scattered about the doorframe and the wall to its right.

Feeling a pleasant contented warmth, she went onto the porch, expecting him to be cowering there, but he wasn't in sight. "Olly-olly in-come free!" She tilted her head, listening, cancelling out the sobbing of the Mexican crawling away up the stairs, cancelling the wind and the flicking leaves. Will's heartbeat was a drum to the girl. He was to the right of the porch around the corner, breathing loudly as if he had just run a sprint.

"Is this going to be hide and seek, Will?"

"No. Where's Amy? Is she dead?" he stepped from around the corner of the wraparound porch gripping a sheaf of old yellowed looking paper in his left hand. He had a nervous look in his eyes—she liked that.

"She's long gone; she hasn't been here for hours. But it was sure nice of her to leave these toys for me to play with." She sniffed at the gun—the man who had owned it was a chronic masturbator. Quickly, she pulled it from her face and looked at it in disgust.

Will blinked, clearly bewildered. "She's gone? What about Lisa? Is she here?" He didn't wait for an answer but started to walk around his sister giving her a very wide birth.

Talitha forgot about the gun in her hand and stepped to her left a few feet, coming to stand in the doorway, essentially blocking his path. "Hold on now, we were talking. Are those the incantations that Luke used?" Will nodded and held them out to her.

"Take them please, I need to see Lisa," he said with a good amount of pleading in his voice. She didn't take the papers, but only smiled at him.

"Sometimes you're just perfect. You use just the right amount of begging to make a girl feel good about herself. I'm sure Lisa's fine...wait." Talitha paused sniffing again, "She hasn't had the baby yet? When...when was it that we took on Luke? How long has it been?"

Will face contorted into puzzlement. "That was last night."

"Last night?" It felt as if it had been months ago. She remembered so many things happening since the fight with Luke. They had met with Lisa at church only a few weeks ago and had gone out to lunch with her. And she had worked on an algorithm for the software she was developing and she was certain that she had shown it to Will...

"That wasn't me," she said aloud. "That was the other me. Will! You did something to me. Or did Amy? Did that witch put a spell on me?" She was suddenly wonderfully furious. She hated the feeling and loved it at the same time. It gave her freedom and strength. "Tell me or I blow your fuckin brains out right here!" She advanced on Will, who backed to the side of the house.

"She didn't do anything to you, but I don't think you want to know what's happening..."

"Hey!" the Mexican that she had shot yelled out with a quaver of pain in his voice. "Get me a phone. Get me a phone or this bitch dies."

Will, to her amazement, tried to rush past her. With a casual strike, she sent him to his knees gasping for breath. Beneath his bruised face, he turned a very red-burgundy. The colors were fascinating.

"Hey! I said get..."

"We heard you, asshole," Talitha called out, angry that the man's whiny voice was disturbing her appreciation for...art. Was what she could do considered art? If not, it should be.

"I'll kill her," he tried.

"One more word and I'll put out your eyes." Her rage was fast becoming insurmountable.

"Stupid bitch." The man muttered this to himself, but he might as well have whispered it directly into Talitha's ear.

"That does it."

She pulled her wheezing brother to his feet and dragged him inside the house. The Mexican was upstairs, moaning. The sound irritated her to no ends and she decided to put a stop to it. Her mood was black and she was simply beyond thinking.

"Lisa?" Will called out in a raggedy voice, as Talitha drove him on toward the stairs. "Hey you, mister, is she ok?"

"Get me a phone or I kill her."

Will tried again between gasps, "Is she ok?" When

silence greeted this, he turned to his sister. "Don't kill him, please. I need him alive. We have to find out where Amy..."

His words didn't register in her mind. She was caught up in a rage that she hadn't felt in years, not since those early days in the asylum. All she wanted was to kill. The Mexican was in a room at the end of the hall, she could hear his heavy breathing as easily as if he were blowing his nasty bean eating breath in her face.

She could smell that he had another gun, but she didn't care. Her brother would act as a shield, and as a battering ram. She threw him bodily against the partially open door and he fell through it stumbling to the floor. The Mexican stupidly shot at Will, but his aim, at chest height, was too high to hit the falling man and a small neat hole formed in the wall inches above Will's back.

Talitha's aim was spot on. Though she wanted to kill him, it didn't mean she wanted it to go fast and her shot struck him in the right wrist. He screamed, but it was drowned out by a roar that ripped from her throat. Like a ferocious dog that had just slipped its collar, she was on him in a flash and over the next minute, she bludgeoned him to death with her bare hands, crushing bones and rupturing organs with every strike of her hammer like fists.

Only when the body ceased even its involuntary twitching, did she stop punching. It had all been very satisfying, deeply so and as she straddled him, she couldn't help gyrating her pelvis a few times on the warm corpse. Feeling a wonderful contentment, she sighed largely and climbed up on the bed next to Lisa. The girl seemed very much asleep, yet Talitha knew better.

Her brother, who had just sat up, blinked away fresh blood that dripped into his eyes; one of his stitches had loosened and sprung a leak. He seemed dazed by his impact with the door and stared at her with red-rimmed eyes. He stared and stared, and it began to affect her newly found good mood.

"What?" she asked, it was more of a challenge than a question. His mouth came open and his head gave a little shake, but that was all.

Just then, a very timid voice called from the doorway to the house, "Hello?" She recognized the voice as familiar, but she couldn't place it. "Hello? Will?"

"We're upstairs," Talitha brought the gun up, sighted it on the door and waited. Her mouth hung open and she breathed light but excited.

"Don't come in here, it's not safe," Will said in a shaking voice, looking back and forth rapidly between the gun barrel and the door.

Now she blew out her breath, exasperated and the gun dropped back on her lap. She looked at him as if he had just spoiled a good joke. "Dang it, Will. Stop being a pain. Who is that, anyways?"

"What are you talking about? That's Father Vogel."

"Vogel?" The named seemed familiar, her brow came down in concentration. "The priest who was at the factory?"

Will nodded, "Yes. Please, put the gun down. You're not right...you're thinking it's all..." He left off uncertain what to say.

"My thinking is fine," she replied, but it wasn't, even for her it wasn't. She felt that her mind could best be described as a little warped. The killing had been fun, but now her mouth tasted like metal, and the odd memories filtering into her subconscious were distracting and aggravating. They were of things she had never done, or never would do: going to church, writing out algorithms, working on puzzles. Puzzles for God's sakes!

"Will?" The priest was at the top of the stairs. "Is Talitha with you? Is she... ok?"

The brother and sister locked eyes. "She's... she's, uh..." His mental state looked to be cracking like an eggshell and he stammered, "She's... she's... not injured."

"You sound disappointed. Are you? Do you wish that

Jose, over there had been a better shot?" She pointed with a tacky red index finger, to the mush that had once been a human.

He seemed to see the man for the first time and paled, his eyes going very big. "No. No I don't wish that, but..." He stopped talking. It seemed that he needed to concentrate in order to pull his stare from the grisly thing lying in a pool of blood. "I...I...I just..."

Father Vogel spoke up again, closer this time but still nearer to the stairs than the door, "Will, shouldn't you be doing something?"

"What are you supposed to be doing? Saving your poor little wife?" Talitha yanked Lisa by the shoulder and she lolled like a corpse in the sea. Her head rolling on her shoulders coming to face Will. From a certain point of view, it was probably disgusting or upsetting at least, and tears began to escape from his eyes, they were pink with diluted blood.

"I can't. I can't do it," he moaned.

His misery had a calming effect on Talitha. The memories ceased to come to her as rapidly as they had and this put her in a benevolent mood.

"What can't you do, Will?"

"I was supposed to tell you...something, but I can't. We have to help Lisa first. She's alive, right?"

Talitha looked at the girl and shrugged. "No less than usual. She was always such a stick in the mud that does it really matter. So what were you supposed to tell me?"

"Nothing," Will cast his eyes down, staring at the carpet.

"Will, you have to," Father Vogel called from down the hall. Closer.

"Yeah Will, ya gotta," Talitha agreed for fun. The more miserable he looked the less strange her brain felt. "What is it ya gotta do?"

"He has to..."

"I was talking to my brother, Vogel. What kind of name is Vogel anyways?" She was only mildly curious. In truth she was waiting for the priest to take two more steps further down the hall, at that point he would be just outside the door. She lifted her arm, holding the gun out, sighting it at the crack of the door. The urge to peek into the room would be impossible for the man to resist.

The floor creaked in the hall once.

"Father, don't come any closer she has a gun..."

Thunder erupted in the room as the gun spat out a spinning hunk of lead. It buried itself in the wall an inch from Will's right ear.

"Will, you're such a pain in the ass, you know that?" she asked amiably; for the moment, her blood lust satiated. Will looked too stunned for words and only sat leaning against the wall while his mouth opened and closed like a fish at the bottom of a boat. Talitha smiled at him. "So what was it you were supposed to do?"

"I...I was supposed to tell you this story, but...I don't think I can."

"What's with you and your stories? Didn't you start one earlier that you never finished?" Her brother gave her a flaccid little shrug. "Hey, I got an idea, Big Bro. You tell me a story and if I don't like it I kill Lisa." Talitha suddenly got excited at the thought. "This will be just like *One-thousand and One Nights*. Remember that? If the girl couldn't come up with a beguiling enough story every night, she'd die. This story thing is a great idea, Will."

Will's pale skin went pasty white now and his eyes darted about. Clearly, he couldn't think of a thing, which only added to Talitha's excitement. Seconds ticked by and his fear was delicious.

She thumbed the hammer back on the pistol, which got him started, but poorly so, "Remember dad, how..."

"Of course I remember my father. It's you who obviously doesn't. If this was mom lying here all dead looking, we both know dad would come over here and take this gun, just like that," she snapped blood stained fingers, flecks of red leaping into the air as she did. "He would put an end to this nonsense right quick. I would get the paddling of a lifetime and a long-ass lecture to boot."

"Maybe not," Will said, taking a long time to reply. "Maybe not, he wasn't always the best disciplinarian. Remember how he used to count to three when we wouldn't listen to him right away."

"I think so," Talitha couldn't quite recall what Will was talking about and suddenly she had a moment of unease. Perhaps this story idea wasn't such a good one after all. There had been something odd about the ending of the last one, but before she put her mind to figuring it out, Will began speaking again.

"Well, you were the reason he stopped doing that. We were at this hardware store shopping for...I don't know what. Remember that Ace by our house? The one that sold brauts and hotdogs out front? You always begged for one, when we left."

"I remember the hotdogs." The smell of those long ago hotdogs came to her and it suddenly made her hungry. Will seemed to read her mind.

"Just thinking about them is making my stomach growl. But they really weren't all that good. It was the smell that drove us nuts, not the taste. They were usually overcooked and the buns were dry as sawdust." Will paused and Talitha nodded; the picture he was describing was very familiar. Now that he had begun his story, it seemed easier for him to go on, "This one time you were playing on a display of plastic door mats inside the store. You know the ones with the fake stubby grass and the white and yellow daisy in the corner?"

It was a rhetorical question, but she nodded all the same. Their family had at least one of those mats outside their house for years.

Will waited for the small nod from her before he wiped his wet nose with his sleeve and picked up where he left off, "Well, they had this big stack of them, three stacks actually. They looked like stairs to us and you were playing on them, even though they slipped and shifted around beneath you. You know how mom was back then, everything was dangerous to her. She said 'Get off there or you'll break your neck.' But you didn't listen and then dad steps in, 'Tal! I'm going to count to three!' Well, all you did was smile huge as if daring him to start counting."

"That was me? That doesn't sound like how I used to be." She couldn't quite remember, but she had always thought of herself as too straight laced to do anything like what Will was saying.

"I'm pretty sure that was you," Will replied and now his voice was more hopeful. "Anyways, dad puts on his mean face and says, all important sounding, 'one'. You only grinned bigger, because you had a plan brewing to outsmart him, which is funny because you were like three years old at the time. So dad scowls even fiercer and says even louder, 'TWO'. At this, your eyes are huge and mischievous and you get into a squatting position. Your plan is to leap up the second dad begins to say three. And he knows this and doesn't know what to do, because he will end up looking kinda stupid being outsmarted by a three year old. Mom starts to die laughing and a second later dad looks like a balloon that just lost its air."

Suddenly Talitha did recall this in full detail. It just mushroomed whole into her mind. "That wasn't me that was Katie."

"Oh, you're probably right," Will replied quickly as if this was a minor point. "Katie did always have a special something about her that kept her out of trouble. Remember the time she tried to make jello in the toilet?"

Talitha smiled at that crazy memory. The little blonde girl had boiled five gallons of water and had slowly poured it into the toilet all the while stirring in six or seven packets of Jello. She had let it set overnight and then purposely kept the second floor bathroom occupied so that her father would get a weird surprise in the morning. Coming out of the bathroom, his face was priceless.

"For a little girl, she was brilliant at getting into trouble and genius at getting out of it again," Talitha said shaking her head. She then looked at the gun in her hand and then around at the room, confused and with growing fright. "Will, I think I'm back."

Chapter 14

Will

"Will, I think I'm back," Talitha announced in a shaky voice; her words were quiet and full of shame and thumped into his pounding head as if they were rocks coming from her mouth. Her first act was to put the gun down gingerly on the stand next to the bed, she then reached over and touched her sister-in-law, "She's alive, and so is the baby."

"Oh God," Will was up in a flash, but his head was none too stable and he tottered for a moment as the room swayed. He stumbled and lurched around the bed to his wife who, despite what Talitha had said, lay apparently dead to the world. Gently he shook her. "Lisa! Lisa!" he called, soft yet urgently. His eyes brimmed with sudden tears. "Vogel, get in here!" Fear caused his words to come out as a harsh order.

The priest rushed in, white faced, but otherwise cool and collected; he too went to the blonde and began a brief examination. He lifted her eyelids, opened her mouth, took her pulse, ran his hands over her head and neck, and then down her spine. Next, he checked her abdomen and chest, after that he just shrugged.

"I don't know what's wrong with her," he said lamely. "We need to get her to a hospital."

"Call nine-one-one, there's a phone in the master bedroom, the first door just to your left in the hall," Will commanded, roughly giving the priest a shove toward the door.

"Father Vogel, wait," Talitha hopped up to intercept the priest grabbing him by the arm. "Can't you smell that? Amy wasn't lying, there's been witchcraft performed in here. It's very strong on Lisa."

The last twenty-four hours for Will had been long and full of pain, his mind felt drained and stuporous. "Right, what was I thinking? Can you look at her?" he asked his sister.

"Me? I'm not a witch," she replied, backing toward the wall.

"Please?" Will begged.

"I guess...I guess I can try." Talitha went to the girl and bent so low over her face that for a moment Will thought she was going to kiss Lisa. Instead, Talitha closed her eyes and breathed in deeply through her nostrils. They wrinkled in disgust. "There's something here." Lisa wore a purple sweater that rode high up on her neck due to the way she was laying. Talitha pulled down the warm material and stepped back. "You didn't give her that did you?"

Around her neck, Lisa wore a strange necklace. It was of laced twine and odd fragrant flowers, small discs of what looked like hammered dimes hung from it.

"No. Do you think I should take it off of her?" Will knew next to nothing about witchcraft. Talitha shrugged, and when he looked at the priest, Father Vogel appeared even more lost. Will doubted it would do any more damage if he did and so with a quick motion, he yanked the necklace off his wife.

Quite literally, thousands of images flashed through his mind in the space of the next few seconds. They came so fast that none was able to actually register on his consciousness. Along with the images there was stinging burning pain in his eyes as if he had looked into a laser and he forced them closed, yet still the pictures came.

"UHHGG!" Will cried out. They were a blur, a machine gun of lights, faster than any strobe. In seconds, his balance went and he swayed a moment before falling over, but strong hands gripped him and gently lowered him to the floor.

"Will, are you ok?" He knew his sister would ask this.

"Will, are you ok?" she asked.

At first he could do little, save moan and roll back and forth on the floor, but then the visions began to slow in pace and when his sister repeated her question, something he knew that she'd do, he was able to nod. Finally, a last image of a man stayed in his mind. It was of a very big Mexican with tattoos running up his neck, he had the eyes of a puff adder, hooded and poisonous, they stared at him.

"What happened?" He knew Father Vogel would say.

"What happened?" the priest asked like an echo.

"Please be quiet for a moment," Will begged, holding out his hand to them. He attempted to open his eyes, however double images surrounded him, he was seeing the room a second into the future. This was layered over the image of the room in the present and it was disorienting as well as nauseating. A few moments later, he tried again and the double images wavered, blurred, and then fused into one.

"I...I think I just got my vision back, you know my second sight. I think that thing around her neck was like a charm keeping me from seeing what was happening here. How's Lisa? Did breaking that necklace do anything for her?" he asked, trying to get up.

"I'm sorry, but there's no change," Vogel replied. "Do you think it's possible Amy Harris has used your wife to open a gate into the Void with a spell? Weren't you in a similar state, Talitha?"

"No, it's not the same spell. Feel her skin; she's not at all cold. And look around us, there's no demon about. This is something different...move over." Talitha again sniffed Lisa thoroughly. She shocked Will by next running her finger along Lisa's gums and then she stuck her own finger in her mouth. "She hasn't been poisoned or drugged."

"What about the other Talitha?" Will asked. "Would she know what this is? I think we should ask her."

Talitha leaned back shocked. "You want me to bring her back? So soon? Will, please no. Look what I did." She pointed at the grotesquely beaten body of the Mexican.

"He deserved everything he got," Will growled as anger flared in him at his sister's refusal. "You won't do this for me? For Lisa? How many times have I risked myself for you? How many of those damn dreams did I put up with for you? Huh?" Compared to his weeping and frustration, the guilt trip and the anger were oddly satisfying to him and they went well with his headache.

"Will, I can't. It would be a waste, even if she knew, there's no way she'd help you. She hates you and Lisa both; I think she would just try to make it worse somehow."

She was right, but perhaps there was another way. "Father Vogel, could you hypnotize the information out of her?"

The priest shook his head. "No, for a number of reasons. Her subconscious is not..."

"A simple 'no' is fine," Will interrupted. He got up and paced the room feeling his emotions spin away from him. All day he'd been holding back a nagging fear of what was happening to Lisa and now here he was and still just as much in the dark.

Talitha tugged his leg as he passed and said, "There's another way perhaps. Since your ability seems to be back, you could look into the past to see what happened here. There is precedence for this; you were able to see the past as it concerned Fredrick Brabec."

Will hesitated, afraid of what he would see, afraid to know what they had done to her. "Tal...was Lisa violated?" He shifted his eyes from his sister as he asked.

Talitha was quick to answer, "No. She hasn't been, not like that. What do you think, will you look?"

"Yes."

Without preamble he sat and took Lisa's hand. Closing his eyes, he sent his mind back, searching.

It was like running into a very dark night. Heavy black shadows were laced by slighter ones and nothing seemed to have form. Further out, just at the edge of his vision, things seemed lighter and he ran forward, hoping. It felt as though hours passed and still the light was only at a distant horizon. He became frustrated and swung his fist through the shadows close to him, but couldn't touch them. They shifted constantly and were unreadable. They were useless, as was his vision. After a time he grew discouraged and bored; not knowing what else to do he wandered uselessly—his steps numbering in the tens of thousands. Time stretched out as he walked, but then suddenly snapped back when he heard his name called. Will opened his eyes and had to blink from the bright light.

"Did you see anything?" his sister inquired in a rush. She looked worried.

"No, it was as if there's nothing to see. It was like that spell not only blocked my vision, but erased the past as if it never happened. How long did you let me stay under?"

"Eight minutes," Talitha replied, anxious that she had made a mistake. "I know that seems like a long time but your heart rate and breathing remained unchanged during the duration. Was that ok?"

"Yeah," he answered somewhat distantly—the eight minutes could have been eight months.

Father Vogel took Will's pulse and gave him a quick once over. The priest then asked, "Talitha, can you track Amy by sense of smell?"

"I could, but not if she drove, which I think she did. Do you have any idea where Lisa hid the sword?" she asked Will.

"No." Surprisingly, Will had plum forgotten about the sword. His concern had been focused squarely on the safety of his wife and child. "Still, I don't think it matters. Amy has to have it by now."

"Does she?" Vogel murmured. "Maybe Lisa hid it deep in the woods. We might still be able to catch up with her."

"Perhaps," Talitha eyes went slightly out of focus and she breathed in deep. Suddenly, she bent over Lisa again and began inspecting even closer than she had before. She paid close attention to her shoes, a pair of very white Nikes. "She didn't go out in the forest in these sneakers."

Talitha hopped up quick and ran from the room. Will guessed she was heading to the master bedroom and he found her with her head in Lisa's closet. "I don't think she's been in the forest in the last week at least, judging by her shoes."

"So where does that leave us?" Vogel asked dispiritedly from the doorway. He was looking down at the hardwood floor eyeing the blood that trailed along from the stairs.

"The bishop hinted that the Church could help out," Talitha mentioned, getting up from the closet. "Could they use some influence and maybe find out where Amy lives, or who these four men were?"

Vogel nodded. "It would take time. Probably a couple of days..."

This shocked Will. "A couple of days? No, we need to find her now. I want you to call the bishop right away, right this second."

"I can't." Father Vogel had an odd embarrassed look to him. "He's still in the air. His plane isn't scheduled to arrive in Bangor until five." Will's mouth dropped open and the priest went on to explain, "Bishop Keenan wanted to have a backup plan available just in case you and your sister weren't successful here."

"And what did the bishop think he could possibly do?"

"He didn't come alone, Will. He brought with him a special paramilitary unit. You see there are certain people, men and women of great faith who volunteer their services in time of need. Thankfully, that need is extremely rare, in fact I've never seen one of these groups in action, but the bishop deemed the incantations important enough to call upon them."

"Do they have any special abilities? Do you think they'll be able to help Lisa?" Will asked in a rush. Hope and relief made him feel a slight bit giddy.

The priest killed the feeling quick. "I'm sorry, but I don't think so. They're just normal people. Most of them have military training, some have medical training and a few like Eric Milner are with the police or the FBI."

"Milner is one of them!" Will no longer felt hopeful at all.

"Technically yes, like I said, they're just normal people. Officer Milner has been very helpful to us in the past and I hope that despite what he has gone through, we'll be able to count on him again in the future."

"Would it help if I apologized?" Talitha asked. She stood meekly half in and half out of the closet, biting her lip.

Will answered before the priest, "No, it'd probably make it worse. But I don't think you have much to worry about, I'd bet that Milner isn't with them, just when he could be of some help." He walked out of the room, feeling the strain of the last few days on him like a weight. The bishop and a few boys with guns weren't going to able to help them out. At the door to the nursery room, Talitha caught up with him and tugged at his shirt.

At first, she seemed nervous to the point of tears. "May I hide the bodies, please? I can maybe put them in the basement or in the trunk of their car. We have twenty minutes before they land and another twenty before they get here..."

"Tal, hold on. Just leave them for now, they can wait. I need your help figuring out where Amy went."

"They can't wait! The bishop will be here soon, and he can't see what I've done." Her eyes were wild in her head and the tears were only seconds from coming. "He'll blame me. He'll think I did all this on purpose or for fun. Please, please, let me move them. Is there a deep lake anywhere near here? I can weigh them down really well. They'll never come back up."

This last she said with such honest conviction that

Will's insides seemed to loosen and turn watery. She had sunk bodies before, he was quite sure of it. The other Talitha had left her many presents, the dead and the dying, for her to clean up.

From behind his sister, Father Vogel asked, "How many bodies are there in the house, *Talitha.*" He said her name deliberately to keep Will from answering. It was a moot point, he didn't know.

"Four," Talitha replied in a whisper.

"Can you recall how each died?" The question from the priest was strange and off-putting. Will looked past his sister; Vogel gave him a little headshake, telling him to keep quiet.

"Yes. I shot the man in the nursery three times and then finished him off by bludgeoning him with my fists." Talitha's voice was low and unemotional, as if she were reading off a laundry list. "There were two in the living room; I killed the first with a kick to the throat, the second I killed with a stone." Her face clouded slightly at this, "I was angry about this for some reason. Oh yeah, right. It was because the stone didn't bounce back like I wanted it too."

"Ok Talitha, you don't have to go on. I just..." Vogel started.

She gave a little laugh, like a short bark. "You should've seen the first one I killed. I chucked this stone, Bam! Right in the forehead and you wouldn't believe, it just bounced right back to me, like it was a tennis ball I had thrown against a brick wall. It was so funny." She smiled at her brother as if she honestly thought he would appreciate what she had said.

His mouth came open and he could only shake his head, confused. First, that he could, in any way, think her story was funny and second, that there were only four men in the home. By the sound of the gunfire, he would've thought it closer to six or seven. He remembered the two in the living room, but he had only stood there for maybe all of a second, before he had dived away. The gunshots had been strange. The first few had sounded like thunder in his ears, but then the noise had flip-flopped. The guns went suddenly muffled, while the bullets that tore through the air all around him had become loud. They zipped past with the shriek of shredding canvas.

The priest spoke up in that very calm manner of his, "Talitha? Listen to me. You weren't here when these men died. Where were you?"

Her smile had faded away. "I don't know. One moment I was outside in the backyard and the next, I was in the nursery. But now, I'm starting to remember what happened."

"She shouldn't go near the bodies, Will," Father Vogel advised. "I'm worried the sight of them may spark a snap changeover. Talitha, the gap between your personalities is closing quicker than I thought it would. I don't have an explanation for it either."

A pounding in his head reminded Will that it still ached and he rubbed at his temples, "If that's the case Father, then I have to ask you a favor. Will you please move the bodies and all of the guns out to where that black car is parked? I would, but I have to keep an eye on Talitha."

The priest nodded easily. "That's not a problem."

Brother and sister waited in the master bedroom until the priest moved the corpse out of the nursery, and then they went to the spare bed there. Talitha seemed drawn to Lisa, she gently massaged the little bulge where the baby lay nestled, warm, and hopefully safe. Her eyes were deeply sad as if this was as close as she would ever get to a baby. He felt compelled to try to cheer her up.

"Just getting broodie?" Will asked.

A puzzled expression cleared her face of most of its worry. "Broodie? What's that?"

"Stop the presses. Talitha Jern doesn't know a word? Oh, you have no idea how badly I want to tell you to go look it up!" Will exclaimed. "But since from personal experience

I know that can be terribly annoying, I'll answer your question instead. It's Australian slang. When a woman sees a baby, or another pregnant woman she sometimes gets that hankering for a baby of her own. That's being broodie."

Talitha snorted, a noise somewhere between contempt and amusement. "First, there's no such thing as a dictionary of Australian slang, so it would be impossible for me to look it up. And second... I'm not broodie, I'm jealous. It feels like I've been cursed. Like my entire life has been one long demented joke, and I'm jealous of this baby. She has a future."

"We hope."

Talitha put her ear to the bulge, but spoke to Will, "You could find out. Without the little charm, you could look into her future; maybe you'll see something hopeful."

"Or maybe I'll see something horrible," his voice cracked as terrifying images of his own making flashed into his mind. His imagination was too good sometimes. "That's why I'm not jumping at the chance. I'm afraid Lisa's future will be as empty as her past day has been."

"That's no excuse," Talitha admonished. "If you rely on me or what little the bishop can do, your wife and child may pay the price for your cowardliness. There could be something that will point us in the right direction."

Will cast his eyes to the floor and studied it for a long time. "I know." He sighed huge and then looked up at his sister. "Five minutes, no more, if her future is horrible I don't want to be there any longer than I have to." She nodded and he cracked a crooked, nervous smile. "Ok, here we go..."

Will heard a voice that sounded like his own say, "You're having a contraction."

"Oh really? I didn't know." Lisa's face was very white and was lined with a grimace of pain. Her mass of blonde curls was tied up in a great blob sitting on top of her head and she wore such a garishly flowered gown that he wondered briefly if they were in Hawaii. They were in a

single occupancy hospital room; its walls were two-tone, pink on top, blue on the bottom. They were alone.

It was an odd feeling being alone. Where was everyone? Shouldn't his parents be here? And what about Talitha? There wasn't even a doctor present. At the very least he had expected a smattering of nurses buzzing around like worker bees. But they were very much alone. Except that is for the technical looking machinery hemming-in the bed and a vase full of newly bought flowers from which pink balloons struggled to get away.

There should have been more flowers.

The contraction had been brief and when it was over, Lisa picked up the magazine that sat in her lap. The cove: a glossy picture of some young starlet shown out at him. He felt his eyes roll.

Will's lips moved, "Would you like some ice?" He hadn't meant to say it, nor had even thought it, but out came the words nonetheless. Will was along for the ride in his own body and had no control of what it did.

"No thank you," she sounded bored and Will didn't blame her. Even riding shotgun in his own body, Will was bored. He supposed that to be good thing. People in fear or danger were rarely this bored. How long had they been there? It felt like hours.

Now Will looked down at a line of paper spilling from one of the machines. He didn't want to do this, but had no choice. What he really wanted to do was get a better look at his wife, to see if she had any scars or bruising, yet his stupid self of the future only stood staring at the procession of paper. After thirty seconds or so, a running blue line on the paper edged upwards. Next to him, Lisa gasped.

"You're having another contraction," he said in a pleasant conversational tone. Will wanted to smack his future self.

"Thank God you're here to tell me these things," Lisa said in between her panting.

Will felt a sudden spin and the scene changed, but not terribly so. The walls of the hospital room faded to white and now Lisa was asleep. The machinery all looked the same, they beeped and hummed as they had before. There were other smaller changes, the flowers for instance had been moved and were no longer in his vision.

In fact, his future self wasn't in the room. The room was empty save for the girl sleeping in the bed. For a long time he watched her, having no capacity to do aught else and in all that time she didn't budge, but slept as the dead. The sun went down and the room grew dark, but that was for seconds only and then the sun was up again.

The blurred ghost like shape of people sped in and out and then it was dark again and still Lisa slept. The light came once more and then disappeared. This repeated itself, faster and faster so that it appeared as if a naughty boy was playing with a light switch. But then it went too fast even for that and soon the light stayed a steady grey. And still Lisa slept.

Her hair grew and a second later, it was shorn practically all away. In seconds it grew again and eventually, like the light, her hair seemed to stay in a halfway stage. However, he knew that it wasn't, he was seeing a year fly by in seconds.

It took a while, but eventually Lisa aged. Her beautiful golden hair turned grey and then white, while her face sank in so that her teeth grew more pronounced.

And then she was dead.

Light flashed brilliant and it stung to see, but Will couldn't blink away and was forced to watch in pain as Lisa's coffin was lowered into the ground. No one stood nearby and no flowers were anywhere in evidence. The view became only an intense black and the only sense that accompanied this was a rushing crackling sound. Then he was alone in the darkness. Lisa had decomposed and was gone.

The utter darkness now became familiar. It was a cold, cold darkness. He was in the Void and he was all alone.

"No!" The word tore from his throat as soon as Talitha shook him out of his trance.

"Are you ok?" she asked, her brown eyes were very large in her face.

Will hopped up without answering, and at first paced the small room, but in seconds, it didn't feel big enough. He hurried downstairs and surprised Father Vogel who was carrying a roll of paper-towels. Will didn't say a word to the priest, but left the living room in a rush, heading for the kitchen.

"Will? What's going to happen?" Talitha called out from somewhere behind.

"I don't know. All I saw were the outcomes for Lisa." The second outcome, where she stayed forever in that unnatural coma hurt his mind to dwell upon.

"There was more than one? Will, come on you have to tell us. We're a part of this too," Talitha swept into the kitchen and then stopped dead, her eyes darting around. She was seeing her past, the memory of how she had killed the Mexican, it gave her a shudder. She came to the table and picked up a pair of scissors that were lying there. Will snatched them from her.

"Sorry," she said with a little embarrassed shrug.

Father Vogel hurried. "You looked into the future?" There was a long unstated, *aaannd?*

Will told them. Viewing the first part of the vision had been only odd, but re-telling it was uncomfortable in the extreme. Talitha had been painfully absent and he didn't leave that part out. She sat spinning a roll of masking tape appearing nervous and sad at once. The second part of the vision was even worse, since it was very likely in that future, none of the three would live.

"I'm sorry," Will said as a way of finishing.

"You're sorry!" Talitha suddenly seethed with volcanic

anger. She threw the roll of tape at his face as hard as she could and though Will managed to block it, his left forearm went numb from the elbow down. "Is that all you have to say? You're sorry? Well sorry doesn't count for shit. What's going to happen to me? Huh? Look into the future and see. Right now."

"That would do you no good, Talitha," Vogel reasoned. "Clearly the future isn't set and by looking into it and seeing your death, you automatically invalidate the vision."

"That's the fucking point!"

The priest remained amazingly calm. "Your death is going to be a surprise no matter what you do. If you invalidate this vision, you're still going to die eventually and who knows, it could be in a much more painful manner. And for certain it will be for a far less noble cause."

"Who gives a rat's ass about noble?" Talitha replied.

"Talitha I want you to know that..." Will started to speak, but had to stop in midsentence. "I was going to say that if I could, I'd die in your place, however I can't say that with any honesty right now." Her brown eyes flashed dangerously, yet he continued, "Why should I? You keep telling me you're doomed to go to hell, why should I risk everything to keep you from hell for a few more years?"

"I told you that you wouldn't understand."

"Oh, I understand. It's because you're afraid," Will answered back in a loud voice. "Everyone else is afraid of the Void, but you're afraid of heaven. It doesn't make sense."

"It's your fault that I'm not going!" At first she seemed all in a rage, but suddenly she looked desperate. "I can't talk about this right now, the stranger is right here with me. I can feel her, it's like she's looking over my shoulder."

Vogel looked sidelong at Will, "Do something, tell her a story."

"You tell her a story, I can't think of any." Will's mind had gone suddenly blank. All that occupied him was the fact that he had left a gun sitting by the bed where Lisa lay asleep and Talitha had an eight foot head start in that direction.

Vogel nudged him and Will shrugged. The priest put on a fake smile. "Will, you should tell her why you've been lying to her all these years. You told her the story of that big dog, but you told a rather large lie in it."

"What?" Unbeknownst to him, Will wore an embarrassed smile.

"You're a terrible liar, Will. But please don't be offended, that's a good thing. People who are accustomed to lying, or who are morally ok with it, are the best liars. The way you lied, it seemed like a very rare thing."

Talitha eyed the men in a strange manner and Will saw the back in forth in her eyes as the two personalities balanced each other out. He had lied, but since Talitha had never known, he didn't know if this was in fact the best way to get her on the right track.

"What did you lie about?" Talitha asked with narrowed eyes.

"It was nothing, really. I didn't cut my foot on glass like I said. That was it, that's all," Will answered.

"Talitha, how did he cut his foot?" Vogel inquired.

"Duh, he just told us this story," Talitha replied rudely. "He cut it on some glass."

"But he also just admitted to lying," Father Vogel answered. "Think back. Do you remember the glass?" Talitha furrowed her brows trying to remember and Vogel continued, "Was it green glass, like so many bottles were made out of back then? Was it clear like the glass from a window? Did *you* step on any of it? He said he came up right behind you. Why weren't you cut as well?"

"No, I don't remember the glass, but I'm sure there was some there." Talitha's eyes darted back forth scanning the table, scanning her memory. "We had just got away from Nancy when I noticed him crying and he was limping and there was all this blood. It looked like his foot had on a shiny red sock... wait, did Nancy bite you?"

"Yeah, but I didn't tell you because I didn't want you to feel bad. I didn't want you to think it was your fault or something."

"But it was my fault. I walked into the ring of death like an idiot and you saved me. And then when I went berserk and knocked you over, I remember you pushing me on." She began to pace, frowning as she did. "You were attacked by the dog so I wouldn't be. Is that right?" He nodded and she went on, "And you did it again with the demon. You risked your life for me. And also with the dreams. You did that for me."

For some reason, she seemed angry over this and out of the blue, slammed her fist into the refrigerator, denting it badly, and showering the floor with pictures and magnets. "That's it, Will. No more. You can't save me anymore." When he started to protest, she held up her hand. "The other Talitha is gone for right now and I don't want her back just yet, so listen. Why I'm going to the Void when I die is my affair. You'll never know the reason, let alone understand it. That being said, no more. You were correct before, I'm a lost cause, so please don't try to save me. I am doomed."

With her face set, Talitha stalked out of the room. "I need a drink. You guys want one?"

"I wish, but we don't keep alcohol here," Will replied. "Remember Lisa's mom was a raging alcoholic?" He tossed the scissors down on the table, where they clanked heavily and came to rest open like a hungry alligator. Inside him, the urge to have a drink rose up demanding.

Talitha popped her head back into the kitchen, she wore an odd expression. "I don't want to be a snitch, but Lisa has vodka here. Somewhere. Down the hall, I think."

Why this was so important considering everything they were facing, he didn't know, yet still he got up quick. "Show me."

Giving the air a light sniff, Talitha went to a little used closet that sat just off the den and opened the door. As she did, a red Christmas ball in a suicidal mood, leapt off a shelf and would have dashed itself to pieces on the hardwood floor below, but Talitha caught it neatly. She nestled it with a jumble of other ornaments, which sat on the tidy stacks of brown cardboard boxes that held their ever-growing number of holiday decorations.

She fished out a bottle of Smirnoff from behind the boxes and held it out to Will. "This isn't a good sign."

It certainly wasn't. Will took the bottle and sighed, feeling that he had let his wife down in some way. A fully formed image came to him: *Lisa sitting at the kitchen table alone on a Saturday night. She poured an exact amount of the vodka into one of their kitchen glasses. He knew that amount never varied. Next, she added orange juice and then in defiance of reason, she put the ice in last. Drops of orange juice and vodka leapt over the edge of the glass and landed on the table, causing little lines to crease her forehead.*

She got up and wiped the few drops with a dishrag and then, neat as always, she rinsed out the rag and set it to dry. Only then did she start to drink.

"This isn't like her," Will said mostly to himself.

"And neither is this," Talitha added pointing to the closet.

Will glanced up from the bottle and looked in. "What? That's how it always looks."

"Actually it isn't," his sister replied picking up one of the Christmas ornaments. It was a small gold bell that tinkled in her hand. "There's not a stray mote of dust on any of these. This little pile was in a box not too long ago."

She said it with some importance, but Will was missing what that could possibly be and she looked up at the ceiling in exasperation. "Do I need to spell it out for you? A box is missing. There is tape and scissors sitting out in the kitchen..."

Finally, it clicked. "You think she mailed the sword somewhere?"

"Yes, hold on." Talitha sniffed at the air, "She still uses Maybelline?" Before Will could respond, Talitha was moving down the hall toward the kitchen she went directly to the door and there next to it on a peg was his wife's purse. Talitha dug through it for a moment. "She went to UPS yesterday and spent forty-eight dollars. What's UPS?"

"United Parcel Service," Will replied in excitement. "It's a delivery company. And the fact that she spent forty-eight dollars means that she had the sword sent over night."

Father Vogel had trailed along after the brother and sister in silence, but now he spoke up, "Does the receipt say where she sent it?"

"No," Talitha replied, but it didn't have too.

Chapter 15

Amy

On the wall, a phone began to ring.

"Don't answer that," Amy ordered. One of her thugs had reached his hand out for it. She couldn't remember this one's name. But to be honest, she could barely remember any of their names except for Pedro and the one who called himself Diablo. "We'll let the answering machine get it. You do have an answering machine right?"

The couple in front of her nodded as one. They were older than she had expected, especially the man. William Jern looked terrible, like he had a disease or something. He was dreadfully skinny and his hair which eight years ago had been blonde was now completely grey as well as sparse. His cheeks were hollow and thick dark bags sat puffy under his blue eyes.

Gayle Jern, whom Amy couldn't help but think of as *Mrs. Jern* was better off. Her hair was still a thick rich brown, dappled only slightly by grey and her skin was a wonderful deep tan. Only about the eyes did her years stack up on her. They were enmeshed in wrinkles and lines that bespoke of the long burden of worry and now fear only added its weight. She looked about to cry.

And that was too bad for her.

Not that Amy was uncaring or unsympathetic, but if she couldn't get that gate open for Ba'al, she was looking at a long stretch, an eternity in the Void. And that scared her badly. Right there, sitting in the Jern's living room she felt her insides thrumming with nervousness. She had looked into the Void on too many occasions not to be properly afraid.

The phone rang a second time and involuntarily she

checked her watch. It was just after three. Nine hours left. Nine hours to fulfill a promise. The phone shrilled again. It made the silence on either ends of the ring uncomfortable and everyone, including the bored looking Mexican thugs wanted to answer the thing. After the fifth, the machine picked up and the room waited in mute expectation, but the caller hung up.

"Where were we?" Amy leaned back relaxing. The phone call had bothered her. It had seemed almost too coincidental that it would start ringing so soon after she had entered the home. It had only been four minutes since her thugs had slipped into the unlocked ranch style home from three directions and found the Jerns sitting quietly in their kitchen. "Oh, yes. You were going to tell me when Katie will be coming home."

"Actually, we weren't. That was an incorrect assumption on your part," William replied.

He was wonderfully calm, and had steel in his eyes. Amy could appreciate this and truly wished her own father had been half the man William Jern was. And that steel should have been enough to stop her own mother from going after Talitha. That had been mistake number one. Instead, her mother should've gone after Lisa. No one would have cared, much less put their life on the line for her. Lisa's mother was a drunk and her father was always away. It would've been a snap, a piece of cake, but that was water eight years under the bridge now.

"Mr. Jern, I only ask because I don't want her walking in here and accidentally surprising one of my men. Look at them. They appear to me a little trigger happy, don't you think?"

They actually looked like a bunch of iguanas basking lazily in the sun. There were six men in the room lounging about the furniture or leaning against the walls and she had to fight the urge to scream at them to stand up straight. Amy hated their slovenly appearance, their poor manners, and most of all, she hated the fact that none could speak passable English. Yet for all that, they were dangerous and fulfilled a purpose.

"She's running track. She'll be home at half past five," William stated, keeping his eyes hard on Amy's face.

"See? That wasn't so difficult," Amy smiled, despite that William's words added to her anxiety. She had hoped the girl would be along sooner, too many things could happen in the next two and half hours. Even a simple thing like a neighbor stopping by for a visit could start a chain reaction that could unravel everything, and she was simply out of time for any new plans.

It would have to be the sword. There was an opening on it somewhere and it was possible to expand it large enough to allow Ba'al to be set loose. Amy just wasn't sure exactly how, though she had an idea. Her mother had been killed by it and her soul sucked directly through it into the Void. Likely, the more souls that passed through the opening, the bigger it would get.

Erosion on a metaphysical, level so to speak.

Amy got up and paced about, trying to release some of the stress building in her. She wasn't really a killer; always, if she could, she had someone else do any actual killing that was needed. But in this case, she was pretty certain that she alone would have to do it. The thought made her neck ache and she rolled her head back and forth trying to relieve it.

A picture on a credenza caught her attention and she walked over to it. At first, Amy thought it was a picture of her mother Henny Harris, but on closer examination, she saw that it was actually a young looking Gayle Jern. Although her mother had darker hair and more up top in the breast department, the two women could have passed as sisters. Amy laid the picture face down.

"I like your home, Gayle." It was nice. It was styled as a sizeable 'T' shaped ranch and had long halls and tall ceilings. The main living area, the kitchen, living room, and dining room were separated by short three-foot high walls, which made the area look larger than it was. All the rooms were fashionably decorated and the floors were covered in white wall-to-wall carpeting. Too bad for the carpet, Amy thought. It was about to be ruined.

"You have what you came for," Gayle pointed, without raising her arm, toward the brown box a few feet away. "Take that horrible thing and go," it came out as a whimper.

Amy sauntered back toward them and tried to smile, but failed, her stress was too great. "I'll do as I please...Gayle." She had almost called her Mrs. Jern, which would've been laughable at the moment. "Have either of you touched it?"

"Not today," William answered. "But I did eight years ago."

Amy eyed the man closer. Was this what happened to a person who touched it? The idea made her nervous. "What about you, Gayle? Did you touch it?"

Gayle shook her head. "No, never. Amy, please don't do this. You could tie us up and cut the phone lines and..."

Amy rolled her eyes, interrupting, "Pedro, have your boys tie them up. Thanks Gayle. That was a good idea. Do you have any more?" When Gayle only put her head down, Amy smiled for real. "Good. Make sure those are tight," she said to one of the men who had come forward. Was it...Pablo? She couldn't remember.

As he tied the couple up, Amy took a hold of the box. She sat herself on the glass coffee table in front of William Jern and stared at the ugly broken blade. Despite the fact that it looked like it had just been pulled from a fire, it emanated cold as if it was an open freezer door.

"I wouldn't touch it I was you," William warned.

Amy did anyway. "Uhg!" She had just put out a finger and barely made contact, but a ghastly sick feeling had run up her arm. "That's horrible. You killed my mother with that?"

"I didn't, but I would have," William answered right

back. "Your mom was a sadistic evil person and she deserved everything that she got."

"Blah, blah, bah. Gag them both." Amy got up and walked away. She didn't want to see their pathetic struggles or hear any of their whining and she wished again that Katie were here. The virgin method for opening a gate was far less messy; a little blood, some hell-bred runes, a rather short incantation, and then step back.

But she couldn't wait. Teenagers were terribly flighty and it would be just her luck that today would be the day that Katie would decide to go to the mall, or stay late and chat up some high-school boy.

Breathing hard and with a face set in grim lines of determination, Amy came back to stand in front of the two; she would make this quick. "Close your eyes, Gayle. You don't want to see this." As she could have predicted Gayle didn't close her eyes but squirmed and wriggled ferociously. "Have it your way then."

William didn't budge an inch, but only stared at her with his hard blue eyes. It was slightly off-putting and because of that, Amy didn't draw the moment out any longer than she had too. With a quick move, she caught up the sword and made to stab him in the chest, however she hadn't counted on the horror of the blade. The quick touch she had given it before was nothing compared to actually grabbing it. The metal was nasty and unnatural and it was an effort to force her muscles to grip the handle and because of this, she made a weak fumbling attack.

Still, the blade drove deep into the left part of his rib cage, but to the side of the heart and low. It went in easy. Perhaps even eagerly.

Beneath his gag, William screamed. A second later, Amy screamed as well. She felt a sick vile suction drawing down her arm—something was pulling her in—drawing that part of her, the true essence of what it was to be Amy Harris out of her and into the blade.

Fear and pain drove her into a frenzy and like a wild animal, she bucked and yanked at her own arm. The hilt of the blade seemed frozen to her hand and if she had an axe, she would've hacked it off at the wrist. Time meant nothing. Only the loss of her soul had meaning.

But fortunately for her, William lost his soul first. She felt it rush down the blade, like a train on fire.

With a shriek, she was able to pull her hand away—back she fell, tripping over the glass coffee table and the sword went flying, clanging against a far wall, but she didn't hear. Her ears were filled with the echoing screams that had come tearing up the blade. There had been millions of them, maybe even billions. Amy Harris, who was at that moment the greatest witch on the planet rolled onto her stomach and cried.

Minutes passed this way, but at length her own sobbing and that of Gayle drowned out the fading echoes and she began to be aware of where she was. The room was cold.

"Someone turn off the fucking air conditioning," her voice was a hoarse rasp. No one moved. Except for Gayle that is. She had somehow wriggled next her husband and cried over him. His eyes were open and his mouth hung slack. He looked as if he had aged thirty years before he died. Amy tried to stand, but was too weak and so for a few minutes she knelt on the white carpet next to a spray of red and looked about blearily.

Her Mexican thugs, those, oh so tough gangbangers had backed away and to a man they no longer looked so sleepy. "Pedro, tell one of these morons to turn off the air conditioning before I get angry." She was very cold and had at some point commenced to shiver. Her words had some effect, a few of the men looked around for a wall mounted thermostat.

"Ms. Harris, I think the cold is coming from that." He pointed at the sword. It lay next to the wall that separated the living room from the family room.

"Oh, right. Then turn up the damn heat." After another minute Amy felt renewed slightly and was able to stand; it was only then that her men began to scurry about. She looked down at Gayle who still cried over her husband. It was a pitiful scene, but pity didn't touch Amy's heart, that was numb to everything save fear. She was afraid to touch the sword a second time. "Pedro, come close his eyes. I don't like the way he's staring at me."

The Mexican strode over and bent over the man.

Amy didn't watch. Instead, she went to the kitchen and found a dishtowel. In her heart, she knew that the thin veil of cloth wouldn't save her soul, only a better strike could do that; a quick clean kill. William had lingered as he had because her aim had been off, but she hoped that the towel would help a little, at least with the cold.

She wrapped it around her hand.

Still, she was afraid to touch the sword. The thing had tried to take her soul and just looking at it sent shivers down her spine. Yet she had no choice. Amy tottered toward the blade and hesitated above it, preparing herself.

"Fuck you bitch! I'm going to be waiting for you. When you get to hell, I'll be there and you better believe I'll be ready." Amy turned back at the poisoned words. Gayle's tears had loosened the tape about her mouth and it hung like a flap of skin from the side of her face. Their eyes locked and Gayle's hate was such a force that it caused Amy to pause. Still the pause was only for a second. On the line, it was either Gayle's soul or her own and thus there was little choice in the matter for Amy. She bent down for the sword. Her dreadful work was not over.

The phone rang.

Everyone in the house stopped what they were doing at the same time and froze. It rang again and Amy felt a sudden touch of worry. A third ring and Amy looked at Gayle. The older lady wore an expression of wonder and hope. After the fifth ring, the answering machine came on as before.

"Mom, dad? It's Will. Pick up the phone, it's an emergency. Hello? Hello? Please listen carefully. Lisa sent you a package in the mail. It should arrive today. Don't open it...*do not* open it. It's the sword, *remember*." There was a pause and Will could be heard breathing deeply. "There are people after it. You need to get Katie and leave. Don't bother calling the police they wouldn't understand and don't try to contact me. I'm heading your way with Talitha, but don't wait for us, we'll catch up to you. Disappear for a few days, use only cash and keep moving. Get in touch with Bishop Keenan from Boston. He'll be expecting your call. I love you. Bye."

"Ha! My boy is coming and he will get revenge," Gayle was in a lather of vindictive righteousness and shrieked the words loudly. "Revenge! You have no clue what you're up against. He has powers that you only can dream about, and Talitha! I hope he turns her loose on you. She's a monster. She's been to hell and back, she'll tear through these idiots like they were babies. She'll kill all of you." Gayle's usually warm brown eyes now blazed in her face.

Her raging speech had the impact of a small explosion. Amy's crew of thugs stepped back uneasily, eyeing each other with silent questions. They knew that Will was supposed to have been killed by now. Seconds went by in silence and then Pedro with a scowl on his fearsome face began barking out orders in Spanish. Whatever he said caused the men to nod subserviently to him; they left the room and went to the kitchen where they stood milling.

"What should we do?" Pedro had returned to the living room and stared down at the body of William as he spoke.

Amy needed time to think. "Post a man at every corner of the house. Call L.A. I want every one of your thugs here as fast as they can."

"What about the police? Won't her son call the police?" This was the first time Pedro had so openly questioned her, but she was in no real position to make it an issue. For one she was weak and still shaking from her ordeal and for two, her reserve of spells were not inexhaustible. There was only so much she could do. In fact, there was very little she could do. Her powers of witchcraft weren't like those from a movie. She couldn't shoot fire from her fingers or lightening from a wand. Her abilities were far more subtle and took time to prepare.

"If he told his parents not to call the police, why would he? No, I don't think he'll will, but I'm going to go find out for certain. Keep everyone quiet—including her." Amy pointed at Gayle.

Pedro nodded and left, going about muttering to the men in Spanish. Amy looked around for a second, feeling slightly shell-shocked.

Her day had begun with such promise. Back in Maine, Lisa's mind had opened easily to her and the memory from the day before of her boxing up the sword and mailing it out was strong and clear. The spell had taken less than half an hour. She had been giddy at the time and it wasn't only because she knew that the ghastly blade had been sent to Will's parents. It was because Amy Harris had completely forgotten about the youngest Jern, Katie.

At fourteen, Katie couldn't be anything but a virgin and the right kind of virgin as well. The church going, mind your parents, eat all your vegetables type that would be perfect for the spell to open the gate. All through the plane ride, the picture of the little blonde pain in the ass that Amy had known, wound through her mind, putting her in the best of moods.

And then as they pulled out of the city of Phoenix heading south and then west on route eight to what was questionably considered a suburb of another smaller city, they happened to catch up to a UPS van. Amy ordered Pedro to slow and fate seemed to be on their side because the van went straight and true in the very direction they were heading. They followed it right to the Jern's home and then parked discreetly well away until it left.

As it drove off, Amy had felt that happy giddy feeling grow. She would get the sword *and* a virgin.

Only, Katie wasn't there and the sword seemed horribly double-edged, biting the hand that would dare to wield it. Not only that, Will should've been dead and Talitha as well for that matter. Even Amy's petty revenge had been diluted by the upsetting gaze in William's dead eyes. They held her guilty even in death.

She wasn't feeling at all giddy now.

Her stomach ached. It was a sharp pain right in the pit. With a quick intake of air, Amy left the room with all the dignity she could muster and after getting her satchel, she went to an unused back bedroom. From inside her bag she brought out aromatic candles and her well-worn board.

After lighting the candles and placing them around the board, she began to force herself to relax, breathing in and out slowly, clearing her mind, thinking only about her focus. For her it was an orange. Her mind swept over every aspect of her imaginary orange. The dimpled rind, the endless loop of the navel curving in on itself. Where did it begin, where did it end? The dimples seemed tiny from far away, but up close, they were huge orange hills...

"Damn!" she cursed. Her mind wasn't letting go, as it should have. From her bag, she brought out a small bottle of amber liquid and drank straight from the lip. The rum was one-fifty-one and burned as it went down. She gasped and then took another swig and gasped again while her face screwed up into an unpleasant grimace. After a third swig she put the bottle away.

Placing her hands on the faded wooden planchette and with eyes closed she tried again. Once more, the orange filled her consciousness and every aspect of it, her mind dwelled upon until she saw the long tan fingers come and grasp it. Manicured nails slid beneath the outer skin and into the rind effortlessly.

"Would you like some?" The words came to her from out of a dream. It was a memory from long ago and the voice was that of her mother's. This was her focus. When the words came to her, she knew that she was ready.

"Mommy?"

The planchette dragged her fingers to one of the four words on the board, 'Yes.'

"Will Jern is still alive. He is coming to kill me. Will he bring the police?" Amy asked in a whispering monotone. She had to remain as serene as possible or her mother would become worked up and unreadable.

The planchette went to the word, 'No' and Amy felt relief drain the tension from her shoulders, but then the planchette began to move quickly, sliding from letter to letter with barely a pause. 'WARRIORS OF GOD'

It was with difficulty that she kept her calm and as much as she wanted another shot of rum Amy kept her fingers on the little wooden pointer.

"Do they have special powers?"

'NO HUMAN'

This was a problem communicating in this fashion. Did her mother mean that the warriors were *not* human? Or did she mean that the warriors were human with no special powers. Amy would have to reword the question, carefully. Even more than when she had been alive, her mother hated to repeat herself.

"Are they super-human in any way?" It was all she could come up with.

The pointer slipped to the word 'No'. That was something at least.

"How many are coming?" Across the bottom of the board were a line of numbers and the planchette went first to the six and then to the seven.

"Sixty-seven!" It had been more of an exclamation than a rhetorical question, but her mother took it as neither and the pointer went to the 'No' and then back to the six and then to the seven.

So she didn't know the exact number. This was a little odd. Normally she either knew something or didn't, there wasn't a middle ground. But did it matter? Really? It was just after three in the afternoon now and L.A. was so close that she figured that she would have a total of seventeen of her thugs in Phoenix by six pm—way before Will and his little posse could ever hope to arrive. She hoped.

"When will they arrive?" Amy asked. The pointer went to the seven and wiggled back and forth between it and the eight. That seemed oddly quick. Amy did a quick calculation and surmised that it was faster than her flight had been by at least an hour. Still it was plenty of time. But enough time for what? She could kill Gayle at any moment she pleased with the Hell blade, only she realized that she didn't want to.

It was so horrible, that she would force herself to wait on little Katie Jern.

"Is a proper virgin coming here today? One that can open the gate?" The pause for the answer was no longer than normal, but Amy held her breath afraid of the answer.

'Yes' the pointer was right on the word. Amy sagged and blew out her pent up breath.

Only two more questions remained: "Is Talitha Jern dead?" This had been nagging in her mind since the morning.

'Yes' the planchette wiggled, but didn't come off the word. For some reason Amy suddenly doubted her mother. Where or even how the soul of Henny Harris came by her knowledge, Amy hadn't a clue, but she had never been wrong. Many times Amy's mother didn't know an answer to a question, but if she ever gave an answer, it would be correct.

Yet on this, Amy worried that she was wrong. "Will Jern says he is bringing Talitha here, tonight. Is he?"

'CANT '

"Will J..." Amy nearly pulled her fingers off the

planchette by accident. It started moving almost as soon as she began speaking.

'HER SOUL IS IN THE VOID'

This was a shock. Miss goody-two-shoes in hell. It was hard to believe. "You've seen her?" The skepticism came out strongly in Amy's voice, yet her mother didn't notice.

'Yes'

That was another shock, there were too many souls in hell for that to be a coincidence. Something odd was happening down there and before she broke the connection, she tried to find out what it was. Unfortunately for Amy, her mother was reluctant or unable to discuss it and she couldn't pursue the issue too far. She had to prepare another spell.

Thirty minutes later Amy checked her make-up and sent a brush through her thick brown hair. She never looked better. And she felt good too. The pain in her stomach had subsided and the weak feeling that had come over her after killing William Jern would be gone in a minute.

"Pedro!" she yelled as soon as she stepped out of the guest bedroom. He slouched toward her with an air of insolence. A number of his men loitered around the kitchen eating the Jern's food and watching her. They seemed to be expecting something of a show and Amy didn't blame them in the least.

They had seen her at her weakest. Screaming, acting like a feeble pathetic girl, letting a bound woman shame her. The men mocked her with their eyes. There were seven of them including Pedro, which meant that only two were actually standing in vigilance, keeping an eye out for the coming virgin. That was about to change.

"Are the cops coming?" Pedro asked without the slightest sign of respect.

Amy smiled and her white teeth flashed as she walked past him toward the kitchen. It was funny to her that so little a thing as ignoring Pedro, their leader, would make such a change in the men. Each of them sat up a little straighter and all were suddenly more alert. Good. She wanted their undivided attention.

She turned back to Pedro.

He had seen a demonstration of her power on only two occasions and it was obvious he needed to see another. It must have shown in her eyes, because he suddenly seemed a slight bit more nervous.

"I only asked cause we need to think about, ya know, gettin outta here."

"But you didn't ask me nicely," she said still smiling. "Where was the *ma'am*? Where was the *Ms Harris*? Where were your manners?"

"Sorry, ma'am." His eyes were a straight up mix of fear and fury. He was being made to look bad in front of his men.

She casually put a hand on his chest. It seemed sexual the way she did it, like it was a caress. "That's ok, Pedro. As long as you learn your lesson. Enoi-aya Findronose," she said soft and far from dramatically.

Pedro's hooded eyes shot up and his face registered a torturous shock. His strength drained out of him and flowed into Amy, so that all her previous weakness was forgotten. For a span of seconds, he shook in place and his great bulk seemed to be held up by the slim elegant arm of Amy Harris. In a moment, however, she pulled her arm back and he slithered to the floor in a state of semi-consciousness.

A very obvious stain spread out from his crotch and an unpleasant smell filled the room.

"Oh my!" Amy exclaimed waving her hand in front of her face. The thugs who had been eyeing her with impertinence only moments before scrambled out of the way, as she went to a closet and took from within it a broom. Bare handed she snapped it in half. She took it back to Pedro and smashed him in the face with it a number of times, careful not to damage him too badly. He would still be needed.

"Diablo," she crooned softly. The man who called

himself Diablo hurried forward and it was good to see that his usual smirk was not twisting his thin black goatee. His attire was as always, black. Black jeans and a t-shirt hugged his blade thin frame. In his eyes, he had a spark more intelligence than the rest of the goons but he also had the black smoke of insanity rising there as well. He liked to hurt people.

"Yes, Miss?"

Amy's lip curled at his accent. Miss came out *meese*. She jerked her head at the limp moaning man at her feet. "Get two men to clean him up. The rest I want watching out for the girl. There are pictures all around this place in case these morons don't know who to look for."

"Yes, Miss."

Men fell over themselves to do as she ordered. Thankful for a reason to get out of the stinking kitchen, Amy walked with purposeful casualness to the living room. The blade still lay against the wall where it had been thrown, she turned her back on it, knowing that she would have to pick it up eventually. Just not yet.

Gayle Jern was uncomfortably cuddled up to her husband's body, looking as if she were trying to protect him. The sight annoyed Amy. It was just so truly pathetic. What good did Gayle think she could do with her hands tied behind her back? The only positive that she could garner from the scene was that somebody had shut William's eyes.

"Diablo! Get someone to move this corpse. Gayle, where do you keep the sheets?"

"No," Mrs. Jern whispered harshly and shook her head pushing herself further onto her husband. Diablo came up, looking sidelong at the sword as if he feared to take his eyes from it.

"Gayle, please." Amy felt a surge of anger at someone telling her no, but she attempted to be compassionate. "Your daughter will be home soon. I doubt that you want her to see her father this way. We need to move the corpse."

"Eh, maim, theese penejo ain't daid." Diablo pointed at William shaking his head. It took Amy a moment to figure out what the man was saying.

"What? Not dead? Is that what you said?"

"Si."

"Uhg! This is fuckin America! When you're in this country, you say *yes,* not si." She shook her head in anger and then turned toward William.

"Don't touch him, please," Gayle whined.

"Oh shut up." Amy no longer felt the least bit charitable. She leaned over the cringing form of Gayle Jern and felt William's neck. His skin was only cool to the touch and not cold as she had expected and what's more, there was a light thumping beneath the man's scrawny chest. This was a puzzle.

William Jern no longer had a soul, least ways not in his body. It was in the Void somewhere—yet the man's body still lived. Amy went to pry open one of his eyes but Gayle interceded with her head, thrusting it in the way.

"Please no. Let him be," she begged. Her eyes were beet red, but they seemed incapable of putting forth any more tears.

Amy shoved her roughly away, ignoring the older lady's bleating. One of Amy's spells, the most horrid one she possessed came to mind as she looked upon the body of the man. The spell was dreadful, even more so than the *Vile Gate*, which brought forth the demon. Its name *Mancipium Donec Nex*, meant nothing to her since she didn't speak a lick of Latin, but what did matter were the very gruesome effects it produced in its victim.

The person's soul was sacrificed to a demon and in return, the gypsy who cast the spell would be able, for a time, to control the victim who would go on in a semi state of life. They became a ghoulish nightmare that was in effect, indestructible, and due to their inhuman strength, basically unstoppable.

It had been the very spell that had persuaded Pedro that she was the real deal when it came to witchcraft. She had chosen a rival gang member and sucked the life out of him with the spell. The demonstration had fulfilled its purpose, but it had also left a nasty taste in her mouth for dealing with the undead.

And now here was William Jern alive without a soul. What could she make of that?

"William, open your eyes." She spoke clear and loud, but his eyes remained closed. Amy tried again louder, "William Jern! Open your eyes!" Nothing happened.

Gayle wiggled to her knees again, "What did you do to him?"

Amy turned away, not wanting to deal with the woman. She was trying to figure out how to turn this to her advantage. One of the problems with the *Mancipium* spell was its relatively short duration. The gangbanger had started off as practically invincible, but over an hour-long period it had wound down, slowly losing its energy, until it finally just fell over and ceased to function.

It was for this reason that she was so interested in William. He'd been stabbed over an hour previous, yet he still looked fresh. Sort of.

"What did you do to him? You have to tell me," Gayle whined.

Amy was tired and more than a bit cranky. She snapped her fingers at Diablo, "Shut her up."

It wasn't a very specific order. Diablo grabbed the middle-aged woman and began slapping her across the face. Tied up, Gayle could do nothing and her eyes bulged and her screams split the air.

"Stop it, you idiot! I said stop," Amy commanded advancing on the man. Diablo backed away, letting Gayle flop to the carpet where she rolled into a ball and began moaning. "Get the hell out of here. Go!" Amy was beside herself, enraged. She paced around Gayle for a few seconds, wondering at the stupidity of these idiot thugs. "Pedro, get your ass in here now."

Pedro was there in seconds, dripping water onto the carpet and wearing nothing but a towel. "Yes ma'am."

"Your men are fucking morons. If we lose the girl, I'm going to hold you personally responsible. Do you understand me?" The big Mexican paled considerably beneath his natural tan and he nodded with vigor. "Good. Now Katie could possibly show up at any time and we can't have her being warned off by people screaming in the house. Get dressed and then...then lay Mr. Jern on the couch and cover him with a blanket as if he were taking a nap. How's that Gayle? Is that good enough for you?"

The woman only wept, crying into the carpet. Amy shook her head, and looked back at the big man. "Get her up. Put her in one of the chairs so that she can't be seen from any of the windows. When you're done with that, I want you to go around to each of your men and instill in them the fear of fucking this up."

"Don't do it, Pedro," Gayle glared up suddenly. "If you do, you'll be dead by midnight. Run away instead. Take your men and run." Her words were spoken with such conviction that it sent a chill through Amy.

The witch stared down at Gayle. "One more word and the gag goes back on for good." Gayle clamped her mouth shut but the defiance was nestled in her eyes to stay. For just a moment, Amy wanted to bring Diablo back in and have him smack the defiance out of her, but instead she twisted around to gaze at Pedro, judging his loyalty. "Here's the deal. We're waiting solely on the girl. When she shows up, we snatch her and take off."

"Yes ma'am. Do we take the two of them?" He pointed at the Jerns. Amy didn't know. If everything went according to plans she wouldn't need them, but she couldn't exactly count on that happening.

"I think so. She's going to be my backup plan if all else

fails. I think if the sword takes a few more souls, the gate will open. It's just I'd rather do it the good ole fashioned way. Now make sure someone stands guard on these two every single moment. I want your man right here on this goddamn love seat and if they take their eyes off of her for a second, I want you to shove their balls down their throat."

"Yes ma'am. May I make a suggestion? You should gag her right now."

Amy smirked. In truth, the only reason that Gayle wasn't gagged was that Amy felt sorry for her. How funny was that? She hoped to become the ultimate power on the planet and still she felt pity. She was being stupid. "Good idea. Gag her and make sure it stays this time. I'm going to be in the back bedroom. Let me know when the girl shows up."

She left Pedro, knowing that he'd do everything she had ordered, and slipped into the bedroom. The Ouija board was still out and Amy gave it a glance. Should she try to contact her mother to ask about William Jern? A great yawn erupted out of her as an answer. It made her eyes drip.

Spell casting was more taxing than she would've ever guessed, but the spell that she had laid on Pedro was one of the worst. She had drained his strength and fed it into her, yet now she was exhausted. The spell was similar to a drug, in that it brought her to a great high but almost as quick, it also sent her crashing down.

The witch was just too tired for the Ouija board, in fact she felt close to swooning. She went to the bed and within thirty seconds was sound asleep. It was deep refreshing dreamless sleep, one that her body needed.

A light knocking woke her and for a moment, she couldn't figure out where she was. The room was dark save for a single sputtering candle and this only coated everything in shadows, making her surroundings even more unrecognizable.

The knock came again and this time was accompanied

by a fearful sounding voice, "Ma'am?"

Right. She was at the Jern's home. "Do we have the girl?" She got up and flicked on the overhead ceiling light.

"Not yet."

What? On her wrist, she wore an expensive gold watch. The time was ten minutes to six. Amy was out of the room in a flash. "Is everyone still in their positions? Did you check that they were keeping out of sight?"

"Yes, ma'am," Pedro sounded desperate to please. He had changed into what must have been a pair of William's sweat suits. Decked all in grey, he looked soft and far less imposing. "I woke you after checking each position. The men are all situated real good."

The pain that Amy had been feeling earlier stabbed again into her stomach, she rubbed it absently, looking back into the bedroom. "Maybe I should consult the spirits." She liked being mysterious by saying things such as, *maybe I should consult the spirits*. It just sounded better than saying I'm going to go ask my mom. But she changed her mind quick. "Show me where the men are positioned."

Pedro nodded and stood back from the door, not moving to show her as she asked. He knew better. Amy swept past him heading to the living room where William lay partially covered by a blanket and Gayle sat trussed up being watched over by Diablo. The older lady looked startled at Amy's sudden quiet appearance and froze statue like, sweat dripping off her brow.

Amy barely gave her or Diablo a glance and went toward the family room that opened off the living room. Behind her, she heard Gayle begin to grunt loudly. Amy ignored it. The family room was smaller and cozier than the living room. It had tall windows and a glass door that looked out upon a deck. The room itself was nicely furnished with two long matching leather couches oriented on a television. A fully stocked wet bar took up one corner of the room and large portraits of the family adorned the walls.

One of Pedro's men sat in one of the rooms big comfortable chairs facing out toward the deck. The man went by 'Jin' Amy recalled. "Anything moving out there?" she asked.

"Nah," Jin replied with a shake of his head. Behind her Pedro snapped his fingers and Jin straightened slightly. "I mean no ma'am."

The witch smiled inwardly at the man's attempt at manners and strolled past him staring out of the window at the beginnings of a very chilly dusk. Soon her men would be at a disadvantage—Katie being able to see in, better than they could see out.

"Jin, come stand just to the side of the window. Right here," Amy ordered. "Pedro, make sure all of the lights are off in the house except the master bedroom and maybe one of the bathrooms."

With that, she left, heading for the kitchen. Gayle kept her eyes down as she passed, making Amy smile again. "You there..." she pointed at a man in faded jeans. "Amador, don't sit right there. You're too obvious. Move around the counter."

Despite the fact Katie wasn't home yet, Amy felt good. She was rested, her stomach no longer hurt and she had actually remembered two of the Mexican's names. This was a small triumph for her. Both men hadn't been situated badly, it was just that as their leader, she felt it a good idea to bark out an order every once in a while to remind them of who was in charge.

After going through the kitchen to the garage and checking on the man there, his name eluded her, she went back to the living room and paused. Katie would be along soon. Any minute in fact, her own mother had told her so. Yet all the same, sudden disquiet fluttered her heart.

Heading toward the guest bedroom where her board still lay on the floor, she called over her shoulder, "Pedro, see that I'm not disturbed. I need to see what's keeping that damn girl."

At this, Gayle began to go crazy, bucking and squirming, as well as grunting beneath her gag as loud as she could. Amy stopped and glanced her way, wondering if it would be worth her while finding out what the ruckus was about. She decided against it, but just then a drop of sweat stung her eye. "Pedro, one more thing, turn down the heat. You're roasting..." It was hot. Way too hot.

Amy ran down the hall to the living room. The hell blade was no longer lying up against the wall as it had. "Where's my sword?" she screeched with her heart booming loudly in her chest. It had taken two seconds but she had gone from relaxed to almost literally panicked. "Who took my sword? Diablo, where the fuck is my sword? What did you do with it?"

Diablo had hopped up at the first of Amy's screams and now he backed away shaking his head holding out his hands in front of him, "I no know. I no know."

Pedro had heard the commotion from the kitchen and came running. "The sword? It was sitting right there, you know before." He pointed at the blank spot on the wall.

"Before what? Goddamn it! I want that sword back right now. Get all your men in here and make it fast." Pedro took off, hissing in Spanish, calling to them. Amy began to pace in a fury. "Whoever took it is going to pay! I am going to fucking kill whoever did this."

"Mmm...mmhm!" Gayle grunted. With a raging snarl, Amy turned to her, raising her hand to slap the tape off her mouth. However, Amy stopped with her hand raised. Gayle's eyes were smiling; she knew who had the sword.

"Diablo, let Mrs. Jern see your knife."

Chapter 16

Katie

At three twenty-six pm, the young blonde in the blue sweat suit looked back for a third time. Her eyes appeared bored and indifferent as if the long ride had dulled her senses as it had most of the other teens. It hadn't. She only pretended so. She sat near the front of the school bus as it bounced along the rutted roads and this was because, unlike most of America, Arizona was still hot even this deep into the school year. All the cool sophomores and some of the cute or personable freshmen who made up the in-crowd sat towards the front. The air condition was more effective there.

The nerds and the forgotten sweltered in the rear.

"It's so stinkin hot." Next to the blonde a rail thin brunette complained, "How can you stand to wear warm-ups when it's this hot out, Kate."

Unlike her brother's long ago failed transition from Willy J to Will, Katie had begun calling herself Kate, two months before on the first day of her high school career and through sheer willpower and blackmail her new name had stuck, at least at school it had.

"I'm fine. It's not even that hot, probably not even ninety degrees," she replied, seeing the sweat in Megan's hair. Since Katie's head was already turned she gave the back of the bus another glance, purposely maneuvering her eyes around Brad Tarleton's handsome face two rows back. He was, as always, trying to catch her eye and it was best if she just pretended that she hadn't noticed.

Brad claimed to love her and was practically a stalker these days. It was a lesson learned for Katie; if you wanted a little fun, don't have it with one of your neighbors. On a not so chance meeting during the last week before school had begun, the two had fooled around pretty good. Now Brad was always prowling around looking for more, but that wouldn't happen. He had served his purpose. Katie, despite being tall and beautiful, sporting a tan the color of warm honey, had never so much as kissed a boy before. Brad, on the other hand was considered a lady's man by all his friends and never denied—and probably started—the false rumors that he had gone all the way at least twice.

He seemed like the ideal boy for Katie's designs and she'd received the kiss she had wanted from him. It had been disappointing, clumsy, and amateurish. It was funny, despite her complete inexperience, she didn't blame herself in the least. She blamed his ill-deserved reputation. And that was a lesson as well.

Katie refused to meet his eyes. Instead, she stole a look at a raven-haired girl sitting along the bus' rear axle. The girl had a flat round face with wide spaced dark eyes, and these were currently locked onto Katie's ice blue ones. They stared at each other until the black haired girl looked away. When she did, Katie continued to stare, examining her. The girl had a reddish brown tan. That was good.

After a few seconds, she turned back to her friend. "That girl back there on the right. The one with the black hair and the white t-shirt, who is she?"

Megan looked back in her most casual and secretive manner, which wasn't very secretive. "Oh, she's new. Her name is like Dominguez, Gomlinglez, or something like that."

"Mexican?"

"Yeah, I think."

Katie dropped her voice low. "Does she have an accent? Does she sound like a Mexican?"

"Yeah, I guess. Why? What's up?" Megan gave her friend an inquisitive look and then dropped her voice to a level just below conspiratorial, "You got a problem with beaners?"

Katie's eyebrows went up, surprised by the question. She realized she must've allowed her undercurrent of suspiciousness to show. With an easy natural smile, she smoothed it away. "No, I don't have a problem with Mexicans. I was just curious as to who she was."

"Well I don't really know her at all," Megan replied wiping a trickle of sweat from her forehead with the sleeve of her pink Izog shirt. "She's in Cindy's homeroom, so she's a junior. Did I tell you that I caught Cindy wearing my jeans again? My Jordashe jeans that I just got for my birthday. She's got a job; you'd think that she could buy her own clothes instead of swiping mine and stretching them out with her big butt."

Megan went on talking for some time and Katie nodded her blonde head at all the correct pauses, but wasn't really listening. Her mind strayed briefly to the Mexican girl and decided she wasn't likely much of a threat and graded her a six. This wasn't about looks.

This was about Katie's obsession with evil.

After the time with the demon, Katie had carried on in her bubbly sweet fashion as if nothing had happened, and no one, not even her wonderfully brilliant father, knew any different. On the outside, she was the essence of sweetness, but on the inside she was cold steel. Those who knew her best, didn't know her at all.

She had seen the demon. She had felt its questing tendrils taste her and long for her in the most horrible way. She had looked into that black pit, the gateway to the Void—and the experience had matured in a way that couldn't have been duplicated. It had also warped her in the same way. The world had changed for Katie Jern.

Evil, once an ethereal, intangible concept had become for her very physically and spiritually real. At six-years-old, she had become obsessed with evil, and she strove to understand it. She knew that demons existed, but what about witches and vampires, ghosts and goblins, what about these? In secret, she read and learned all she could, including everything that had occurred and what was currently occurring with her family.

It hadn't been easy, and in order to learn all she had, it took listening at keyholes, reading private letters and skimming through doctor's reports. In the end, she had found out the truth.

Katie's mother was secretly convinced that their family was cursed. To her credit, Gayle had kept this secret buried deep, but Katie divined the truth. And from the very start, she had shared her mother's conviction.

They were cursed. How could it be called anything different? Her murderous sister had been driven insane. Her father was quite visibly dying, while her mother was dying as well, but just less noticeably. When William went, Gayle would go shortly after. And her brother, Willy J, with every visit he appeared to shrink, not physically, but spiritually. The dreams that he endured were corroding his very soul.

Oh yes. They were all good and cursed.

Yet everyone pretended otherwise. No one had ever spoken to her about the demon, nor had they mentioned Talitha's problems other than to say she was sick. The topic of her father's coming death was avoided altogether, as were the hell dreams. All of these subjects were strictly taboo. They were trying to protect her, to shelter her. They needn't have bothered.

In her mind, the truth would have been a better shield to defend her.

The bus braked in its usual jolting fashion and a number of kids got up and filed in solemn procession off of it. Brad Tarleton was among them. He gave her a wave and she gave him a smile, not wanting to be purposely rude, but it was also a small smile so as not to lead him on.

"You coming to the Dojo tonight?" Adam Gustafson asked as he passed by. He was a tall gangly sophomore and they took Taekwondo classes together. He loved her madly and had since she'd moved out to Arizona during the second grade.

Her homework load was light and though she had run four miles that morning she was up for another workout. "Yep, I'll see you there." There was no question that he was going. If she went then he went. He would accept a pummeling at her hands as if she were doling out kisses.

Like everything else in her life, her karate was fueled by her warped obsession and thus she was far from the ideal student. If her sensei hadn't needed the money, he likely would've kicked her out of the class after her first year. She barely took any time to learn the flowing ballet like Katas, or in fact any techniques that she felt would be suspect in a fight. These would include any of the fancy spin moves, where an odd landing could put her at a terrible disadvantage.

She went to the Dojo three times a week strictly for two reasons. The first was for heavy bag work, where she perfected her skills and tried to increase her speed and striking power. The second and more important reason that she went was for sparring, which was simply in essence, mock combat between two individuals. Because she frequently disregarded the 'mock' part of the combat, she wasn't allowed to spar with any of the other girls anymore. This was fine with her. At five feet eight inches and one hundred and thirty pounds, she was even too much for many of the boys to handle.

"I can't believe you let Adam sweat all over you every week," Megan whispered. "Gross, gross and more gross!"

Katie gave a little fake embarrassed shrug. "I suppose you're right, but he doesn't really have any friends and I don't want to mean."

"I say you need to start being mean."

The bus jerked away from the curb and Katie cast her eyes out of the window as she always did. The next stop was hers and the bus would pull up just about seventy yards from her driveway. Out of an ingrained vigilance, Katie kept her eyes out as her street approached.

"Cindy saw you running this morning. Isn't it way too early to get ready for track season?" Megan asked. Though the brunette was slim, it wasn't due to any exercise and she seemed to dislike that her best friend spent so much time at it.

"No, I only have five months to get ready," Katie had meant for this to be a bit of a joke, but her words fell flat out of her mouth. They were pulling up to her stop and instead of seeing her driveway empty as always, there were two long cars parked outside of her house and her attention was riveted on them. A man in black leaned up against the nearer of the two. He glanced up toward the bus and as he did, his hand went to his mouth, stayed for a second, and came back down to his side.

"Megan, can I get off at your stop?" Katie whispered with some urgency, slumping down in her seat. The man was smoking! Her mother would never have allowed that within five hundred yards of her home, not with the way her father had been feeling lately. There was something wrong. This time she was sure of it.

"Sure, why..."

"Mr. Jenkins? I'm getting off at Megan's stop, if you don't mind." Mr. Jenkins shrugged indifferently and pulled away even before he had a chance to stop.

"What's going on Katie?" Megan asked, eyeing her as if hoping for something juicy.

"Uh...uh, it's my grandmother," Katie lied. "She would freak out if...uh, she saw me dressed in sweats. She likes me in dresses and high heels."

"I can't say as I blame her, if I had your figure, I'd never wear sweats." Megan blew out in exasperation. "I can't wait till my boobs start to grow."

Now it was Katie's turn to be exasperated. The two of

them had this conversation a dozen times already and she really wanted to focus instead on what she was going to do about whoever was at her house. It's probably nothing, she told herself. Aloud she said vaguely to Megan, "You only just turned fourteen. They'll come in, don't worry. Just look at your sister."

"How can I not? She parades around the house naked, showing them off."

Two minutes later, the bus began slowing down again and Katie motioned for her friend to get up, only she wouldn't and Katie, feeling deepening anxiety, stepped over her. "Sorry, I'll call you."

She was the first off and without ceremony she began jogging back the way the bus had come, her big freshman backpack smacking into her every second step. The land this close to the Sonoran desert was rugged and lonely and seemed comprised solely of dried out gullies, nasty choking scrub brush, and windswept hills. As soon as Katie crested the first of these hills, she tugged her backpack off, unzipped an inner pocket, and pulled out the four-inch jack knife she kept hidden in a nest of tampons.

She stashed the bag under a thick stand of scrub and took off in a loping run, thankful that Megan's bus stop was basically all uphill from her own. First, she ran along the lee side of the hill for about a quarter of a mile away from the road until she saw a good spot to head toward her house. Even from a mile away, the house was visible and obvious. It was the only one on this side of the road and looked like a lonely fort in the middle of Indian country.

As she closed on it, the land flattened somewhat and at moments the house was visible and at others, such as when she ran down into one of the many gullies and fissures torturing the landscape, it couldn't be seen at all. At about a hundred yards she slowed and began to use as much cover as nature could provide. A steep fissure ran to within twenty yards of the deck in their back yard and she used it to get as close as possible.

When she could go no further, she slowly peeked her head up, using an arrayed cactus as cover. There was a man, Hispanic by the look of him, framed in the glass of her family room window. For a moment, he stared out into the desert and then turned away. Katie had never seen him before. Her anxiety reached a new deeper level within her, seeming to sit smack dab in the middle of her chest.

She didn't know what to do. It was very possible that this man and the other one she'd seen had every right to be at her house. They could be friends of her parents. Or contractors of some sort, it wouldn't be the first time. But then again it wouldn't be the first time that she had over reacted and freaked out for nothing. Once she'd called the cops on a plumber. And another time she had been exactly two seconds away from getting caught snooping through the truck owned by their landscapers. They had hired someone new. Someone, who in her mind, had skin a little too light to be a proper landscaper.

To Katie, he had a sallow tint to him and that had been enough to brand him as gypsy. She hated and feared gypsies with a passion. But in that circumstance, the man was just getting over a case of jaundice and it turned out to be nothing. Yet as always, it was better safe than sorry. Only she had been sorry so many times that lately she had begun to worry that her obsession had turned into paranoia. Not the silly teen paranoia which was all about self-aggrandizement and the egocentric: *everything is about me* attitude. No, she worried about her actual mental state.

There were just so many more people in high-school and she had begun to see *gypsies* at every turn. By her second week, Katie had started keeping a list and rated every person in the school based on their threat level. Janitors, teachers, the football coach, all were on the list. Every kid that was new to her went into her book, but then she began to add old acquaintances from middle school. Kids that she thought she knew, but who now began to look different to her.

Even her best friend Megan was on the list and was rated as a two. After all, there was a chance that she could be coerced or blackmailed. But blackmailed into doing what? Whenever Katie could step back away from her obsession, she could see that it was unhealthy and getting worse, but she couldn't seem to stop herself.

It was a compulsion. The raven-haired girl on the bus, who had been rated as a six, would be unknowingly subject to a rather personal investigation. Discreet inquiries would be made as to where she lived, where she came from, who her family and friends were, and what her parents did for a living. Her knowledge of Spanish would be tested by Katie, who was fast becoming fluent. The rating of six wouldn't drop unless all the questions had been answered in a thorough and complete manner and then, if the girl was lucky, the rating would go to a four.

The men at the house, who had done nothing as far as Katie knew, had already subconsciously been rated as nines. It was a scary rating. Scary for Katie. Her mind was on the edge of paranoia and she knew, but pretended that she didn't, that if one of them made a false or sudden move while she was too close, she could very well bury her knife in his belly.

She looked down at the knife. The blade was out and shining at her. She folded it closed, not knowing when she had opened it.

"It's probably nothing," she whispered. Not for a second did she believe it and wouldn't until the men broke out saws and hammers and began building a cabinet or some such, and even then there would be doubts in her mind.

It was an obsession. And the obsession ran all the way down into her toes, so that as the man turned away from the window, Katie darted forward without even thinking. She sprinted for her house keeping her eyes locked on the man's back ready to dive to the ground if he so much as twitched in her direction. Her feet were quick and light, guided by her peripheral vision and she was at the deck in seconds, crouching low at first and then crawling along so that she was hidden by the patio furniture.

Her mind began exploring realistic sounding excuses as to why she was there just in case her mother came out, but then voices came to her from one of the open living room windows. She crawled closer.

A woman's voice came out with startling clarity, "Ugh! That's horrible. You killed my mother with that?"

Katie froze. The voice was known to her, but she couldn't place it just yet, especially since what had just been said was so bizarre and unexpected.

"I didn't, but I would have. Your mom was a sadistic evil person and she deserved everything that she got." That was her father and he sounded...strong. Even angry. To hear him like that, so much like his old self, settled the flame of fear that had been whisking about her insides. Whatever was going on, Katie knew that her father would take care of it.

"Gag them both."

The fear that had just been subsiding erupted again inside of her and now it was much greater. She had to know what was going on and she decided to poke her head up to see, but just then a different man went and stood by the glass door that led from the deck to the kitchen. The deck was a large square that took up the inner angle where two of the wings of the house came together. There were two doors that opened on to it, one to the kitchen and the other to the family room and she was trapped between the two, hidden only by a wicker couch and a barbeque grill.

She hunkered back down and began to tremble from head to toe. The realization struck her hard—her father wasn't suddenly going to take care of things like she thought.

The woman spoke again, "Close your eyes, Gayle. You don't want to see this." There was a pause and Katie's heart stopped beating. What didn't she want to see? What was going on?

"Have it your way then," the woman added.

A strange muffled roared, followed a second later by a woman's scream split the air. It went on and on and Katie began to whimper, tears dripping down her face. All her Taekwondo training was forgotten, as were her lists, her vigilance, and hyperawareness. She was no longer anything that she thought she had been. Gone was the woman on a mission who had prepared herself for the next attack on her family. In her place was a fourteen-year-old girl who above all wanted to run away.

Sobbing came now. It was her mother crying out in wretched misery. The sound was of the deepest grief and Katie knew what it meant, her father was dead. Now she began to cry in earnest as well, complete with great slobbery tears and a hitching chest, but she was afraid of being heard and in desperation she clamped her hand over her wet mouth. In a minute, she was able to control herself to a degree, but her mother wouldn't stop crying and it was a pain that went right to Katie's soul. So Katie took her hands from her mouth and covered her ears and closed her eyes.

There was nothing about this she wished to hear or to see. Mumbling got past her fingers yet still she cringed defying the brutishness of the world, letting her tears drain down her face in silence. But then the phone rang and its shrill noise penetrated into her awareness.

Hope flared at the sound and she removed her hands from her ears and waited. Everything seemed to wait; the house, the wind, even the insects enjoying the heat stopped what they were doing. Nature itself paused to hear who had called.

It was her brother, Willy J. In that brief phone call, he explained everything and now Katie knew who the woman was. It was Amy Harris and she was here for the sword. Katie's immature mind reeled, but then her mom started screaming about revenge, and about Talitha being a monster and Will's powers.

It seemed to light a fire under the people in the house but it didn't help Katie at all. Her mom was going to die, just as her father had and Katie would have no one. She would be alone, just as the desert.

Because of the awful screams, Katie guessed that Amy Harris had used the sword on her father and it wasn't something she wanted to hear a second time. She loved her mother dearly, however she feared anew for her sanity. If she heard her mother die in the same way as her father, she figured her mind would simply cave in on itself.

She had no choice but to make a run for it.

With slow, slow movements, she poked her head up, only to drop back down again. There was another man in the kitchen. A second later, there was a small thump almost above her—one of the Hispanics that she had seen earlier leaned against the window. Fortunately he was looking out at the tired view and not down.

She froze in place. For a very long time, over an hour, she laid there with the man above her. For some reason they hadn't killed her mother, which was a relief, however it was only a slight one since the men above her seemed to be settling in and Katie realized she would have a long wait beneath the wicker couch. Because of the angles of the windows, she felt relatively safe there, yet she knew that if anyone were to actually come out onto the deck she'd be in big trouble.

As she lay uncomfortably, she pondered all of what had happened and what she'd heard and guessed that the sword wasn't exactly what Amy had thought it would be. It was Amy's scream that had mingled with her father's—clearly it had hurt her in some way. Katie's reaction? She grinned with barred wolf teeth.

But if they weren't going to kill her mom, what were they waiting for? It seemed odd that they were hanging around, since they had the sword. It made no sense. Unless they were waiting for Willy J and Talitha. They'd be fools if they were. In the early days after the demon had come, Katie had seen what her sister could do. She had somehow grown cruel and monstrously strong. Talitha threw men twice her size around with ease and broke bones as if she were snapping twigs. Only Willy J seemed able to control her.

He could see into the future now. He could see all her punches coming and he was fast. Nobody seemed quicker. And he was big. So if they were waiting for her brother and sister, they were only waiting around to get their butts kicked.

Unless they had help coming. A thousand goose bumps tented upwards on Katie's skin. Perhaps they were going to bring the demon back. The girl feared the demon more than anything, more than any gypsy-witch, that was certain. The demon was in her every nightmare. It was the reason beneath her paranoia. And if they were going to bring the demon back, that meant they weren't waiting for Willy J or Talitha, hey were waiting for a virgin. They were waiting for her—Katie Jern

A movement in the kitchen caught her attention and she saw that for once no one stood looking out. Quickly she turned to see if there was anyone above her staring out of the living room window and that too seemed clear. To be on the safe side she rose and peeked into the room. There was a thuggish looking Mexican in the love seat, idling playing with a long knife, and on the couch her mom bound at the wrist and ankles lay across the dead body of her father. Tears sprang again to Katie's eyes, but she blinked them back.

Now was not the time to cry. Now was the time to be strong, as strong as she could be. Amy and her foul gang were waiting on a helpless, innocent, little girl and if Katie wanted to save her mother she would have to be anything but helpless, or innocent for that matter.

She made to duck back down, only at that moment, she

saw the sword. It lay as if forgotten against the wall next to doorway of the family room.

How very strange that it was just sitting there. The thug who sat in the love seat turned slightly and gave it a queer look. He acted as if the sword would jump up and stab him on its own. Katie realized that the man was definitely afraid of it and since no one else had picked it up, she guessed that they all were. A smirk enveloped her face at their cowardice. Her brother wasn't afraid. He had possessed that blade for something close to four years and yet he didn't shy away from it.

Their fear of the thing gave her a touch of courage and Katie began slithering backwards beneath the couch. Her plan was to crawl away and then call the police from their nearest neighbor, the Tremens, who lived just about a half mile away on the other side of the road. But unfortunately, just as she came abreast of the family room door someone strode into the kitchen. It was Amy Harris.

The newfound courage in Katie turned into a fire of hatred, burning her insides. Amy's back was to her and just then, Katie could have wormed her way off the porch and fled, but she didn't. Eight years ago, her father hadn't run away, nor had her mother. They had saved her.

"Pedro!" Amy called.

At this, there was a general movement toward the kitchen by all of the men and Katie saw that the family room was left unguarded. Without hesitation, she reached up a sly hand and pulled the door open toward her and slipped in. She crawled low so as not to be seen by the group in the kitchen and went to the three-foot wall that separated the living room from the family room.

"Are the cops coming?" one of the men, likely Pedro, asked. His tone bordered on insulting.

The words seemed very loud to Katie and they stopped her just as she was about to take a glimpse over the wall. Now there was a pause and this time she rose her head up the slightest amount and looked. The kitchen was crowded about with a number of men, and it was a bit of shock to the young girl to see that one of them carried a gun stuffed down the back of his waistband. This was something she hadn't noticed before and it sent a sour shiver running in her guts.

The look on Amy Harris' face also gave her a turn. She wore a smile of nasty contentment, as if there was pain in the offing and that she would be on the giving end.

The smile seemed to bother the man Katie thought of as Pedro as well. "I only asked cause we need to think about, ya know, gettin outta here."

Katie now shot her eyes in her mother's direction hoping that Gayle would see her, but she was looking back into the kitchen wearing a fearful expression. Katie ducked back down and searched around the edges of the carpet, a few feet away she found a paperclip and poking her head back up saw that everyone's attention was still on the kitchen. She tossed the clip at her mother.

Gayle jumped in surprise and then the mother and daughter locked eyes. It didn't seem possible, but to Katie her mother appeared to grow even more terrified at the sight of her. It was unsettling. It made her second guess herself.

'Run!' Gayle mouthed the word. 'Now, run!'

Katie shook her head, no. She would run, there was no doubting that, in fact she dearly wanted to run even then, but first she would do everything she could to free her mother. Unfortunately, there didn't seem a lot she could do.

Dropping down again, she crawled to the doorway, hoping to be able to dart around it and get into the living room quick, only it appeared impossible. Of the knot of men in the kitchen, two of them, wearing matching looks of unease were facing right at her not twenty feet away. Luckily, their attention was focused away from her. They were looking down at Pedro, who was currently lying on the ground, moaning lightly.

Just then, Amy came into view and began beating the

dazed looking man with the shaft of a broom handle. Katie was so shocked at this that all she could do was stare. It was a dreadful cruel scene, devoid of any humanity and just watching it sucked almost the last bit of courage and determination out of the young girl. She pulled back again behind the low dividing wall and tried to control her breathing. She was close to hyperventilating.

With a second glance around the corner of the door, Katie began to practically pant. She had a clearer view of the men in the kitchen and saw that *all* of them carried weapons. Some had pistols only, but quite a few held large black military style weapons. Whether they were machine guns or assault rifles, she didn't know, yet for some reason these words began to take on an importance to her causing her fear to escalate.

There was no way that she was going to be able to save her mother. Not then. There were too many men nearby and the house's open floor plan meant that sneaking about would be next to impossible. It would be all she could do even to save herself. The door that led to the deck was in view of the men as well and though she could make a dash for it, the guns made her too terrified to even try.

"Get two men to clean him up. The rest, I want watching out for the girl. There are pictures all around this place in case these morons don't know who to look for."

The Girl! So they were waiting for her. It was one thing to guess at this, but hearing it for herself knocked the wind out of her chest. A second later, Katie heard a soft footstep approaching and a shadow fell across the doorway and with it came the scent of a woman's perfume. Amy was just on the other side of the wall, not three feet from her. Now Katie was thoroughly terrified, her heart thundered within her and an uncontrollable shaking took over her body. Moments before she had been close to hyperventilating and now it felt as if she couldn't breathe at all.

"Diablo! Get someone to move this corpse. Hey, Gayle.

Where do you keep the sheets?" Amy was talking about her father, and had used the word corpse. Her father was dead. She had known it. Katie had heard the horrible scream, she had seen the body. But corpse? Was he now a corpse? That couldn't be right, could it?

The word corpse acted like a gradual eclipse in her mind, slowly shutting off all thinking so that nothing much made sense. Corpses, gypsies, swords, escape. Everything began to form into a stew of images, which whirled around inside her until her insides were a complete mush.

Thankfully for her, instinct took over.

Her instincts told her that she had to hide. She had to crawl away and find a place to cower. At the moment, it was all she was capable of doing and with only the slightest whisper of her sweat pants sliding on the floor she slithered back behind the long couch that sat up against the wall. There she curled up as best she could.

"No!" her mom whispered the word, but it came to Katie's ears clear as day. What was she saying no to? Were they going to kill her now? Was she about to be stabbed with that horrible sword? And what did the sword do? Why did Amy want it so bad? Was it magical? Did it have powers?

The sword did have a power she realized. It had turned her wonderful father into a corpse. A corpse. The word was so terribly upsetting that she felt like vomiting. And now her mother would be next. She would be just like her dad, a staring, vacant-eyed corpse.

This was too much for Katie. She yanked her hood over her head and stuffed her hands in her ears and tried not to think about anything. A stray dust bunny sat near at hand and this she focused on, crying silent tears. It helped a little and she pretended not to hear her mother's pleading voice, or the sounds of her being smacked around, or her heart wrenching sobs. She pretended instead that she was nothing. A dust bunny too.

Chapter 17

Will

A shout had Will half-awake and hearing his name a second later got his bleary eyes blinking stupidly. He had been dreaming about a river. The water of it was slow moving and it held the reflections of surrounding hills on its glittering surface.

"Huh? What?" he asked one of the bishop's men. At the moment, Will couldn't remember the man's name. The river was fading quickly from his mind, but all the same, he knew that river. It was so familiar.

"It's your sister," the man said and the words caused the river to evaporate in his mind and the dream left him.

"Will, get this priest away from me!" Talitha's voice rang out over the steady drone of the Gulfstream IV's two burly jet engines. They were riding in easily the fanciest and fastest jet Will had ever had the pleasure to sit in. Everything was leather and shining brass. It was on loan from the cardinal and Will didn't want to give it back.

"Coming," Will answered, guessing he knew what the trouble was. Before he had come back to his seat to nap, Father Vogel had begun a form of hypno-therapy on Talitha. Though it would've worked better on Will. With the humming of the engines and the priests droning voice, he had been quickly yawning.

Just as he was about to climb out of the leather chair, he saw the priest heading his way, blinking as if in surprise and holding his hand to a blazing red cheek. "Your sister is reluctant to proceed with her therapy," Vogel said, understating the problem masterfully. The purpose of the therapy had been to attempt to channel Talitha's more diabolical memories toward memories that were innocent.

The idea not being to suppress the memories but to manage them. He had used the example, "Instead of picturing a lion, you will imagine a cat, and then you will envision a playful kitten." It had seemed to start well; Talitha did like kittens after all.

Initially, Will had been reluctant. While they were drinking their screwdrivers in his kitchen, waiting on the bishop, Father Vogel had broached the idea of hypno-therapy again. "I think your reasoning not to allow this, Will is no longer valid. Talitha has done what you needed her to do and with the unit the bishop is bringing with him, you no longer need a personal killing machine."

That wasn't necessarily so, but it was likely. Talitha had sniffed out a total of three other men that had left with Amy Harris and if they were anything like the four who had stayed to be killed, he wasn't terribly worried. They had the look of street toughs, and their pathetic aim suggested that they weren't trained professionals. Still, Will had hemmed and hawed until the unit showed up. There were four of them and each was slim and of average height. They carried themselves and their military style weapons with authority, running their hard looking eyes over everything around them. Will was impressed by their maturity, as much as by their bearing. Two were running grey through their hair, while the youngest had to be thirty at the least.

For the first time in a few days, Will felt the smallest reassurance. The bishop less so. Will adamantly refused to hand over the incantations since his wife and unborn daughter were still in peril. Nor would he allow the police to be called. He sensed desperation in Amy's actions as if she were gambling everything on getting that sword and he was afraid of what would happen if she were backed into a corner. Instead of involving the police, he planned to use the bishop's contacts to find out where Amy had been staying and perhaps more importantly, where she might be going.

In the mean time, Will was going to Arizona where his

gut told him that he would find Amy. The reason for this was his little sister, Katie. Amy had practically told him that she wanted to bring Ba'al back by using the sword, but Amy wasn't a fool. It was very likely that due to her virgin status, Katie would be held in reserve as a backup plan to whatever Amy had in mind. After what had happened to Talitha eight years ago, Will's insides went queer at the thought. Yet this was his main hope in catching up to the witch. Having Katie and perhaps his parents as hostages meant that whatever Amy was going to do would likely be within driving distance of Phoenix.

The bishop, not wanting to implicate the church in the many illegalities that were likely going to take place, stayed behind in Maine to co-ordinate the various searches. The most important of these was the difficult job of narrowing down all the places associated with great death in and around Phoenix. Rich in old blood was how the gypsy Adrina Fortini described their home back on Governor's Island and this same concept had to be applied to a large portion of the desert state. Will tried not to think what a daunting task it would be and instead said a quick prayer every time his mind wandered over the near impossibility of the undertaking.

The initial mission that Will had laid out for the unit seemed quite simple and easy in comparison. It was most likely in vain, but they were going to Will's parent's house on the off chance they would find his family held hostage there. That was the best-case scenario, but also the least likely. The next best situation was that they would find a few more of Amy's thugs hanging around. The men of the unit were under orders from Will not to shoot to kill if at all possible, he wanted a chance to interrogate them. Unfortunately, the most likely thing to happen is that they would find the place deserted. Because the unit seemed so capable and Amy's thugs so unskilled, Will figured that the biggest problem he would come across would be controlling his sister.

This was why he had finally allowed the hypno-therapy

to occur. "Being slapped in the face is a sign of reluctance?" Feeling as if he were at least partially to blame for Talitha's actions, Will tried to make light of the fact that the priest had been hit.

Vogel gave him a slight smile and then worked his jaw around a bit. "In order for this to work, she has to want it and I don't think she does. It doesn't make any sense."

"I agree," Will replied with a sigh. "Does it seem to you that she has become kinda closed off? It's been getting bad all day, but ever since she found that vodka, there's been a wall up."

"I think I need to sit down," the priest looked weary. He collapsed into the nearest seat and rubbed again at his face. "I barely know her. But I suppose...yes. She does seem quieter than she had been. It could be that she's remembering more."

"Will that trigger a change over to her worse side?"

Vogel thought for a while, looking down the back of the plane at the pretty girl. "Possibly."

Beside him, bundled in a blanket so that she looked to be just sleeping, Lisa lay as if dead. Will touched her cheek gently, "Watch her, will you? I'm going to talk to Talitha." The priest nodded and Will heaved himself up, checking his watch. He was surprised to see how long he had napped, there was only another two hours left in the flight.

"Will..." for some reason Father Vogel seemed suddenly a little nervous. "Would you mind terribly if I administered last rites to Lisa? I'm not suggesting that there isn't hope for her, by doing this."

"Go ahead, please. Anything you can do for her would be great."

Will left the priest and squeezed up the aisle, giving a smile to each of the four men as he passed. They nodded in return, but generally averted their gaze from his battered face, perhaps embarrassed for him. The men were tense and each fiddled with or cleaned their weapons and had done so almost continually throughout the plane ride.

"What kind of gun is that?" he asked the leader of the unit, a man who went by the name *Abe*. It was short for Abraham which itself was only a code name. All the men had biblical code names, but tended to shorten them somewhat.

The man sitting next to Abe, the youngest of the group answered for him, "It's a *Caw* fifteen."

Will had never heard of such a weapon. It looked like an M16 but smaller and more nimble. "A Caw fifteen? I've never heard of a Caw before. Is it new?"

All the men in the little unit laughed as if this was quite the funniest thing. Will glowered until the eldest of the group, a man with a tight set of wrinkles running from the edges of his eyes, and grey at the temples of his brown hair spoke up, "Zeke here is from *Bhaaston*, Massachusetts. So don't feel bad that you can't understand him. They talk weird there. It's a CAR 15. Just like an M16, only it's better in an urban setting. Less range, but better handling in close. I'm Jake."

"Will Jern." The man held out his hand and Will shook it firmly, perhaps a touch too firm since he was still a bit miffed about the raucous laughter. "You guys have any questions about what we're up against?" Will had hardly spoken to any of the men other than to outline the bare bones plan of his.

Abe, the smallest of the men at maybe just over five and half feet in height, and the second oldest looking, replied, "Yeah we have tons of questions. You really didn't give us much to go on, other than to say you expected our opposition was to consist of three men and a woman and that none were to be killed if at all possible. What kind of home are they going to be in? Bi-level? Ranch? Is there a basement? What kind of neighborhood are we going to be fighting in? "

The Bostonian, Zeke, who had a fine thick head of black hair, which set off a pair of inquisitive blue eyes spoke before Will had a chance to answer any of Abe's questions. "An' what kind of weaponry will they have? Pistols like the othah fellahs?"

"What about the demon?" Jake added, causing all the men to nod in agreement. "The bishop said there was a demon. What do we do about that?"

The fourth man added nothing; he was a dark haired Hispanic. His code name was Timothy, which in no way jibed with his coal black eyes that bored into Will; those hard eyes made the big man a trifle uncomfortable—Will tried not to look him as he spoke, "First, I don't know what kind of guns they'll have. Pistols probably. Secondly, the house is a ranch, it doesn't have a basement, and the closest neighbor is at least a half of a mile away. It borders on the Sonoran desert, which has some sand dunes, but is mostly hard baked and craggy. The house is shaped...like a capital T."

"But what about the demon?" Jake persisted. "What do we do about it?"

"Hold on, just a second," Will paused, wondering how to proceed. He hadn't thought about what would happen if the demon was there already. It would be chaos that was for sure. "If the demon is already there, you shoot to kill, everyone but the woman. Don't hesitate, just start shooting."

"But what about the demon?" Jake asked again.

"The demon? I wouldn't bother shooting at it. There will be a big column of black smoke, but that is just some weird effect. The demon will actually not be there at all; it will still be in hell. The smoke only marks where the gate to hell is."

Their guns would be useless and that meant someone would have to challenge the fiend, and that someone would likely have to be himself. Forgetting briefly about his sister, Will sat down again, feeling far older than his twenty-five years. Could he go against the demon again? Doubt struck him heavily, making his insides quiver uncomfortably and instead of seeing his past victories as a sign that he had a chance that he could win yet again, he saw instead that Talitha wasn't the only one cursed. Depression tried to sinks its ugly teeth into him, but he gave a shake to his head. "You know I could be wrong about shooting it. It won't hurt to try. But I do know that everyone will need to be baptized again and Father Vogel will need to hear your confessions. Father Vogel... do you have everything that you need? The proper vestments? Oil of Chrism?"

"I have everything I need, Will," the priest responded in a vague manner from four rows away. Just then he was kneeling in the aisle, praying over Lisa.

"The four of us have been to Mass this morning and have already confessed..." Abe began, but was interrupted by Jake who elbowed the man in the side.

"Yeah, there's nothing like confessing to a bishop! You should have seen Zeke coming out of the confessional. His ears were so red, I could've lit a cigarette on them." The four laughed easily again, yet Will couldn't find it in him to do more than crack a lopsided smile.

Will nodded. "Ok then, good. So if the demon's there, and trust me there will be no doubt in the matter if he is, then the men Amy has with her have to die. And they have to die quick. The witch will have to die as well, but she just can't be shot. You have to take her hand and the hand of...her victim." He had to pause as he felt his throat tighten up. "There will be a girl there...uh, blonde and cute. She's gonna look asleep or maybe even dead." A second time he had to stop for a moment to collect himself. "Someone will have to tie the Father's stole around her hand and that of the witch's hand and only then can you kill her. I hope that I will be the one to do it, but if I can't, then one of you will have to. And if you do, there'll be a moment where you're going to be between two worlds. Our world and hell. You have to call to Katie, the blonde girl I mean. Call her and bring her out."

"When you say witch, what do you mean exactly?" Abe

asked running his hands through his thinning blonde/grey hair. "A real witch? Despite how worked up Bishop Keenan was, I'm having trouble accepting much of this." The others murmured in agreement.

"The woman who has the sword is for real, though I'm not quite sure what sort of spells she can work. She did that." Will pointed to his wife. "It's not a coma. There's nothing physically wrong with her at all, only she can't wake up. Amy did something to her."

"What are you going to do if Amy has used the sword instead of a spell, huh?"

Will jumped. Everyone jumped. While their attention had been on Lisa, Talitha had come slipping up the aisle, silent on her still bear feet. Will turned and a wave of goose bumps broke out all over. She was right behind him. Her hand came down on his broad shoulder and gripped the trapezious muscle that sloped off his neck. It was a hard grip that brought with it a sense of vulnerability; she could kill him if she wished.

Her warm brown eyes were in a state of flux and her smile was simultaneously knowing and confused. She knew she could kill him as well, only it appeared that she didn't know if she wanted to or not. This ambiguity, coupled with his clear defenselessness sent a shiver down Will's back and it broadened her smile. However, the confusion in her eyes deepened and she walked her odd smile further up the plane, exposing her back to her brother and the four men. They had fallen silent at the sudden appearance of his sister and each had tensed. The unit had been briefed on Talitha. And in an effort to instill in them a proper respect for her abilities, Will had shown them the bodies of the four thugs she had killed. Seeing them piled like a slop of human spaghetti caused some eyes to widen.

Talitha went a little further and stood staring down at her sister-in-law. "I don't know whether to be sad for her or happy." She looked back at her brother shaking her head.

"Lisa gets to sleep through all of this. It almost doesn't seem fair. We take all the risks and if we prevail against Amy, then she gets to wake up all perky, like a pregnant Rip Van Winkle. But if we fail...we die horribly and she sleeps right through it."

Beneath the thrum of the jets, there was a silence in the cabin at this.

"I'm not kidding," she continued when no one spoke up. "I don't know what I'm supposed to be feeling right now. What about you guys? Is there a consensus concerning this?"

Father Vogel looked up at her from where he had been kneeling. "Talitha, you don't have to feel one way or the other. I feel a little of both."

Will nodded at this, but Talitha frowned, the corners of her full lips edging far down. "That's silly...and wishy-washy and stupid. Shouldn't you have to pick one? Sad or happy...it's only two choices. It should be just like yes or no? White or black? Is it better like this or like this?" Behind her eyes, thunderstorms began to swirl. Will fought to remain calm; a small jet, six miles in the air was no place for a battle. She continued growing louder, practically screaming. "These aren't tough choices you know. Either you're happy for her or sad. It's just stupid thinking you can be both. You can't be happily-sad or sadly-happy. Damn it! What the hell's wrong with you people?"

She was in a bizarre rage and tramped back down the aisle knocking into the men with sharp aggressiveness, looking for one of them to react.

"Maybe I should go talk to her," Vogel suggested in the middle of the embarrassed silence that had followed Talitha's tirade.

"You'll keep your ass down at that end of the plane, if you know what's good for you," the girl yelled. Will gave the priest a little shrug and started to get up. "You too, Will. I don't need your ugly face making me sick, thank you. If you're going to send anyone, send that hunky dude with the blue eyes instead."

Everyone looked at Zeke, who didn't budge. "Should I go?" he asked Will in a whisper.

"No..." Will started.

"Yes!"

"No, stay here," Will insisted, putting his hand on Zeke's arm. Talitha had been standing with her hands squarely on her slim hips, but at this, she flopped into her seat and looked out the window with a sulking air.

After a moment, Abe spoke quietly, "Your sister brought up a good point about the sword. What do we do if the demon has come through already? I mean it'll be different than with the spell, right? From what you say, the spell opens a gate and it only looks like the demon will be there, but if she's used the sword that means it'll actually be there, correct? And if so, then what?"

The question wasn't hypothetical. After his father had stabbed the sword into the gate, thinking he was actually attacking the demon, the sword had a nasty feel to it. Yet that was nothing compared to how it felt after Will had used it to kill Henny Harris. It had grown far colder and there was a voracious sucking feeling to it now. In Will's opinion, it wouldn't take too many more deaths to create an opening in it large enough for something to come through. And who knows what would happen then.

Will shrugged. "I don't know what we do. Run away maybe?"

The men were silent on this suggestion and each looked to be considering their own ideas of what would happen. Will checked his watch; they were landing in two hours. Sidling up to Father Vogel, he squatted down and asked in a hushed voice, "What do you think? What do we do if the demon is actually there? Not just the opening to the Void, but the real thing?"

Vogel sent his fading grey eyes into Will's blue ones and stared. "We don't run from it that's for certain. We fight it. That's what these men are here for. That's what I'm here for."

With an effort, Will stopped himself from rolling his eyes; the priest had no clue what he was talking about. Will had seen the thing down in the Void and just recalling the horrendous sight gave him the chills. "With what? What do we have that can fight the demon?" Fear tended to make him snappish.

"With courage. With faith in the Lord..." Will's loud groan interrupted the priest. Vogel didn't get upset however. "These are the tools that God has given us, Will. They'll be enough. You of all people should know this. You have been given gifts from the Lord and..."

"Gifts? You call what I have a gift? What about Tal? Is she gifted too? How bout Lisa? Is her eternal sleep some sort of gift as well?" Will made to get up, but the smaller man grabbed his left hand, not knowing that Will's fingers had been recently dislocated. Immediate pain shot up Will's arm and he grimaced. The priest seemed not to notice.

"Yes. Clearly you don't understand the gifts that..."

Angrily, Will jumped in. "You can't mean my visions. It's you who doesn't understand; that was part of the gypsy's curse..."

"No, I don't mean that either," the priest replied in the most calm attitude. Will was thoroughly perplexed and Vogel smiled. "The Lord has spoken through you. Remember what you told the bishop and me? You told us what occurred when you were in the Void. In order to deny Ba'al Zubel the body of your sister, the power of the Word of the Lord came from your lips. These lips right here." Vogel touched Will on the lips and he was too stunned to react and actually blushed. "And the lord has given you the power to cast out demons. Last night you cast out Ba'al Fie-ere from your sister with nothing but simple words. And then there's your dreams that you take from Talitha."

"That's no gift. That's pure and literal torture."

Vogel shook his head. "Really? I would think it was a wondrous blessing...for your sister. You don't see these things as blessing, but I do. It can't be any more obvious to me that God has blessed your sister by having you as her brother." Will made to argue this but no words came from his open mouth and Vogel went on, "And you can't deny that the Lord has touched you personally."

Will had to suddenly blink back tears. "But I don't want this. I want to be normal and live a normal life."

"That's your choice. All along you've had the option to walk away. To pass the cup from your lips. And you still can. When we land in Phoenix, the pilot will take you anywhere you want. You just have to ask."

Will closed his eyes and breathed out heavily. That would never happen. He was burdened by too much responsibility. Who would find a way to cure Lisa, or save Katie and his parents? And who else but him could control Talitha? Certainly not the priest, nor the soldiers, despite their training. And who among them could challenge the demon?

"You know I can't walk away from this."

"Yes and neither can we." Vogel indicated the other men and Will was surprised and quite embarrassed to see that the four men had been listening in on their conversation. He didn't like the looks they were giving him. They reminded him too much of the look that Father John Santos had worn minutes before he had died in Will's place. Like he was special or extraordinary. At the moment, he felt far from that. He felt tired and had a headache.

Abe spoke up, "Since we aren't going to run, it only leaves one choice; fight. We just need to know how. Will your visions tell us?"

"No. Amy...the witch, has discovered a way to block them."

Vogel spoke up with some excitement, "She used an odd looking necklace to keep him from seeing what was going on back at the house in Bangor. It had leaves and little metal dangling things hanging from it, so if you see someone with anything that looks like that, you should...uh...you know."

"We'll take care of him," Abe filled in the blank in a nice manner. "What about your sister? She was supposedly stuck in hell for all that time. I bet she knows how to deal with a demon."

Will had no clue whether Talitha would know and he was just opening his mouth to say exactly that, but Vogel stepped in, "It's too risky a subject. It might bring out her own demon."

"You mean the one that he," Jake pointed at Will, "supposedly exorcized out of the girl?"

"Yes, but it's complicated."

"I'm sure it is, Father." Jake wore an on odd expression. "All the same, the bishop, and you, and this guy here." Jake again pointed at Will. "You all think she's dangerous. Now I don't know anything about exorcisms except what I see in the movies, but if she's still so dangerous why are we bringing her along? Especially if we can't even ask her a few questions? What good is she?"

"Jake's right. I'll go talk to her," Will said, coming to a quick decision. Judging by the look on his face, Vogel wasn't happy. "Father, please. Don't give me that look. You've tried the hypno-therapy, it didn't work and we're running out of time and options." Will started to go up the aisle and just then Jake tugged at his shirt.

"Just in case?" He held out a large black pistol. Very much Will was tempted to take the gun, only he didn't think he'd be able to pull the trigger if push came to shove. Not the least reason for this was the fact that they were traveling at six-hundred miles an hour in a relatively small plane. A missed shot could realistically bring it tumbling down out of the sky.

"No thanks, but if anything happens to me, don't

hesitate. Shoot for the abdomen. It'll stop her without killing her." Jake gave him a skeptical look and Will shrugged. "She heals fast."

"Sure center mass, no problem. Tell me, she do all that to your face?"

Will had avoided looking into mirrors all day. As an answer, he gave Jake his swollen, lopsided smile and went to the back of the plane. Talitha sat jiggling her legs up and down in a fury of speed.

"Just go away, Will." She hadn't turned around. "I don't know anything helpful."

"I didn't think you did." Will came and sat down across from her. It was a dangerous spot since he would have precious little time to react if she went crazy or rather if she went semi-demonic. Only he was tired and part of him just didn't care. "That came out wrong. You know lots. We both know that. It's just I doubt that you know how a demon from the Void would react on this world. The physical world I mean."

"Yep, I don't know." Talitha kept her face down. "Will? Why do you like me? And don't say it's because I'm your sister." That was exactly what he had been planning on saying. It was the standard answer to a question like that. Her eyes came up and bored into his. "I want you to really think on this. What about me was worth all the pain you've gone through?"

This was an embarrassing time for his brain to draw a blank, yet that was what happened exactly. Everything he came up with sounded lame in his mind and before he could come up with a good reason, she asked another question which had his mind turning in a different direction.

"Did I ever tell you how I escaped from the asylum?"

"Yeah." And he didn't really want to hear it again. He wondered what this had to do with her previous question, which he had still to answer.

"Then why do you still like me? I wouldn't like me. In

fact I don't like me...I don't. I really and truly don't. That's why I'm wondering, why do you bother?"

She began crying softly. Her eyes were just turning red, her lips were a little puffy, and with her pretty sundress and bare feet, the overall effect was that she looked like a little kid. She looked like the kid he had grown up with. The one that was a pain in the butt and hung around him when he wanted to be alone to smooch his girlfriend. The little kid who always seemed so smart, that it made him feel stupid every time he opened his mouth. The one who got the front seat on every car ride and the better gifts on Christmas. He loved that girl and he couldn't explain why. He just did.

"I'll tell you why. I was in the first grade and you were in kindergarten, this was back before you and I were in the same class..."

"You don't have to tell me a story, Will. I can control my thinking now. It's my emotions that are getting the better of me."

"You asked why I bother and I'm telling you, so hush." She snorted in a most un-lady like manner and wiped the back of her hand across her nose. With this small display, even more she was that little girl. "This isn't a long story, only a memory. I remember coming home from school and you had raked this pile of leaves into a great mound. You were so tiny back then, that the mound was piled higher than your head. You had worked all afternoon on making that pile and then instead of jumping in it like a normal kid, you waited for me to come home and gave me the first crack at it. We had so much fun jumping in the pile and then re-raking it back up. Even to this day, I can still smell those leaves when I think about it."

"I don't remember that. I'm so stupid. I can tell you the name of every man who has served as Vice President of the United States, but I can't remember jumping into a pile of leaves with my brother." Her tears that were a light trickle came in a gush now. "I've wasted my life! Why did I do that?

Why? And now..."

"And now, what?" Will coaxed.

Talitha only made a growling sound of frustration and got up to pace. "You already know what. I'm going back to the Void, and I don't want to hear it from you. No more why, why, why! Fuckin A! No more why."

"Fuckin A?" For some reason he found that humorous and began to chuckle. "Since when do you curse, Miss *I can control my thinking*?"

"I've explained to you that it's my emotions I can't seem to get a grip on. You should try listening."

"Have you tried meditating? It worked for you in the Void," he replied reasonably. "It might also help with your thinking. You're not in control like you say. Just a few minutes ago, you were asking hunky Zeke to come down here. Remember? That doesn't sound like the Talitha I know."

"Yeah well that Talitha is dull. She never had any fun. When was the last time she jumped in a pile of leaves?" Will's brows came down and he began to think back, but Talitha paced up to him and put her hand on his shoulder. "It was a rhetorical question, Will. And yes, I've tried meditating and all I get are new memories. Real special ones too: me killing some guy, me setting a house on fire, me fuc..." she broke off quick.

Despite an effort to not react, Will felt his eyebrows pop up. "Uh...that's why you should be talking to Father Vogel. The therapy should be able you to help redirect your memories..."

"No," Talitha interrupted plopping back down in her seat. "I have to deal with the demon in me in my own way. Suppressing or avoiding will only put that off and I don't have much time."

"Wait. First off, there's no demon in you it's all just neural paths and a personality disorder."

Talitha shook her head. "Yes, but the end effect is no

different. When I become the other Talitha, when I use the neural paths that she created to form her personality, can you tell the difference?" Will's mouth came open uselessly. "By your look, you clearly cannot and no one could. I could go down into the Void and they wouldn't know either. We are the same. Ba'al Fie-ere and I are the same."

"Have you tried praying on this? You used to pray quite a bit."

"Praying is for people with hope and what's more, I'm out of time for prayer."

Will sighed. "You're being obstinate. First off, prayer gives a person hope. It's not the other way around. And second, there's always time to pray."

"According to you there isn't. I wasn't in either of your visions. Can you think of any reason I would miss the birth of your baby girl? Because I can only think of one: I'm going to die soon. And why should I pray? God has blessed me already. He gave me you, my own personal savior." She let a small, sly smile creep onto her face and Will felt his cheeks go red.

"You heard that, huh? What a bunch of malarkey, Father Vogel doesn't know what he's talking about."

Talitha stared again out of the small square of a window. Beyond the blinking light on the tip of the wing, everything was black. "I don't know, Will. You've been blessed. It's undeniable. But as much as I appreciate all that you've done for me, I can't help to think that I haven't been. I don't see anything that has occurred as a blessing. Yes, you saved me from the Void, but my judgment day has only been put off a while longer."

"I've told you that God doesn't judge."

"And you may be correct about God, but what about everyone else? All the angels and saints? What about all of my victims?" Will could see her eyes start to cloud up again, she swiped at them with the back of her hand. "They'll judge. I know it."

"And I will judge you too, Tal. And I'll tell everyone what a wonderful person you are."

"No you won't. You have no idea. Of everyone, you'll be the last to do something like that." She gave him a smile that dripped with agony. "But who knows? Maybe I'm wrong. Having witnessed the miracle of you using a word like obstinate, I now think anything is possible." The pain emanating from her was too palpable to even smile at her little joke. "Will, I think I need to be alone for a while. When I said I could control my mental state, I meant that I could control it for a little while. I think we're heading into more trouble than you realize and I need to be able to set my other side loose and then maybe get it back bottled up again."

Something was odd about his sister. Momentarily, her affect had changed from angry and fearful to something else. Embarrassment, or shame perhaps. He couldn't tell. There had been something in her eyes and he paused, staring at her, trying to fathom a sudden puzzlement within him, but she blushed and looked down.

"Do you want to me to control my personalities or not?" Talitha asked, still keeping her eyes averted. "If so, I'm going to need some time alone."

Before he got up and moved to the front of the plane, he smiled at her, warm and friendly. It was a dishonest smile however, one that was full of lies—just like her words had been. He *knew* it. She had lied to him about controlling her personality. But why?

Chapter 18

Talitha

Talitha felt the excitement building in her chest and it was with the greatest effort that she put a lid on it. Though it didn't quite work—a part of her was eager and the car ride couldn't go fast enough for her liking.

"You should be the one driving, Will," she commented. Her brother could drive like a bat out of hell when he needed to...or when he was forced to. She could make him drive. There was that option. The idea just popped into her head, fully formed, complete with visuals of her using her right elbow to crush...

"Stop it!" she hissed the words under her breath. Only she couldn't stop it. There was a part of her that was beyond her ability, or in fact, beyond her desire to control anymore. Her other personality, her other self...soon to be her only self had begun to lust for the pain that they each knew was coming. The four gangbangers back in Maine had all died far too quickly. It wasn't their fault, she blamed herself and her brother. His was supposed to have been the slow death, only he had started in with his dull stories and she had quite forgotten herself. Next time...

"Abe, can you please roll down the window?" she asked with a hint of desperation. "I need some air." In the back seat of a Ford Taurus, Talitha rode sandwiched between the leader of the unit and her brother.

The slim soldier gave her a long look as if unsure of her motives before replying with a tight smile, "Sure thing, Miss Jern." Without taking his eyes from her, he rolled down the window.

The desert air helped. It flowed over her open senses and she breathed in a thousand fragrances. There was more to the barren wasteland that most people realized, and she could smell the many animals hiding in and around the scrub. Even the scant vegetation was more varied than it appeared and in minutes she categorized thirteen native plants, though she knew not their names. And then there were the people. They were out there. Or perhaps they had been. She caught traces of human aromas: sweat, musk, sex, blood.

"Do you mind?" Abraham asked practically in her ear. Only then did she notice that she had leaned over to get closer to the window and was almost in his lap. He wore a strained look.

"Oh, sorry." Talitha retreated back to the middle and now her leg began jiggling again. Faster and faster, and she let it go. To try to stop it would be to have to deal with the reasons why it was going in the first place: fear and excitement. Though it was mostly excitement, there was so much blood to be had. She had been born in blood. There was so many screams to pull from so many throats. She had been born to the sound of screams. Misery was her reason for existence...her purpose. Pain was pleasure, and cruelty, her love.

"Are we almost there yet?" She began to rock in her seat. Earlier, at the hospital, it had felt as if someone had been watching her. A stranger creeping around corners to spy on what she was doing, how she was acting. Then at the house, it felt like someone was always right behind her, trying to glance over her shoulder. But now that someone was in her, trying to see with her eyes and trying to use her hands for itself. She felt like a girl crossing an iced over pond. Every step brought more and more cracks which zigzagged away. Beneath her, under that thin ice, the water was dread black and deep and oh so cold. And the ice grew thinner with each step onwards. And *she* was there under the ice, waiting.

"We'll be there in fifteen minutes. Are you ok?" Her

brother peered his battered face at her. She had done that to him. It had been skillfully done, especially considering she had worked in complete darkness, striking blindly with nothing but the sound of his breathing to hone in on. It made her smile. She fought against the smile.

"No. I'm...nervous, about what we're going to find out at mom and dad's house." This was true, but also there was an undercurrent of the fear of death. In a manner of speaking she wasn't really afraid to die, she was just afraid to die still as Talitha—as herself.

"Me too," her brother replied evenly. His tone was calm yet his blue eyes held plenty of fear. A part of her was bothered to see him so afraid, mainly because of the way it affected her. It fed into her anticipation and she felt a little zing down low between her legs, involuntarily she rubbed herself against the seat cushion. Embarrassed, she turned away to look across Abe at the night speeding by, and wished again that she was riding with the priest. Father Vogel never seemed to show even the slightest fear. Excitement, yes, plenty of excitement, but not fear.

"Does Father Vogel remind you of dad at all? The way he seems so fearless?" Talitha asked, feeling a sudden sense of loss. It had been a few years since she last had seen her father.

For the first time since they had slid into the back of the car, Will took his eyes from his sister and glanced into the cooling desert. "No. Dad was...you can't even compare the two. First off, dad knew what he was fighting against and he still went after the demon. And when he was in the Coast Guard, he didn't just know the risks, he lived the risks. He had men swept overboard during storms, he saw helicopters crash and planes ditch in icy waters, but still he always went out. You ever see dad hesitate for a second?"

She hadn't. "You're right about dad, but Father Vogel is an exorcist and he says he has gone up against two demons. That's pretty brave."

"I'm sure it was and I'm not calling him shy. I'm just saying he's not in dad's league when it comes to bravery."

"I miss dad," Talitha said, feeling an unexpected need to cry. "I miss mom too, but right now I need dad to tell me that everything will work out. I want him to say in that big voice of his, *don't worry, Tal honey. I'll take care of this silly witch that's been bothering you.* You know he was the only one that I didn't..." The tears that had been threatening, fled as she bit back the horrible words that had almost come tumbling out of her mouth.

Talitha's eyes darted to her brother and her breath caught in her throat. He was peering at her with sharp intensity and his blue eyes were like drills, driving into her head, searching for her dreadful secrets. She turned away and looked across Abe toward the window yet she didn't see the desert night. She felt her brother's eyes still on her and the air from his nostrils blew across her thick dark hair. He wouldn't stop staring.

Will had powers, and she wondered, fearfully, if he could see into her memories.

Just then, she felt that someone else was looking too. That someone was looking at her secrets, looking at her crimes. Suddenly her mind opened up so that she could see herself, whipped bloody standing in the blackest dungeons, surrounded by horrible gibbering creatures. All their eyes were insane with a lust that hurt her to see. They cried out to her, urging her on. *Hit him, hit him!* They jeered and chanted, yet she didn't raise the whip that she held in her own hands. As she hesitated, a crack sounded across her back and she fell to the floor crying out from the pain.

Ba'al Zubel was there. He was tremendous and horrid. An ill wind, rank beyond the vilest sewer or the greediest charnel house, swept forward wherever he turned his gaze and just then, it was upon Talitha. The demon raised his whip again and she flinched and trembled in fear. Her whip was nothing compared to his. Hers looked more like a buggy whip than anything that could be considered torturous, while his was heavy and branched into three barbed and metal bound heads. Each was sharp and glistened with her blood. Straggles of her flesh hung upon the barbs and the pain it caused was like fire and acid. The fiend Ba'al drew back the whip, further.

It would fall upon her again, just as it had already to a number that was beyond count. Yet she could make it stop, if she wished. Her agony could end. All she had to do to stop the pain was to use the whip. It was very simple. Bring it back and let it fly. She had done it before.

"No!"

Talitha forced the memory away and that feeling of being watched and controlled from the inside, diminished. She saw that Abe stared at her quizzically and she realized she had spoken aloud. "Sorry. I uh, was just thinking of something." In response to her embarrassment, the capillaries in her cheeks dilated and her cheeks flushed a pretty pink.

Quickly she glanced away and saw lights in the distance far down a long sloping hill. On the south side of the road, there were a smattering of them, well spaced, some as much as a mile from their nearest neighbor. On the north side, a single light shown well away from the rest. Her brother pointed at it.

"We're down on the right. You can just see it now." For half a minute, he stared at the lights and then with a long tired sigh he faced his sister. "Really, are you going to be ok? You seem so...on the edge." She didn't answer him right away. Her death was down that hill. *It will be tonight*. Her mouth went dry at the thought and she swallowed and stared at the innocent twinkling lights with growing dread. Will took her hesitation to mean that she wasn't going to answer, "Tal, hey? Will I be able to count on you? Are you going to be able to control yourself?"

Her voice was a little thing, "Yes." She would keep

herself under control until the timing was right. That was her biggest fear; that the timing would be off. "I'll be ok, only I don't think it would be advisable for me to be too involved in death. In light of...you know."

"I know." Will's face turned sour in the dim light. "I'm scared for you, Tal. I thought after last night, you'd be ok. But it's like the demon never left you."

She felt the presence in her mind flare up and it stared through her eyes. It made her world feel hazy and out of sorts. She had to blink a few times before her vision cleared. "There's no demon in me, but it doesn't mean I'll be ok."

"I get it. Can you please do me a favor? If we get out of this ok, will you at least try the hypno-therapy?"

To lie was a sin, but it was a sin that she could live with or more accurately, it was a sin she could die with. "I will. You should consider turning off your headlights, soon or they'll see you coming from miles away." This she added just to change the subject.

Will nodded. "Zeke, in about a mile there'll be a road heading off to your left. When you get to it slow down and turn off your headlights."

Zeke flashed his eyes to the rearview mirror and gave a little nod. Beside Talitha, Abe blew out a long breath and sat up straighter. Everyone became more tense and the silence of the next couple of minutes grew heavier than it had been. At the junction, Zeke slowed and flicked off his lights. Behind them, the glare of the following car disappeared and now the two-car parade traveled on slower. Yet still the lonely looking house on the right seemed to come closer faster than Talitha wanted. The closer they came to it, the harder her heart beat and she had to actively work to keep it at its normal thirty beats a minute.

When they were half a mile away the road sank into a trough and Will spoke up, "Ok, this is good. Pull over, Zeke." Little was said for the next few minutes as the soldiers piled out of the cars and checked their weapons.

Will went back to the other car to look in on Lisa while Talitha stared up at the stars. She loved the stars and already she began to miss them. A part of her hoped to see a shooting star and if she did, she would wish upon it just as she and Will had done on so many nights in their youth. As they stood there, a wind sprang up and blew her hair back.

"A strong wind, that's a good sign," Zeke said with a nervous smile.

For some reason this bothered Talitha. "Is the wind a sign from God? Or is it just a phenomenon derived from the unequal heating of the earth's surface?"

Zeke's brows came down and his eyes showed a touch of anger, but his leader stepped in between the two quickly. Abe gave her a tight little smile and had his hands out as if to make peace. "We're just happy for it, because it will mask the sound of our guns. See those houses way down there? Because of the hills and the wind, they won't hear a thing."

Talitha knew this. She knew how far the sound of gunshots carried, just like she knew how far screams would carry and she didn't need to be told this by some stupid grunt. "Whatever," she replied and was about to turn away when she saw the hands that Abe held out to her shook a little. She also saw Zeke swallowing, like he was about to be sick. Jake was working the bolt of his CAR 15 back and forth as if it were a compulsion and Timothy sweated in the cool night and darted his black eyes all over the landscape.

They were anxious, if not downright afraid. The stranger within her surged at the knowledge and she wanted to scoff at them and spit in their faces. An unholy malevolent smile split her face wide and showed all her hungry teeth. She was so close that she could kill them all in seconds and the first that would die would be Zeke. She would send those pretty blue eyes of his deep into his skull and then...

A light, like a line in the sky, etched in a blaze across the heavens. It was there and gone again in a fraction of a second and it stopped her breath in her throat. A shooting star. The thing inside of her seemed to retreat from the sight and her mind was her own again. It was her turn to shake.

"Tal."

She jumped at her name, her body momentarily out of control. With a feeling of intense guilt she looked back to see her brother right next to her.

"Are you still ok?" He gave her an inquisitive look and it helped her mind to see that he wasn't nervous. He had his game face on and his eyes were the color of steel.

"I'm...good."

"Great. I need you to do a spot of reconnaissance. We need to know if it's really just Amy and three goons, got it?"

She nodded, but Abe stepped forward. "I want to send Jake with her. He has tons experience at this sort of thing."

It was an idea. She could bring Jake and leave his body in one of the fissures that had been ripped into the land by the hand of God...

"No. He won't be able to keep up, sorry but all he'll do is slow me down." *And piss me off, and die with my fist in his chest*, these words she bit back. Her hands clenched with such force that her nails dug into her palms. She had to hold on for only a while longer.

"No offence, but I think we need to keep an eye on you." Despite being far older and the actual leader of the unit, Abe looked to Will for a reply.

"No, she goes alone." The men of the unit grumbled in silence sending angry looks back and forth between themselves. Will ignored them. "Just circle the place at a distance and find out what you can. Don't try to go in; your other personality is too unstable." With a sudden move, Will sent his arms out to grab her and she was within a twitch of crushing his sternum, when she realized that he was just going to give her a hug. She felt like a cat being hugged by a wolf and it was all she could do to let it happen. "Good luck," he whispered.

"Thanks." For a moment, she was too much in shock to

do much more than look at her brother. It felt like a lifetime since she had been hugged by him. It was odd. He nodded at her as way of telling her to get going and she didn't need a second invite. She ran off into the desert, happy to be away from them. Her emotions were all over the place and having to deal with Will and the unit was making it very difficult to concentrate on being herself.

The night helped. Talitha stretched out her stride, feeling better as the air flowed over and around her and in seconds, she was a hundred yards away and virtually invisible. The moon would be almost full when it rose for the evening, but that was an hour from happening and without it, the night was a dark one. Had she been anyone else, she would have stumbled a dozen times already. The land was hard baked and rugged, filled with sudden drops and sharp rocks, cacti and low thorny shrubs. Her bare feet flew by all this with nary a twinge. Though Maine was a far more gentle state, it had been years since she wore shoes to run through the woods, something that she dearly loved to do. On these runs, clothing was generally disregarded, but she kept hers on that night.

After a minute, she slowed and crossed the road to keep it between her and her parent's house. The two-lane black asphalt was too close and anyone with any sense would have posted at least a lookout facing in the direction of the road. She moved away from it, giving herself plenty of room and as she drew closer to the house, she began dodging from shrub to shrub, until she found a good vantage. To all appearances, the ranch home looked empty, it was early in the evening, yet no lights burned within it and no noise could be heard, even by Talitha.

However, she wasn't in the least way fooled. She knelt peering through a heavy bush and within a minute her eagle like eyes picked out movement in two areas of the house. There were more of them than that, only the wind that the soldiers were so happy about was playing havoc with her sense of smell. She ducked low and scurried a hundred yards further on. Here the wind ran over the house and blew directly in her face. It took a few minutes of studied breathing to pick out the scents of at least nine people for certain in the house, and one maybe.

Two were her parents and seven were unknown males, but the last, the scent of Katie was harder to judge. Her aroma came at Talitha, but though it was strong, it should've been stronger, like that of her parents. Of course, there was a chance that Katie was locked away, or perhaps hiding, or maybe buried nearby. Amazingly, Talitha had to stop and think about how she felt about the idea that her little sister could be dead.

"That's bad...or is it sad?" she asked the mute night sky. It should be both, she decided. "But why? Am I sad for her or for me?" This was harder to answer. Both were based on emotion and that was one thing that was slipping right away from her.

"You are sad because we didn't get to kill her."

With a start, Talitha spun around fully expecting to see someone behind her, but there was nothing but endless desert. Still, she stared about, feeling as if there was someone right there. "It's all in your head!" This she hissed at herself in anger. Saying the words helped. "It's all in your head," she repeated and took off in a low sprint heading further out to the west of the house. It was all in her head, for now. But too soon that wouldn't be the case. The other Talitha was coming and this one, the one who used to be so sweet was doing all she could to hold her back, again, for now.

The far west side of the house was taken up by a large pantry, a laundry room, and the three-car garage. Talitha had to scramble slowly along the slope of a hill eighty yards from the house to keep it in view, but it paid off as she saw a face framed in one of the glass panes of the garage door. It was a man's face and though she saw him clearly, she was invisible to him as she moved on to the back of the house stealthy as a cat. Here was the length of the T, it held the four bedrooms and at the first angle, she saw another two men peering from windows. Two more men were situated in a couple of different rooms facing out of the next angle, this held a wide deck that sat with a scattering of furniture upon it.

A long few minutes went by as Talitha paused to see if anyone else would show themselves and when they didn't, she dashed off for where she had left her brother. She didn't get far; unexpectedly she came upon a new scent and a large grouping of unsullied tracks. In a flash, Talitha was down on her knees sniffing at the ground. Katie had come by here, but she wasn't alone. Amy and seven or eight men had trouped along with her, heading in a northeast direction.

A long time Talitha considered where they went and why. As she did, standing staring out along the tracks, her pretty face turned into a harsh mask of anger. Amy had her sister! What a waste of a fine virgin! Useless moronic Amy was going to call the demon and knowing her, she would just screw it up. Talitha fumed in silence and had even began to sprint down the trail of footprints when another shooting star zipped by low in the horizon.

"Oh God." Talitha stopped in a daze and her hand went to her head. "It's too soon damn it." She couldn't make the change just yet. Instead, she tore off, flashing across the desert in a dead sprint crossing the half-mile of broken land in a minute and a half.

"Will!" her call had her brother scurrying from the second car and in a moment she was surrounded by men, Father Vogel among them. She gave them the layout of the house as well as the dispersion of Amy's thugs and the entire time she kept her eyes down, not daring to look into Will's or the priest's faces.

"How old was Katie's trail, could you tell?" her brother asked.

"A half an hour at least but likely closer to an hour. They could be four miles away by now."

And I'm the only one who has any chance of getting there before it's too late, before Amy goes and fucks this up. What I wouldn't give to have Katie for myself. I would force Ba'al to set me up in hell right. I would make the Void my kingdom!

The thought staggered her and she forced her face into a mask that she hoped would convey some sort of neutral look instead of the intense shame that she felt.

"An hour's a long time. Maybe Zeke and I should go with Talitha and..." Will began, but Abraham cut him off.

"No. We can't afford to split up. The layout of the home and the disposition of the bad guys, makes me worried. They'll have overlapping fields of fire no matter what direction we take. Either we all go after Amy or we all attack the house, but we don't divide our forces in the face of a superior force. That's just basic."

"I say, while we take on the guys at the house, the girl goes alone after Amy and gets a rundown on that sitch and then reports back. She wouldn't be any good otherwise, it's not like we're gonna give her a gun or anything," Jake offered.

This was exactly what Talitha wanted and it brought a thrill running down her back that she couldn't seem to stop.

Will had his eyes down to the compacted dun-colored dirt. "Fine. That's the plan then. Talitha get going and hurry back." Talitha couldn't stop her eager feet, they started off even before Will finished speaking. He grabbed her and brought her around. "Look, if the demon isn't there, do what you can to take out Amy. Can I trust you with a gun?"

She pictured shooting her brother in the eye and watching with a smile as his brains exploded out the back of his head. Her face turned a dead pale that was visible despite the night and somehow, she was able to shake her head, no.

"I understand, I think," he paused seeming unsure of

himself. "Tal, it's going to be ok. You aren't going to the Void again. I won't let it happen. Do you hear me? Stay Talitha. Stay yourself. Don't change to the other girl, please." She nodded, but looked terribly unconvincing, which caused Will to have second thoughts. "Maybe you should..."

"No, I can't stay. If I waste any more time, Katie is doomed for sure. You take care of those bad guys and don't worry about me, I'm in control." The words were a shock to her own ears. They had come from her mouth, but she hadn't spoken them. And now it was Talitha that felt as if she was peering over someone else's shoulder. No! It's too early. She tried to scream this, but nothing left her lips.

Will nodded at the stranger and the stranger smiled in return, playing her part to perfection. A second later, she was racing off across the desert, sniffing the air. Talitha struggled to get control of her body back, but it was in vain and when the stranger stooped and found a round smooth rock that fit the palm of her hand so nicely. Talitha's thoughts began to dissipate beneath an avalanche of hate and malice. It felt as if she were drowning in a black evil and slowly she was being sucked under.

Chapter 19

Katie

For ages Katie laid there behind the couch with her hands stuffed in her ears, waiting for the horrible screams of her mother to creep through the cracks of her fingers, however, other than a few slaps, Amy and her thugs had left her alone. Eventually, Katie became bored and tried to listen in on the conversation of the Mexican thugs. Every ten minutes or so, the leader of the gang came around to check on Diablo and the man sitting in the family room. Pedro would usually give just a short pep talk but the thugs were nervous about Amy and the sword.

"Can you get that thing away from me?" Diablo asked in Spanish.

Pedro snorted, "I'm not touching it, and if you do, the White-witch will have your balls."

Were they talking about the sword? Was it still sitting up against the wall around the corner from her? Katie didn't like it there either—it gave her the creeps thinking it was so close.

The thug in her room asked, "How much longer we gotta stay?"

"We'll leave soon...I hope," Pedro replied. "When the witch finds the girl we take off."

The girl...they meant her! Was Amy using spells to find her? The very idea made Katie want to up and make a mad, stupid dash for the family room door. Only, that was impossible.

The thug in his chair sat eight feet from her, and wouldn't budge, not even to use the bathroom. She had to get out of there—the couch would not hide her from spells. When Pedro left again, Katie, moving with the stealth of a mouse, inched out from behind the couch and peeked into the living room and saw the top of a man's head in the chair just in front of her. Another man could be just seen standing in the deepening shadows of the kitchen.

Inwardly she cursed. Escape this way was even less likely than trying to rush past the man in the family room. She was just about to turn away when she felt the cold. It came from just to her left and turning, she saw the dread hell blade. The metal of it was black and burnt looking. Unwholesome. It repulsed her, she leaned away from it, and unknowingly her face contorted and turned pale. She wanted to creep back away from it, but a part of her realized that despite its ugly appearance, the thing was an actual weapon. One that was feared by the Mexicans as well as by Amy.

Reaching out her slim arm, she gently grabbed the sword and came very close to gasping. It was horrible. Worse than she could have imagined. It drained her arm of warmth and life. Her stomach began to churn and she wanted very badly to vomit. The blade was poison. It was death. Even so, she brought it around the corner with a cringing face and Katie's hand was near about frozen to the hilt. It hurt bad to hold, and it made her breath hitch in her throat. Very quickly, her entire body was trembling. She half slid, half-crawled back to the scant safety of her hiding place behind the couch. Once there, she set the sword down as gently as she could, so as not to make any noise and only then did she rub her hands together. Yet still she shivered. The broken hell blade had such a vicious cold to it that being so close sucked away her warmth and she began to fear that if she didn't do something, she would freeze to death.

She pushed it further under the couch, but that barely helped. In desperation, Katie slithered backwards to get as far from it as possible and saw to her delight, one of her sweatshirts she had tossed behind the couch only the day before. This she wrapped around the sword as best as she was able. It was a horror to touch, but once the cloth was between her and it the cold decreased rapidly.

Katie then laid back and went limp with relief. Going for the sword felt like the right thing to do, but it had also been terrifying and exhausting. Her hand still stung, except for where there was a numb swath that ran across her palm. She rubbed at it some more and worried that somehow the sword had tasted her and now knew her. It was a chilling thought and she scooted the sword bundled in the blue sweatshirt further from her.

A commotion from the other room reached her ears. There was a murmuring and then an odd sounding series of grunts.

Amy Harris walked into the family-room a second later. "Anything out there moving?" Although she was already snugged down into the shadows, Katie tried to borrow further under the couch. If it had been possible, she would have crawled beneath it completely, but as it was, with the room hung with growing darkness, she was quite invisible where she was. Now all she had to do was keep her teeth from chattering so loudly. In her fright, they clicked together going a hundred miles an hour, but she couldn't seem to control them, nor could she control her hands and arms and chest which shook as if an earthquake was going on within her.

Only when Amy left, breezing out of the room, did the young girl sag back onto the floor in relief. The relief lasted only a few minutes and then Amy screeched.

"Where's my sword?"

Suddenly the entire house seemed alive and people began running towards the living room. Katie didn't know what to do with herself. They would search the house for sure and it would only be a moment before they thought to look behind the couch. Grabbing the wrapped sword, she slithered to the far end of the couch and raised herself up just the tiniest amount. The man who had been sitting in the family room, stood in the doorway, he seemed very nervous, with wide eyes and hands that kept up a constant motion as if he didn't know exactly what to do with them.

Amy was screaming at her men, but Katie barely heard, she was too busy focusing on the door. It was just too far away to make a break for it with the man right there. Therefore she slunk down again, grabbed the sword and crawled across the far side of the room and came up behind the second couch and moved to the end nearest to the door. Now all she needed was two seconds and she could be out the door, booking like mad out into the Sonoran. She even knew where she'd go. There was a small trail that led...

"Diablo, let Mrs. Jern see your knife."

Katie's heart stopped, and try as she might, she couldn't breathe. It was as if her entire chest had seized up.

There was a grunt from the living room and then her mother's voice rang out, "Sure let's see that stupid knife, but don't get too close Amy. He's the one who has the sword."

"No. The beech es...lying. She es lying." Diablo sounded as if he couldn't make up his mind whether to be angry or afraid.

"Right. Why would I lie? What would I get out of it?" Gayle replied with a quivering voice. "He stuck it in the back of his pants and went out front. He doesn't look too smart to me; it's probably just in one of the cars." Katie realized her mother must have seen her grab the sword and was trying to get their attention focused away from the back door. Katie readied herself to make a run for it.

There was silence for a moment and then Amy said, "The real question is, why would you tell me the truth? Which I really doubt that you just did."

"Only because...I...I," Gayle was clearly trying to find a good lie and Amy wasn't in the mood to mess around.

"Diablo take off one her fingers. I don't care which."

"Good! Come on Diablo you stupid jerk!" Gayle screamed at him in a fear-warped fury. "Do what you want. I know which one of your men took..." She began to scream.

Tears ran down Katie's face but her mind was hard like a rock. She wouldn't waste what her mother was doing for her, she would run. Only she couldn't. As she peeked, she saw that the man who had been in the doorway had turned slightly away from the scene in the living room and was partially canted toward her.

Her mother's screams seemed to tear at her vocal cords but she was still able to wail, "It was Pedro! It was Pedro. He said he would free me!"

"Stop!" Amy shouted. Gayle's scream subsided into a blubbering and soulful weeping.

"She's lying. It wasn't me."

"It had to be one of you idiots! Pedro, give me your gun."

"But..."

"Now! You...Jin put your gun on the ground, Diablo, you too. Step over there and face the window." Katie cursed to herself again. They would be able to see her easily if she ran.

"One of you three took my sword. You were the only ones on this side of the house. Now did anyone see one of these three leave se?" There was silence. "So that means the sword is still in the house and that means I'm going to find..."

Katie ran.

If she had to guess, she figured they would start their search in the family room and work their way down the house and that meant she was out of time. Noiselessly, she dashed to the door, yanked back on the knob and tore out of the house. Without looking back, she sprinted across the deck and just then, a huge sharp sound that seemed more like an explosion than a gunshot erupted behind her and glass flew around her speeding feet. A second one followed the first but then there was only screaming as she hurtled the deck's three foot railing.

Cries of "Run!" from her mother were intermingled

with Amy shouting for the men not to shoot. The family room door crashed open a second later and the desert air was disturbed by the sound of heavy steps tromping across redwood boards.

Into the last of the evening light, Katie sprinted for all she was worth. Her legs pumped like mad and sandy dirt kicked up behind as she ran fast than she had ever in her life. At first she could hear them behind her gaining...gaining, but then after a few hundred yards, the sound of their feet drifter further and further back. A glance back showed there were four of them, running in a ragged line with their heads bent down low. They wouldn't be able to keep going much longer. But then neither could she. Her breath came in huge gasps and her feet started to weigh her down. No longer was she springing over the gullies with the athleticism of an antelope, instead she was down to a plodding jog.

Yet she was still faster than the out of shape bullies chasing her. With her lead over the men growing, she decided to alter her plans somewhat. Originally, she had meant to hide in the desert and loop far out before coming back to one of the homes a few miles away, where she would call the police. But now, with her huge lead, she saw she could make it to one of her closer neighbors.

At the next low rise she came across, Katie broke from her northeast route and turned sharp to the right and set off with all her dwindling strength for the road that looked like nothing more than a black stripe across the tired landscape. Past it, lights twinkled in the gathering dark. They looked closer than they actually were and five minutes of stumbling up and down ravines seemed to bring them no closer. The good news was that the four men who had been dogging her, had either given up, or had kept going in the direction that she had originally been taking.

The bad news was that as she neared the road, sucking wind and holding her hand over a stitch in her side, a black continental came idling up slowly. It was one of the two that had been in her driveway. Katie ducked down behind the nearest bush and watched as a man carrying a long gun hopped out. The road sat further down on a gentle slope and it had been a bit of a blessing for weary Katie to jog down it, but now the slope became a curse. The man with the gun was a few hundred feet off to her right, which at first seemed a good thing, but as he started up the slope, he decided against going straight up it, instead he walked slowly in a diagonal. He would pass very close to where she hid.

With little choice, she turned and started up the slope again; her legs were heavy as stone and just as stiff. It was one thing to go for an easy early morning jog and quite another to sprint for your life in this hard land. Ducking from shrub to shrub and running along the floor of the little ravines was slow work and each time she turned to see where the man with the rifle was, he seemed no further away. Though with the dark it was hard to tell. She wished she could find a cave or at least a large bush to hide beneath, but the desert was painfully barren with only the many folds and gullies giving her any cover.

The slope eventually ran out and there before her was the harsh rugged Sonoran. It had been her playground for years and she was just about to dash forward to lose herself among the hills and fissures of the broken landscape when a movement thirty feet in front of her caught her eye. A shadow moved among the low scraggling bushes: it was one of Amy's thugs and he moved with care to be quiet. Katie ducked down quick and watched as he kept going, oblivious of the girl so close to him. She could barely wait a minute after he passed to get moving again—there was the sound of someone scrambling up the slope in her rear.

The minute of rest helped and she was able to jog away to her right, once again heading northeast. Yet very quickly, she became tired again and took to plodding along. This was strange for her and at first she chalked it up to the fact that she had begun her get away with a full on sprint, however that had been practically twenty minutes prior. She should have recovered from that, not fully since she was still moving but more than she had.

It was as if she were being drained of energy. It was the sword. Even through the thick sweatshirt, the thing was cold and she took to switching hands every ten or fifteen seconds as they went numb. The night was cooling as well; Katie began to shiver despite her exorcise.

Up a head, there was a sheer outcropping of rock. It was a place she'd been to many times and was about three miles as the crow flew from her house. She staggered on towards it and ten minutes later, she pitched up panting, leaning up against the rock. Eagerly she set the sword down and after a minute of rest, she climbed as high as she could to get a good lay of the land.

Almost immediately, the young girl saw a blaze of headlights turn into her driveway. Hope that her brother had finally arrived surged in her and she turned her ear hoping to hear the crackle of gunfire that would let her know that Will was even then saving their mother. But the house was too far away and she had no way of knowing if it was him. In her heart, she didn't believe it was. There had been two cars that had pulled up and as far as she knew Will was only coming with Talitha, who couldn't drive as far as Katie understood.

She settled in, feeling relatively safe—no one could sneak up on her. Minutes ticked away and after twenty or so, a flash of light briefly lit the desert about a mile away, it was back along the route she had taken. A few seconds later, a fine crackling report of a gunshot came to her ears. This repeated itself a few more times and then stopped.

She hoped they were shooting at each other. That would be good. Yet she couldn't count on that fact and she decided to get moving. Climbing down the rock, she picked up her loathsome burden and began jogging more closely north. A dirt trail that ran east to west lay in that direction and she planned to take it east for a couple of miles and then strike again south where there were more houses. Her jog lasted for only a few minutes, after that the sword sapped her energy and she took to walking and then a few minutes later to stumbling. She didn't get close to the trail. A mile from it she saw headlights heading from the east and she stopped. Was it her brother, who could see the future and might have found out where she was, or was it Amy using some sort of spell to find her?

It was fifty-fifty. Katie ran back the way she came, reeling in fatigue and soon tears started to course their way down her cheek, she couldn't go far. Even if she ditched the sword right there she was practically done in, and she was far too afraid to throw the sword away. What would happen if they found it and killed her mother with it?

Behind her headlights grew brighter and the sound of an engine roaring came across the waste. Katie tried to hurry faster but she ended up sprawling in the dirt. Forcing herself up, she looked back in time to see the headlights click off. Where could she go? The desert was wide and empty, with nowhere to hide. The tall bare rock that she had partially climbed was the only thing in sight; it beckoned to her and she made her way back to it.

When Katie finally arrived, she climbed with frozen hands as high as she could, but it was nowhere near as high as she had climbed before, perhaps only twenty or so feet from the ground. Sheer exhaustion stopped her and she rested on a shelf of rock. It was supposed to be only a halt of a minute or so, but when she turned to move again, her muscles cramped up in her legs and she knew there would be no going any higher.

The sword she pushed as far from her as possible and she sat back, leaning against the rock shivering with fear and cold. The only good thing about her spot was that due to the angle of the shelf, she had protection from bullets, at least as long as the thugs stayed on the ground. However, there wasn't much chance of that and since there were a number of ways up the rock, she could be attacked from more than one direction at once, she felt painfully vulnerable.

With a light *snick*, disturbing the quiet air, she brought out her jackknife. Once she had been quite proud of it and the gleaming blade professed to this, but now it seemed pathetic and practically useless. She tested it against her thumb. It was very sharp and this was no surprise, since she had honed it herself in preparation for a day very much like this one.

She had trained to fight. She had hardened her body and her mind. She had prepared like no child her age would ever consider. Her state of readiness had been fantastic. Yet it had all been for nothing. Just then, Katie lacked the strength to run or to fight. The most that she could hope for was to have the strength to die.

Could she do it?

Suicide was a sin. An unforgivable sin according to the priests. It was throwing away God's greatest gift—in essence, throwing it back in his face. But the alternative! Sucked into the Void as a plaything of Ba'al. She wouldn't go that way.

"Katie!" Amy's voice called out. She sounded very close.

"I'm sorry, Lord." Taking the razor sharp blade in her right hand, she made to slice into her left wrist.

A sound came from just below and Amy said, "I know you're up there, Katie."

With her shaking hands and the suddenness of the voice, the blade slid into her wrist almost smack dab in the middle, missing her radial artery by almost an inch.

"Uhhh!" It hurt very badly and she had to clench her teeth to keep from screaming.

"Now what do you think you're trying to do?" Amy asked conversationally. "Are you trying to hurt yourself? Are you thinking you can get out of this by killing yourself? Don't be stupid. It'll take you too long to die. Diablo, go and fetch her."

"Si." There was a scrambling of someone climbing up the rocks.

"No stay back, or..." Katie didn't have anything to bargain with.

Amy seemed to know this. "Or what?"

Katie grabbed up the sword and shook it so that the cloth fell away from the blade. It was so cold and nasty that she had to hold it out away from her. "Or I'll use the sword on Diablo. I have it right here in my hands and I'll do it."

The sound of climbing stopped on the rocks.

"You should know that whatever you do, you're just plain fucked," Amy said with a hint of irritation. "If you try to kill yourself by jumping, you're going to hell. If you use that sword, guess what? That's right, you're going to hell. If Diablo fetches you down here, you're going to hell as well. Face it Katie, you are one fucked little virgin. But..."

With each count of how she would end up in hell, Katie's spirits sank lower and lower so that when Amy said *But*, despite herself, Katie felt the smallest glimmer of hope. "But what?"

"Well it's like this. I can make it real tough on your family if I want to. I can make them all suffer. I can use the sword and send them to hell, or I can I can make it quick and natural. A bullet in the back of the head."

Katie, who had been feeling small, grew quickly angry. "That's your deal?"

"Yeah. I'm going to get what I want one-way or the other. I'm going to open a gate and that's that. I'd just rather do it the easy way," Amy replied reasonably. "I would even let them live, if I could trust them not to interfere. Do you think I can? Do you think ole Willy J is gonna sit back and do nothing?"

Katie was silent at this. If Will could, he would stop Amy.

"Just what I thought. Now I'm on a time crunch. This

has to be done tonight, or it's my ass heading off to hell, so what do you think? Do you want them all in hell with you or will you come along peacefully?"

Katie knew that she was indeed fucked, still it was nearly a minute before she answered. Amy had given away too much. Time crunches were made to be exploited.

"Yes, but..." She paused again dragging out the seconds. She had aces up her sleeves: Will's capacity to see the future, Talitha's superhuman abilities and she, little Katie, had her guile and her jackknife. This she slid down her sock. "You'll make their deaths quick? You promise?"

"I'll have my men shoot to kill." Almost like magic, a gun fired off to their right. It was surprisingly close, perhaps only a hundred yards or so. There was a pause and then Amy, with a little tremor in her voice, called, "Get down here now, or all bets are off."

Katie's confidence escalated. "If that's my brother then you're in more trouble than you realize."

"Why? Because he can see the future?" Amy laughed at Katie's silence. "He can't see my future, and if that's him, he's in for a rude surprise. Besides Diablo, there are seven other men surrounding this little outcropping and another up with the jeep."

Now Katie was sorely vexed and her confidence sank to a new low. Without his vision, her brother was just another man. She cast a last glance at the sword and purposely left it on the rock shelf when she climbed down.

"Where's the sword?" Amy demanded. The thought had come to the young girl that she would try to make a run for it when Diablo went for the sword, but Amy held a pistol in her hand. It was small and mean. So it was that Katie jerked her head to the shelf.

"I didn't want to have to touch it again," she said as way of an excuse.

Without being asked, Diablo climbed up for the sword. Amy called up to him, "Whatever you do, don't throw that thing down here. I don't want to get stabbed on accident. Just carry..." A man's scream of pain cut in on Amy. It came from around to their left, almost behind them. It rose up high and then cut off quick.

Though Katie felt that she should've been in some way elated that a possible rescue was taking place, the scream had chilled her. She didn't think that it was her brother out there; she had a feeling that it was Talitha. And Talitha stalking human prey at night wasn't something she wanted to see.

"What is it?" Amy hissed up at a wide-eyed Diablo.

Diablo shrugged, which could barely be seen. Seconds later a long string of automatic rifle fire lit up the sky to their right.

Amy spun. "What the hell! Is that guy even shooting at anything?" Who knew? Amy stood looking angry and confused in equal proportions. She gazed back to the north where the jeep sat parked. It seemed far away. "Get back up there. Go on get climbing," she ordered her hostage.

Katie was glad to. She had seen her sister when she was in one of her moods—Talitha could be a holy terror. The climb was short and Diablo pushed her to the side of the ledge. Suddenly she felt quite exposed and the drop very steep. To keep her mind off the nearness of the edge, she looked out into the desert. At first, nothing could be seen, but then someone began firing again. Whoever it was sprayed the surrounding landscape with bullets and then in the fading light of his gun he could be seen to turn and run.

After that, the night swallowed him up and nothing more could be seen from that direction. Amy watched nervously with eyes that couldn't get any larger. "If that's Willy J, how's he countering my spell? And if he can, what does that mean?" She gave Diablo a shrew look, but turned to her hostage and said, "Katie, skootch back from the edge a bit. You don't want to be too close."

The girl was all too happy to get away from the edge,

but she wasn't happy when Amy smashed her on the back of the head with her pistol. It sent her flopping face first on the ledge and the dark desert got darker still. However, she didn't lose consciousness. Her world spun and little came into focus and less made any sense.

"Diablo, look at this in my hand."

Despite the sharp pain in Katie's head, she wanted to see what was in Amy's hand. The very idea of it was strangely demanding and she rolled over slightly to see.

"Ohh." It hurt to move and there was no question about getting up, it would be impossible to even try. So it was that Katie was disappointed and did not see what it was Amy held. Something twinkled in the witch's palm and Diablo looked quite stupid just standing there staring. He seemed frozen and moved not a muscle. Feeling let down at having missed it, Katie let her head flop to the side and groaned a second time as the darkness spun and tilted around her.

For the next few minutes, the young girl could do little but lay there trying to right her mind. She could hear as Amy crawled about the ledge, whispering in a cruel sounding language. It was unnatural and it soured the air and brought bile rising in her throat. Fearing that she would vomit, the young girl struggled to a kneeling position and began to retch like a dog.

"Not here you idiot! Over the side." Amy was in a fiery mood and this had Katie turning to look at her perplexed. She wished that she hadn't. In the past couple of minutes, Diablo had died, though he bore no obvious wounds. He was dead and that was a certainty. His eyes were open, but there not a flicker of life or intelligence in them. His skin had gone gray and now sagged from his bones, forming odd layers of wrinkles below his eyes. He smelled foul. How it was possible the young girl did not know, but Diablo smelled like he had been dead a week a more. Now Katie had to vomit, there was no stopping it. Like a sophomore after her first kegger, she staggered on her hands and knees to the edge and heaved up everything that was left to her stomach.

There wasn't much.

Amy continued through this to hiss out her venomous language, until at last the thing that had once been Diablo began to move. First, his head swung this way and that and then one by one his arms raised and lowered.

"Good," the witch said with a great deal of satisfaction as well as relief. "Now take up the sword and kill anyone who comes near to this rock." Without a word, the bizarre creature of Diablo bent and took up the short broken sword and began to climb down. Once he was out of sight, Katie felt her nausea regress.

"What did you do to him?"

"Never mind that. Just be glad that it wasn't you." Amy looked to have aged ten years and sat with her back to the pinnacle of rock, her body sagged in exhaustion. There was silence between the two for a minute before a final cry went up in the desert. It was a long harsh scream and went on and on. The person died slowly. Katie felt that she wanted to be sick again and as the scream kept going Amy didn't look much better.

"What the hell is Will doing?" the witch asked.

"That's not Will. He'd never do that to someone, he's far too good of a person. That's Talitha."

"What? How do you mean? Talitha is just...she's just a girl."

The screaming ended and then there was the sound of someone begging and the word please began to be repeated with unsettling repetition. Katie realized she was now almost as afraid of her rescuer as she was of her captor.

"No, Talitha is something a lot more. She'll tear that thing you made into shreds. Talitha's unstoppable." Katie had great confidence in her sister's ability to kill.

"Don't be too sure about that..."

"I'm quite sure. And then she'll come up here and do the same or perhaps worse to you." Katie's self-assured manner had Amy looking worried.

"Oh Aaaaameee?" A girl's voice, sweet and sounding very young, called out from the night. It sent shivers down Katie's spine. That sweet girl had just killed who knows how many people, yet it sounded like she was out after dark playing hide and go seek.

Katie leaned over the ledge and looked out, but saw nothing. "We're over here. Amy's a witch and she made some sort of thing..." she was interrupted.

"Shut up or so help me I'll shoot you through the spine." Amy had her little gun pressed against the lower part of Katie's back.

"Shooting someone in the spine? Nice...very nice." The voice had moved closer, but still remained unseen. "Well, look what you made, Amy. That's a *Draugr*. It's real cute, but really, do you think it will save you?"

"How does she know that's a Draugr? Is she a witch?" Amy whispered to Katie.

"I wouldn't bother whispering, Amy. I can hear you just fine. And let me tell you how I know that's a Draugr. It's because someone's dumb-ass mother was a whore-bitch and sent me to the Void. You can learn all sorts of stuff down there if you listen and watch and learn. And you can become! I've grown, bitch! Everyone else turned into the rotten filth that is trod upon and pissed upon and bled upon, but not I!" The voice was loud and triumphant. It edged nearer with each word and Amy pulled further back as it did.

"Don't come any closer! I'll kill your sister. I'm not kidding, I'll do it." Amy's fear came out in her voice, which trembled. The gun dug into Katie's back.

"I don't think you will. In fact, I know you won't—you need her. Don't you?" The voice of Talitha drew off to their right, but because of the rock, she was still unseen. "You told Will that you were on a time crunch, but I know what that really means. Ha-Ha! You were always so stupid. You made a deal with a demon and it's looking for payment. So you can't exactly just up and kill her." Amy was quiet behind Katie, breathing heavily and thankfully, the pressure of the gun relaxed. Talitha continued, "But I have all the time in the world. I can just sit out here and wait. I bet that time crunch of yours is going to expire here pretty shortly."

Katie cast a glance back at her captor. Beautiful raven haired Amy Harris had been transformed in the last few minutes. She had wild eyes, pale skin, and shaking hands. Her lips trembled and her whole demeanor was that of a trapped animal. Her little controlled world had turned upside down simply by the presence of someone more foul and evil than she.

She was desperate. Katie could see her mind working, yet there were few options left for the witch. To give up her hostage would certainly mean death. To send the Draugr after Talitha was a risk as well. The girl had killed seven armed men in the dark and whatever the Draugr was, Talitha didn't seem too worried about it. And to wait meant what exactly? That a demon would come and claim her soul? It was no wonder Amy looked to be falling apart.

If Katie had been in her shoes, she would've sent the Draugr to fight Talitha and then would have tried to make a dash for it. She dearly hoped Amy would do this since it would be her best chance at escape from both of them.

There was another choice that Katie hadn't thought of.

Amy leaned to the edge. "Diablo, run to the Jern's. Use the sword, kill everyone there. Go!" Like an automaton, the Draugr ran off without a word. Katie watched it go and it was with a shameful sense of relief; both it and the sword were horrors her young mind could barely cope with.

"Bye Draugr, have fun!" Talitha called after it. "I don't know if you can be anymore stupid, Amy. You may not be able to hear the screams and gunshots, but I certainly can. Our dear Willy J is over there with some soldier boys right now. I don't think there'll be enough people left alive to come close to freeing Ba'al. Maybe a few of the smaller demons sure, but not Ba'al, that thing is huge!"

"But..."Amy started to say but stopped, fearing that Talitha was right.

Katie feared it as well. "Tal, forget about me, I'll be alright. Go after the Draugr; don't let it kill mom and Will. Please," she begged.

"Mom and Will?" Talitha repeated with slight touch of incredulity. "I don't know. That doesn't seem worth the trip. I gotta tell you—me and Will, we get along about as well as a cat and a dog. And frankly, I would rather see him in the Void, than out of it. He's always fucking with me. Keeping me from having any fun, ya know? And mom? Eh."

"What do you mean, eh?" Katie demanded. "She's your mother, Tal."

"Well, she was always so nitpicky. I note that you didn't suggest that I go save our dad. Is he out bowling or something?" For the first time since Talitha had begun speaking there was the slightest hesitation.

"He's dead already," Katie replied. The word corpse flashed through her mind and it made her chest ache to think it.

"He's not dead yet," Amy cried; hope made her voice rise the slightest bit. "But he soon will be if Diablo gets there before you,"

"You're lying...I don't think...you can't kill my father," Talitha hesitated. "He's far too strong... and you're just..." Her voice had changed from the imperious commanding tone to one of confusion. Katie had seen her sister change from one personality to the other a few times years before and it sounded like this.

"What's wrong, Tal? Was dad supposed to be alive?" Katie strove to keep the fear out of her voice; she knew the evil Talitha thrived on it.

"Y-yes. Will was going to save him...he was supposed to..." Talitha broke off again.

Katie glanced at Amy who was slowly pulling herself

back together and the young girl realized that for a second there she could've grabbed the gun from the witch, but that moment passed. "What was Will supposed to do? Do you guys have a plan?" Katie asked.

"Yes, he was supposed to save mom *and* dad. And I was supposed to kill Amy and take the virg..." This time Talitha didn't falter in her words—she clamped her mouth shut hard.

The word 'take' didn't register on Katie. She took a shaky breath and rallied her courage. "Tal, forget about me. Go and save mom and Will. Run!"

"No, I can't," Talitha said in a small voice. Gone was the braggadocios snarling of a minute before—she had thankfully changed. "I can't do it...I can't leave you to the same fate that I went through."

It was good to hear Talitha's voice the way she always remembered it, but it hurt Katie terribly to have to say, "No darn it, leave me! The sword is way worse than anything Amy can do me."

"I can't. You don't know how it will be. The Void is horrible beyond..."

Katie's courage had peaked when Talitha made the change to her nicer personality, but the peak didn't amount to much and was even then slowly dribbling away. With her courage went the strength of her voice and she whispered, "Tal, I'll get out of this, somehow. Please, now go."

"No, I can't," Talitha said with conviction.

Time was getting away from them. The thing, the Draugr had run off with great speed. "Do you trust me?" Katie asked the voice in the dark.

"What? Do I trust you? Katie...I don't really know you. I haven't seen you since you were six years old."

"You're right, you don't know me. I may not have your strength, or Will's vision, but I saw the demon, Tal. And I'll fight no matter what, and besides, if you save Will, he'll find me and he'll save me." Talitha was silent and seconds ticked by, and with their passing Katie grew more anxious. "Talitha! Go now or you'll lose all of us. Trust me, please."

"Ok...ok. I will, but I'll be back, ok?"

Talitha started to run away and then the last words that Katie ever heard from her sister came to her faintly: "I love you, Katie."

"Love you too," Katie whispered. She cast a look at her captor; Amy held the gun directly on her; it never wavered even for an inch.

The witch smiled in a sudden relaxed manner. "That was a close one. You did the right thing you know. Better just you in hell than your whole family, right?" It didn't feel so right, not just then. In fact, the girl felt sick but regardless, she nodded in a slight way. Amy nodded back; there was an evil glint in her eyes. "So you gonna fight, like you said?"

Unable to look the witch in the face, Katie dropped her gaze down at the rock they were sitting on. After her long fear-laden afternoon and her exhausting sprint through the desert, she was done in and just then, felt too weak to do much of anything let alone fight. She shook her head, no.

"That's what I thought," Amy replied and the smirk in her voice was audible. "Katie?" The witch paused until Katie raised her head like the scared child she was. "Look at what I have here in my hand."

Her mind screamed for her not to look, but the little thing was so very shiny in the dark night. The thing was interesting as well, so much so that her mind swelled, taking in all of its intricate details and she quite forgot about the gun pointing at her midsection, and she forgot about escape, and even the fact that very soon she would be sacrificed to a fiend from hell and that her soul would be sucked into the Void for all eternity. It was just so shiny.

Chapter 20

Talitha

To the girl flashing across the rugged night desert, the dark wasn't an issue. As plain as day, she could see the cacti, the jagged rocks and the odd, tar-smelling bushes, and she leapt or dodged them without slowing her fantastic, frantic pace. Her long brown hair drew out behind her like the pendants of an olden day frigate, flowing and dancing with the wind of her passing. Her long tan legs stretched, extending beautifully and when she sailed across a gorge of some twenty feet, it was with the grace of a gazelle. To anyone but herself she was a sight. A beautiful girl.

In her mind, she wasn't and could never be. There was blood on her hands. Literal, actual blood. There was blood in her hair as well, and a fine spray of it across the slim perfection of her neck. She had killed with ease that night. The thugs that had been arrayed around the lonely spire of rock looking to keep a little girl from escaping, had gone down one by one, unaware that something horrible had been stalking them. Unaware that is until the stranger controlling Talitha had become bored over the silent and quick manner in which she murdered. Then she had allowed for some pain, not as much as she would have wished for, but still enough to get her feeling hot and randy.

The memory of her sexual excitement over the screams and the desperate quiet begging sent a spasm of disgust across her back and shoulders. She wanted to spit. She wanted to take a very long hot shower and scrub away her guilt and sin. And most of all, she wanted to pretend that it hadn't been her. It hadn't felt like her; while the killing had been going on, it had felt as though she were deep underwater, watching helplessly as her hands had crushed throats and beat in skulls.

It had felt like her other self, the stranger, who was even now watching her again. Sometimes it seemed as if the stranger was in her and at other times it was as if she were being shadowed, only steps away, so that she wanted to turn as she ran and look back. Fear stopped her, she was afraid to see that she was alone, afraid to come to the conclusion that there was no one else culpable, that it was she who was the real killer.

Talitha sobbed aloud as she ran, confused at who she was and why she did things that she never would have ever considered. On one level, she understood that she was possessed by a second personality, but on a more basic level, the blood on her hands was still wet and stank of copper, the smell of which was driving her crazy. Yet despite her bewildered mind or perhaps because of it, she sped faster than she had ever before. The desert floor zoomed beneath her sprinting feet and after barely two minutes, she could see the Draugr far off. It had a near insurmountable lead and if it were to gain the house before she did, her family would be dead within seconds. Or at least part of her family would.

Katie might never die. To judge by Will's dreams from the day before, it would seem that her little sister's body might someday end up in cold storage, while her soul, used like a wedge to prop open the gate, would forever be tormented in the Void. The thought of leaving her behind made it hard to keep going, since Talitha had been there herself and knew the terrors that the girl would face.

"You might as well turn back," the stranger demanded. How badly it wanted Katie! This was the greatest reason that Talitha had abandoned her little sister to her fate. With her, the stranger would have the power to control the gate, in essence, the power to control Ba'al Zubel here on earth. That was a power indeed, a great evil power. A power that could turn Talitha into a demon just as Ba'al Fie-ere.

The stranger reared up, growing stronger at the thought.

Talitha had to forget Katie. The girl was doomed no matter what. It was sad but true. She didn't even have the option to run away, Talitha had smelled the fragrance of witchcraft all about the rock and knew that Katie was laid upon with a beacon. There was nowhere she could run that Amy couldn't track her down. She was doomed and Talitha forced herself to put the girl out of her mind. Instead, she concentrated on her own running.

Into her bloodstream, she began to pump dangerous levels of adrenaline and noradrenalin. She constricted blood flow throughout her body so that quickly her arms went numb, but her legs felt fresh and invigorated. She blazed even swifter, faster than any Olympian could hope to run. A minute passed and then two more, and still she kept up her pace. There could be no slowing. The Druagr wouldn't. Or so at first she thought, but as the minutes passed and she drew closer, she saw that it was moving in a shambling unnatural waddle and though it hadn't exactly slowed, it still wasn't as fast as it could have been. Oddly, it made detours around the large formations of bushes that she routinely leapt over without a problem. Because of this, Talitha saw that she might catch it after all, but it would be oh so close.

With the slim possibility held out before her, she threw everything she had into the final mile and was only dimly aware that she was leaving bloody footprints laid out behind her as the tough skin of her feet shredded under the blistering pace. Soon, in spite of the great control she had over her physicality, her heart thundered in her slim chest and her breathing became harsh. The cool night air burned like fire in her lungs, but she would make it, she would catch the thing. Yet at what cost? She had put her entire self into the sprint of three miles and she rightly gauged her exhausted body to be on its last reserves. She didn't think that she would have anything left to fight such a monster. Yet she had no choice.

At a little over two hundred yards from the house, she

closed on the thing and with each long stride, she drew closer still, until finally, Talitha was near enough to lash out at the thing's legs and this sent it stumbling head over heels. So tired was she that the action staggered her as well and she nearly went sprawling, but managed to stay on her feet. It was a good thing she did too, for the once-human was at her with barely a pause to right itself.

The Draugr was a blasphemy. It was possessed with unholy energy giving it speed, strength, and vitality out of any proportion to that of the human it had once been. Talitha had never seen one, yet knew much about it, though she had no idea how. The knowledge just came to her in a flash and with it, the understanding that she wasn't likely to prevail against it, at least not as Talitha, not in her present state. She had a much better chance of survival if the killer inside her were to take control and undeniably it wanted to. It was large in her mind, powerful with evil and desire. Even as the Draugr sprang up and sent the hell blade slashing at her face, she felt her mind shifting between herself and the stranger.

This time Talitha fought back against the stranger.

What would it gain her to destroy the Draugr only to have the stranger, that evil beast within her, in control of the blade and so close to her parent's home? Talitha knew what the killer would do and decided that it was better to die and have her mottled soul sucked into the Void than to have her own hands further soiled with the guilt of killing her own family. Therefore, she strove in a battle of wills to retain her awareness, even as her body fought just to stay alive.

Quickly, it felt as though her body was losing.

Her chest ached with each breath and her feet stung and bled where razor sharp rocks had penetrated the skin. Her legs shook uncontrollably and when the Draugr sent the blade in a hacking slash at her face, they wobbled her backwards and only barely did the black sword miss. She felt the cold of its passing and it froze the sweat beading on her forehead. As she stepped back, Talitha stumbled in her weakness and made to catch herself with her arms, but they were dead weighs, still numb from oxygen deprivation. The best she could manage was an awkward pin wheeling.

A second later, the creature attacked again and Talitha was still not even close to being balanced. She felt quite a bit as though she were a large penguin with her arms unable to rise above her shoulders. A lurching ungainly backwards momentum was all that she had and she didn't think it would save her, especially when her feet struck one of the large creosote bushes and she fell full into it. In a panic, Talitha began kicking out, forcing herself further into the bush and amazingly the Draugr stopped, seemingly confused.

It turned its head this way and that, apparently searching for the girl who was only a step away. Next, it moved a few feet to the right, but still it couldn't seem to see the girl with the wonderful tan and the floral print sundress among the leaves and sharp stems of the bush. Eight wonderful precious seconds slipped by as the thing went to and fro searching for her. In that short time Talitha sent fresh oxygen rich blood flooding down her arms, right into her finger tips, and down into her legs. The eight seconds were a godsend, but what she really needed was five minutes resting on her back and a quart of Gatorade.

That was not to be.

Abruptly, the Draugr forgot about her, and dashed off in the direction of the house intent on its primary directive, the killing of everyone there. Talitha pulled her weary body out of the bush and stumbled after. Thankfully, a long gully detoured the creature and Talitha, after leaping over it, stood in its path, with her chest heaving and her muscles trembling. She knew the Draugr would attack with strength, speed, and endurance that was greater than her own, and she knew that it would kill her. The reason was simple; she was down to her last reserves of strength and not only that, she lacked ferocity and a killing instinct, these had always been the attributes of her other self.

As expected, the fiend attacked. It hacked left and right with the blade so that it was all Talitha could do to dodge or block the blows sailing in faster with each swing. More and more she was forced to let her instincts dictate her actions, until she began to feel a hatred for the creature. This feeling was so intense that it came as a surprise and only then did she realize that her instinct for fighting had slipped into a lust for fighting. This wasn't a desire that she had ever felt before.

Too late, she saw that the stranger had control. This other self dodged and fought with such skilled technique that Talitha worried that she might actually win the fight, but then in her exhaustion, her foot caught on a rock and she faltered to one knee. The Draugr's next attack couldn't be evaded and she brought her left arm up to block the sword from striking her. Her forearm met the forearm of her enemy and the force of the blow almost paralyzed her arm. It fell limp to her side. Now she was too close to the Draugr for any dodging and her only option was too fall back.

Down she went with the much stronger Draugr on top in a dominant position, and without pause it drove the blade down at her face again. It was a terrible sensation for Talitha to watch as if from a distance, as her body was attacked. She felt helpless seeing the black blade pass within an inch of her face as her head swung hard to the right to avoid it.

The stranger inside went wild with animalistic fury, the feeling erupted throughout her body, she bucked and heaved, but to no avail—the Draugr was to strong and she too weak—and the blade came again.

With almost no room to evade it, the blade sank into the side of her neck, just above the sloping trapezius muscle. Immediately she felt her essence, her soul being drawn along into the sword. There was no fighting it. She tried and the stranger tried, but a leaf in a tornado had more control of its destination than she, and down, down, down she felt herself being pulled into the great black Void.

Chapter 21

Will

Will wasted no time preparing himself mentally for the confrontation with Amy's thugs, but Father Vogel was another matter altogether. After Talitha sped off in search of Katie, the priest, decked out as if for Mass, began a final prayer for the men. At first, Will thought it to be a good idea, but it turned out that Father Vogel, unlike most priests, lacked eloquence. He might have been a first rate exorcist and certainly knew psychology and the workings of the human mind, but when it came to exhorting the men and comforting them in times of peril, he was a touch dull and worse, long winded.

After five minutes, Will began to fidget. At the start of the prayer he felt good, relatively calm, however as the time ticked away he started to get nervous, though judging by the four men of the unit, he shouldn't have been. They stood coolly with bowed heads as Vogel went on and on in a seemingly endless procession of words. After eight minutes, Will not only was nervous, but he also became agitated at the delay, this took the outward expression of him tapping the side of the pistol that he had picked up in Maine. Within him was the desire to check once again the number of rounds in the magazine. He had done this three times already, the first time only a minute after he had loaded the thing.

A craving for Wild Turkey came upon him, which he attempted to dismiss, though without any real success. Too many times in the past eight years he had used the alcohol as a crutch and now he felt jittery going into a battle without it. Glancing surreptitious at the men, he wondered if any of them were carting about a hip flask or its equivalent, yet nothing looked obvious and he knew he would be too embarrassed to ask.

A long and loud sigh escaped him. It was much louder than he had expected it to be and it caused Father Vogel to glance up. In chagrin, Will dropped his head back down so quickly that his chin thumped against his chest. A few seconds later the priest wrapped it up crossing himself.

"Amen," the five men said in chorus after crossing themselves.

"Ok, fellas the plan's quite simple," Abe began with some authority. "Diamond formation, Timothy takes point until we bear up to about a hundred yards. Zeke on the left. I take the right, Jake in the rear. Mr. Jern are you still coming?"

"Yeah." The word was a whisper. His nervousness was so pronounced that he didn't trust himself to speak and was glad that the dark hid his shaking hands.

"In that case, I want you off to Zeke's left by at least thirty yards. Please, don't shoot over anyone's head. If you have to fire your weapon make sure you know where each of your squad mates are before you do. We'll be attacking what you have described as the family room first, and we know where the other men are arranged about the house, so if you see flashes coming from one of the other rooms, or if you see someone come out, don't be afraid to shoot. Just whatever you do, don't shoot south to north because you may be shooting at one of us. Know what you're aiming at, got it? And one more thing, check that your safety is on till you're ready to fire."

Will nodded though no one could see it. "Yeah." His hand went to the butt of the gun that stuck in his waistband and he forced himself to pull it back without checking the load. "Can I get a moment, if you don't mind?" Will jogged over to the other car where Father Vogel stood and after giving the priest a quick tight smile he ducked in and kissed his wife on the lips. They were agreeably warm and soft.

"Love you," he whispered, staring into her face.

"I'm sorry I'm not much of an inspirational speaker."

"Huh?" Will pulled his tall frame from the car. "What did you say, Father?"

Father Vogel looked odd in his Easter vestments out there in the night desert, he also looked uncomfortable. "I was just apologizing for not being such an inspiration. I was never really such a good public speaker. I think it may be why I was shipped off to exorcism school."

"There's such a thing?"

Vogel laughed quiet and dry. "No. It was just a joke. I'm sorry. I'm just a little nervous."

He wasn't nervous near enough, in Will's opinion. If Ba'al was there at the house, it would destroy the priest as soon as it could. "I think we all are, so don't sweat it. In fact, I could use some of that sacramental wine."

The priest smiled at Will's half-joke and then the two stood looking at each other in embarrassed silence. Despite the cooling night, a small trickle of sweat ran down the side of Will's face, he reached up to wipe it away and it seemed to break the moment.

"Good luck," the priest said with some solemnity.

"You too." Somewhat stiffly, the two men shook hands.

"Abraham? To whom should I give my stole to?"

Jake came up out of the dark, giving the priest a little start. To add to his dark clothing, the soldier had painted his face black as well. "I'll take it." With some ceremony, the priest removed the stole kissed it once and after folding it neatly, handed it over. Jacob stored it away neatly, tucking it in his shirt. There was another heavy silence.

"Ah we gonna do this, ah what?" Zeke called impatiently in his Boston accent.

"Yes. Timothy, get going," Abraham spoke in a low tone. He was closer than Will realized. "Watch your spacing and keep your shots tight. Mr. Jern, if you don't mind..."

"Please. It's Will remember? Not Mr. Jern."

"Right. Will it is. Get going. Keep low. Stay abreast of Zeke. You don't want to get either in front or behind. Someone can get hurt that way."

This, Will thought was actually supposed to be a joke since they were heading off to hurt all sorts of people and so he smiled in appreciation. However, Abe didn't. He just glared about with a hard face, making sure everyone was moving off into the right positions.

As Will left him, trotting to the far left of the little formation, he heard Abe giving last minute instructions to the priest, "Keep the lights off and don't move until you hear shooting. Then creep up until you hear two shots and then a pause and a third. Bang, bang...bang. Like that, got it?"

He assumed the priest got it since he moved too far away to hear the acknowledgement. "Zeke?" In the dark, the camouflaged man was impossible to see.

"Over here."

"How am I supposed to keep abreast of you when I can't see you from ten feet, let alone thirty?"

"Every few seconds, I'll make this sound." Zeke let out a little chirping noise, *sweeip*. "Just orient on that. Good luck Will."

"You too."

Will, slinking low, walked out toward the road for about thirty paces and hunkered down. His breath came and went heavily, his sweat continued to trickle down his forehead and his eyes were wide, straining in the dark. The need for a drink was becoming a physical force within him. He could do this with half a bottle of whiskey in him, but he didn't know if he could, dry.

Sweeip, sweeip. The noise was ahead of Will and to his right; Zeke was already fifteen to twenty paces in front of him.

Hurrying forward, he stumbled and fell, cutting his hands and dropping his gun, "Damn!" This he said aloud, but wasn't worried about the noise; the house was still a way off.

It was quite dark and had a sad gloom about it and if Talitha hadn't reported that there were men in it waiting with drawn guns, he would have very much considered it vacant.

In haste, he picked himself up and after finding the gun a few feet in front of him, began again more carefully. A while later, perhaps two hundred yards, he realized he hadn't heard the chirp sound in some time. Did that mean he was too far in front of Zeke or too far behind? There was no way to know. A thrill of anxious panic swept him for a moment and he ducked down not wishing to be taken for one of Amy's men. For a long minute, he squatted, sweating beside a bush, and feeling altogether unlike himself.

The cause of his puzzling anxiety was almost certainly the Wild Turkey, or rather the lack of it and he was very embarrassed to come to that conclusion. Forgetting completely the hidden bottle of vodka that Lisa had sipped from on Saturday nights when he was with his sister, Will worried what she would think if she knew that he was at least situationally an alcoholic. He was mentally upbraiding himself for his weakness when he heard a soft noise coming from the north, not at all the direction that any noise should be coming from.

Closer it came and Will brought up the gun. *Sweeip.* Will practically deflated in relief.

"Zeke?"

"Yeah...sorry. I went too far to the right. I think you need to move back to the left."

Will hurried away, not wanting Zeke to see him even in the dim light. There would be nothing but shame if any of the men could see how badly his hands shook. It was strange that they did, he wasn't even that scared. The men of the unit had assault weapons and training, while the thugs he had seen so far were pathetic, and really, Will didn't see that he would be much use other than to draw some fire his way.

His only plan at the moment was to get in close and squiggle up to the border of the lawn that sloped upwards to the house. From there he could fire some shots into it, if he felt the need to distract some of Amy's men. If they fired back, they wouldn't likely hit him if he kept low, which he very much intended to do.

At two hundred yards the chirping slowed in pace, meaning that Zeke was likely crawling from bush to bush and Will emulated the idea, moving on his hands and knees. With painstaking slowness the house drew closer, as it did his anxiety increased until at fifty yards, he couldn't go further. A barren swath of desert lay between him and the equally open yard. Sometime in the last few months, his father must have cleared the area of scrub and now there was half a football field of coverless exposed ground between him and the house.

Slowly Will poked his head up and saw with further dismay that this openness extended as far around the house as he could see. What were they to do? What was he to do? He had no clue; there had been no contingency plans for this sort of thing at least that he was aware of.

Did he dare try slipping over to where Zeke was? He thought better of it. He was the least trained of them all and worried that he would give away their position. Instead, he would wait for them to come to him, which was something he fully...

From the house, a long rattle of machine gun fire sent Will sprawling face first into the hard dirt. They had machine guns! The sound of guns firing off to his right sounded next. Suddenly gun blasts were coming from everywhere in the house and the din was amazing. For seconds he hugged the dirt, but then after a short time realized that no one was shooting anywhere near him, and he lifted his head to see.

Two men in black were crouched in front of the family room, keeping low away from the shattered windows. They were men of the unit but he couldn't tell who they were. The man furthest to the right, crawled to the corner of the house and snuck a quick peek toward the wing of the ranch that held the bedrooms. He was rewarded with a burst of machine gun fire from one of the rooms. Off to Will's right a man from the unit was obviously training his gun in that direction and a short pop, pop, pop sounded and the machine gunner fell back firing his gun into the ceiling.

Now for a minute, nothing happened except for a bit of sporadic firing from inside the house and Will wondered if he should move up on the left as he had planned, but only just then, a figure in black streaked diagonally across his vision. It was Zeke. The man sprinted and dropped a bare half second before bullets tore through the air. Will was back to lying as flat as possible since Zeke was almost directly in front of him and the bullets missing him were coming uncomfortably close to Will. More gunfire from his right silenced one of the gunmen shooting at Zeke. This caused almost every gun in the house to spray the desert out to his right, giving Will the opportunity to clear the area behind where Zeke lay. His only options were forward or to move to his right.

Forward across no man's land seemed too crazy.

He crawled along to his right, toward where shots still ranged out, but didn't get too close to whoever was shooting since intermittent gunfire zinged in every few seconds. Instead, he snugged up behind a cactus and watched as the men from the unit worked as a team, popping up here and there, taking a shot or two, and then dropping again. The fire from the house dwindled with each passing minute until there seemed to be maybe only a couple men left alive and it was Will's guess they were holed up in the kitchen.

"Will?"

The way his name was spoken sent a chill down his spine. The man on his right was hurt and badly too. Will crawled as quick as he could to the man, his fear for himself having disappeared in a second. It was Jake. He lay on his side and blood that seemed altogether too black spurted from a wound high up on his chest.

"Will," the man repeated. "Is it bad?"

The bullet had entered in the hollow on the left side of his neck between his throat and his collarbone. There wasn't an exit wound as far as Will could see. "What should I do, Jake? Tell me what to do?"

"I'm not Jake. My real name is Tony...Tony." His voice faded as he spoke. "You have to find my wife...she's...she's." Will put his fingers over Tony's mouth, quieting him.

"Hey look, it's going to be ok. We'll find your wife, no problem and I'll tell her what hospital you're at, ok?" Tony nodded in a small way and Will continued, "Now I need you to keep quiet." Will bent down looking into the wound and because of the dark was unable to see a thing, so he then reached in with his finger and right away, he felt a fine pulsing spray. It wasn't huge, but there was an artery nicked.

This spelled trouble.

"Cover fire!" Abe yelled from near the house.

Will plucked Tony's knife from its sheath and cut a portion of his own shirt away. He then rolled it up and stuffed it rudely into the wound causing the injured man to groan weakly.

"Cover fire!" Abe screamed again.

"That's you," Tony whispered.

"Me?" Will looked down at the CAR 15 lying on its side like a dead fish. He grabbed it up. "What does he mean by cover fire?"

"Just shoot at the house. Don't hit any of our guys."

Will sighted down the length of the barrel and fire purposely high to get an idea what the gun would feel like. It was fantastic. It was painfully loud, as if tremendous explosions were occurring right beside his ear and yet there was almost no kick to the thing whatsoever. He lowered his sights and fired down the length of the house raking it until the gun quite unexpectedly stopped firing. A small port on the side of the gun sat open where it hadn't before and Will guessed he had run out of bullets.

"Do you have..."

Tony's eyes were closed. Will reached out to feel for a pulse and discovered one that was light and thready. He wouldn't last much longer and unfortunately there was nothing more Will could do for him. Something whispered passed his head and he glanced back to the house and saw flashes of light twinkling from deep within it. Someone was shooting at him, but oddly, he couldn't hear the gunfire and he wondered briefly, as he searched the various pouches on Tony's belt for more ammo, whether the men in the house were using silenced weapons. It didn't much matter to Will if they were.

Tony was out of ammo, which was neither here nor there with Will since he had no idea as to his efficacy with the CAR 15. With the dark, he had no clue whether he even hit the house, let alone shot through one of the windows.

"Cover fire!"

"I'm out of bullets," Will yelled back. As soon as he said it, he regretted that he had. It just wasn't something to announce to everyone. Feeling stupid at his error, Will grabbed the pistol that he had laid aside and charged forward stooping at the waist. It seemed like a very long run out in the open. Six seconds later, he came gasping up the side of the house and threw himself to the ground near Abe.

"That was real stupid!" Abe growled. "Don't ever run in a straight line like that again. Is Jake ok?"

Will shook his head. "No. He's hit and he'll die if he doesn't get to a hospital quick."

Abe and Timothy shared a look and as usual, Timothy was quiet. Abe called out, "Zeke! Cover fire!" This was met with silence. "Damn it!" Abe took a deep breath, "Ok. Timothy, I'm going to lay down some fire you go around and enter through that other door. Keep your eyes peeled. After you're in, I'll come through the glass right here. Cool?"

Timothy nodded affirming the plan, but Will wasn't in

agreement. "What about me? What should I do?"

"You stay right here, and don't do a thing till I give you an order."

Abraham's terse reply angered Will, who was unaccustomed to being commanded about and who thought that waiting was a sure fire way to let Tony die. Besides, he knew the house better than the other two men and instead of waiting for who knows what, as soon as Abraham began shooting, he found the clearest area of the broken window and scrambled through it.

Coming down into his parent's family room, he landed on a body and feeling squeamish, crawled over it. Two more bodies were to his left. He didn't look for long at them. Gaping holes raged out the back of their heads and it turned his stomach to see.

The family room was full of blood and noise. Bullets zipped through the air back and forth above his head, striking walls and furniture and glass and nick-nacks. There was no other option for Will than to slither along as low as he could, and he did, making it to the half wall that divided the living room from the family room just as a lull in the firing came about. Only then did he realize how harsh and rapid his breathing came and went. For a moment he wondered if he were hyperventilating, but then he saw the body of a Hispanic man laying in the doorway of the adjoining rooms and all thoughts of his own breathing left him.

The man, clearly and undeniably was dead. There was a small hole above his right eye and another hole, large enough for Will to put his fist through, on the side of his head. Head wounds seemed to be the order of the day in the house and the very thought kept Will from venturing to peek above the wall. Yet if he didn't, and just sat there what was his purpose to coming into the house at all? He would have to rise up eventually to fire his gun, but the dead man kept drawing Will's eyes to him. The death dealing injury was strange, and morbidly his mind pictured the bullet ricocheting around the inside of the man's head before exploding outwards. He ogled the man for a few more seconds before he realized that the man had about his neck a strange necklace of beaten disks of metal and entwined plant stems.

Without hesitation, Will exposed himself to the possibility of gunfire from the kitchen and reached out to snatch the necklace. The second it broke a storm of light seared across his mind. Images flooded his consciousness and he reeled backwards, crying out in pain.

And he *knew*.

Yet at that moment, he didn't know *what* exactly. As before, the future and the present intermingled to such a degree that for long seconds where bullets tore the air and guns rattled back and forth, nothing made sense. Visions doubled over themselves until he squeezed his eyes down hard and only then was there the relief of darkness.

But this was different than how it had been that afternoon; when he had closed his eyes then, the images still had come to him. Now there was only darkness, and the darkness worried him. It was an empty darkness, devoid of thought and feeling. Quickly he opened his eyes, but for a second the darkness hung with him. It was a coming darkness.

Was he going to die? Is that what the darkness meant? He had known the possibility of his coming death all afternoon but possibilities were not the same as realities. Possibilities could be shrugged off and perhaps dealt with at another time. This was far more immediate. It would be soon.

Unless.

He could just sit there huddled behind the wall. Surely, he would be safe if he did and truly he didn't know Tony all that well. And the man could die either way no matter what he did. He could be dead already for all Will knew. And

Zeke as well. Rationalizations came to him by the score and his desperate mind lapped them up without question. But then...

The door to the deck came open just to his right. A dark man with very white eyes and bright teeth crouched in the opening, it was Timothy. Only his name wasn't Timothy. And he wasn't a quiet man as he seemed. His name was James and he loved to laugh. He was a real person. James stood up and fired a short burst of gunfire over the living room couches and into the kitchen. Suddenly his face contorted and blood sprayed from his chest coating Will. He had been shot in the back. One of Amy's thugs leaned, propped up and bleeding, firing through the master bedroom window from across the 'T'. The man had been thought to be dead, by everybody.

This was about to happen. And it did far too quickly. Forgetting about any fear he had for himself, Will jumped to the door, which opened like magic in front of him and there was Timothy, or James rather, squatting down. Behind him, across the deck, a man popped up like a jack in the box, bringing a heavy black pistol to bear in a quick motion. There was no time for anything other than to grab James and yank him hard into the living room. Gunfire erupted and almost simultaneously, blood and gore drenched Will's face. James toppled over atop him with muscles that twitched and danced grotesquely for a few moments and then went still. Unfortunately, Will had saved him from being shot in the chest only to doom him to being shot in the head.

Sickened by the feel of the man's dying spasms, Will struggled from beneath the corpse and as he did, he *saw* another Hispanic rise from behind the kitchen counter. It was maybe two seconds from happening and he knew he had the choice to jump behind the low wall again or to fire his weapon. The safety of the wall was too alluring and he turned in that direction, yet he was brought up short by what he saw in the living room.

His once proud father, William Jern lay upon his back and stared up at the ceiling with eyes vacant of life. Across his chest, Gayle Jern laid, shielding him with her body as best she could, her eyes were terrifically red and swollen from crying, and they looked altogether desperate in her need to protect her husband.

White-hot anger leapt in Will. His mother's face had been ill-used as evidenced by dark bruises that ran along the left side of her cheek and temple. Her hands were tied and bled freely where the rope had been cruelly bound. For a moment mother and son locked eyes. With his own countenance swollen and dreadfully bruised, she didn't recognize him, yet there was no time for reintroductions or explanations because at that moment, one of the gunmen in the kitchen popped up and began firing. Will had seen it coming and made up his mind.

With the air ripping with sound of bullets tearing though it, Will calmly thumbed off the safety and fired back three times. Unfortunately, knowing the future and shooting straight were two different talents and he only possessed the one. Every one of his shots went high and to the right. He could see them causing little holes to appear in the cabinetry, but the man ducked down before he was able to correct his aim.

"Cover fire!" Abe screamed behind him. Will took this to mean that he should fire and he did, sending bullets as low as he could across the counter top. From his right more gunfire erupted and Will returned fire in that direction. Then there was a loud ringing silence. Tense seconds slipped by where nothing happened.

"Will?" It was a whisper. Without turning, Will knew Abe had been hit. He could picture the wound in his mind, Abe had been hit just above the right elbow. Unless the man was ambidextrous, the injury spelled trouble since Will had proved himself a poor shot. He glanced back to see the small soldier with a pistol in his left hand, gingerly hugging his right arm to his chest.

He nodded at the soldier with a show of bravado, but the soldier only growled in stern quiet manner, "Get your ass out of that doorway before you get shot."

It was a smart plan and Will scurried to the front of the couch that sat against the dividing wall and crouched there, looking back and forth from the door where James had been killed, to the kitchen where two gunmen remained. He kept his gun out swinging it back and forth in a short arc.

"If you want to hit anything, use two hands," Abe hissed. In a flash Will complied and wondered if that would improve his aim any. He would find out quick. One of the gunmen hopped up and began firing through the doorway he had just vacated. Will came up slightly out of his crouch and squeezed off two quick rounds. He missed both times.

A second later, the front door banged open.

"Did one of them leave?" Abe whispered. The whisper sounded very tired as if the little man was almost asleep. Will risked another glance back and saw a great stain of blood covering half his chest. The arm wound was bleeding worse that he would have guessed, and it gave Abraham a pale grey appearance.

Someone called out in Spanish from the front of the house, answering Abe's question. A return answer came from the person in the master bedroom and this was followed seconds later by the man in the kitchen. They were effectively boxed in.

"What are we going to do?" Will turned to Abe with the question, but stopped as he saw that the man had slumped over, unconscious. "Oh my..."

Surrounded by dead bodies and with the lives of at least four people dependent on him, it was no wonder that for just a second, panic swept across him like a wild fire in the wind. The gun began to jitter in his hands and just then a man with black hair and dark features poked his head up from the deck looking through the shattered window into the family room.

He was there for but a second and Will wasted a bullet shooting and missing. The man called out and Will could guess that his exact location had just been announced.

Crawling over broken glass, he hurried to the bar, which sat nestled in the corner. Facing out, he had ninety degrees of room to cover. It was too much for one man, especially if they came at him all at once, which they surely would. Back and forth, he tracked the gun while his breath came loud, and fast. In and out, faster and faster, he practically panted as he waited for the men to come at him.

They would come out of the darkness and they would bring it with them. That darkness was death. He had foreseen it and it was near upon him. His hands began to shake even worse and he had to prop them up on the bar so that he had any hope whatsoever of shooting straight. A picture on the bar fell with a small clatter that ended abruptly and for some reason it made him wonder about how many bullets were left in his gun.

He had no idea and was too frazzled to even attempt to count the number of times he had pulled the trigger. Ducking down he slid the old magazine out of the pistol, and began to search about in his pockets for the second one. To his horror, the second magazine wasn't so quickly found and ten precious seconds slipped by where he was utterly vulnerable before he located it in his inner jacket pocket.

Snick. The sound of the bolt sliding home calmed his nerves a bit and he breathed a great sigh of relief before peeking out from behind the bar. The man from the deck fired two quick shots and then ducked down. Both of the thug's shots hit the bar and both went right through it, the second grazing his arm at the shoulder. The slight wound didn't hurt a lick but the fact that the bar was so flimsy scared him badly. So badly that he decided that his only option was to go on the attack, but the idea of stepping out of hiding and exposing himself to gunfire from three directions kept him from budging.

He prayed for a vision.

It was likely the only thing that would save him. With seconds slipping by, his hands grew sweatier and when no vision came to him, he wondered if he should attempt to force a vision. Only, how would he get himself out of it again? He would be lucky if he had a minute left to him and sadly, he had to put the idea aside, fearing to be still in the vision when Amy's men came. Instead, he counted in a whisper, preparing to jump up and attack three men at once.

"One...two..."

Bamn! Bamn! He jerked in surprise. Someone was shooting from off in the desert. His first thought was that Talitha was out there. The idea sent a chill down his back. If she were out there, instead of tracking down Katie it meant that there was a better than even chance that the winner of this little battle wouldn't live long enough to enjoy the fruits of their victory.

Bamn! This shot struck one of the east facing family room windows with a loud crack. She was shooting at the house? Will guessed that it wasn't his sister out there. A gun would be the last thing that she would use, her evil side preferred killing with her hands when possible.

What about Tony? Perhaps he had regained consciousness and...

"Mmmmmh! Mmmmmh!" It was his mom grunting out a warning; someone was moving through the living room. Who needed a vision when he had Tony and his mom?

Will did. Knowing the attack was coming had frozen him in place for the barest second, but then he heard a thud and a groan from the living room. The man there had kicked his mom! His anger thankfully came roaring back and he sprang from behind the bar prepared to shoot the man in the living room. Only with the dark, it was quite hard to see and it took a moment to note the slinking shadow moving toward the doorway between the two rooms.

Will fired four times and the shadow went down to the

ground. Quick as a wink he turned and fired twice toward the deck and two more vaguely behind him, he then dove over the wall. Bullets seemed to chase him as he went and he fetched up hard against a chair, awkwardly he untangled himself and fired three times at the shadow that lay groaning in the corner. With that, he poked his head up just in time to see flashes from behind the wall of the family room and down he went, crawling for the kitchen.

Behind him, his mother grunted out helplessly. It hurt to leave her like that, trussed up and entirely helpless, yet there was no choice. To stay meant death for both.

More gunfire crashed throughout the house but it didn't seem to be directed at him and Will was able to scurry toward the wing of the house that was comprised of bedrooms. He took the first right into the master and went to the window and prayed not to miss. There was a man on the deck ducking up and down trying to look into the living room.

Will steadied himself and fired three times purposely aiming low. The man appeared to jump as if stung and then he crumpled and lay unmoving. Will didn't dare to waste any more ammo and ducked down as bullets headed his way. He crawled toward the hall before jumping up and doubling back in the direction of the kitchen. A great part of him felt a growing excitement, there was just one man left, and a lucky shot could end this in a second. Thus, he hurried forward just as that very last man came around the corner from the living room. At twenty paces, the two men opened fire at the same time. Will threw himself violently to the right as his gun blasted once and then twice. Both men missed and in the space of a second were both out of ammo. Now there was an awful moment between them.

The Hispanic had feverishly bright eyes and very quick hands. Will had dropped his only other clip and therefore he charged only to be brought up short when another gun flashed into his opponents hands. *The darkness was coming.*

Will suddenly had the vision that he had prayed for, a piercing light and then darkness.

And so it went. At the last moment, Will tried to dodge, but at twelve feet, there was little chance of the man missing. The light. A brief flash of pain shattering his skull. Then darkness, only darkness.

Chapter 22

Talitha

There was no helping it, no possible way to stop the scream that tore from her throat. The scream was reflexive, born from an instantaneous terror that applied itself to her entire being and rode in a blaze across her nerves like cold dread lightning. But what was one more scream? It mingled with the millions of others and was lost in a second.

Talitha, high up on the rim of the Void, looked down into its vast stretches, and saw the multitudinous demons feigning to writhe in an ecstasy of sadistic pleasure. As well, she saw the countless souls in their self-enforced exile going through the motions, screeching and crying and begging, all for an audience consisting solely of their own little minds. Nothing had changed. The illusion of hell was as it had been, full of hate and misery and fear, but most of all, denial. After all, it was the key ingredient to self- deception and without it, where would these lost souls be?

There was the illusion of hell and then there was the great Void. The Void was everywhere and endless, and as the name would suggest there was nothing to it but emptiness and more emptiness, and still the illusion of Hell with its horrors and pain was far preferable to that emptiness. The terror of the Void was indescribable and subtle. It unmade souls. It turned them into the shadows of finality.

Talitha knew all of this, and because she had experienced the Void as no person had ever before, both from within and without, she understood it to a greater degree than any. Yet she was still subject to its horrors as much as the least soul and she trembled and cried in fearful misery. Her dual-mind split upon the idea of the Void, with the remnants of the demon that had been in her demanding to go down into the pits, demanding to be named, while the girl within her, Talitha Jern, terrified to the core, would deny the Void if she could. However, for her there was no other way and no other path, and far, far up above it all, she was monstrously afraid.

Though there was nothing around her, it was as if she clung to the side of a mountain, and a great fall awaited her were she to slip from its precipice. She had no idea how it was that she held on, but the bitter cold of the Void smote her causing her weakening muscles to quiver, yet at the same time a warm howling wind struck her from the rear, threatening to cast her off the invisible peak and dash her among the vile atrocities below.

She turned from the inevitable and looked back in the direction from which the wind coursed and was startled that she could actually see the world that she had just left. There was the Draugr, with the broken blade in its hand, the point of which was through the side of her neck. And there as well was her body, with her face contorted in an ugly portrait of misery. The scene appeared frozen, with nothing stirring as if all the world waited for the actuality of time to perform its appointed duty and move on to the next second.

Unable to shift her eyes away, Talitha stared for an unknowable span of time. Every aspect of the scene she took in, including the somewhat mystifying and embarrassing realization that she wasn't wearing underwear. The little sundress, that the saleslady at the airport had looked down her nose upon, sat very high up on her hips exposing all, and this had her worrying what people would think when her body was discovered.

The eternal scene of her last moment on earth was sad and depressing, yet what lay below her was infinitely worse so she ignored that as best she could and stared at herself and thought upon the things she might have done or at least should have done. Her mind drifted over her family, she should have loved them all more dearly, she thought of friends whom she should have treated more fairly. She had many regrets and it was these which began to spur on the stranger within her. Grief and guilt fed it so that after not too long it began demanding a return to the Void. It had a strident evil voice and it pecked and berated, incessantly. It would not be denied for long.

Talitha had looked upon her coming time in the Void with the dispassionate logic that had always defined her and she had come to the difficult conclusion that it would not make sense to enter the Void as herself no matter her current readiness to confront its evils. The Void was eternal, and eventually it would wear her down as it had before. Evil begets evil. That was nowhere more true than in the Void and it was a certainty that her own evil side, what once had been an entirely separate entity but was now only a byproduct of its creation, would prevail over her and take control.

That was a given, there was no alternative and no fighting it, that is unless she made what could only be a brief stand just to satisfy honor. But she wouldn't even do that. Common sense would prevail and instead she would hide herself away in the breast of the stranger, hoping against all reason that she would be saved a second time. Yet it would take more than a miracle to do it again, since no being in the universe would risk everything just to save a demon.

In the guise of the stranger, Talitha would be a demon soon enough. She knew the demon world. She knew their weaknesses. Their lust for power. Their tendency to gamble too much on false alliances and she knew, as well, how she would go about exploiting it. All it took was cunning and desire, both of which the stranger had in abundance.

These thoughts transfixed her and caused the stranger to grow bolder in its attempt at possession. Its will had grown strong and she could feel her fingers peeling back against the nothingness that she gripped. Despite the great height and regardless of the horrendous pain the fall would inflict, the stranger prepared to hurl herself into the Void.

"Not yet!" she pleaded, holding harder to the nothingness. The fear at the prospect of the fall, at entering again the Void, and at losing her identity, possibly forever, drove her near to hysterics. "Please, not yet!" she wailed.

The stranger emboldened to a greater degree by the pitiful begging was able to pry Talitha's left hand fully away. She pin wheeled with it in a desperate attempt to keep herself from falling.

The stranger laughed with her voice and then said with an air of casualness, "Let go. Don't waste anymore of our time. Let yourself go."

It was an odd thing to say and Talitha's mind clung to the words. There was no such thing as time in the Void. It was a word without meaning. A thousand years was the same as a second, which equaled to a month. Time had no substance and no boundaries. There was no earth to spin, so that days were undefined. There was no sun to revolve around, which meant a year had no value. A second or an hour could be as long or as short as a demon wished it to be. Talitha allowed the concept of time to flourish within her and it trailed along the synapses of her mind and as contemplation took hold, the stranger receded. It was a creature of action and death, not one of cognition.

Flush with this petty victory she cried out, "I am still Talitha!" Yet the victory was short lived.

Similar to a car crash, she felt herself flung forward in hard jolting manner and then...just like that, she was in her body again, out in the desert.

Confusion was her second sensation behind the screaming pain of the wound in her neck. The pain was all-encompassing and rendered her incapable of thinking beyond it. Nothing in her life or her death had ever compared, which was indeed something. It was as though her soul had been ripped like a sheet and each fiber that parted from its neighbor carried its own individual agony straight to her mind, where instead of being glomped in with the rest, she felt each as a singular unrelenting torture. The pain was cacophonous beyond the describing and thankfully short.

Amazingly, the Draugr withdrew the blade from her neck, whereupon the sanity destroying pain completely disappeared and in its place was blessed numbness. The nerves that ran along her left shoulder and neck were destroyed beyond any hope of repair, and after that pain, she couldn't have been more thankful.

Now came the confusion and questions. Why did the creature pull the sword from her? Why did it save her life? Why was it still night and what was the day? How long had she been in the Void, staring at her body? Weeks or days? These came to her as she watched, happily at first, as if in slow motion, the black blade drawing back from her. It raised up high, paused above her face and then without warning came plunging back down faster than she could blink.

This answered her first query, the Draugr wasn't trying to save her life at all. In its mindless attack, it knew nothing of souls, only of beating hearts and hers had never ceased its heavy drumbeat. Her soul had been snatched from her body and sucked to the very brink of the Void, but hadn't crossed over. This insight hit like a flash as did the understanding that if the blade struck her again, there would be no coming back.

Feeling remarkably composed after all that had occurred, Talitha yanked her good right shoulder hard to the side at the same time, she brought the flat of her palm across her body and just barely was able to direct the blade away from its intended course. Instead of driving down into her left eye, it sunk soundlessly into the dirt next to her ear. Time indeed was an oddity to the senses. Again, as if in slow motion the Draugr reared back to strike, this time Talitha used its momentum against it, shoving out hard with her right arm. Though the creature was possessed of unholy strength, it still weighed only one-hundred and sixty pounds and her shove almost toppled it off of her. It flailed backwards with the strength of her push, giving her another second in which to grab its leg, and this she used to catapult the Draugr into an ugly rear summersault.

In the space of a breath, the two opponents were up facing each other and Talitha had a half second to take stock of her situation—her future never looked more grim. Hours or days might have passed in the Void, but only a fraction of a second had passed on earth and so she was quite unrecovered from her long dash. She gasped for breath and wobbled on shaking legs, the ghastly wound in her neck bled freely and with her broken left wrist and destroyed nerves, her left arm was all but useless.

The Draugr was her match in strength but greatly exceeded her in its ability to absorb damage, she could punch the thing for the remainder of the night and not seriously affect it, and nor would it slow from exhaustion or blood loss. Their speed was equivalent as well, though an outside observer would have given the edge to the girl, but that was illusionary. It seemed this way because Talitha held one great advantage over the Draugr and that was in the area of intelligence, which she used to anticipate and analyze the creature's attacks.

It moved in again; amazingly fast, dreadfully strong, merciless, and vicious. Four times the evil blade hacked at her, blistering the air with its intense cold and she gave ground, dodging about back and forth, using up her dwindling reserves of energy. This couldn't last much longer. Her body was fading, but her mind, perhaps slapped into focus by the dread reality of her fate was still composed and saw in the Draugr a great oddity.

The vile thing attacked with horrendous power, yet also with one-dimensional unvarying repetition. With its last swing, she had been too slow and exhausted to dodge far enough away and there had been an opening for the Draugr to reach out with its left hand and tear out her throat as she slipped away from the blade, but it didn't avail itself to her destruction. This she puzzled over until the order Amy had given came to mind. *"Diablo, run to the Jern's. Use the sword, kill everyone. Go!"*

That was the reason she was still breathing in the desert air. Had the creature used all of its not insubstantial abilities, she likely wouldn't have lasted more than seconds against it. And there also was her single slim chance, and if she were to live past the next few minutes, she would have to find some way to exploit it. Only the Draugr pressed her so closely and with such blazing speed that not once could she see an opening to strike back.

Still she had the resource of her mind at her disposal and she determined that if an opening didn't present itself then she would have to create one. Without waiting for the next attack, Talitha turned and ran. Hot after, the Draugr came and in her exhaustion, the thing was within a second of catching her when she spied the good-sized bush that she had hid in only a minute before. This she jumped full over.

The Draugr charged around it, only to come upon a completely naked Talitha Jern. It cared not for such things, as she knew, and slowed not a bit while it brought the broken blade back for another great swing. Though it strained at the weaken fibers of her courage, Talitha waited the onslaught and only at the last minute did she fling the balled up sundress at the fiend's face. With ease, it slashed the dress aside with the blade.

Talitha struck. The blade had flashed right to left and as it passed she leapt in with a bone crushing roundhouse. Now, the Draugr could in no way feel pain, nor would a fractured bone do much to slow it, yet for all its hell bound ruggedness, its human body still operated along the normal laws that govern our world. Talitha's kick was sent at the things left knee, cracking it square in two and torqueing it off to the side. No longer was the simple pulley action of the opposing muscles of its leg capable of moving it in anything close to a normal gait.

Ecstatic for the moment, she skipped back out of reach of the blade as it swung back at her and looked for another opening, while the creature lurched after. With the gunfire dying out in the house, she felt a growing sense of urgency but she couldn't leave the Draugr even as debilitated as it was. There was no guessing at what rate it might heal itself, she would have to brave the blade and destroy her enemy as fast as possible. In front of her, a rock the size of a baseball sat partially embedded in the dirt, in a second she yanked it out and stood poised to hurl it with all of her considerable force.

Indifferent to its body, her opponent staggered on and she waited until it was almost upon her before she threw it pointblank into the things face. Her aim had been to take out its left eye and she succeeded so admirably that after retreating again she stooped to find more rocks. The rugged landscape had birthed millions of rocks so that ammunition was plentiful and soon she had blinded the creature and crushed in part of its skull. It kept coming.

Since its joints were the closest thing to a vulnerable area that it possessed, she moved in like silent lightning and destroyed its other knee with a driving sidekick. After this, with the creature flopping about blind, lashing out robotically with the sword, she went to work on its elbows. A bit of patience and deft strikes had them both broken in a minute and after that, it was only a simple yet disgusting matter of breaking all the bones in its right hand for it to release the sword. Pathetically, it still squirmed in complete silence, attempting to come after her; she withdrew from it with a great deal of disgust contorting the beautiful features of her face.

The look wasn't singularly for the Draugr, the sword too added to her discomfort. Not only was it blistering cold, its foul touch reminded her of the Void, and that sparked the return of the stranger, who grew in her mind becoming larger in seconds. Never in her life had Talitha been more worn down, this wasn't just physical, though she still breathed in and out like a furnace bellow, and her muscles shook—fatigue struck her mentally and spiritually as well. Her mind was drained, and she felt depleted and empty to the core. The stranger knew all this and decided that right then, it would challenge her for control. Ultimate control.

For the last eight years, it was she, Talitha who was the dominant personality within her. On a daily basis, she was in charge and the other soul that had resided in her had to resort to trickery or fatigue, or chance, to gain control. But now, the stranger wanted it all. She wanted to call the shots and make decisions and more than that, she wanted to live! She demanded to live.

The onslaught in Talitha's mind was an avalanche of consciousness. It struck her brain like a seizure and she collapsed, twitching, the sword dropping from her hand. Synapses began firing at an unprecedented tempo so that facts warred upon supposition, ideas and opinions surged against each other, hypothesis encountered refutation and all clamored to be deliberated upon. For every up, there was a down, a black for every white. The two personalities clashed striving for dominance and her physical self was caught in the middle. Talitha's hands became hooked claws and she began to bubble and froth at the mouth.

What such a clash came down to was desire. Which personality wanted to live more?

The stranger had a hunger for life. Yes, it wanted to go to the Void and become named and contest for supremacy there, but it also wanted this life, the real one. She thought of it as being wasted and it was this more than anything that spurred her on.

On the other hand, Talitha seemed to be living, simply to delay her coming time in hell. She was alive because she was afraid of death and this was why she was losing the silent battle. There was no denying that deep inside she had long ago let go of her life.

The stranger grew stronger with every passing second, crushing the girl's will and she barely fought back, she was done.

And then she heard—as if through someone else's ears—pop, pop, pop of gunfire. It had been going for some time, but now that she was no longer brawling the Draugr for her life, or sprinting across the desert or battling to save the last vestige of herself, she understood what it meant. A gunfight was raging room to room throughout her parent's house. But in truth it meant more than that, it meant her brother was in trouble. And she loved him.

And just like that, she realized she had a reason to live.

The tables were turned on the stranger, who fought back resolutely, but Talitha was too powerful and sent it scurrying once again to hide in the crevices of her mind. There was no rejoicing over her triumph, since it was a shoddy triumph indeed, both Talitha and the stranger knew what had really occurred was simply a postponement that couldn't last much longer.

Not only that, she lacked the strength to rejoice, she barely had the strength to stand. The battle had left her wilted and damp with sweat and drool, her insides quivered as if she were about to be sick and her muscles protested even holding up her slight frame.

Reeling like a drunk, she went first to her dress, but didn't slip it over her head. Instead, she wrapped the sword in it and doing her best to ignore the fantastic cold she staggered off in the direction of the gunfire.

Strobe lights looked to be going off within the ranch house, back and forth they seemed to duel, but when she was fifty or so yards away it ended with a long pause and then a single flash. A second later the dampened rumble of the last gunshot rolled down to meet her and she stopped, scanning in the windows for movement, but the house, at least from her angle, looked remarkably still. And foreboding. Without the gunfire, the house lay cloaked in an eerie darkness. The last gunshot hung in the desert air with a depressing quality. She waited for more, yet none came and the thought that the final bullet fired had come from an executioner had her running again. It wasn't anywhere near her normal running style. There was no grace to it at all, her legs felt like broken stilts that had been taped together in the middle.

But she staggered on. Bloody prints following after her as did dead silence, she was a shadow tottering across the landscape, moving as quick as possible despite the pain in her torn up feet. They were in poorly suppressed agony and when she hit the thick green grass that bordered the house, she had to hold back a sudden cry of pleasure. Nothing had ever felt so cool and comforting in her life. She couldn't pause to enjoy it. Instead, she leapt through a partially destroyed bedroom window, almost stumbled on a body, and sliced her feet even greater on broken glass.

In the shadowed room, her senses came alive: she heard the sound of a gun being loaded with a fresh clip, she saw the bodies strewn about, she smelled the blood and the pungent fumes from spent bullets, and she felt even the small vibrations of a man walking upon carpeted floor. He was working his way from room to room and she had his position fixed in what she took to be the family room. Exiting from the bedroom, her fatigue caused her to trip and she thumped, first into one wall before ricocheting off onto the opposite. This she clung to and it held her up as she wobbled her way toward the kitchen, but a sight there stopped her.

Her brother lay in a heap at the junction where the kitchen and hallway met. His head was soaked with very bright fresh blood and covering his face and chest was a thick chunky looking grey substance. She knew very well the odd metallic smell of human brain.

A tiny whisper escaped her numbed lips, "Oh, no."

She wanted to go to him and cry over him, but there was still a killer to deal with and her mother could possibly be alive. Though this seemed like a long shot. Talitha forced her eyes from the body of her brother, but as she turned the corner and looked into the living room she had to stop once again, stunned by the sight.

More bodies, more blood, more brains greeted the girl. The room was such a nightmare of death and carnage that for a moment Talitha had to check her hold on reality. It looked like a scene from the nastiest pits in hell and it was with an effort of her crumbling will that she pushed herself on.

The one man left alive, whom she had heard walking about, stood over the body of another. She knew the man's scent. He had been at her brother's house, and now he was here, killing, murdering, executing. Without a thought to her state of undress and in complete silence, she ran in a shambling stride through the living room before vaulting the low wall; and the man was unaware. His focus was on aiming down the length of the assault rifle that he carried. Talitha struck it with the hell blade and sent it spinning away before he knew what sort of terror was upon him.

In the dark, with her wild hair looking black and skin that glistened with the blood of many men, her teeth shown fiercely white and hungry. No succubus or vile Huldra of the lower planes could have caused any more fright in the man and a fear induced mania seemed to light the man's eyes from within.

Perhaps this was why he fought with greater speed and strength than she had experienced from a normal human in a long time. He was on her in a flash striking wildly, hitting her twice, and sending her sprawling. She could barely protect herself, her body was worn, broken, and bleeding, she had no use in her left arm, and her right was numb from carrying the sword, and this she no longer held, it had thunked heavily to the carpet after she had hit the man's gun.

With no real way to protect herself she started kicking

backwards to give herself room, but he jumped full upon her and easily pinned her arms over her head. And then he very stupidly paused. Shock crept into his eyes at her nakedness, but amazingly the shocked look evolved into a leering one. Up and down her slim body, he gazed and she felt the depravity within his soul as his manhood gave a forceful pulse against her thigh.

Talitha went limp. Other than her heaving chest, she let all of her muscles relax. It was precious seconds that she needed. Seconds where her body could recoup just the smallest amount and the perversion atop her gave her just that as he fumbled with his belt. More seconds were a gift as he struggled his pants down one handed. He paid for those seconds with the loss of his left eye.

Just as he thought he would slip into her, she yanked her right hand out of his loose grip and punctured his eye with her thumb. It went into the socket, right to the webbing of her palm. He screamed and with the last of her strength, she toppled him sideways, rolled and ended up atop him. The charred black hell blade was right there; she snatched up the horrid thing and brought it up for the killing stroke.

But she was stopped with a word, "Talitha."

The voice was ragged and unpleasant and barely human. Turning, she saw a lurching bleeding man heading into the living room and instantly thought it was the Draugr coming for her again.

"Where's Kay...where's Kay..." The man stumbled against the couch and then fell over it, to lay on the ground unmoving. It was her brother.

The shock of seeing him alive sent her mind reeling, "Will? Is that you?" She had trouble believing her eyes. "Will?" He didn't answer. Unthinkingly she tossed aside the sword and crawled off the moaning thug and went to her brother.

The outward appearance that he presented was far, far worse than the actuality of his injuries, which apart from a minor scratch along one shoulder, consisted entirely of a deep nasty wound—a long furrowing gash along the side of his skull. On closer examination, her questing fingers discovered his skull to be intact and she almost wept with relief. The grey matter drying on him was not his at all.

"Miss?" Behind her.

Suddenly she became aware of her nudity and grabbing up her fallen dress she spun about, pressing it to herself. Abraham, looking dead pale with eyes that were half closed said, "Jake is out there...in the desert. Please go find him."

The man appeared so far gone that modesty was no longer an issue. Talitha yanked the torn sundress over her head and went to him first.

"No..." With mouse like strength, he tried to push her away.

"Shush," she ordered in a kindly voice gently putting his hand down by his side. "I'll make sure that you're going to live first." Abraham's wound had perforated his upper arm, completely passing through the bicep and she didn't need to feel about in the wound to know that his brachial artery had been damaged. The spray pattern of blood was like writing on the wall, literally. With him still protesting weakly, she took from his military style web belt a sterile field dressing. This she stuffed into the wound without regard to his pain and then cinched it down tight with the light green sling that came with it. He groaned in response and she only pulled it tighter, before tying it atop of the wound. She then laid him on his back and propped a couch cushion under his feet to lessen the degree of shock that he was very likely even then experiencing.

Now she would go check on Jake, or so she thought.

"Mmmmmh!" Gayle Jern had worked herself to a kneeling position and was looking over the wall.

"Mom!" Jake was forgotten momentarily as Talitha hopped over the wall. A long dreadful looking knife lay on the floor and she used it to unbind her mother. "Are you ok?

Are you hurt at all?"

"Only my hands...I think they're...never mind. Are you alright? You're all..." Gayle looked at her daughter with wonder and dismay. Talitha couldn't have looked too good.

"I'm..." she was about to say fine, but in truth she was nowhere close. The wound in her neck wasn't natural, the edges of it felt dead and she feared that it would never heal. However, she wasn't going to burden her mother with that information, at least not then. "I'll be fine. I'm a little worried about Will. A bullet grazed his head, but he's got tough skull. You know how hardheaded he's always been." Talitha's pathetic attempt at humor had been predicated on how her mother had looked to almost faint at the news of her son being shot.

"And Katie? Do you know where she is?"

If her mother's desperate imploring tone hadn't been that of one begging for good news, she might have told the truth. Instead, all she could stutter was, "I, uh... I, uh..."

"What? Where is she, do you know?"

Talitha was able to answer this with honesty and she shook her head, no. "Mom...listen to me. There's a man in the desert. One of the soldiers. He may need my help, ok? Wait here. Keep an eye on Will and that man there." She pointed at the Hispanic, who lay curled in a ball clutching his face.

When her mother nodded, she ran off in a stumbling manner, thankful not to have to answer the question concerning Katie, because just then it felt like a mistake having traded lives the way she had. Talitha feared how her mom would react when she heard the news about her youngest daughter. The little girl was special to Gayle...to all of them.

"Jacob?" she whispered, tracking the scent of the man. Behind a glump of bushes she found the man on laying on his side. He didn't look good, even worse than Abe. "It's Talitha," she said kneeling down next to him.

"Did we win?" came his whispered reply.

"Yeah. Quiet down, don't talk." She tried to examine his wound, but there wasn't anything to see. Other than a little hole in the hollow of his neck, his injuries were all internal.

"My chest... it feels full. I'm having a lot of trouble breathing...and I can barely talk."

"I know, that's why I told you to hush." Talitha looked at the wound again, but had no idea what to do. Though she knew anatomy and physiology, she was clueless past the basics of first aid. "I think it would be best if I moved you to the house. I think..."

Just then, two gunshots went off in the house. Talitha was up in a flash, but Jake stopped her, "Wait."

"No. I'll be right back." Another gunshot thundered out, and with it, Jake looked to relax. "Was that a signal?" she asked and Jake nodded. As if to affirm his answer, headlights flicked on in the direction of the road and an engine roared into life.

"It's the priest," Jake whispered.

This response was a bit of a letdown. Though Vogel was a smart and competent man, the wounded men needed a surgeon and fast. "This may be uncomfortable." Talitha bent down with her good arm, grabbed the harness of Jake's web gear and began dragging the man at the quickest pace that she could manage back to house. After the night she had, the fifty yards felt like a thousand and she was huffing and light headed by the time she had her charge pulled into the blazingly bright living room. Father Vogel had beat her to the house and was in the process of examining Abraham's wound.

"Tal," Will was sitting up against the couch looking slightly cross-eyed and dazed. "Where's Katie?"

"Not...now." Her breath was ragged in her chest. "Where's the...phone? We have to call an ambulance." This was greeted with an awkward silence. An ambulance meant the police would soon be involved and there were plenty of ramifications to that. "Jake is going to die if he doesn't get help soon."

"I'll call," her mother volunteered before hurrying from the room.

As soon as she had left, Will whispered, "Tal, where's Katie? Is she alive?"

Her heart seemed to shrivel at the question, yet stoutly she relayed her story, watching all the while as her brother's head sunk lower upon his chest with each passing syllable. She finished lamely with, "I'm sorry."

"My soul for Katie's?" Will asked in misery, ignoring the fact that his wasn't the only one that had been saved in the bargain. "You don't know what a bad trade that is. Katie was so smart and sweet and beautiful...and fun...and ..."

"And so are you, and so is mom!" Talitha, who never liked her judgment questioned, began to get angry. "Also what about Jake and Abraham, what about them and their souls? That's four souls for one and besides...we still have a chance to save her. It has only been what, twenty minutes since I left her? More than likely we still have time to save her."

"Amy has my baby?" Gayle stood letting the wall hold her up. She looked on the verge of collapse.

Talitha only glanced her way for a second before dropping her eyes, nearly overwhelmed with guilt. "Yes. But you would've been so proud of her. She was very brave and strong."

"I am proud of her, just like I'm proud of you, Talitha." The words struck her like a slap and she blinked in surprise and then she blinked harder to fight off the tears that began doubling her vision. They came regardless and as she cried, her mother came and held her. This only made her cry harder.

A minute passed and then Will called them to their senses, "We have to leave. The police are coming. Many of them, and if they catch us here, we'll never save Katie. Mom,

I'll call later when..."

"I'm coming too. No don't give me that look!" Gayle was suddenly angry. "You don't see yourself the way I do. Look around us. Look at your poor father! Look at your sister! Look in a damn mirror! My family is being beaten down, one after another and there's no way I'm going to sit by all helpless and let it happen any longer."

"Yes, Mom, you're right," Will replied. In a much quieter voice he asked, "What's wrong with dad? Did he get stabbed with the sword?"

Talitha had known right away he had. She could smell the wound from the moment she walked in. The odor of corruption was as peculiar and singular as it was stomach churning; it matched the sick smell that emanated from her own neck. Her mom nodded, confirming what had been obvious to her.

"Then he's coming as well," Will declared in a commanding tone. "No hospital will be able to save him if we can't. Father Vogel, please help Talitha with moving my dad. Go to the garage, right through there," he pointed past the kitchen. "We'll take the Jimmy. Abe, the first ambulance will arrive in eleven minutes, will you and Jake be ok for that long?"

Though he looked as though he were about to pass out again, the man nodded. "Yeah, Jake is one tough guy, don't worry. I need two things before you go. My real I.D. is in the car... I'm CIA and the I.D. will save me a bunch of tough questions. And...Zeke is out there still. If he's still alive, please bring him in here."

Will agreed that he would honor these two requests, but as he could barely walk without falling over, it was Gayle who fetched the I.D. and Talitha who found Zeke. He was quite dead, having been shot through the heart. He was a sad sight and it affected Talitha more than she had expected. She closed his once pretty blue eyes and since there was no one about, kissed the man on his cooling lips. It seemed like a fitting farewell.

Chapter 23

Will

Six minutes later: "Pull over...there's a dirt road. Do you see it? Go up it a bit and then kill the engine and shut down the lights." Will *knew* the emergency vehicles would be led by a state patrolmen and sure enough within seconds, red and blue lights danced in the desert night looking gay and festive rather than urgent. More lights were strung out in a long line behind the first and the Jimmy sat dark against the dark and all but invisible.

"How do we find Katie? Can you *see* where she's going to be, Will?" his mother asked. She sat in the front seat next Father Vogel, rubbing her hands together constantly. This had as much to do with anxiety as it did with pain. Where the numbness hadn't faded, pins and needles of returning circulation burned her miserably.

In the back seat, next to a scary looking, blood covered Talitha, Will answered, "No, Amy has placed some sort of spell over herself to keep me from seeing her future and that seems to extend to anyone near her." He spoke in a whisper. Everyone else's voice seemed normally pitched, but his own was like a shriek in his mind. So far, this was his only real after effect of being shot in the head, that is except for the double vision, nausea, dizziness, and whomping migraine.

"Maybe she didn't put a spell on herself, maybe she put a hex on you or us," his mother replied with a touch of mania raising her voice. "I think she cursed us, or maybe her mom did. Can't you feel it? Nothing has been right for years. I mean, take your father for instance and Talitha. All this time they've been under some horrible curse. And now Lisa too! And you also, Will. Your poor face..." she began to cry and seemed near to hysterics.

"Mom! We'll figure this out, ok? Calm down." Will looked around for support, but no one else said anything. Talitha was oddly quiet and sat with her eyes closed looking as if she were meditating rather than asleep, while Father Vogel looked completely stunned and had from the moment he had walked into the house and had seen the place littered with bodies and sprayed with blood.

"I don't know if I can be calm." Gayle hugged her hands to herself. "I can't stop thinking about my little Katie and what's happening to her. It feels like my chest is going to explode. We have to find her and save her, please. Can you do anything?" She touched the priest on his arm and he looked away from the dwindling lights at the woman.

The priest was very pale. Even in the dark his skin seemed to stand out as whiter than anyone's. "There are people working on finding out where Amy may be going. We should find a phone as soon as possible."

"It's safe now to go," Will whispered. "Keep heading east and in about ten miles, on the right is... a, uh..." In his mind, Will could picture the gas station but the name escaped him.

"Texaco," Talitha supplied, still with eyes closed. "And don't touch that. Just leave it alone."

Will's hand had gone to the makeshift bandage that his sister had wrapped around his head. It felt heavy, like a water-laden log sat upon his shoulders. "Texaco, right. They have a phone booth there."

For the rest of the trip to the gas station, no one spoke, or so Will assumed. He fell asleep, resting his head on his sister's slim shoulder and only woke when the priest exited the car and Talitha called out to him, sounding very much like a kid begging to her dad, "Can you please get some milk and a sandwich and Doritos, if they have any?" Gradually and with small groans escaping from his throat, he pulled himself up; Talitha gave him a guilty smile. "I need nutrients."

"It's ok." There was no way Will could eat.

From the front seat, their mother looked back. "Will? I don't trust myself to stand just yet; can you look back and check on your father?"

Turning his head was a chore and elicited more groans. In the cargo area behind the second row of seats, William Jern's long slim form lay curled around Lisa's small one. He looked so terribly old, while she, in the longest sleep of her life, appeared younger than her years. The dichotomy in their appearances didn't end just there. She seemed at peace and looked as if he could wake her with just a kiss, while his features held pain. The muscles in his face were taunt, frozen into a grim expression of agony.

Will could only look for a second before turning away. "There's no change."

"What about his wound?" She seemed afraid of her own question.

With a grunt, Will turned back and lifted up his father's shirt, "It doesn't look good. The black around the edges is spreading." The hole where the blade had torn into him gaped large and ugly, all about it the skin was blackened. He couldn't look on it for long either and after only a second covered the wound again.

"Necrosis," Talitha whispered. Her face told Will plainly that she feared greatly for her father.

Gayle saw the look as well and doubled down on it. "What does that mean?"

Talitha took a deep breath before answering, "It's simply the death of tissue, such as skin or muscle and once it's dead it can't heal itself. But the wound can be debrided and once it's done then healing can occur. Will, the necrosis bordered the wound by about an inch before, how much is it now?"

"At least double that."

Shock widened his mother's eyes and etched a line across her brows; mutely she turned back in her seat. For many minutes, the Jimmy was quiet until a faint siren came to them. An ambulance followed a minute later by another came streaking across the desert heading off to the east. The silence and tranquility of the night settled again on them and they each sat back lost in thought. Will glanced at Talitha...she looked to have bathed in blood. Could some of it be Katie's? With a shiver at the thought, he asked his sister. "What happened to your neck?"

"There was a Draugr...do you recall the thing last night that Luke had become? Amy created one of those and it stabbed me with the sword."

This didn't ring true and it showed on his face and in his words. "Tal, that thing last night was tough, but...but I can't believe that it could do that to you."

"It did. The power of the witch determines the power of the Draugr. I get the feeling that the witch from last night was nothing more just a fortune telling gypsy than any sort of real witch."

During this short conversation a frantic excitement began to light a fire in their mother's eyes. "Tal, how did you live when you were stabbed? I mean you're awake and talking, is there a spell or whatever you can use on your dad? He was stabbed too and...he's not dead, go feel him, you can hear his heart beating and everything. He's still alive, but he's gone at the same time..." Gayle's voice just sort of trailed away as Talitha lowered her head shaking it back and forth.

"No, I only lived by accident. The Draugr stabbed me but pulled the blade out before my soul could be fully torn from me. I'm sorry about dad. I'm sorry for everything." Tears ran across the dried and cracked blood on her face.

Will reached out and held her hand, and was just about to speak when Father Vogel emerged from the store carrying two large brown bags and wearing a grim look. All eyes were on him and it seemed as if none in the car dared to breath.

"I got you a ham and cheese, it was the freshest looking

one," he said handing back both of the brown bags. He then gripped the wheel with both hands and stared out the front windshield it was a moment before he spoke and they all expected the worst. "According to the bishop, there are forty-six possible sites within an hour of our location that Amy could have taken Katie."

"Forty-six!" Will exploded, sending a dagger of pain deep into his head.

"Yes and if we expand that further to two hours, the number almost triples. Of course, we don't know for certain if the criteria we have established is..."

"Shut up. Just shut up," Will growled. "There's no way. Forty-six places in three hours and thirty-six minutes. It can't happen."

His mother looked practically dead from defeat but said, "You don't know that, Will. We could get lucky."

A laugh of derision leapt from his throat and he didn't even try to stop it. "Lucky? Since when have we ever been lucky? We're cursed. You said so yourself, and I for one believe it. Talitha does too and I bet wherever Katie is, she would agree as well."

Oddly, Father Vogel smiled. "We both know you're not going to give up hope. Now look at this list I jotted down. Which should we go to first?"

How badly Will wanted to shred up the list, instead he closed his eyes for a second before speaking in the calmest voice he could manage. "Talitha, when Henny opened the gate, how long did it take, do you remember?"

She shrugged. "It was so hard to tell, she had this shiny thing and I was forced to..."

He held up a hand. "Just ballpark it for me, please."

"Twenty, maybe twenty-five minutes?"

"I was wrong then. At the most, we have an hour and a half to check forty-six places. You see now why, I'm so upset? Amy's not going to wait till the stroke of midnight just so we can swoop in and save the day. She's gonna get this done as soon as possible!" Will's voice had crept up and he ended practically shouting.

"So you're saying we should try one of the closer ones," Vogel replied with annoying calm. Will put his head in his hands, feeling the pounding of his blood increase in tempo.

Talitha piped up in a small voice, "It's worse than you realize, Will. Amy has at least a thirty-minute head start on us, which means we have only an hour to find her. But..." she paused and glanced at her brother. "We still have you. Could you try to look at the future of these addresses? You should be able to see all but the one she is at. We'll use the process of elimination."

"I could try," Will said excitedly. "Let's see, twenty-thirty Valencia court... twenty-thirty Valencia court," he closed his eyes and reached out thinking *twenty-thirty Valencia court*. Nothing happened. He tried to relax, rolling his shoulders a few times and then made a second attempt. Still it was only blackness or maybe blankness that he was able to view. "It's not working, I can't see anything," he said dejectedly.

Talitha tried a good-natured smile, not realizing how fiendish she appeared layered in blood as she was. "Perhaps we got lucky and that's the address she's going to. Try another, if you can see that one then we'll know."

He tried the next address, but it was as black as his mood. "Nothing. I don't know if I'm being blocked or if I just can't look to a place I really know nothing about. I mean these are just words to me."

"Then what do we do?" Gayle chimed in. "Can the Church do anything?"

Vogel's calm became strained with embarrassment. "Very little just yet, but by tomorrow or maybe the following day we might be able to narrow down where Amy has gone. I know that won't do that much for your daughter now, but..."

But nothing. The priest could only do so much and

everyone knew it. A heavy sigh escaped Will. He didn't blame the priest, and he tried not to blame God, he just wished for a break.

His sister sighed as well. "Tomorrow will be too late. According to a vision Will had yesterday, Amy will move the body. I mean Katie, she'll move Katie and hide her. We might still be able to find the gate, but without Katie and Amy present it would be a waste."

"So what do we do? My baby and my husband, how do we save them? Just tell me and I'll do it, I'll do anything," Gayle turned her pleas to each of them. They all looked away. "Could we find another gypsy? One that could find Katie with magic or something?"

Talitha answered, "No, it would have to be a witch who is stronger than Amy. We would never be able to find one before..."

Will cut across her, "There's a gypsy who may help us...Adrina. Maybe the dead have the answers. I heard that was a thing, communing with the dead."

Talitha's eyes narrowed. "It is, but she's in the Void. How do you plan on speaking to her, Will? You won't be able to look into the future to do this. There is no future in the Void, time is meaningless."

"I'll do it the same way you split your soul in half."

Vogel was all interest. "How did you do that?" he asked Talitha.

"I just did." There could be no explanation for such a thing, beyond the one she had given. Now, there was real concern in her eyes. "If you do this, you might not make it back; in fact it might be impossible to make it back."

"You told me hell is voluntary."

"Not if you're being held against your will! Adrina challenged Ba'al Zubel, it's not something he will likely ever forget and that means she's in the Pits at Rek." Her body flared with goose bumps at the name and a shiver went down her back. "There is no escape from those foul dungeons."

She didn't need to tell him about the Pits. The cold black holes where torture and pain had been first conceived were well known to Will Jern and were such a terror that they couldn't be risked. She was right about that.

"What about Henny Harris?" he asked. "We know Amy has been using her mother for information. Henny wouldn't be in the Pits, would she?" There was a lot of hope in his question.

Talitha was slow to respond, but finally declared, "Maybe not...maybe not. In fact, probably not. Souls are traded for all the time. In your dream, Will, were you sure that the demon that was trying to come through the portal was indeed Ba'al?"

"No I guess not, but it was very big."

"The size of it in your dream is irrelevant since clearly whichever demon it was had been feeding on the light of the world directly through the gate. In fact, just like the thrust to weight ratio limitations placed on engines in space travel, where the point of diminishing returns is..."

"Talitha!"

"Sorry," she replied sheepishly. "What I mean is that the demon sucking on that gate grows constantly, making it just that much harder for it to fit through. With that said, the demon could be any of the many thousands and not necessarily Ba'al Zubel."

"Then I'm doing it."

Gayle looked confused. "You're doing what exactly? Going to hell? No, I forbid it. You'll just have to find another way. I... I might have lost two members of my family tonight, I'm not going to watch you die simply on a hunch."

Will tried to explain, "I'm not going to die, ok? It'll look just like I'm asleep..."

"Like your father?"

"No, nothing like that. I'm going to slip down there on the sly, find Henny and...and I don't know what, but I'll think of something. And then." Will snapped his fingers. "I'll pop right back."

"And you two think this is a good idea?" she asked looking from her daughter to the priest. Talitha averted her eyes, but nodded.

Vogel clasped his hands beneath his chin and gave the impression of pondering on the idea in depth. "I can't say if it's a good idea or not, however I don't have another and time is getting very short." Silence greeted the truth of this until Gayle started nodding with great reluctance.

"Ok. Do it but please be careful." She put her arms over the seat for a hug and though it hurt to oblige her, he did and happily so. Hugs may not be so frequent in his future.

"Alright then, I suppose I'm going to do it...Father, head north. Most of the addresses on that list were in Phoenix and if I know Amy, she'd rather open a gate where there's at least the possibility of good dining nearby rather than in one of the dusty little towns around here."

Talitha looked grave. "You make too many assumptions. Amy may not have access to this list. She may know of only a single place and for all we know that could be in Alaska. While you're in the Void, make no assumptions, question all that you see or feel. And...and..." Tears sprang up with a surprising suddenness. "Come back to me, please. I won't last a day without you. Please say that you will?"

She was again that small little girl, his sister from a long time ago and despite his monster headache, he felt tears brewing as well. "I will, Tal. I promise. I promise to come back, heck you know that I don't even want to go. Now... how long should I stay under?"

"Thirty minutes?" Talitha replied.

The answer was like a kick in the stomach; he had been considering half that. "Thirty minutes is a long time in the Void."

"It is, but if you're not done and I try to pull you out, are you likely to go back?" Her logic as always was unassailable, there would be no going back for seconds.

He breathed out loudly and tried not to appear as terrified as he really was, for his mother's sake. "Fine, a half hour then." The brother and sister looked at each other and both knew that thirty minutes could not only feel like an eternity, but might become one as well. His insides began to quiver in fear. "Ok, I better start... or I might, you know, not start." He gave his sister a quick kiss on the cheek and then did the same for his mother all the while diverting his eyes and holding the fake smile of a seasoned politician on his lips. "Love you two." He swallowed and every one could hear.

"I love you, hon," his mom replied through a strained smile of her own. "Be careful, and if you find your father..." The smile slipped away from her face and was replaced by pain. "Set him free. I don't think he can come back here, not after all this."

Will nodded, blinking rapidly, fighting tears. He turned to his sister and watched as Talitha took command of her own features, which had been starting to warp from her fear for her brother. "Love you, Will. Remember that and remember as well, hide your light. It's all an illusion down there, become a part of it, at least outwardly."

He nodded to her, though he was unsure of exactly what she meant. After giving his wife a quick kiss and touching his father on his skinny arm, Will leaned back against the door of the Jimmy and prepared to head into the very worst place imaginable, but he couldn't, not with his mom, sister and a priest staring at him.

"Do you mind? This is kind of a private thing."

They each looked away and he settled in more deeply and closed his eyes. Unlike the house on Valencia that he had tried and failed to see, he knew the Void well. Countless times he had stumbled through it during his dreams, walking with trembling legs to his next torture. That was a torture in itself and the demons knew it and enjoyed the spectacle. He had also seen the Void in person, standing high above it on the great blade. So it was that as he closed his eyes, his mind was easily able to reach out and feel the dire cold of its boundaries. Yes, entering the Void wasn't the problem.

Chapter 24

Katie

The little sparkling light stayed with Katie, dancing, glowing first brighter here and then running brighter there, changing colors in the most delightful manner; it was all that she cared about. Distantly she was aware of other things about her. For instance, she knew she'd been carried down from the rock and then lugged across the desert by a scary, dangerous looking man with thick eyelids which covered pitiless eyes.

She knew as well that the jeep they were bouncing around in was her father's. Amy had need of a four by four to track her down out in the desert and had stolen it without a second thought. And Katie knew that Amy still had in her hands the small, but deadly looking gun, and it had been pointed at her ever since the big Mexican had dumped her into the back seat of the jeep. But none of this mattered to Katie as long as she had her sparkly light.

The light was like an intriguing maze or a puzzle that compelled her to find its hidden origin and she chased its many dazzling tangents only to be led astray and forced to start again. At length, it seemed to her that she had been down every streak and had hunted down every waltzing mote. After this, the patterns began to repeat and she became bored and instead of studying the light, she looked to the negative image that surrounded it.

Initially this consisted of only a tiny black margin, a bare outline only and then as she investigated it further, the margin grew until the light shrunk smaller and smaller, and seemed but a dot. And then she blinked and was aware again.

She found her face pressed up against the window of

the jeep, it was very cold and soon annoyingly so. Yet Katie refused to budge. She tried her best to remain still and take in everything around her with just her periphery, only there wasn't much to see. The desert at night was empty and one cactus looked very much like another. Minutes passed and they zipped by a road sign that proclaimed Tucson in eight miles. Her neck stuck at an angle for so long, began to hurt. Still she refused to budge, but then the jeep struck a good-sized pothole or perhaps an armadillo and bounced enough for her to shift her head as if by accident.

"Katie?" Amy leaned in closer and gave the young lady a keen eye, before sitting back. "You can stop your playacting. I can tell the spell fizzled."

Katie's head had fallen at an odd angle and since she was getting quickly car sick, she straightened and glared over at her abductor. Her urge to be sick grew worse, and Amy noticed.

"You look a little green in the gills."

"Yeah well, you look a little stupid," Katie wasn't proud of the remark, but she was very afraid and it was the best she could do.

It made Amy smile though. "You don't have to be that way. This is going to happen. No one can stop it, not Will, not Talitha...you know, you never did finish telling me about your sister. About how she got all strong."

"She's just PMS-ing. You know with the cramps and the bloating, she can be real bitchy. I'm sure *you* understand that."

Amy's smile drooped. "Fine. Be a pain in the ass." She turned to the window and stared out for a few moments. It was just long enough for Katie to drop her hand down to the side of her leg, but not long enough for the girl to grab the knife hidden in her sock. Amy was nervous and talkative. "I could make this much harder on you. You know that, right? I could have Pedro come back here and bash your face in. He'd do it in a heartbeat and probably smile the whole time."

"Then do it." Katie was determined to be obstinate. Her reasoning was that any action that diverted her fate in even the slightest way had to be good, and that included a beating by Pedro. Perhaps a police officer would happen by, or a concerned motorist would stop to help and she could escape out into the desert. "I dare you. Hey Pedro, why don't you show me how tough you are? Come beat up a little girl."

Pedro only drove, silent and watchful, flicking his hooded eyes to the rear view mirror every few seconds. He would be a hard one and Katie worried that her knife wouldn't be near enough to kill him.

Amy only shook her head in disbelief at her little outburst. "I think it's about time I gag you."

"I think it's about time you try. I'm not afraid."

This brought another derisive laugh from Amy. "Oh yeah you are. You're sweating, your voice is pitched way up high, and your eyes are all crazy. But that's ok, that's normal. I'd be afraid too."

"You *are* afraid," Katie shot back. "All that you just said sounds like you described yourself." She glared hard at her captor for a moment and then dropped her eyes, her determination was granite-like, but it was built on a foundation of fear and was even then being undermined. "What...what's going to happen?"

"Well, physically you won't be hurt at all," Amy replied, trying to put the best possible spin on the horror that Katie would face. "The spell itself is very quick, a couple of minutes only. Setting up is the longest part."

"I meant what happens when the spell starts."

Amy tried to mask the truth in her eyes with a big fake smile. "Oh, right. Well...a demon will come. Wait, I'm getting this backwards. The spell is two parts, one part opens a gate, and the second summons the demon. Your part is actually very important. Your soul is what maintains the gate, so that means you won't be hurt, but at the same time you won't be let go either, sorry." Her condescension was nearly as poorly done as her lying. Clearly, there would be lots of pain.

"And me being a virgin? Does that really matter? Wouldn't the demon want someone more like you? Someone skanky?" Katie actually wanted to know, but the dig just came to her and she didn't really try to stop it from coming out. In the front seat, Pedro's shoulders twitched.

The witch glowered looking ready for a nasty catfight, but after a moment she forced the sham smile back on to her face. "Look, I don't make the rules and believe me, I wish it could be just anyone. This would have all been so much easier if I could just pick up any old girl, but that's not the way it is. It has to be a virgin."

"Oh," Katie looked out the window, poorly lit suburbs whizzed by but went unnoticed. Depression had slipped over her in so stealthy a manner that she didn't realize it until her shoulders had slumped and her forehead had thumped against the cold window. But it didn't last more than a few minutes and her fear returned at Amy's next few words.

"Pedro, your exit is coming up. We're almost there and soon this will be all over," Amy said in a soothing tone, but it sounded like she was trying to convince herself rather than Katie. It would have been near impossible to sooth the young girl just then. Perhaps the only thing that could was if her brother was to show up, riding a white horse.

"When my brother comes to rescue me? Will the demon still... arrive?" she asked.

Before answering, Amy took a nervous glance out the back window, there were no headlights to be seen, not even tiny distant ones. "He's not coming and if he were, he'd be way too late to do anything."

"But if he..."

"He won't!" Amy barked and the gun in her hand gave a little twitch. "I'm sorry but Willy J isn't coming to save you. Even if the Draugr hasn't killed him, he has no way of knowing where we are and even if he knew, he won't be able to catch up in time."

"Could you just humor me?" Katie pleaded. Pedro had just turned off the highway and her fear had escalated. It thrummed in her chest and without realizing what she was doing, she began cracking her knuckles, one after another.

"If you stop doing that, I will," Amy said, indicating the finger popping. Looking sheepish, Katie stopped immediately. "That's so freaking annoying."

"I stopped."

"At the light turn right," Amy ordered and then looked over at Katie. "Really, I don't know what would happen. It won't be good for any of us, that's for certain."

"But..."

"Look, I don't know," Amy snapped. "Let's just see what happens. Now if you don't mind please shut the hell up. I have to concentrate." Yet she didn't concentrate, she fretted. Over the next ten minutes, Amy checked her watch a hundred times, looked back to the streets behind them on a dozen or more occasions and jounced her knee up and down nervously in rhythm to an unheard jackhammer. She even took to checking the pistol in her hands, pulling out the clip and eyeing the bullets lying snugged up close to each other.

All of this did nothing to help poor Katie's own growing fear. By degrees, it increased, until she was sure that her heart would straight up burst. Only Pedro seemed calm, taking turn after turn until Katie had no clue in what direction the highway lay. Eventually they pulled up in front of what looked like an abandoned ranch. There were a few dilapidated and dusty outbuildings that sagged or leaned waiting only on the right gust of wind to send them toppling.

At Amy's direction, Pedro pulled the jeep up to what appeared to have been a barn at some time, the boards that remained to the structure had long before turned an ugly grey. Its windows were broken and jagged and behind these the dark was an impenetrable black, the overall impression was that the barn had many gaping hungry mouths. Even

Amy paused at the sight, her eyes very wide.

"Keep her here, keep her quiet. I've got to consult with the spirits and make sure this is the right place," Amy commanded.

Pedro and Katie watched the woman walk to the building, in silence. But silence was not what the young girl needed. "You should get a better name. Pedro is kinda...stupid. It's not tough sounding at all. You could be Diablo." As she spoke her hand slid down her sweats in the most casual fashion she could affect, her knife was inches away.

Pedro turned to her, freezing her questing hand. "That won't work. I have a friend named Diablo."

Katie knew this of course. "Yeah, but he's dead now. Didn't you know? Amy turned him into some sort of zombie thing. It was real gross and I'm sure my sister has shredded him up by now."

The man's hooded eyes narrowed even more. There was danger behind those implacable eyes, but not berserk mindless danger. Pedro was clearly a killer, but didn't seem to be a pure psychopath. "You seem very brave," he said. "You know she's going to sacrifice you? That you're going to die? Perhaps you should be praying," he advised.

"Yeah, but what about you? You think this is all going to end well for you? If my sister and brother don't hunt you down, I bet Amy will turn on you next. If you were smart, you'd take off right now. Just ask yourself, do you truly trust the witch?"

He gave a little snort as a way of an answer, clearly he didn't.

It wasn't much to hang her hat on, but the girl knew desperation intimately. "Yeah me too. I know she was lying about the pain and all. I saw what it did to my sister...it's going to be..." Katie broke off. "But maybe it won't happen the same, I can still be rescued."

"No, your brother's walking into a trap. Ms Harris has

powers; she seemed to know all about him and how many men he was bringing along. Somehow she knows everything."

A pain struck her deep in the chest. It was so bad that Katie wondered if it was possible for a fourteen-year-old to have a heart attack.

"She doesn't know everything. She doesn't know that you're second-guessing yourself. I know that you're just as afraid of Amy as I am, and I know that you want to help me." In truth, she didn't know this, but it was her only hope. "Please help me. We can be gone before she even knows, ok? Look, if you don't we're both doomed. Your soul is going to be right there next to mine burning in hell, is that what you want? If not then drive, please."

Pedro looked thoughtful for a time and then turned to the steering column. The cold in the jeep grew and minutes ambled slowly on and still the big man just stared at the leather bound circle.

"Pedro, are you all evil? Is there nothing about this life that you care for? Not even yourself? You know that when you're in hell, you'll have nothing, you'll be nothing. But it's not too late for you." Katie heard the fear in her voice. The words gushed out of her in a rush. "All you have to do is put the car in gear and drive away. Leave Amy behind, leave your past behind. You can do it. I know you can...God knows you can. God has given you a great opportunity. He's put my life in your hands; he's giving you a final chance to turn from the path that leads straight to hell. Drive away, please. Save me, please! If you do you'll be saving yourself as well."

Briefly, Pedro looked back, his eyes now full of doubt. However, he didn't drive away.

Now Katie had a terrible dilemma on her conscious. Her hand traced the outline of the knife in her sock, she could have it out in a matter of seconds and she guessed her chance at killing Pedro with it hovered well below fifty/fifty.

With his huge thick neck, the target if she were to make the attempt, the possibly could even be as low as one in ten.

Did she strike now while she had a chance, even a poor one, or did she wait to see if he would come to the right decision and drive away? Did she kill in cold blood or did she give the man a chance at repentance? Her hand slipped into her sock and felt the hard unforgiving steel and just then, Pedro shook his head as if he were in the middle of some internal battle. It was only a slight movement, but it was a start.

"Pedro, please. Make the right choice. I need you." The words were an admission on her part. She wouldn't strike down a man poised to turn from evil. She put both hands on his shoulders, "Please."

The knife remained hidden.

Chapter 25

Will

Will closed his eyes. Leaving his body behind, he stepped down into the Void and was immediately surrounded by beings and creatures, which pawed at him and his light.

They were everywhere, above and below, hands reaching for him, some were clawed spectacles of horror, others were human, but grey and rotting. Many of these last would crumble at his touch and cries of pain would erupt when they did. He was pressed in upon. Pulled and pinched and bitten. It was all too much and all too unnatural. Panic had his chest in a flutter, and in seconds, the closeness of the souls was too much for him and he tried to run—it was like running underwater. Slow and pointless, for as soon as he left one set of miserable begging hands another found him.

Even his breath was sought after, and creature after creature fought to force their face into his and drink up the fear that came panting out of him.

A terrible thing that sprouted many heads threw down the last of the others and came before him. All the heads had dead blank eyes, many of which were ruptured and ran with a viscous milky substance, but the heads weren't entirely devoid of life. Each had active hungry mouths, the lips of which were black and blistered and they opened wide to him. A harsh rotting stench smote Will, tipping his mind over, sending him screaming in hysterics.

This excited the many-headed thing and it pressed itself onto Will and now he felt the mouths sucking and biting on his flesh. Will went wild in panic and thrashed and kicked but the creatures only bit or sucked harder and he was pinned beneath it. Madness began to overwhelm him and he screamed again but this time pathetically, blubbering to be let go, crying to be released. Over and over he begged but to no avail and he felt himself dwindling beneath the many teeth, he was being eaten alive.

Still his cries were not unanswered.

A greater darkness came forth and the dreadful head-creature fled before it, as did all the rest. It was a demon. It came upon Will in a rush like a giant black shadow and it completely engulfed him. It was everything he was not and he was everything that it wanted. The demon brought Will in close and the horror that was the demon's face made the many-headed creature seem angelic in comparison and Will screamed again in harsh misery and madness. His world above, his family, his coming baby, Amy and the sword were all forgotten in that time. Only the demon and its overpowering evil mattered to Will. It was everything and he desperately wanted to die to free himself of it.

The demon, however didn't want that. It loved its newfound soul in the hateful way of demons, and wanted the misery to last, so it withdrew it face. Will immediately went limp and found himself in an odd partial consciousness. He could see and hear but couldn't move. The demon carried him in one of its great clawed hands through the Void and Will saw many visions that threatened to break his mind wide open—so he closed his eyes and was surprised to find that this did nothing to stop him from being able to see. At first, he thought this was just how it was in the Void, but then he recalled his sister. Her beautiful face came clearly to mind and he remembered her telling of her time in the Void and never had she been able to see with her eyes closed.

Will closed his eyes again and still was able to see all, just as before and he wondered if this was a form of his vision, his special talent. Foolishly, he tried to see the future. In a flicker, his body went into spasms and for long seconds he screamed with an inhuman voice until his throat shredded from the violence and his mind clicked over. It was like a circuit had blown and he ceased to think or to see and he lay there without knowledge of anything. After some time, he felt a stirring and a cold painful touch on his face. He recognized the demon whose countenance held the closest thing it possessed for concern, which happened to be anger. Its rage was familiar, leading Will to begin to remember all that had happened to him, including his vision of the future.

His future was all misery and pain. Endless misery and pain.

Depression smote him like a hammer and he lolled again in the grip of the demon, which infuriated the thing even more. Apathy was perhaps the only sin in the Void. The demon demonstrated its rage by shaking him and squeezing him until Will felt his ribs snapping, he was then flung down and stomped upon by the beast.

"Please stop, please," he begged in a tiny voice. The demon didn't, yet it didn't stomp him to death either. It was too cagey for that. Only when Will began crying like a child in his pain did the demon relent and it scooped him up again to recommence its journey. For a long time, Will moaned as his broken limbs jarred and grated against themselves, the pain was intense of course, but Will, who generally wasn't effusive when it came to such things made sure not to hold back. He was learning.

He realized that he would have to hide his true feeling if her were in any way to survive.

Just then, Will remembered what his sister had advised about hiding his light. How long ago that felt. It had been hours at least and the idea that he had dallied in his panic and had failed his sister threatened to sink him again. Out of fear of the demon, he rallied the remnants of his spirits and as he did the black of the Void shrank back in the slightest. This amazed him and he brought his hand before his face and saw that he did in fact glow. The warmth of the light filled him and he was glad for it and he wished to bath in its soft radiance, but the demon saw it also and gloating over the light, brought him up to its horrid face. The face was terrifying and Will didn't so much as hide his light as much as it fled within him.

The demon chuckled at this, happy at the display of fear. Will was happy as well, not only did the demon go back to its journey, but also he had felt the light. Long ago, Talitha had told about the physical properties of light and how that it was actually made up of matter, that it had weight and something called "rest" mass. All that he had got out of the explanation was that there was more to light than met the eye, but now, he could feel the light. It was like warm water inside of him.

Gently he drew the light deeper into him and as he did, the Void seemed to gather about him thick and viscous. The demon was oblivious and failed to notice until after Will had the light of his soul balled into the tiniest knot and this he covered over in darkness of his own creation. All that remained of him was his shadow and it was nothing to slip between the great claws of the demon and slink away, blending in with the darkness. Behind him, the fiend suddenly raged in an unintelligible language and searched high and low, but soon Will could no longer see the beast.

Blessedly alone, he wandered in a daze, pondering the possibilities left to him. They were only two, flee the Void as fast possible and find some way to live with his guilt, or stay and find Henny Harris. He glanced around, the cold was eternal and absolute, the dark infinite, the fear all-encompassing, and the screams innumerable, he despaired. There seemed to be no way he could accomplish his task even if he wished to.

Some time passed and Will began to walk faster through the gloom. It was silly, but he was afraid to be alone. Every shadow bore the resemblance of a demon and apparitions hung on his periphery, disappearing every time he turned his head. Strange sounds came to him as well. Whimpers and wailing, every sort of misery, his loneliness was so great that he chased the noises but it was like pursuing echoes.

Another noise came to him, different than the rest. Water on water. It was a tiny drip, drip, drip noise and he followed it to the source. It was a man. The little skin that remained on his body showed that he was a white man of middle age; his eyes were a deep red and tears descended from them without effort, dropping to a pool of them that had gathered at his feet. Beyond the trickling from his eyes, the man didn't move and could have been a statue, so still he remained.

Will didn't know what to think. "Excuse me?"

Never before had Will seen a man react with such a passionate fear. As if attacked, he screeched like a girl child and tore off into the dim, caterwauling horrendously. Will loped along after, easily keeping pace. Now the Void was a maze of shadows, some deeper than others, some thicker as if they were made from black silk and all came together in the most bizarre kaleidoscope of shapes. At times these resembled the night forest and at others a craggy desert, but mostly it felt to Will that he was underground—so it was when following after the skinless man.

Around shadows that loomed from the black floor like stalagmites and over sudden and alarming drops into nothing, Will stalked after the man, only to lose him quite unexpectedly. One moment he was there, the next, only empty shadows surrounded him. Will tore at them, but they only shifted like fog and after a few moments, he was quite turned around and had no clue which way he had traveled from.

A sigh escaped him, and renewed despair had him sitting amongst the shadows.

Drip, drip, drip. Off to his right the same sound as before. Hurrying after it, again Will came upon the man, but now he looked much changed, his skin was healed nearly completely. It was as if years had slipped by in seconds.

"Hey there. Wait, don't..."

The man took to his heels a second time, but on this occasion, Will was more prepared and due to the man's newly grown skin, far less squeamish. He tackled the man, who was surprisingly light, as well as weak and held him pinned.

"Just relax, I won't hurt you."

These words were lost on the man who continued to squirm and wiggle beneath him. Will attempted to wait the fellow out patiently, yet ages seemed to pass and still the man bucked in a most annoying fashion. It was all Will could do not to punch him in the face and finally he barked, "Stop it damn it!"

The man wilted into acquiescence, staring up at Will with teary eyes. "Tell me your name," Will demanded, lightening his tone only by the barest margins.

"Uh...Uh, I'm..." The fellow looked stumped by the question. "I don't know. I don't remember."

"You don't remember? How long have you been here?" Almost immediately, Will realized the question to be intolerably foolish. Time was meaningless in the Void. After a few more seconds of sputtering, Will waved his hand in dismissal. "Never mind how long. Can you at least tell me does the name Henny Harris sound at all familiar?"

With a great deal of skepticism the man asked, "There's a demon with that name?"

"No, she's a person, a soul."

"A real person? With a name?" For a time the man looked thoughtful. "Henny Harris, Henny Harris. I don't think so. Why do you want her? Did you kill her? Or did she kill you? Are you on revenge? What are you going to do to..."

His questions were asked with a hungry malicious tone and Will was considerably irked by them. "Shut up! Why I'm looking for her is my own business."

"She did something to you, didn't she?" The man's look

was insufferable and before he knew what he was doing, Will smashed his fist square into the man's leering greedy face.

In the time it took for Will to draw his fist back a second time, guilt struck him heavily, yet he held back the apology that had formed on his lips. Instinctively he knew it would be taken for weakness. Instead, he held his fist up threateningly. "How would I find her? What would you do to find someone?"

The question was beyond the man. He simply couldn't conceive of any reason to ever purposely look for another individual. This was transparent, but so too was his childish conniving mind. "You could, I suppose, ask a demon. I know where one is, Zoderath, Lord of the Chrystal Plain...it could tell you for sure. Here give it this," the man tore at the new flesh of his thigh and pulled a long peel of skin and blood from his leg. "Tell him I sent you...he's so...uh, nice, he'll tell you."

Murder grew in Will's heart and he fought back against the unfamiliar desire. "And how would I find..." He was loath to name a demon; it seemed filled with dangerous potential. "How would I find this demon?"

"How? What do you mean how? How do you think?"

Oh the savagery that welled in William Jern Jr. at the man's impertinence. This time it couldn't be denied, his fists brutalized the man's face, turning it into a bleeding mush. When Will could finally stop himself, he stared in horror at the creation of his unbridled lust to destroy. Where this need came from, he didn't know, but it was now a part of him. He hated it and now he hated himself and he hated the miserable little creature cringing and mewling before him.

"Sorry, please no more, no more," the man begged unintentionally throwing fuel on the fire burning in Will. With an effort, he got off the man and stomped around, concentrating on the shadows until he felt that he could face the soul.

"Tell me plainly right now, how do you find a demon?"

"Well its easy...you just...uh, you just," the man now looked perplexed not to be able to put into words what he had considered so simple. He started again, "All you have to do is say the demon's name and then head off, you'll find the demon sooner or later, or it will find you if you take too long."

Will tried to recall if that was how it had been when he had dreamed Talitha's dreams of her time in the Void, he didn't think it was. In his vague fading dream memories, he saw himself as his sister, dragging her feet along with great reluctance and usually crying over what was to come. He never remembered calling any names out, and for that reason, he eyed the man with suspicion. "And this Lord of the Plains demon, are you going to run into him now that you've said his name?"

The man lowered his chin, "No, Zoderath has sold me. I'm to go...to go..." the rest of his words stuck in his throat along with a strangled cry. A moment of sympathy swept over Will and he grabbed a hold, it was the closest thing to his old self that he had felt so far while in the Void.

"Never mind, I think I get it," Will said in kindly response to the man's painful silence. With the ever-changing landscape, there had to be some way to navigate the Void, yet the overwhelming background din of screams and cries had Will guessing that the physical act of saying the name was little more than a device to focus the mind on the particular demon a person sought. This information was interesting but his problem, of course was that he wasn't searching for a demon, but for a soul and from what he had learned from the demon Ba'al Fie-ere and what had been reinforced by the naked man, souls in the Void were nameless.

Henny Harris was no longer Henny Harris in the normal sense. Will tried to wrap his head around the concept, only to find it beyond him. How did a demon trade for a soul if that soul couldn't be named? Did they use numbers instead or vague descriptions? It was stupid system, whatever it was. Thinking down this line made him lose whatever sympathy he had been feeling and now he felt irritated and snappish.

He turned to the nameless man. "Thanks, you've been a great help. See ya." In his foul mood, Will had meant this to come across as sarcasm and he was sure he had said it in as rude a way as possible, but the man seemed not to notice one bit.

He jumped up and pawed at Will. "Hey don't go. We were just talking... hey, I got an idea! Maybe you could take me with you."

Will shrugged him off. "Why would I want to do that? Look at you! You don't know who you are or what you're doing. You don't even have clothes on for goodness sake."

"Neither do you!"

It was a shock to look down and see that the man was correct. It took the steam out of his anger, "You're right...I never noticed." For a while, he could only stare at himself and couldn't help but think that something wasn't quite right. His skin was grey and pale, but other than that was unblemished and appeared as it always had. Holding his hands up he examined them front and back, noting that other than his wedding ring no longer wrapped about the ring finger on his left hand they appeared normal. He flexed them and balled his hands to fists, they stretched and curled in a completely ordinary fashion. And that was the problem.

Two of his fingers on that left hand should have been shooting pain from the small movements, since only the day before they had been dislocated defending himself from Talitha. Yet they were completely healed, as were the ribs that he had heard snap when the demon had grabbed him. A quick check of his head and face, had his puzzlement complete. There was nothing physically wrong with him.

He should have been glad for that, but his spirits couldn't reach that far. Wasn't hell supposed to be all about pain and suffering? One would think that his pain would have been greater not gone altogether. He pondered on this for some time until the unnamed man interrupted his thinking by grabbing his hand suddenly.

"Hey...uh, mister? So what do you say, can I come along with you? I'm so lonely...no one's talked to me at all since I got here, except the demons that is." On his knees, the man pawed and touched, stroking the skin of Will's hand as if he were a king. Will yanked it away, disgusted by the sin-filled feel of the man.

"Don't touch me...don't ever touch me!"

How quick his emotions leapt to mountainous rage. Inside Will, the urge, the want, and the need to hurt the man bloomed like the deadliest flower. The man saw it in his eyes and began to back away with his hands out in supplication, but Will couldn't hold his anger in check and if he had a belt, he would've whipped the man bloody with it, just as if he were his own child. His hand came up to strike and a belt appeared looped in his palm, it whipped back in a fine satisfying imitation of cat's tail.

Will paused just as the belt slapped against his own back. There was a slight pleasurable sting to it, almost an erotic feel. Suddenly he recalled what Talitha had told him in the parking lot of the church back in Maine, *I like hurting people, I get off on it. You see in the Void, there is only one pleasure allowed and that is the pleasure in causing pain.*

Desire and cold reasoning split Will in two. To give in to this lust and whip the man who had done nothing wrong seemed absurd, but a part of him couldn't help rationalizing—clearly the man had done something wrong, he was in hell for a reason after all.

"What are you here for?" Will asked.

The man was anxious to please. "Because you chased me here."

Will's hands fists became as stone. "No, I meant what are you in hell for? What did you do to get here?"

"You don't know? Really? You haven't heard? No one told you? Then it was nothing... uh, uh, uh, it was nothing. An accident is all it was. And...and, I didn't even do that, I was framed, right? I was framed, that's what happened. It was an accident and I didn't do nothing, and I was framed...so I didn't do nothing."

This only piqued Will's curiosity all the more. "I don't believe you. You did something. What was it?"

Deathly pale as he was, the man suddenly went flat white and looked as if he was close to being sick. "Like I said, it was an acci...I mean I was framed. I wasn't..."

Rage washed over Will, and he reached out taking a hold of the man's hair and forced him to his knees. The belt was back in his hand, but this time the buckle was huge, it would shred the man's face with barely any effort on his part.

"You are a liar!" Will filled with self-righteous fervor seethed at the man, "And a murderer! I can smell the blood all over you. The blood of innocent little girls. What do you have to say for yourself?"

"It's not what you think... if you had seen them flaunting it. They wanted it. And besides they weren't that young, ten isn't young..."

The fire of hatred burned out of control in Will and he silenced the man using his belt. It felt so good. After a dozen lashes, he paused to see the ruin he had created. It was a good start, but the man certainly deserved more.

"No please, please stop," the man entreated. "I didn't do nothing wrong."

"Nothing wrong? Look around you jack ass, you're in the black pits of the great Void. You had to have done something to belong here." Will's logic was impossible to deny and the man didn't try, instead he sidestepped it and threw Will into turmoil with a question of his own.

"What about *you*? What did *you* do? You're here too, so you must have done something."

How dare the man question Will! He wanted to rip the

man's smug face off with the belt, but just as he brought the belt back again, a perfectly preserved memory came to Will. It was like movie it was so clear. In fact, it was better than a movie, he could feel the cold biting at his exposed skin, and he felt the air whistling by, snatching at his hair. There he was in the attic of their house on Governor's Island and there was the gate to the Void and beyond that was the demon, Ba'al Zubel. He could see it all just as it happened eight year ago. There was Adrina Fortini and he hid behind her like a coward and he could feel her bony, old lady shoulders as he pushed her forward, against her will. She shivered in tremendous fright. He could hear plain as day, her pleading with him, begging for her life, begging not to be killed in so horrible a manner.

And he watched as he shoved the lady at the demon and he stared as her limbs were rolled up, crackling and popping, breaking in a thousand places. Her face was the perfect rendition of pain...and he saw every terror writ line etched deep upon it.

It was all such a clear crisp undeniable memory that he was thrown down by his guilt. The man came and towered over him and judging by the look in his eyes, somehow he seemed to know all about what happened. Will went to his knees beseeching the man for understanding and compassion.

"No...that was the way it was supposed to be. She wanted me to... to... she was supposed to face the demon. She wanted that."

"Oh right! Sure, she wanted to be killed in such a horrible manner. You're as guilty as the rest. You're the one that should be punished." The naked man now held a whip of his own. Its many heads glinted and gleamed with the razors attached to the ends. It was a very menacing thing and Will began edging backwards away from it.

"Really you don't understand. It had to be that way..."

The man lashed out with the whip, it came flying at

Will and there was no way it could miss. He tried to scramble away, but the many heads tore into him. He screamed, surprised at how bad the pain was.

As the man drew back the whip again, he asked, "What about the witch, you nasty bastard? Smashing her head into the wall? Was that fun for you? Do you enjoy torturing people, you sick, sick bastard?"

The man's words dredged up a full clean memory that Will had long ago suppressed. He saw himself carrying the prostate body of Henny Harris and he heard the vile words coming from her possessed lips. Mountainous goose bumps covered his skin and he could feel the complete revulsion that had turned his face into a mask of horror. He watched as the memory played itself out, how he slammed the woman's head against the wall. It was sick. Far more grotesque than he could ever have imagined and it paralyzed him long enough for the man with the whip to strike again.

Will screamed in pain, but also in misery over his terrific guilt. He fled into the shadows with the man hot on his heels, but Will wanted to hide and the dark took a hold of him and soon he was nothing. Black on black. Ages he hid, reliving his sins. How many and how enormous they seemed to him. They were anchors around his neck and for a long span of timelessness, he could do nothing but dwell on their every detail. And always in his memories, the great demon, Ba'al Zubel, lingered about the edges as the ultimate cause, and Will affixed all of his sins to the fiend.

At first, he raged in defiance, "It wasn't me! It was Ba'al. It was all its fault!" Yet despite the rationalizing and the blame, the weight of his transgressions never grew less, they swelled even greater and brought him lower in spirits. As the rage wilted, he became covered over in the dark matter that made up the Void. It was like the web of a great spider and in its wicked strands, he became entrapped. Struggling did nothing, nor did crying, yet he couldn't help himself and did both, fluctuating between harsh anger and pitiful blubbering over the injustice of his predicament. The tears that fell from his eyes were pure globes of misery and as they rained down on the shadows, the shadows fed upon them and grew even greater about him, binding him so that all movement was impossible.

Panic over his virtual imprisonment now added its grip on his soul. He began screaming for help, "Is anyone out there? Hey! Anybody? I'm stuck, please...I need some help. Anyone? Please, I can't get out of these..." Will's voice trailed off as movement caught his eye.

Distant shadows appeared to sway like the tops of trees billowing in a storm as something vast brushed them aside. It was a terrible something, a ponderous leviathan of tremendous proportions and it ranged about the gloom. Its size dwarfed the man making him feel tiny and weak so that instead of struggling to free himself of the shadows, he now burrowed deeper into them, purposely covering himself over. Only his eyes could be seen and they were large white circles in his pale face, they watched in horror as the thing circled about, searching. Even compared to the perpetual dark of the Void, the thing was deep, deep black and it made all the shadows seem lighter than they were.

It was the purest evil. An ill wind flowed off of it and brought with it a horrid stomach-churning stench that Will recognized. The creature was Ba'al Zubel. It was out there, searching, hunting for the soul that had dared to say its name. This was the way it was and this is the way that it is. The Void is infinite. Its boundaries all but unknowable, and a soul could lose itself forever if it wished, but to think on a demon, or worse, to say its name was an invitation. Or in some cases, like to that of the greatest of demons, it was a challenge.

No being in the Void ever spoke the name Ba'al Zubel. No one dared.

Cowering in the rat's nest of his own making, Will began to understand what a fool he was to have said the demon's name. Deeper he slunk, trying his best to be small and inconspicuous, but all the while the beast drew closer. Nearer it came, until it stood nearly above him and the black steel of its clawed feet rung out as if they had clashed metal against metal. In the greatest fear, Will quaked and trembled. Fear defined him. Fear of the demon. Almost too late did he realize that his fear of the demon was what was had drawn it in. He was still thinking about Ba'al Zubel.

Yet how could it be otherwise?

How could he not think about anything else? Especially since it was so close. In desperation, Will tried to push his mind away to another topic, but always the demon forced its way into his thoughts. He could feel what passed for its mind prying about the shadows for him. It was like a dentist probing in a rotten tooth. He could think of nothing else and he knew that he was doomed. He had called the prince of demons to himself and he deserved the fate of a fool.

What an idiot! He chided himself in silence. If only he had called out to a different demon, he might've stood a chance, he had escaped the other demon after all. Perhaps it wasn't too late. Perhaps he could still call one and maybe they would fight and he could make a run for it. Nervous excitement had him breathing again and he bent his mind on a demon and wished so hard that it bordered upon praying. He wished for it to come to him with all possible speed.

Zoderath, *Lord of the Chrystal plain, please come to me.* Zoderath*!* Zoderath*!* His mind sung out with the repetition of religious fervor. It felt blasphemous in the extreme, but just then, Will couldn't have cared less. Over and over, he called to the demon, but in vain.

Zoderath did not show itself. The plan was stupid, Will concluded, feeling fresh tears bind him to the shadows. No demon probably had ever attempted to come between Ba'al Zubel and its victim. No demon, except perhaps his sister, Ba'al Fie-ere. She had defied the great demon once and earned her name. It was at least a hope.

Ba'al Fie-ere! Ba'al Fie-ere! Come to me. His mind intoned.

Above him, he felt the shadows suddenly swirl about, it was similar to smoke in a wind. Looking up he saw Ba'al Zubel raking back the layers of shade, searching. With tremendous fortitude, Will bit back the childish scream that rose to the top of his throat. He ducked his head and closing his eyes, pictured Ba'al Fie-ere at the second he had sent her back to the Void. It was a moment he would never forget. Her look of hatred snarled her pretty features, turning her brown eyes to black pits and her white teeth into fangs.

Ba'al Fie-ere! Ba'al Fie-ere! Come to me.

Ba'al Fie-ere did not come either, however, the more that he thought about her, the more the shadows loosened around him, until finally, he felt himself drop. Through many murky layers of the Void he passed, seeing bizarre half-formed images before finally he landed. Again, it seemed as if he was under ground and he stood in a rough-hewn tunnel of black earth. Above him and far away, the great demon, perhaps feeling him slipping away, roared in a fury. The sound was tremendous and was still too close for Will's liking and so he began jogging down the passage that seemed to take him most clearly away from the beast.

As he ran, he put thought to his many problems. The first being that the tunnel he was currently jogging through very likely would bring him either to Zoderath, Lord of the Chrystal plain or to Ba'al Fie-ere. Neither destination appealed to him, and so he stopped and stood wondering what he should do. He was supposed to be looking for the soul of the gypsy Henny Harris.

"Henny Harris, Henny Harris," this he took to chanting to himself and with the picture of the witch in his mind, he set off once again down the tunnel. Soon the tunnel branched, which gave him a spark of hope that he was heading away from the two demons, but then he came to another spot where he was forced to choose a left or right tunnel. To make it simple, he went right and for the next few minutes he came to series of forks in the passage and always he went right and as he did, the tunnel grew less rough and eventually, it became made up of dusty heavy square stones.

This all made him very nervous. It felt as though he was walking along in a sprawling dungeon and the feeling became a certainty when he came upon a large iron gate. It very nearly blocked the passage, but it was open enough to allow Will to slip through if he wished. Yet Will did not wish it. He was quite certain that if he were to walk through the gate that it would close behind him and for a long time he stood indecisively just outside of it. Finally he came to the conclusion that the gate represented too much of a risk and he turned away from it.

A second later, it clanged shut behind him. The noise sent Will's heart into his throat, yet he was for the moment relieved at his decision, thankful that he hadn't been trapped on the wrong side. Going back to the gate, he gave it a hard shove just to satisfy himself. It didn't budge. A heavy breath of relief escaped him, but it was a momentary thing.

"Oh jeez!"

From where he stood, he could see a trail of footprints in the dust. They had been made by a human and he didn't need to match them to his own bare feet to know that he had left them. Somehow, he was now on the wrong side of the bars. In a flash, he spun around and stared down the passage, but he could only see into the gloom so far.

"Henny Harris. I want Henny Harris," he whispered. *Henny Harris* came whispering back. It seemed too clear to be a proper echo, and he froze in place with his back to the bars, expecting to see something coming at him. Nothing did. He was alone with his fear and his heavy breathing.

" Henny Harris," this came out barely above the sound of his breath and when he had waited many seconds and no echo was returned, he was able to relax the tiniest amount. Next came the hard part, letting go of the bars and heading down the corridor. This took a while, but once he did, he scurried forward and didn't look back. The stone hall went on straight for a very long time and ended eventually in a T. Will looked both left and right and was surprised to see that in both directions there were doors leading from the hall.

Going to his right once again, he went straight away to the nearest door and high up on it was a small set of bars so that he was able to look into a room. The door was thick and the lock and hasp that sat upon it were constructed of heavy metal so that even before he looked in, Will knew he was about to see into a prison cell. It could be nothing else.

In the room, lying on its side was a creature that was vaguely human in appearance. It was mottled grey in color and had a long sloping pig nose and very small black eyes. These looked at Will with what he took to be deep suspicion and for a time both stared at the other. There were other doors to look into and Will glanced away first, feeling slightly rude for having stared at the thing for so long. With quick light feet, he crossed to the next door and saw that the lock of this one was undone, unsurprisingly the room was empty. The next held the remains of some poor creature and since the stench was so overpowering Will stayed only long enough to wrinkle his face.

After that, he found one that held a human, a man. He was in his early thirties, blonde and blue eyed, tall and broad, he was strikingly handsome. Looking at him made Will feel inadequate and he subconsciously touched his face where he had been beaten by his sister so badly, however the swelling had disappeared altogether. This gave him a slight boost to his confidence.

"Excuse me? I'm looking for a woman named..." Too late he recalled how no one had names in the Void. "Uh... she was a witch and she lived in New York. She was a about five and half feet tall..."

The man interrupted, "What did she do to you?" His chiseled features had formed themselves into an unpleasant knowing smile. He even raised an eyebrow in anticipation of a juicy story of murder.

Anger immediately leapt up in Will's breast, but he swallowed it back. "Nothing. She didn't do anything to me. I'm looking to her for help. Now, she was around thirty-eight when she died so she's about middle-age now."

"Middle-age? Are you stupid, or what?"

"I'm new here."

The man sat back with a big grin. "Fresh meat, huh? Well you've come to the right place because I know all sorts of information, but you have to give me something first. What year did you die?"

Will was most eager to answer, but another voice, the exact match of the blonde man's spoke up from the next-door down, "Don't listen to that liar. You trade information down here and he'll suck everything out of you and give back nothing. I know because he did it to me."

The blonde became strident, "He's the liar. You shouldn't listen to him. Now, since this is a private affair, I suggest that you whisper. What year was it that you died?"

Will stepped back from the door and looked upon the blue eyes that stared out from the little bars with suspicion. The two voices were so alike that he had to assume that he was speaking to the same person somehow. To satisfy his curiosity, Will went to the next-door down and was amazed to see another of the grey pig-nosed beings.

"You were smart to come to me," the pig-nose said, sounding exactly like his fellow prisoner. "I have a great deal of information that I've been holding back for..."

Rudely, Will walked away. When the grey creature spoke, his long nose flapped upwards and it had caused him to get sick to his stomach in an amazingly short time. He made his way back to the blonde and spoke to him with authority, "We will trade information. I came here in nineteen-eighty-eight. Do you know the gypsy I was referring to? She died eight years ago and like I said she was about thirty-eight at the time."

"All gypsies deserve hell and I would never purposely speak to one. Are you a gypsy?"

The man's condescension grated. "What a waste of a question. No, I'm not a gypsy. My turn. How is it that you and that thing sound so much alike?"

The loss of the question angered the man. "You're the one that sounds like that thing, not me. Maybe you two are related. That's not a question, just a guess." The man paused to see if his jibe had angered Will, but it didn't and Will only stared patiently awaiting, until the blonde continued, "I know that in nineteen forty-five, the Furhur was forced to commit suicide, but was he alone when he did? Was there anyone with him, anyone that might know where he is now?"

"I won't answer that until you answer my last question." In truth, Will didn't know if he could answer the man's question, he remembered that Hitler had a girlfriend of some sort and that she had died with him, but he was pretty sure there might have been others, but who they were he didn't know.

"I answered your question," the blonde said with some defiance and an even greater portion of anger.

Will didn't like the man. "Hardly to my satisfaction."

"That's not my issue. It's yours."

From the next room the pig-nosed thing called out, "I can tell you why we all sound alike."

Despite his revulsion, Will went to the thing. "I'm afraid, I won't have much information that you can possibly desire."

"You could tell me a story...anything would do. Do you have offspring?"

Will was loath to mention his coming child to any being from the Void, but he was also reluctant to go back on his word. "I have a baby girl on the way. Two months."

"Is two months a long time?"

Suddenly, he feared that he had been down in the Void

well past sixty days and in desperation, he tried to calculate how long he had been there. It was impossible to know. Feeling lower than he had yet felt, he mumbled, "It's not long at all." There was a silence between them.

"I have heard that human offspring are grown inside another human and that they eat their way out. Is that true?"

"No."

"You are an idiot!" the human in the other cell called out. "He's asked you three questions and hasn't answered a single one of yours. He sounds like a Jew. Ask him if there are any Jews where he's from!"

The creature's large nostrils flared wet and pink, and it spoke with its tiny eyes downward, "Well it is true that my information is likely worth quite a bit more than your simple anecdotes. I would think another couple of..."

Will had enough. In a blink of the pig-nosed creature's beady little eyes, he shot his arm through the bars and grabbed the long nose with one hand and pulled back with vicious strength. The thing made a small strangled trumpeting noise.

"Why do you two guys sound alike?"

"Oh! That hurts...stop please and I'll tell you."

"You'll tell me right now," Will replied and added a twist to his wrist for emphasis.

"Oh! All the lower creatures speak the same language and sound the same. The demons don't want to bother themselves with translations or dialects."

"The girls too? They sound like the guys?" For some reason this struck Will as very strange.

"Oh! Please stop...please." Will squeezed harder in response to the request. "Oh! No the females all sound like females. There is one in the next cell. She is young and tasty, you can ask her to prove that I'm not being dishonest."

A young girl?

The vision of his wife flashed in Will's mind and letting go of the long nose, he raced to the next cell, yet despite the fact that it was locked, there didn't appear to be anyone in the little room. Jumping up to the bars Will pulled himself up so he could see in properly. A girl, young and blonde was doing her best to hide against the wall, it wasn't Lisa. Yet the little that Will could see of her was painfully familiar.

"Katie? Is that you?"

"Go away! You're nothing but an illusion and I don't believe in you."

"No Katie, it's really me...it's Will."

"La,la, la! I'm not listening. La, la, la."

Will's arms grew tired and slumping down he inspected the lock closer. It was large and crude, strong but possibly easy to pick if he could find something to pick it with. Glancing around the hall, he saw nothing that he could use.

"Hey Katie..."

"La, la, la, I'm not listening!" she began again drowning him out. It was annoying and it set his teeth on edge.

"You shouldn't listen to him, little girl," the grey pig-nosed creature called out to Katie. "He's the demon in disguise."

Now Will was truly angered and he launched himself in a fury at the cell door that held the nasty looking beast. His shoulder slammed into it, causing it to rattle appreciably, so much so that it had practically come crashing down. Immediately he forgot the beast and ran to Katie's cell and threw his shoulder against it. Three times, he repeated this before the hinges snapped and the door fell in awkwardly, still hanging by the heavy lock.

Katie, clearly believing him to be the demon, went mad with fear. Around her neck she wore a thick metal collar and from that, a chain went to the floor. Once Will had seen someone walking a cat on a leash as if it was a dog. It was a sad thing to see, as the cat was quite incapable of understanding the concept of a leash and hurled itself about in the most extreme manner in an attempt to free herself. Katie looked eerily similar to that cat and Will worried she would hurt herself.

Will jumped on her, easily pinning her. She felt so light and weak, also her face seemed younger than he remembered and briefly he wondered what his own face looked like. "Katie, it's really me, your brother. I'm no demon. Look me in the eyes, ok?"

She barely glanced. "Liar!"

Will was desperate to get her to see the truth, and he showed her in the only way he could think of to convince her. For the barest second, he allowed a little of his light to show forth. Just a glimmer, but it was enough to blind them both for a few seconds. When he could see again, he noticed that the little girl had latched onto him and was sobbing into his chest. Her grip about his waist was formidable.

"Are you dead, too?" she asked him.

"No, I'm not and neither are you." Sadly, Will explained what was happening and what his purpose had been in coming to the Void. As he spoke, he grew more glum, his purpose was now useless. Katie had already been sacrificed to the demon.

"I'm not dead? Shouldn't I be happy?"

Will tried to smile to reassure her, but couldn't. Being trapped in the Void, meant happiness would be beyond her forever. Her best hope was for Will to go back to his body and then rescue her as he had done with Talitha. Yet after all the pain and death, as well as the evil, malicious insanity affecting his sister, he wasn't at all eager for the opportunity. In fact, in his heart he knew that if he had to do it all over again, he wouldn't. After every sacrifice that had been made for her, Talitha wanted to go back to hell. What a waste. What a waste of lives and pain.

He loved his little sister, but he wouldn't—couldn't do it again.

"Come on, I'm going to get you out of here."

"We're going back to...earth? How?"

"No, not earth, not back to your body. I'm taking you to

heaven." He was shocked when she pulled back suddenly on his hand.

"What? You're not going to rescue me properly? You rescued Talitha, but you won't rescue me? Why? Is it because you love her more?"

"No, it's because I love you so much that I won't put you through what she went through. To save you means to leave you here, alone. It'll feel like thousands of years before I get back and Ba'al Zubel will torture..."

"Don't say that name!" she hissed. "We're not in those dungeons...we're trapped by Ba'al Fie-ere."

"Ba'al Fie-ere? How is that possible?"

Katie only shrugged. Was being trapped by Ba'al Fie-ere worse or better, or did it matter at all? Will started pacing in the small cell, back and forth. "I guess it doesn't matter what demon is holding us, we still have to escape."

"But my body?" Katie clutched herself and it was then that Will first noticed that she was just as naked as he was. He looked away.

"I'll find your body back on earth and I'll find a way to close the gate. Now come on, before she knows I'm here." Will took his littlest sister by the hand and pulled her into the hall. Faces strained at the bars of the other cells as their occupants pushed themselves up to get a peek at them and soon whispers came.

"Take me with you, please."

"Take me! I know the way out."

Take me. Take me. Take me. Up and down the corridor voices cried in hushed tones.

"Don't listen to them, Will. They're all liars," Katie informed him. Her pretty face looked savage as she glared at the different prisoners.

He didn't need her advice. The begging of the other prisoners rankled him to no end and he felt a good deal of hate building in his soul. It bothered him that he liked the feeling and it made him wonder how any part of Talitha was still good after all the time she had spent here. He began to run, pulling his little sister along. She began to bother him as well. Katie was slow, huffing, and puffing, stumbling.

"Come on, faster! It's all in your mind, your body isn't even here, and besides you told me you ran track. This should be nothing."

"In my mind?" Katie frowned a little and looked to be concentrating, soon she began running as fast as Will. In the end, it hardly mattered. It was all a set up. One second, he was dashing along the passage, taking left after left and the next, just as he saw the beginning of the shadow lands outside the dungeons, he was thrown to the ground and Katie's hand was separated from his.

In a daze, Will climbed to his feet and saw that a heavy barred door has sprung up between him and his sister. Her hands reached out for him between the bars in a pleading fashion, she was crying in miserable fear.

"Will, please...break the door! Break the door! I feel her coming."

Somewhere behind her in the dark, a high cruel laugh rolled down the stones of the corridor. Without hesitation, he launched himself at the door, but this time it didn't budge. He attacked it in a fury of anger and frustration, and still nothing. His sister was trapped.

"Don't leave me," she begged. "She's coming...she's coming. Can't you hear her? Can't you feel her?"

"Quiet down!" Will snapped, his own fear making him angry. "You need to calm down right now. If I can't get you out of there, you'll have to do it yourself."

"I don't know how."

"Shush! I'm going to tell you. Somewhere near or maybe in the Void, there's a river that you can go to. While you're there nothing can happen to you, no one will hurt you. Just don't look in the water."

"Why not? What happens?" Katie had settled down with such rapidity that Will looked at her sharply. Large endearing tears hung from her eyelashes and they sparked a distant memory of her that was just out of his grasp.

"I'm not sure exactly what happens, but it appears, well, rather dreadful. There's something in the water or actually on top of the water that caused..." Will had to stop. Katie was leering at him with such intensity that she barely looked like herself. A faint whiff of suspicion suddenly drew him back from the bars.

"What?" she demanded. "What's wrong? Why'd you stop?"

"I don't know," Will said with honesty. Something wasn't right.

Katie swung her head around to look down the tunnel behind her. There was nothing but unconquerable darkness in that direction. She turned back. "Will, I don't think we have much time. I need you. Please, tell me about the river. How do I get there?" Despite her vigorous movement, her tears still hung on to eyelashes as if they were glued there and suddenly Will remembered where he had seen those tears before.

Years ago, long before the coming of the demon, he had let slip to Katie about the truth of Santa Claus. She had not believed him, and had gone, not to her parents, but to Talitha whom she revered for her knowledge. Talitha told her the painful truth and those tears had slid to the edge of her lashes, but hadn't fallen.

Her look there in the dungeon on the edge of the Void was identical. Too much so. Will stepped back even further and like a cold mist, the shadows of the Void began to curl about his ankles.

"Since when do you call me, *Will*?" he asked and now the shadows covered his knees.

"Aw shit," the little girl cursed. She stood and waved away the bars as if they were smoke. "What gave me away?"

"Just the fact that you're an evil bitch and Katie isn't. Ba'al Fie-ere, right?" Surprisingly, Will wasn't all that afraid, but all the same, he took another step back.

"Ba'al Fie-ere in the flesh...so to speak. Do you like it? The skinny nubile look?" She posed in a sick erotic manner wearing the guise of their young sister.

"Please stop it. It's just annoying is all," Will asked the demon as nice as he could. "Do you have Katie? Here?" He tried to put a placating smile in his voice.

"Not yet, but soon...very soon and what's more, I will have a gate to the world. My very own gate. Thanks to that moron, Amy Harris and our dear little virgin sister. Truly, I haven't been this happy in an age." Ba'al Fie-ere stretched and as she did the tan skin of Katie tore into sick bloody ribbons and a great black beast erupted up and up. She towered high above him and he barely stood as tall as her knee. Her skin was velvet jet and looked deep and soft. An irrational part of him longed to reach out and touch her, but he fought the urge, afraid of what would happen. She was very beautiful, breathtakingly so, and he stood perfectly paralyzed in awe of her, all he could do was stare.

She chuckled at the stunned look on his face and the sound of her laughter was vaguely musical, a combination of tubas and bass violins and deep thrumming drums. "Do you like the new me?" Will could only nod slightly and her smile broadened so that he could see the rows of tremendous white teeth filling her hungry mouth. "You are looking at the new tyrant of the Void, well almost. As soon as I get my gate, it will happen."

There was a pause and it seemed to him that she wanted him to clap or cheer. He could bring himself to do neither and when he only stood there feeling lost, she glowered and then swatted him into the shadows as if he were a fly. It hurt terribly bad, but he still had the presence of mind to limp deeper among the dark trees of the shadow forest that surrounded her dungeon.

"Don't bother trying to hide, Will. I can feel your thoughts. You can't stop thinking about me, which is very flattering, but also rather stupid. There you are..." A hand the size of a loveseat grabbed him about the middle and hauled him above the tops of the shadow trees. "That was fun and here is your reward."

Her skin, when she first picked him up, was as soft as he had expected, but now it became hard as tree bark and she squeezed. Odd sounds came from his crushed chest and ruptured lungs; she smiled down at him in a motherly way. "Now don't go thinking you're going to die so easily. Here in the Void, you can be readily healed. Now if we were in my dungeons, it would take quite a bit longer. The difference is that out here, we're in no man's land and each individual can command the shadows to a degree and really what are we if not shadows?"

The reality for Will was that he was now almost beyond thought. His mind was all about the racking pain in his chest, as his broken ribs slid against themselves with each of his shallow breathes and her words were wasted on his ears. Ba'al Fie-ere didn't notice or care, she blew gently into his face and he could feel his lungs re-inflate and his breathing become easier. It was such a relief, that he almost thanked her.

"Tell me about the river," she asked gently. "How do the souls get there and how do I get them back?" She waited with quiet expectation as if she was just curious, but Will could see the eagerness behind her eyes.

"I... I...the river is... is," his words came stumbling from his mouth. He hadn't been afraid before, but now he was very much so. He had a feeling that no demon knew about the river and that to give away its secret would be to give away his only chance at escape. "I... there is, uh...uhh-ooooh! Stop, please." The demon had squeezed again at his delay. "I've only been there in my...your old dreams. I'm trying to remember how she got there." The demon's eyes narrowed slightly, but she relented and her hand opened up slightly and the phantom air of the Void rushed into his lungs.

Will thought about the river and its gentle flowing water. He pictured its neutral grey sky and the surrounding hills garbed in their uniform of verdant greenery. The image in his mind was very real and in moments, he realized that if demon hadn't been holding him so tightly, he would be able to go to the river right then. This was his chance at escape and all it would take was for him to get her to relax her grip but he didn't see her doing that voluntarily. Moreover, there no way he had the strength to force her hand, and again, she was too cagey to be tricked into doing it.

But he did have something that might work. He had his light.

Chapter 26

Will

When he released it, the light was beyond blinding. It was far greater than the glimpse he had shown the masquerading demon. In the sightless Void it was an explosion of radiance. Ba'al Fie-ere didn't just open her hand, she practically threw him from her and this was perfectly fine with Will. His body floated out into the shadows, but his mind was on the river and in what seemed like seconds he felt the sand of the shore against his skin.

It was grating and coarse and warm. It was wonderful. Will laid upon the sand for a time and tried not to think about much of anything. However, that could only go on for so long and when his mind began to operate again, he began to worry. How long had he been gone from the world? How long before Katie was sacrificed? Where was his father? Will pulled himself up, making sure to keep his eyes from the river, it was terribly calm and dangerously glassy, almost as if it were a millpond rather than a river.

A number of souls were scattered at wide intervals along this near bank. They kept to themselves, not fearing their neighbors but fearing what their neighbors would see. Most were women, but there was also a smattering of men among them and they all, men and women alike, worked steadily, mindlessly keeping to their chores. Some washed clothes, while others cleaned endless piles of dishes. Will watched one young lady who had only a small pile of plates on the sand next to her. Perhaps no more than eight all told, yet that stack never diminished though he stared for what had to be ten minutes.

She looked very sad, but in fact, it was remorse that she was feeling mostly.

He turned his back on her. All the souls along the river had that look. Their guilt permeated the air, something he hadn't noticed in the one dream he'd had of the river. After the fear and hate of the Void, the guilt was like a vacation. At first that is, then it began to settle on him as well. It began like a barely perceptible layer of dust but gradually it came to weigh on him like a heavy blanket of soot that ate away at his calm. Walking and seeing the other souls, helped. He was like a sheep in a herd among them. Their culpability and remorse matched his own and he strolled along, walking forward but never looking straight ahead. No, he kept his eyes up the bank and used his periphery not to stray too close to the water.

As he passed them, he would turn and smile at the people and frequently they smiled back, especially if their water was good and stirred. They desperately wanted to be normal again and so did he. One man in particular looked very normal. Instead of cleaning anything, he fly-fished. It seemed a nice way to keep busy and to keep the water rippling as well. Will watched him for some time, secretly wishing he could take a try with the pole.

"Have you ever caught anything?" he asked the fisherman. At the river, people wore clothes and this man wore a vest with a good hundred tiny pockets worked about the material. He also had a hat that was dutifully covered with many tiny flies.

"Nope."

"You look to cast that fly pretty good. Did you used to do this... you know before?"

The man's jaw clenched at the question. Bringing up *before* was clearly something that should be avoided, "Nope."

"You would never have known..."

The fisherman interrupted, "Fishing is supposed to be a quiet sport."

"Right." Will took the hint and moved on. The river

seemed endless and he began to fret over the time he was losing. He was still at the river, strolling along its sandy banks for just one reason, he was afraid to go back into the Void. The demons and quasi-demons, the evil souls and the bizarre creatures all made his stomach churn and the very thought of going back would stop him in his tracks. He had another fear as well, he was afraid he was imperiling his soul for nothing. He was after one nameless soul out of billions and even if he did find Henny Harris there wasn't much of a chance that she would help him.

"If only I could find, Adrina," he said

Finding Adrina was another impossibility. Feeling low he dallied, shuffling the sand with his toes near a young woman. She was small with delicate hands. They were likely the hands of a killer, yet he walked past, putting his back to her, unafraid of this murderess. This idea struck him as strange. While in the Void he had feared or hated the least soul, but at the river he smiled at people whose sins had to be very great indeed. Why was it so?

He turned back. "Excuse me ma'am? Who did you kill?" It was a great assumption on his part.

"Lots of people." That she even answered was a surprise.

"Why? Did you like killing?"

A short bitter laugh, an expression of the vast pool of misery within her, barked out before she replied, "No. Not once. I hated it and I hated myself."

"So you are sorry for your sins?"

"With all my heart."

"Then walk away from here and go to heaven."

She laughed with a great deal of mirth over this. "Are you a demon who's lost his way, and have come to torment me? I can't go to heaven. There's no place for me there."

"I'm not a demon, I'm just a..." he nearly said that he was just a boy, but stopped himself. Sometimes he forgot that he had grown up at some point. "I'm just a man, just a person like you. I've killed as well. Twice, and like you, I'm very sorry that I did, but..."

"But? You're sorry, *but*...but what? You are either sorry or you're not. There is no but."

"I killed an evil person once, to save the life of another. I'm sorry that I had to do it, but I would do it again without hesitation."

"I suppose that's a good but. What about the other life, though? Was that person evil as well? Would you kill that person again if you had to?"

Their conversation was quite a surprise to Will. He didn't think that he could open up so easily to a stranger in this way. However, her last question froze the words on his lips. Would he still kill Adrina in the same grizzly fashion if he had to do it all over again? "I think so. But...but only because the outcome couldn't be guaranteed any other way. You see, it was very complicated."

"Are you sure it was all that complicated? Murder rarely is," the lady replied. "We make excuses, sometimes outlandishly stupid excuses. And we rationalize and justify and in the end, all we are, simply put, are murderers."

"I don't know if I am one," Will said in a voice so quiet, he didn't think that the woman heard.

She laughed, this time with more actual conviction that she found something humorous. "Then you are the one who should walk away. Just be prepared to face your victims once you arrive in heaven. It's not easy."

"What? You've been to heaven? And if so, why are you here?"

There was no laugh in her this time, only a long drawn out breath that gave hint at the defeat in her. "I never actually made it all the way. I crossed the Void, hiding myself from the innumerable demons and avoiding their web of lies and deception. I crossed the endless Void only to end up here. Of course, I was amazed at the hills and the light and the river. I stood in awe of all of it and I knew on some basic level that heaven lay waiting for me just across the river. I knew it. I could feel it. So I went down the banks... and ...you know the rest."

Will knew. There was a compelling need to go near the water, to look into it. Even then, with his back to the woman, as he faced up the bank at the wooded hills, he felt the tremendous urge to turn and look. It was almost like a deep thirst that could be quenched only by the sight of the water. He swallowed feeling his throat tight and dry and nodded in understanding.

She took up her story with the movement of his head. "I looked once in the water and after that I couldn't force myself to look again. Still, I couldn't go back to the Void, not to those horrors, so I did what everyone else did, I cleaned and for as long as I could, I delayed the inevitable. But eventually, by chance or by accident I would see into the water when it calmed and I would see my crimes. The water never lies or distorts, it always shows the truth. Over time, I began to come to grips with my sins, bit by bit, image by image and I believed myself ready.

"Steeling myself for whatever was to come, I strode into the water and at first it was simply water, warm and wet, a complete delight. I made it halfway and suddenly the water became very shallow, perhaps only an inch in depth, and I stood with just the soles of my feet covered over. Raising my head, I saw that the light had grown brighter, fuller and I cried out in joy. I even turned and cried out to the other souls on the far bank to join me. It was then I saw that the river all about was flatter than I had ever seen it. My joy turned to anguish as every sin that I had ever committed reflected up at me all at once...and...and I was forced to take them in and I relived each of the horrors that I inflicted on others. Now I cried out in the most dreadful misery. But even then, I couldn't go back, and sobbing, I fled toward heaven.

"By the time I gained the further bank, I had destroyed myself. I was a pitiful thing not worthy of the least pity, I consisted solely of fear and remorse. Unfortunately, the fear in me was the greater. I began toiling up into those hills and the sensation of being so close to heaven was wonderful, but also terrifying and it took so, so long to climb. Not because it was a great distance, but because I dragged my feet every step of the way, afraid of what they would think of me. Afraid of the looks that I would get. Afraid that I would hear the whispering behind my back when I passed. Afraid that of all the souls, I would be the only guilty one. And as I trudged, I realized that there was no way I could look the victims of my atrocities in the eye.

"How could I have possibly done the things that I had done to my victims? And their children? What misery did I cause them? And all their friends and family... they would all know what I've done as well and they would judge. I couldn't take another step onward and I couldn't stay there since I didn't deserve the light that had been warming my face, therefore, I turned back. I've been here at the river ever since."

Her story was story was dreadfully sad. "Do you think you'll ever make another try?"

"Yes...when I can face the river again. When I can look into it unblinking...when I can find the courage to look my victims in the eye. Only then will I try. And when I do, I will crawl up those hills naked, on my hands and knees, begging for forgiveness and praying for mercy."

They were silent together for a long time and Will knew that the river was flat behind them, he was afraid to turn.

"So are you ready to face your victims?" she asked in a throaty little whisper. "Are you even ready to face the river?"

"I'm not here for that. I don't have the time to waste."

Again, her laugh came and this time it was biting and cruel. "You think it is a waste of time to say you're sorry?"

"No, that's not what I mean. I'm not here for forgiveness, I'm here looking for someone."

"And you have found someone, me." Will began to

interrupt, but she laughed over him. "I don't think it's possible to find anyone in particular in the Void. For starters, no one wants to be found, especially by any old acquaintance. And then there's the fact that we are all nameless. It's one of the first things a new soul does. They try to forget who they were and what they did to deserve hell. Sorry."

"It's not your fault."

"Was this person you're looking for a victim of yours?"

"In a manner of speaking."

She made a little scoffing noise. "Humph! Either they were or they weren't. Why do you want to see this person?"

"I need her help, badly."

"You want help from someone you killed? That's nuts. And you think there is someone *here*, in the *Void*, who would bother to help you? What do you have to trade for this help? It better be good."

"I have nothing."

Behind him, she laughed very hard and he could see her shadow drop down. Careful not to look at the river he glanced back and saw that she was rolling on the ground crying and laughing. Will walked away in frustration and anger.

Running up behind him, she called out, "Wait! Wait! I didn't mean to laugh at you. It was just..." she began to chuckled again. "I'm sorry. It's just funny. You don't see how funny this is?"

"No. To me it's very serious. Lives are at risk, souls are at risk."

"Ok...ok, that is serious. I'm sorry, I won't laugh, I promise." In good faith, she took a few deep breaths to show how calm she was. "And besides, maybe I can help. I've seen all the people around the river, you could describe this lady to me."

It seemed like the best plan he had heard yet. Will described Adrina down to the smallest wrinkle, omitting nothing and all the while, as he spoke, he kept his back to the woman. So far, he liked her and was afraid that if he were to look too closely into her eyes, he would see her evil murdering soul hiding there.

"I'm afraid your description isn't very helpful. There are very few souls who want to be seen as old, it's a subconscious thing. People take on the appearance of themselves at the age they thought they looked best at. Stupid, huh?" She didn't wait for a reply, "Did you know her when she was younger?"

Feeling dejected once again, he shook his head. "No, thanks anyways."

"Wait, hold on. There's still one way I might be able to help...but, it's... it's really personal." She paused in obvious embarrassment and stuttered when she got going again. "I...I...you could... Darn it! It's like this, despite how a person might alter their age, their eyes never really change. If you are up to it, I could look into your water and see if I recognize your victim's eyes."

Will was almost speechless at her intrusive request and for a while, the most he could do was shake his head. "No way, that's too much. You're asking way too much."

"I know, but if the situation is as dire as you say, you may not have another choice."

She would see his murders, she would *know* everything! Will grew suddenly suspicious. "What do you hope to get out of this?"

"Just what you are offering, nothing. Look, I'm trying to get to heaven. My husband is there and so are my two sons...at least I think they are, I hope they are. And I would do anything to be with them. You see? I'm just trying to be good."

Could he do this? She would see and know everything. Will was suddenly more nervous than he had ever been in his life. "You won't like what you see... and you won't like me much either...just try not to judge." He wanted to go on, for there was a terrific need within him to explain his actions, to justify his weaknesses.

She wouldn't let him. "Don't say any more. The water is flat, just walk up to it, and look for as long as you can. If I know her, I should be able to recognize her quickly. Go on."

Will was somewhat soothed by the tone of her voice. She was authoritative and knowledgeable and so he turned finally to the water. All the length of the river was flat as a picture, except just in front of the few souls in sight, where tiny ripples tickled its surface. The ripples died out quickly and none reached the water in front of Will. His head was up and he looked far out at the water in the distance, trying for the moment to ignore the motion below him. Just feet in front of him, colors swirled on the water. They drew his eyes impulsively; he had to look, it was impossible not to.

Yet he dallied, sweating despite the neutral air until the lady came and stood next to him. A small gasp, hardly more that a sharp breath, sucked between her teeth. She had seen something and his shame was complete. Now she knew what sort of man he was. Against his will, his chin pivoted downward and he saw too.

The water was so smooth it could've been a pane of glass and the reflections on it were not just vibrant, but alive. It was like a parade, it was so captivating. He saw himself carrying the prostate form of Henny Harris and he knew what was about to happen and he had to choke back a sob as he began to bash her head against the wall. It was horrible, he was totally without mercy or justification and the only feeling that radiated from his younger self was an abundance of sickening cowardice. It was writ all over his face, and Will wanted to scream at his younger self and condemn him, and call him out for the weak thing that he was.

But he couldn't. His chest was completely locked and not a sip of air could go either way. He barely noticed. Next to him, the woman watched Will's most contemptible moments in silence. The lack of critique was mocking and judgmental and he began to hate her, but then the river showed the last painful moments of Adrina Fortini and she broke her silence.

"Oh my God!" In his periphery, he saw her move away and his shame and disgrace was so great that he stayed and saw the horrors that he had committed rather than go to her. It was his hope that when he was done witnessing all that there was to see, she would be gone. In the water Adrina died, the breaking of her bones was loud in his ears and he wanted to vomit. The next scene was of Henny Harris laying defenseless and he watched as he plunged the hell blade straight into her chest.

After that his shoulders drooped, he thought that the memories were over, however the water began the scenes anew.

"No!" The word came out in a single loud desperate gasp. Stumbling forward into the water, he splashed down onto his knees gasping and crying like a wretch. The spell broke and the water was only water. He hammered it with his fist.

"You fucking coward! You God-damned coward!" he screamed as his own wobbly reflection. Anger and humiliation infused his soul and he dripped tears into the river, one after the other. He sat there afraid to look around—afraid that everyone had seen the dreadful show.

Only the urgency that time was slipping away made him look up. The woman had left him, but hadn't gone far enough away. She knelt in the sand with her back to him, her shoulders were shaking and he could hear her sniff every couple of seconds. Knowing that he did that to her brought back the remorse and he dropped his eyes back to the water, which was a mistake, another vision had begun brewing. It was a rerun and he lurched out of the water to escape it, heading away, hoping that he'd never see the woman again.

"I'm so sorry," she called out to him. It was practically yelled and he stopped for a moment wondering what could she be apologizing to him for. Behind him, he heard her walk across the sand and then a slight crunch told him she had again sunk down. The word 'sorry' was strange to hear. Perhaps it was the way she had said it, but it held more consequence than he had ever attributed to it before. Almost as if compelled by the word, he turned to look at the kneeling woman, she had finally faced him, however her hands were pressed to her face.

She seemed so small while he felt gigantic, and powerful. Only a moment before he had been a pathetic cringing wretch, now he loomed above the girl with the authority to add to her misery or to reduce it. She had given him that power.

"What are you sorry for? I don't understand." Her face was buried in her hands and tears slipped from between her fingers. The woman was truly sorry for something. It began to make Will uneasy.

"In the water, I saw the true coward and it wasn't you. I was the coward and it was because of my fear that you had to...do that."

"What? Who are you?"

"I'm... I'm...I don't know."

Will had to pry her hands from her face, which was young and completely unrecognizable to him. All except the eyes. She hadn't been lying about that. He was looking at Adrina Fortini. A young Adrina Fortini.

Unable to draw breath in properly, Will could do little but whisper, "You're Adrina, I...I killed you."

"I remember now. I'm Adrina."

Silence.

Neither looked at the other but only down at the sand. For his part, Will was waiting on the inevitable. Blame, condemnation, accusation, he would accept them all without denial. How could he not? The water had shown them both what he had done and there had been no lie to it. He waited for the charges that she would level against his soul, yet the wait drew out and as it did, he began to feel faint.

"I was ready to forgive you, Will." This was how she started and it was like his heart shrunk with each word, collapsing in on itself. "I wasn't at first. At first, I raged against you and blamed you for everything. And...and I even thought I wouldn't have been in hell if it wasn't for you."

Will nodded. This was what he had been expecting. It would get worse. You don't use a little old lady as a human shield and expect gratitude from her.

"It took me a long time to forgive you in my heart, but now..." she let the words drift away.

Here it comes. Damnation. She would rightly damn him for his crimes. He just wished that she would get it over with, but she began to cry again and he didn't blame her. The scene in the water had been horrible.

"But now, after seeing that. I'm the one who has to beg forgiveness. What happened was my fault. I was supposed to confront the demon first, only I was so afraid, that I couldn't. I was..."

Will had to interrupt. "Stop! That's complete nonsense. You did what anyone else would have done. It's no sin to be afraid."

Adrina's eyes flashed. "You're right. I did what anyone would've done, I cowered like an idiot and nearly got us all killed. That's why I'm the one asking for forgiveness. You did what you had to do, and it was the right thing to do. And the only reason you had to do it was because I failed. After all my talk, I let you down. So I'm not going to forgive you for anything, Will. Instead, I'm going to thank you for your bravery and for making the hard choice. You made my pain and sacrifice worthwhile."

"But..."

Adrina was as feisty as she ever was. "No buts. I mean it, there's nothing for me to forgive."

In silence, Will stood stunned as his emotions spun about inside him. The chief of which was a joyous euphoria and it was an effort not to break into a little dance. Forgiveness was the rarest thing in the Void, it was a gift of the greatest value and was never given lightly. Quite literally, he felt a burden lift from his soul; it was almost as if he could fly across the river had he wanted to.

"Thank you, Adrina. This means a lot to me." A smile came to her lips but it wasn't matched in her brown eyes, these showed signs of strain. And now there came between them an uncomfortable silence. They stood facing each other, yet she wouldn't meet his gaze, Will couldn't understand what was bothering her. "Are you ok?"

Her lips grew tighter against her teeth, she shrugged.

"No really, what's wrong?" he asked as he scanned her face for a clue. Only a second ago, she was what he had always thought of as her normal self, then she had forgiven him and now this. There was pain in her bearing. He wanted to press her for an answer, but by the way she was acting, he knew it would be useless. She shrugged again in answer to his question.

More silence followed, which became unbearable to the young man. "Thanks again for forgiving me. I don't think I can ever...oh!" The answer came to him. She had asked...no, begged him for forgiveness too, and he had done nothing. "Are you worried about forgiveness? Adrina, look, you did everything you could, and more. You stood up to the demon and...I would have died if you hadn't, he was killing me, seriously. I can't even believe this is an issue. The fight wasn't even yours!"

"It is an issue, Will. You suffered because of me. If..."

"Ok, ok. Fine. Adrina, with all my heart I forgive you. Look me in the eyes if you doubt me." She was so small that she had to crane her head way back to see his face. A moment later she smiled a giddy little smile, he did the same. "Was that really necessary?"

With a glance to the river, her smile faded and she became serious again, "Yes it was. Never assume forgiveness." Adrina turned from the river and wrapped her arm in Will's without asking. "So, big strong Will. Why do you need my help?"

Despite her younger looks, he couldn't help feeling as if he were walking with his grandmother. "Would it surprise you that I have demon troubles again?"

She answered this with a laugh. It was wonderfully cruel free and made him feel giddy again. "Don't we all."

It was his turn to laugh and for the moment, it was though they were strolling down a Carolina beach, looking for the perfect seashell. Unfortunately, it didn't last. Will began to tell the story of the last few days, about Luke and poor Father Alba. About the sword and the dead children, about Talitha and Amy Harris; as he spoke, he grew cold as if the words were leading him closer to the Void. When he was done Adrina began to pepper him with questions, one after another, many of which dealt with how he came to be in the Void, without having died, something which fascinated her. The questions concerning Talitha's situation were saved for last, it was something she had trouble grasping.

"You say she split her soul in two? One part all good, the other all evil, how?"

A shrug was his response. "Even Talitha doesn't know. She just did it."

"And now instead of an evil soul fighting for control of her body, she has a split personality, one of which is totally evil?" Adrina shook her head in disbelief. "Your Talitha either bears the greatest curse of all of us or she's part of one those television soap operas. She's doomed either way."

The attempt at humor earned her a small crooked smile from Will, who only displayed it as a courtesy, his good mood had all but disappeared with the recounting of his story. "So any clue how we can find out where Amy is taking my sister, Katie?"

"I wish that was your biggest problem. Don't be mad,

but the sword is by far, more important than your sister right now. The danger to the world posed by a gate created through a spell of Amy's will take years to materialize, but the sword, that is something else all together. If a demon hasn't already, one will find that opening in the Void very soon and feed off of its light, its heat, its energy! It will fast become powerful enough to influence both this world and yours."

Will stopped walking. "That may be, Adrina, but I can't let what happened to Talitha, happen to Katie also. I won't." Their eyes met in hard stare, Adrina dropped hers first.

"Will, please..."

"No. First off we don't know how to destroy the sword, so what you're asking is moot anyways."

"I have an idea on how to do that."

Will's anger began to bubble up. "Good and I'll listen to it, but first tell me how I can find where Amy has my sister. And don't even think about lying right here so close to that river."

Her eyes, which had been a warm brown, flashed darkly. "How dare you! I don't have to give you any answers if I don't choose." Another silence came between them, a hard seething quiet. Will was first to break it.

"I'm sorry about accusing you like that. It was stupid and wrong." Asking for forgiveness so near the river was a strain unto itself. Adrina was thankfully quick to reply.

"You're forgiven, Will. We both know I have a history of withholding certain information," this she said with a sad little smile. "But not this time. I swear." Now her expression became one of pain. "I don't think I'll be any help in finding your sister. I'm sort of trapped here. If I go back to the Void... I go back to the pits at Rek. I can't do that. It's so horrible." The pain in her face increased.

Will put his hand on her arm. "Could I find out the information about Katie myself? What would I have to do? Is there a spell or something?"

"There is, but you told me Amy was countering your visions and you told me that she is short on time. This means she's gone all out protecting herself from any sort of clairvoyance, unless she's very, very stupid that is, which I doubt. The time issue is the other reason I won't be able to help you. Without spells, the only other way to find information about the living is through the dead. You would have to find someone who is recently deceased who knows where she's going. Would her thugs know?"

"They might." His stomach suddenly flared in nauseas pain—the chances that Amy would tell her thugs where she was going next were close to zero. "Her mom would know, I bet."

Adrina's head nodded in agreement, but her face registered more defeat. "Yes, likely. But would she tell you? Hardly, and then there's the issue of even finding Henny in the Void, which is nearly impossible. And even if you do, you'll have to get past her demon captor, Ba'al Zubel probably..."

Will interrupted, "No, it's Ba'al Fie-ere...my sister, kind of. I think she has Henny."

"This demon has Henny Harris?"

"Yeah. Ba'al Fie-ere said she was going to get a gate using Katie and since Amy has Katie..."

"Then Fie-ere probably has Henny," Adrina finished. "There must have been a trade, but a really bad one, I'm thinking. Or the demon lied to you. They do that, you know. But it doesn't matter, since getting around any demon in this situation will be practically impossible. The demon will keep Henny very close until the gate is open and once it is, that will mean your sister will probably be beyond your help or mine."

"So there's no hope in finding Katie?"

"I don't think so. Not before the gate opens. But maybe she can come here and cross over."

A sharp pain lanced through Will's stomach. "I

accidentally told Ba'al Fie-ere about the River. I'm sorry; I thought I was talking to Katie. Do you think a demon can come here?"

Adrina shook her head. "No, but it might make it imposs...very difficult for Katie though. Ba'al Fie-ere will try to corrupt her as soon as she can." Will's head drooped and Adrina grabbed his arm. "There's still hope. If a soul dies in the dungeons and pits of hell, it will re-emerge in the Void. Maybe she can come here then. Does Katie, the real Katie know about the river?"

When Will shook his head, Adrina's face fell and there was silence between them. Will's stomach began to hurt with ever-greater intensity and in seconds, he was sitting on the ground clutching himself. "I can't give up on her. There's no way."

"You have to. Katie will have to save herself. She will have to find a way to come here on her own and you have to let her go. Destroying the sword is more important just now. Let Katie go, for the greater good."

"What about Lisa and my baby? Do I sacrifice them also for the greater good? And my father's soul? Just leave it down here as a plaything of some demon? How many of my friends and loved ones have to die before I become part of the greater good?" Will's words were venom and a small part of him was ashamed, the rest, however, was simply furious that Adrina was correct.

"Who else can destroy the sword? If you don't close that tiny gate now, over time it will become impossible. You have to see that."

"I don't!" Will's fury mounted. "We can throw the blade into the deepest part of the ocean or...bury it down a bottomless..."

"No!" With a quick step, she was right on top of Will and gripped his arm tight with nails that dug into his skin. "None of that will matter. You could send the blade into space if you wanted, but still the demon would feed on the light of a billion stars and over time it would grow and put forth its will and the blade would be found. The longer you wait, the harder it will be."

"I can't."

"Please?"

"Look..." There was no use arguing with her. "How bout this, I make an attempt at finding Henny, if I can't get anything out of her, it'll be a lost cause either way and I'll do what I can to destroy the sword."

Like magic, Adrina released her claws from Will's flesh. "Ok, but don't dawdle, Ba'al Zubel is strong enough without being fed pure energy."

"How do you know Ba'al is in control of the gate?"

A smile came to her. "My gut, mostly. The great demon keeps close watch upon its rivals, it will know if one becomes inordinately powerful and it'll move to confront it quickly." For some reason she turned from him and faced away downstream. "Now about destroying the sword...you'll need a virgin girl and a gypsy."

"What? No, no, no!" Will spun her around, something that was very easy since she was so tiny. "You're not going to ask me to sacrifice some poor girl!"

She wouldn't look up into his face. "Maybe you won't have to. She might live, you never know." This was said without enthusiasm and Adrina pressed on quick, "Listen, find a gypsy, you know what they look like. There are more around you than you realize and don't be fooled if they have a last name like Jones or Smith. We've been hiding our identities since the days of Moses. Second, find a virgin and remember the spirit has to be pure...even a nun will do, the younger the better, or at the least find someone who attends church weekly. Third...you have the incantations of Henny's, use them to open the gate and once it's open simply stab the blade into it."

He had listened to her go on, stunned into silence at the idea of perpetrating such evil against an innocent girl, but the last part about sending the sword through the gate struck him as insane. "That's your plan? Hand over the blade to the very demon that wants it most?"

Adrina nodded. "It's a gate into the Void itself. Once it's in the Void, it'll be useless. Picture the front door of a house. Go through it and you move from outside to inside the home. You go from rain or snow, to warmth and light, you see? Take the same door and put it here on this beach, you go from sand to sand, it serves no purpose whatsoever."

The two were silent for long spell, neither looking at the other. Nor did they look into the water. Will grew more depressed the longer he stood there. How could he open a gate? How could he ruin some poor girl? "I have to go," he said eventually.

"You do, time is tricky in the Void, and it almost always runs against you. I'm sorry I wasn't more help and I swear, if I could tell you how to find Katie, I would."

"I believe you. Good bye Adrina."

For her, it wasn't quite time. She leapt toward him and hugged him tight and he returned the embrace, again marveling how small and insubstantial she was. When she looked up at him, her eyes were red and wet. "Come visit me again, please. It's lonely here...I mean it's better than the Void yeah, but it still is lonely."

"No. I won't. You're going to cross this river again. Put your trust in God and you'll be fine." Will detangled himself from her. "Now, I really have to go. Thanks for your insight and uh, the suggestion." He didn't see himself damning a young girl to hell no matter what.

Adrina saw it in his eyes. "*You* trust in God. You've made hard choices before, you're going to have to do so again."

Will nodded and gave her a last smile before he turned away. The hills were in front of him, but they were illusionary. "Goodbye and good luck... I'll try to come here, if..." If he was killed, that is.

"Ok good, that sounds real good." She was crying, perhaps in relief, perhaps in sadness of his leaving. "Be strong, Will."

"I'll do my best," he replied, and gave only a quick look back, worried that he had wasted far too much time already. With a single step, the warm sand turned to deadly cold shadow.

Chapter 27

Will

The cold that struck him like an icy gale was depressingly familiar, as were the shifting shadows that danced in rhythm to his fear. Those shadows hid things. But just barely. They gave him glimpses of tortures and pain, like an evil strip show. They showed only enough to bring his fright to a crescendo and for a moment, his heart quailed in fear, and he froze in place with his eyes darting about. However, this was familiar too.

Fear was nothing new to Will Jern.

The emotion had been an acute intense companion of Will's for days, and chronically, for years. Off and on, for eight long dreary years, it skulked in the depths of his mind to come rearing up at his weekly visits with his sister. This had inured him to a degree and after a few minutes of his heart pounding in his chest, he forced his fear into the background of his subconscious and started walking into the dark Void, ignoring the sights, the screams, the feel of blood suddenly splattering him or squishing beneath his bare feet. Even if he had the time, there was nothing he could do for any of the poor wretches around him.

Time was his biggest issue. There was no way to judge it in any way other than to realize that Adrina was correct. In the Void time worked against a person. If there was pain, it would draw out. If there was a deadline, it would speed up. Will forced himself to relax. He would find Henny, or he wouldn't and worrying would only hurry time along.

Fixing his enemy's face firmly in his mind he began whispering, "Henny Harris, Henny Harris." Much faster than he expected, the shadows turned into wicked black trees and thorned bushes, a path twisted among them. He followed as quick as he dared and soon he came to a castle of immense proportions.

Against a midnight sky, tall straight spires stretched away beyond heavy stone battlements and closer, just at his feet a terribly dark moat opened up. Its depth was immeasurable. Off to his right, a bridge extended across the moat and as Will came to it, he saw that it stood quietly unguarded. In fact the entire structure seemed empty without a trace of motion or noise, but all the same Will knew that eyes were everywhere upon him.

His relaxed mood began to crumble at the sight of the dark castle and he hesitated, afraid to set foot upon the bridge. But across it was his destiny for good or for evil and resolutely, with his face set in hard lines, he practically sauntered over it, daring the demon. Once across he wondered how easy it would be to go back, but as he watched, the bridge faded to nothing leaving only a very long fall behind him. Onwards then. Upon gaining the castle proper, he took the first door that lead to stairs. Stairs that led downwards, that is. Henny would be nowhere else beside the dungeons.

Down the fearfully steep staircase and then along a low ceilinged black tunnel, Will walked, knowing his goal would be soon upon him. He didn't hurry, though he very much wanted to, instead he reminded himself of the courage his father had always shown and pressed on, until actual light could be seen up ahead. This was no illusion. After the varying shades of black, it was a marvel to look upon and by the warmth of the light, he knew he had found a living person.

He also knew that he had found his father. Now Will moved with more haste and slipped quietly up to the chamber where his father lay. The man no longer looked so dreadfully skinny, nor as old, quite the opposite. His shoulders were thick and wide, his arms bulged with muscles, and his eyes were a startling blue.

They were a skeptical blue however.

"What now?" William Jern wasn't quiet in the least.

"Shush," Will whispered, darting to the edge of the room, which was circular and decorated in mottled shadows all along its walls. Other than his father, the place seemed deserted, but Will was loath to step in to the room fearing a trap. "It's Will. Are you ok? Can you get up?"

"I'm fine, *Will*. Thanks for asking, now why don't you tell me what you want?" His manner was strange enough to keep Will from entering the room.

"Dad, please. We have to get out of here."

"Sure, just unchain me and off we go," William held up his leg and showed off a large chain that ran to an eyebolt on the floor. Without hesitation, Will charged into the room and threw his strength against the chain. It seemed about to stretch when a loud clang rent the air behind him, he didn't bother looking back. As he had suspected, his father was part of a trap. Instead of panicking Will got his legs under him and pulled at the chain with all the strength he could muster.

Tunk, the bolt snapped off and he was thrown back to the ground. In a second, he was up again, facing whatever menace had trapped them.

The shadows, filling out into the three dimensional likeness of men, came off the walls and formed ranks around the father and son. In their hands, the shadow-men carried thick spears, which they leveled inwards. Will was surprisingly unfazed and his father was so relaxed, he hadn't bothered even to get up.

From the floor, William drawled out, "This is the worst play ever. I can't tell if this is supposed to be *Cats* or *The Sound of Music*. Just please tell me you'll be serving drinks at intermission." This was so odd that Will had to look back at his father a second time just to make sure that it was indeed him.

"Always the brave Commander. You know I enjoy that so much." This was spoken by a slow heavy voice; it stirred the air so that the shadow men seemed to flicker as they stood and as the wind of the words struck Will, he went cold and couldn't suppress a shiver.

"Who are you?" he called out. The originator of the voice lurked back behind the phalanx of spearmen and had yet to be seen.

"Oh, shut up!" William cried and Will was shocked to the core when he realized that the words were directed at him. William went on indignantly, "This is your worst attempt yet, Ba'al. Why don't you just torture me and get it over with?"

Ba'al? Worst attempt? What was happening here? Will's mind ran around in circles trying to play catch up, he wasn't nearly successful. "What's going on?" he demanded after a moment.

His father ignored him, but the creature he referred to as Ba'al explained, "William doesn't believe you are his son. He thinks you're nothing but an apparition, which is understandable since I've been playing so many fun games with him. He's quite a distraction."

Father and son looked at each other; William shook his head still disbelieving. "Have him put on his little show. Are you supposed to be here saving me from the evil demon? If you are, get to battling."

Confusion had Will stammering, "I am...I think, or at least I thought I was." His mind was suddenly all turned around. The demon strode closer, it was Ba'al Fie-ere and her skin was still as black as jet. She was a bit of a shock to Will. He had been expecting Ba'al Zubel, the tyrant. Yet it hardly mattered, he could no more defeat this demon than any other. At least not without the power that he had once felt burning inside him. The power that he had used to defeat the great Ba'al.

The power of the *Word of the Lord.*

It was something that he was acutely aware of *not* feeling and it left a hole in his heart. Did this lack of power mean he was abandoned by the Lord? Was it a one-time shot and he would now have to win out on his own?

Ba'al Fie-ere intruded upon his thoughts before he could come to any sort of conclusion, "My dear brother, of course you're here to do battle. Where would the fun be if you weren't?" Her voice was now that of her twin back on earth, Talitha. This more than anything else fired his blood.

"Then step out from behind your little phantom men and face me!" It was an empty threat, but for some reason Ba'al hesitated and without saying a word of direction, the shadow men advanced.

"No. Sorry, Will. We've tried that before. You'll flash your little light and run away. But don't worry, these creatures won't hurt you, they'll just drain you so you can't pull any little tricks."

Now William looked concerned. "You have light? Let me see it." His ability to command with his voice was still impressive enough for Will not to hesitate. A weak stream of light gently blew back the shadow men, he could've done more, but he held back. William's blue eyes were ablaze. "Will, are you dead?"

Before he could answer, Ba'al spoke in a voice that shook the gloom with her sordid happiness, "He's not! Isn't that great? His body is somewhere else and his soul is mine! Ha ha! This is far greater than even I imagined. Your souls are wonderful. Look how bright you are! And soon I'll have Katie as well. Who would have thought Amy Harris could have been so handy."

"And the tyrant? Henny was Ba'al's witch. Is he going to sit back and let you take her?" Will asked, hoping to find a flaw in her thinking.

"Who do you think I had to trade with to get Henny?" The fifteen-foot tall demon looked to be getting worked up, not in exasperation, but in exaltation. Ba'al Fie-ere wanted them to know how clever she was. "And do you know what I gave up for Amy and her mom?" Both Will and William looked at each other, and shrugged. All Will knew was that it had to be something big. She gave a little laugh. "I gave up the gate that opens onto the sword. You know the one that sucked you into the Void, Father."

This produced a low growl in William's throat. Will on the other hand was almost, but not quite, speechless, "That was the dumbest trade in the world. That sword is a source of eternal power."

"Despite what you think, I have to assure you the trade was brilliant. Think about it, now that you...or rather Talitha has the sword, how many more souls are going to come through? I'm thinking none. I'm also thinking that very soon the sword will go into a lead lined box and be placed into cold storage as close to absolute zero as humanly possible. Ba'al is going to be dreadfully angry just how little he got for this trade."

William spoke up, "You don't look too worried."

More laughter from the demon. It made Will remember and miss Adrina whose laughter had been soft and musical.

"Why should I be worried? Look at your little girl now, Father." The demon suddenly grew sixty feet and became a vile monstrosity to look upon and her voice was a cacophony of harsh discordant notes. "Not only did I force the great Ba'al to name me, but in a short time I've become very near its equal." This brought on another booming laugh and the two men cowered, clutching their ears. The demon quieted and diminished back to her giraffe size. "Not yet," she admonished herself. "I can't reveal myself just yet. Not until I have Katie and the gate."

"How did you do this? How did you get so big?" Will asked.

"Oh, I bet you of all people are shocked, after how terribly you screwed me over." Her gaze was hard, full of malevolence, and Will took an involuntary step backwards. "You have no idea what you did to me when you cast me out of Talitha. You left me the weakest of demons. I had nothing. Nothing except my wits, and I needed all of those just to survive, especially when I humiliated the tyrant for a second time by stealing the souls of Jim Anderson and that pathetic Brabec girl right from under his nose." She laughed in joy at her triumph and grew giant-like a second time, however it was only for a moment and then she returned to her normal large size. "Ba'al was in the greatest fury and hunted me to all ends of the Void, yet always I managed to slip away and this was mainly due to the fact that I didn't really want to stay in one place either way. I was hunting too, you see.

"I was after the sword's gate. From the moment you sentenced me to hell, I knew that I had to control it. I thought it was an everlasting supply of power and with it, I could become the greatest of demons. My problem was that I couldn't find it; I search everywhere and in truth for a while I was truly stumped. It should have been more obvious, it should have stood out against the black as the tiniest star. But, there was nothing. So I changed tactics. Perhaps I had misunderstood the mechanics of the gate. I now searched out the blackest sections of the Void and was quickly rewarded for my efforts. The gate had been completely covered over by muck!"

Her knowing look was lost on the two men. "Muck? What do you mean?" William ventured.

"Uhg, this!" Reaching down she brought up a handful of the ever-present shadows that swirled about their feet. "This is muck... it's like hell mulch. This is what happens to your soul when demons no longer can have any fun with you. You just sort of wear out as an individual and become, muck."

"And that doesn't bother you?" William's face was set and a heavy pulse beat in his temple.

"Of course it does," the demon rejoined. "It happens to some of the best souls. You get a good screamer one who really feels the pain and then poof...it's like they suddenly don't care." William went red over this and the demon only laughed. "Stop being such an idiot, Papa. This is the way it is and you aren't going to do squat to change it." She drew herself up menacingly and Will stepped in front his father.

"Ba'al Fie-ere, you were telling us how you found the gate?" Will was still in desperate need of information. Nothing she had said so far had been of any help.

The demon smirked showing teeth the size of sabers. "Always the peace maker, Will. Always the hero. Do you think you will actually be able to escape this time?"

It didn't look like it, just then, but he had his light still and it gave him hope. "I'll try. You know I will, but right now, I'm interested in your story. How come the...muck had covered the gate over? Was another demon trying to hide it?"

At his admission, she smiled. "*Try* is the crucial word, because there will be no escape." She paused but Will held his tongue and forced an expectant look on his face as if her story couldn't be any more exciting. With a shrug, she continued, "I actually worried about another demon as well. It's without shame when I tell you that as the newest demon in the Void, I was one of the weakest. I would be a plaything for any other demon who happened upon me, so I nosed about the web of muck with trepidation, but it turned out that like bugs to a light, the muck just sort of gravitated to the gate. It was a perfect situation. I was hidden by endless layers of darkness and I controlled the gate. I grew very strong, very fast and soon I didn't fear any of the lesser demons. Yet, my growth hit a point of diminishing returns.

"I continued to grow, but at such a slow speed that it was almost a waste of time to sit huddled around the gate...but then Dad came popping out!" The demon offered William a large benevolent smile, which he refused to respond to. "At that point, the gate bloomed with energy and I took it all in! It was amazing, and I wanted more. It was like a drug. And then Talitha came, and with her another blast of energy, but it was smaller than before and my growth was far less. And what's worse, she stood poised at the gate and was somehow able to go back into the world.

"All of this made me realize that though the gate was a great thing, it was a dead end. I had to assume that Talitha now possessed the sword and that no more souls would be coming. And when, Daddy dearest told me about how Amy was after our sweet innocent little Katie, bam! My little plan was hatched. The tyrant, having been burned twice now in its dealing with the Harris' was eager to make the trade. What a moron."

"You're not so smart as you think," William jumped in. "You don't know Katie; she's tougher than you were at her age. Not only that, you have misjudged your brother before and I think you're misjudging him now. He will escape, and he will find Amy and stop her."

Remarkably, the demon didn't fly into a rage. "Wrong on all accounts. Even as we speak, Amy is in the middle of the incantations to open the gate. So even if Will does escape back to his body, he'll have what? Twenty minutes to find Amy. I doubt that's enough time."

Will doubted it as well. It meant that they had to be traveling, right that second to the exact right location and that any deviation or delay would mean failure. "Tell me! Where is she?"

The demand brought a cruel smile to the demon's lips. "First tell me, where are you? Where's your body?"

"We should be in Phoenix by now," his reply was far more quiet, little more than a whisper.

"Oh, that's too bad. You're going the wrong way, she's in Tucson."

Ba'al Fie-ere's fake pity lit a fire beneath Will. "You're a liar! Where is she?"

"Me? A liar? I guess I am, but unfortunately for our little Katie, I'm not lying about this. But if you don't believe me, you can ask another source...Henny?" To their left, the phantom soldiers drew back and Henny Harris appeared, rising out of the shadows; she was younger and more beautiful than Will remembered, yet her eyes were haunted and afraid. The demon gave her large fake smile. "Henny, where's your daughter?"

"Where would the great Ba'al like her to be?" Henny's voice quivered and she kept her large brown doe eyes stuck to the shadows that made up the floor beneath their feet.

"I want the truth, Henny. What city?"

"Tuscan."

If Henny was lying, she was an actress without equal. Will felt so weak, he almost sat down, instead he looked to his father.

"We'll figure something out," William whispered, his own face looking grey beneath his hardy tan. It didn't seem likely that they would. There had been fifteen or sixteen addresses scattered around Tucson that had fit the criteria, and Father Vogel was currently driving directly away from all of them. By the time Will was awakened, if that was even now possible, they would be an hour away. He had failed. Remorse struck him just it had at the river and the feeling made it hard to care too much about his own coming tortures. They would be horrible, he was sure, but just at the moment he couldn't bring himself to care.

Will turned back to Henny and found that she stared at him with an intense hatred, something he really couldn't blame her for, especially after having seen what he had done to her on the staircase. "This may sound stupid, but I'm sorry about knocking your head into the wall as hard as I did. I was scared to death and I wasn't thinking about the pain I was causing you."

The apology baffled her and her mouth came open a few times before she got her emotions squared away. "Fuck you! Your apology doesn't mean crap to me. You're going to pay for what you did and I'm going to laugh along with your every scream." Henny grew larger and more fierce looking as she spoke, but then she twirled and threw herself on her knees in front of the demon. "Please, I beg you. Let me torture him first. I've earned it, helping to get Katie for you."

"Earned?" The demon laughed and grew again. "Tell me, what is the going wage for a slave?" Ba'al paused as if Henny could give a satisfactory answer to this and when none came, the demon reached out with one of her oak tree sized arms and snatched Henny from the floor and held her high over their heads, her arms pinned, and her legs kicking. "The answer is no, Henny. But here is the payment you deserve for your insolence."

The monstrous demon turned the struggling woman on her side and with a hungry greedy look in her eyes bit off Henny's legs and chewed on them in ghastly pleasure. Screams and blood rained down on the two men, who stood stoically with matching looks of horror, until with easy indifference the demon tossed aside the body. Henny lay crumpled and disfigured, whimpering in the shadows and Will, despite knowing what an evil person she was, wanted to go to her, but his father put out a hand and stayed him.

Ba'al smirked at this and then spat out a long thighbone. "Watch over your daughter, Henny. Make sure Amy doesn't screw this up, or else."

"Y-y-yes g-great Ba'al," the woman stammered. She then very slowly dragged herself away, leaving a long nasty trail behind.

With satisfaction, Ba'al watched until she disappeared in the dark and then she shrunk back down, this time becoming her normal height so that the shadow men hid her completely. She couldn't be seen, but her presence could be felt and her voice heard easily, "I think it's time we had some fun with you, Will. Get you primed for your sister."

Will had a second for this to register before the shadow men charged with black spears leveled, their grim faces pitiless. A brilliant flash of his hidden light, staggered the first wave and they seemed to come apart, falling to pieces in silent agony. Unfortunately, behind these, a second line charged through the debris and though Will was able to destroy those in front, spears from a third line flew through the air striking him and knocking him to his knees.

The spears weren't designed to puncture his flesh and organs, rather they absorbed his light and drained his strength. The fight was short and bloody, both men were beaten until they could barely move. Will's light was no longer the bonfire that it had been, it felt like little more than a candle, and he was afraid what would happen if it went out altogether.

"Enough!" the demon cried. "We don't want to kill them." At some point, she had grown again and now that Will was no longer even a tiny threat, she loomed over the two men. "Still think you're going to escape, Will? You still think that I'd allow that to happen?"

"I will." He had meant it to come out as a challenge, instead it was a whisper that only had the demon smiling larger. He struggled to his feet and then helped his father up. "I will escape. I know about the river and I can cross it...I think."

"Oh really? You think so?" Ba'al didn't look too worried. "While you were gone, I made inquiries about this river. You ever wonder why Talitha didn't cross?"

"What river are you two talking about?" William asked.

Will answered his father before he answered the demon. "Somewhere on the border between heaven and hell, there's a river...it's got trees and hills and everything. In order to cross into heaven, you have to get past this river, but..."

The demon jumped in, craning her long neck down to put her giant head close to Will's face, "But the river shows you all the evil that you've committed. That's why Talitha couldn't cross it. She's far more nasty that either of you realize. Your little girl, William, can swing the whip with the best of them." William's lips pressed together and his brows came down to rest just above his eyes, but he said nothing.

"Sins committed in hell aren't sins at all," Will rejoined in defense of his sister, not at all knowing the truth of his statement. Common sense seemed to dictate the fact, however.

"Not sins? Are you on a 'time out' from morality here? Is that what you think? So by your pathetic reasoning, it will be ok with God, if I boil you two alive. I won't have to be worried about forgiveness, since it wouldn't be a sin, right?" She chortled over this for some time and Will began to worry that she was correct. "Even for you, Will that's kind of stupid. You had to wonder why Talitha always had trouble looking you in the eye."

Will had wondered that exact thing on many occasions, but he wasn't going to give the demon any satisfaction. "Whatever she did, I'm sure she was coerced."

"Of course she was! She was beaten to bloody pulp, roasted over a fire like she was a hotdog, she was given the works, and she became willing to do or say anything to stop the pain—though she did take a lot of punishment before she finally gave in...the first time. After that it got easier and easier to break her."

"So...what? She was made to torture people? Why? Are you demons so lazy that you can't do it yourself?" William's umbrage looked to be a source of amusement for the demon, who laughed her wall-shaking laugh.

"No, not just *any* people, she tortured family and friends. She took such delight tearing the skin from loved ones you'd have thought that she was a demon herself and you Will popped her cherry. She held firm despite the pain for a long time but it was on an illusion of you that she first gave in to temptation. And as for why Ba'al Zubel made her do this, it was for fun, simply for a laugh."

"That's a lie," Will said with a short hard laugh of his own. "There's way more to it than just fun. Demons like you and Ba'al Zubel can't stand even the least bit of goodness in a person. You're embarrassed by it, because you know that its contrast makes you look small and petty and pathetic." The demon bared her long teeth in a smile. It was a deadly smile that spoke of revenge for his audacity and Will took an involuntary step back, practically hiding behind his father. "There was another reason as well that she was made into a torturer. The tyrant was afraid to lose her, right? She told me once that hell was voluntary..."

William interrupted, turning to his son with skepticism, "What? That can't be right."

"It is, Dad. If you can escape from her," he pointed, indicated the looming demon. "You could search out the river if you wanted and cross over. That's why Ba'al Zubel forced her to do such terrible things. He chained her to the Void with her own sins."

"Finally you show a spark of intelligence," Ba'al Fie-ere rumbled. "And as a reward, I'll let you go first." From seemingly nowhere, she produced a long handled whip. "Let's start with a classic. Come on and take it, Will. Don't be shy." When it was clear that he wasn't going to budge the demon tossed it in front of him. A moment later, she produced a second whip, this one was long and mean, barbed with shining metal. It made Will shudder in fear just looking at it, this brought a smile to the demon's lips. "Time to get your hands dirty, Will. I can't have you running off to heaven if I get overzealous and accidentally kill you. Now since this is your first time, I'm going to give you a very fair deal. You'll give your father a hundred lashes with that tiny little whip or I give him two hundred, with this. Now isn't that fair? Won't you be doing him a favor?"

His mouth came open and hung there. She took that as a yes. "Good. I'm glad you're being reasonable. One other thing however, if any of your lashes fail to draw blood, you'll be whipped twice by mine."

William stepped in front of his boy, looking remarkably composed. "Your little scheme won't work, Ba'al. I love my son and I forgive him for anything that he may be forced to do." The man then turned and actually smiled. "I hold you entirely blameless, Will. Let none of what's going to happen, hold you back. I want you to go to heaven no matter what. Now let's get this over with." He gave Will a gentle push toward the whip.

How could the man be so calm? With the fear drenched gloom and the shadow men standing all around them with spears ready and the demon leering in, a spectacle of vile perversity, Will was a bundle of nerves. His body shook so badly that it took an effort of will just to stumble over and pick up the whip.

"I don't think I can do this," Will said, speaking mostly to the fifteen-foot long strip of leather that sat with unnatural comfort in his palms, he was afraid to look up. And this was for a number of reasons. The first was he feared that the demon, as a master deceiver herself, would see the deception in his eyes. Just as he had bent down to pick up the whip, a plan had come to him, unfortunately not a very good one. He decided that if he could accomplish nothing else, he would free his father. And that meant killing him, something that even if the demon wasn't standing so close, wouldn't be an easy thing to do. In his prime, his father was a bull of a man, but that was nothing compared to the fact that Will loved him with all his heart. It would be a mercy kill he had to remind himself.

The second reason he feared to look up was he knew that if he hesitated any longer, the dreadful whip that Ba'al Fie-ere held would come lashing at him. Purposely he waited as if in indecision and clenched his jaws in anticipation.

"Will, look out!" His father's warning came a half second before the whip struck.

The pain was an incomparable fire that ran a line from his left ear, which tore completely away, and down his back diagonally. He gasped at the intensity and went weak, dropping to his knees, but before he could scream, the whip struck again and then again, and he writhed on the ground in a vain attempt to avoid the blows. Ten lashes of unimaginable pain left him a whimpering bleeding wreck.

"I don't have all night. Your sister is coming soon and I haven't even picked out something to wear." The demon sat reclining on a tremendous throne, which had appeared from nowhere. She looked to be in no hurry. "Now, get up and give it a try. I think that soon you'll come to like it." As she spoke, she ran her whip through her lips tasting his flesh and blood. It was all Will could do, not to vomit at the sight.

"Y-y-yes ma'am," he said with a voice that shook and got to his feet as hurriedly as he could, though his legs threatened to buckle beneath him.

"Address me as the Great Ba'al!" she thundered and he cowered with his left arm up, very afraid that she would whip him again, if she did, he worried he would lack the strength to kill his father.

"Y-yes Great Ba'al," he shook and swayed and cringed in real fear. So far his plan wasn't working so well, his father had just stood there as he had been whipped, the opposite of what Will needed. He had to somehow get close to his father without rousing suspicion. There would be only one chance at this.

The Great Ba'al liked what she saw and smiled benignly. "Good. Now, Daddy has been naughty. Punish him, or else."

Will looked at his father and was surprised at the hard look that William had for him. "Stop messing around, Will and swing the whip, damn it!"

"I..." Will began.

"I said, swing the whip, now!"

This is going to hurt, Will thought to himself and sent the leather lash past his father's right arm. He missed. Purposefully. There was barely enough time for him to grimace in fear and cast his left hand up to protect his face, before Ba'al's whip descended down upon him. It was like a lightning strike. The pain seared into him yet he stumbled forward, trying to get near enough to his father on the off chance that he would have the strength and will to kill the man. By his fourth step, the demon lashed his legs, dropping him to the ground, after that there was only agony.

"Stop! Stop it now!" A familiar voice roared out. The whipping stopped, but the pain stayed and he cried on the floor among the shadows, embarrassed, but only vaguely so. The pain was that great. "Pull it together, Will. Don't let her win." William was a red blur above him. "Come on be strong."

There was almost no strength left to him, he shuddered and whimpered, and the demon sat enjoying the misery and William came down on one knee and held him close. There was something wrong with Will's vision and when he touched his own face, he found that his left eye was missing, as was a great deal of his skin. The pain was too much for him to care.

Eventually the demon spoke and when she did, it seemed to clear his mind and he was able to think past the pain, "We all know what you are up to, Will." He swallowed hard, afraid that she actually did. "You just want to take the punishment; you're trying to protect our father. I would call that noble, but just look how it makes him seem? He looks like a pathetic coward. You're all bloody and crying like a bitch and he looks as good as new, almost like he's using you as a shield."

"Will, please...you're going to have to use that whip on me. I-I can't stand to see you in this much pain," William whispered, his voice cracking with emotion. "Please, do it for me?"

Will nodded and put out a hand to be helped up, but when his father hauled him up, he could barely stand. Fortunately, Ba'al gave him another minute before she became impatient.

"Enough stalling! Whip him good, Will. I wanna see you bloody up his pretty face." Ba'al threw one of her huge legs over the armrest of the throne and smiled down on her prisoners.

"Yes, great Ba'al." Will turned to his father, "Could you kneel down, please? And just try not to move, ok? No matter what... don't move." With his one good eye, he gave his father an exaggerated wink, after a flash of puzzlement, William nodded.

Now was Will's only chance. Another whipping would take too much out of him. Taking a deep breath, he ran the leather through his hands, formed it into a coil and before his soul could protest the patricide he was about to commit, he dropped it over his father's head and yanked it as tight as he could around his neck.

Chaos erupted around the two men. Ba'al leapt to her feet and the shadow men charged with black spears pointed square at his chest. Will wasn't entirely defenseless, he still had some light left within him, and he released it in a blinding silent explosion. The radiance of it wasn't much compared to how powerful it had been, but it still smote the rushing shadows, sending them scattering.

"Go to the river, go to the river," Will grunted through his clenched teeth, pulling for all he was worth. For a moment, he thought that he would succeed. His hands stung from the amount of pressure he was exerting and his father's face went from pink to red and then to a deep purple and just when he was sure the great man would finally succumb to asphyxiation, the leather whip turned to smoke in his hands and Will toppled backwards.

Ba'al laughed hard. "These are my shadows, my playthings. I command them, they obey me. I created them and I decide what shape they form. Oh, but what fun that was, watching you play the part of the hero. Now get on up, don't just lie there crying. I think that since you were so bad, your father should spank you."

Will stood, tears of frustration did indeed drip from his chin, and his heart was heavy with defeat. "You may control the shadows, but you do not control me."

"Are you going to strangle your dad with your bare hands?" she asked standing. Ba'al rose to her full height now and he barely came to her knee. "Do you think that I would allow that? You think I would sit by and let you kill such a prize?"

Instead of answering her, Will looked at his father, who knelt in front of him with his back ramrod straight, his shoulders out, and his head up. It seemed as though the man would never be cowed. Except that he would. In the end, the infinite grinding hate and the constant fear and pain would wear down even this heroic man, turning him into just so much soul mulch. Will couldn't allow that to happen, he would kill him in any way he could.

By training, he was indeed a killer, he had learned from the best, by the very demon that stood above him.

Every week, while in the body of his sister, she had sought ways to strike him down, though many of these attacks he had seen coming by way of his *vision* and had avoided them without the need to fight. But he had learned nonetheless. He had seen the thousand moves, the precise angles of attacks, the ferocious focused power that could kill in a blink of an eye.

It would need to be a clean death and a very fast one.

"I love you, Dad." It was all Will had time for. He took a large step back and then pivoted, before driving his right leg out, throwing his entire weight behind a bone crushing side kick. His foot smashed into the back of his father's neck with the force of a sledgehammer. There was a horrid cracking noise and his father flung out his arms and pitched forward onto his face, spasmed once and then lay there in shadows unmoving.

"No!" Ba'al's scream of outrage surged through the shadows sending them spiraling around him in a froth. A second later, Will was struck by something and went sprawling, he was unaware of pain or any emotion.

Curiously and blessedly, he felt completely numb.

The vast figure of Ba'al Fie-ere stooped and picked up the body of William Jern and it lolled in her hand, its head looking like only strings were keeping it from dropping away. Fire grew behind the black of Ba'al's eyes. "You will pay! You'll pay, you'll pay, you'll pay!" She stamped her foot like a toddler in a fit and then threw down the body as if it were a broken toy.

Her deadly whip lifted and came at Will, the sound, a powerful crack, woke him from his numbness and pain shot across his body. Soon his whole world was only pain and the one thing that Will could care about was saving the one eye he had left. Above all else, he had to see for himself that his father had died, that William was really and truly free. But that eye was in jeopardy. Ba'al seemed determined to shred every inch of skin from his body and already he had lost his fingers off both hands.

Just then, a new sound blasted through the hell that Ba'al Fie-ere had constructed. It was as if two pieces of metal had thundered together in a massive clash. The sound was like electricity and vibrated and tingled the very shadows. Ba'al's whip stopped half drawn back and she stood as a statue.

"The Gate!" she cried.

Before he knew it she strode away, leaving him penned in the circular room that he had first found his father in. Gone were the shadow men and the throne. A body lay in a heap near one of the heavy brick shadow walls, and just as Will focused on it with his single eye and saw that it was his father, it faded into nothing.

Will wept in joy that his father was now free and he wept in misery from the scores of wounds that covered his body, but above all else, he wept in sadness. He might have saved his father, but he lost him as well, gone from his life was the one man that he had ever loved and the one person that he respected over all others. A thousands tears fell from his one eye, before he was able to think on his current predicament: Katie would surely be joining him soon. This dread thought brought a fresh wave of tears.

Poor Katie. She was doomed and that was almost certainly unchangeable, the gate was being opened even then and after that, her body could be hidden anywhere. Perhaps worse, her soul would be Ba'al Fie-ere's plaything for an eternity since there was no way that the demon would fall for any of Will's little tricks now.

But that didn't mean he wouldn't stop trying, nor would he stop trying to escape.

Unfortunately, that wasn't going to happen just then. Will dragged his body to the nearest wall. On some level, he knew that it was little more than shadows and illusion, but his reality told him that it was concrete, heavy and thick. He tried to will himself past it as he had before, but it remained solid. When that didn't work, he tried meditation, only his pain was too great to concentrate on anything else. After that, he laid there on the frozen concrete, clueless at what to do. Depression laid such a good hold of him that now the idea of escape seemed ludicrous, but it was just then, that Will heard a sound. It was very faint and seemed to come from all about him.

"Huh?" It hurt terribly even to make that one noise, his bottom lip had been nearly sheared away and it dangled grotesquely.

"Will?" His name floated out of the shadows and he grew afraid again, certain that it was a gypsy calling him as part of some evil spell.

Hands shook him, "Will?" Now the gypsy was louder, more urgent, and Will suddenly recognized the voice.

"Mom?"

"Yes," Gayle said. She leaned over him, shaking his shoulders and staring into his blue eyes with her big brown ones. He was back, back in the world.

Chapter 28

Will

The air in the back of the SUV felt like it had come straight from an oven, all the same, Will shivered violently and his skin sprung armies of regimentally aligned goose bumps.

"Will! Are you ok?" Gayle was practically shouting. She turned to her daughter and asked her, "Is he going to be ok? Is this normal?"

Before Talitha could answer, Will managed to blurt out, "I-I'm ok. W-w-where are..."

"We're in Phoenix. The first address on the list is right there." Talitha, looking listless and pale, pointed out the window, however Will didn't look. They weren't even close to where Amy held Katie. Talitha leaned her face next to her mother's. "What happened? Did you find Mrs. Harris? Did you see dad at all?"

Due to his many wounds, being back in the world was nearly as painful as being tortured in the Void and Will, with some urgency, struggled to get up and only answered his sister with a vague, preoccupied, "Yeah." He then turned to look at his father, lying curled around Lisa. The man looked dead, but also more at peace, no longer did his mouth gape and the lines of fear had relaxed. He looked younger than he had. Will checked, but there wasn't a pulse to be found.

Everyone watched him in silence. "I found dad down there, he was trapped by Ba'al Fie-ere and I...I freed him." A lump the size and consistency of a pinecone lodged in his throat and it was a moment before he could go on. "It was so terrible there and he was very brave and...and so strong. But...but he's no longer in the Void. I think he's in heaven now." Will felt an almost uncontrollable urge to break down and cry like a child, but his mother hugged him close and he was able to hold it down inside of himself.

"You did great, Will," she said, pulling back and leaving the side of his face wet from her tears. "What about Katie? Did you find out about her?"

He told them what he had learned, and the news about Katie stunned the little group, each stood mutely save for the constant sniffling. Finally Father Vogel spoke up, "We should check the building either way. After all. I'm sure demons are notorious for lying."

"Sure it wouldn't hurt," Will agreed. In his heart, though, he was only putting off the very difficult choice he had to make. "Tal can you smell Katie or Amy."

"No, there's nothing."

"But we're still so far away," Gayle pleaded, unable give up hope. Her eyes were almost black with the dark of the night and her Arizona tan very deep, Will tried not to stare or even think about what she looked like just then.

"Tal and I will go and check the place out, Mom. Please stay here with Father Vogel, just to be on the safe side." He gave her another hug and sat her back down in the front passenger seat before turning to the building they were supposed to check out. They were in a low rent office park, where storefronts faced the street and goods were warehoused in the back.

After a single glance, Will's stomach rolled over. A killer had worked as a welder there and had used his arc torch for horrible purposes, the man had been dead three years, but the smell of burning flesh was fresh in Will's nostrils. It wasn't the only thing that he saw. He *knew* that the building was empty, yet he went to it regardless.

"We both know Amy and Katie aren't here. Why are you wasting our time?" Talitha asked when they were still twenty yards away. "Shouldn't we be trying to get in touch with the bishop and maybe the police, to try to track them down?" Her mannerisms were odd, jumping slightly from personality to personality. She looked on the verge of giving up the fight against her evil side and Will knew that he would have to tread carefully despite the sensitive questions that he had to ask.

He kept silent until they got to the front of the abandoned business and then he asked in a soft voice, "You're a virgin aren't you?"

At first Talitha looked shocked at the question, but hot anger was quick to follow, and it made her voice quiver, "You know that I'm not. Why do you want to know? What did Ba'al Fie-ere show you?"

The place was deserted as he knew that it would be and he waved the priest and his mom over, only then did he answer, "I'm not talking about Ba'al Fie-ere or whatever you want to call the other being that lived inside you all those years, I'm talking about you, my sister. Did *you* ever make love to a man, by your own volition?"

"Yes...I mean no. Damn it! I never did. It was always her, the other one."

"Why didn't you?" She started to protest and he repeated himself, as calm as he could, "Why didn't you Talitha? I need you to concentrate."

Talitha took a long deep breath and closed her eyes before answering, "Before, I was too young. Sex is supposed to be the physical aspect of love itself, not a way to inspire the emotion, which so many people wrongly presume. With Brian, I was just about ready and then the demon came and when I returned, it was with my other self along. She made even the idea repugnant."

As she finished speaking, the priest rolled the Jimmy up and Talitha buttoned her lips on the subject with embarrassment. Their mom hopped out quick and peeked nervously in the window, her reflection was so black that it reminded Will of Ba'al Fie-ere. This left a bad taste in his mouth and he walked away to look at his wife one more time.

"No one's in there," Gayle said coming around to Will. "What are we going to do now?"

"Katie is beyond our help, Mom."

Gayle sunk to the pavement. "No! You've got magic powers, use them. You too, Talitha. Go find my baby girl, go find your sister."

Will half expected this to set off Talitha's other personality, however his sister only looked more weary than he had ever seen and sat down against the building with her chin dragging on her chest. They all looked done in, save for the priest, who hovered nearby keeping silent. Will was quiet as well. He was afraid that he was now at the cross roads of his earlier visions, whichever way he turned from here would decide if his wife would wake, or die years from now in her endless sleep.

He was in possession of the hell blade and it was his clear duty to destroy it. At the same time, he had an obligation to his sister and an obligation to destroy the gate that was being created through the energies of her body and soul. It seemed impossible to decide which route to take, but only because one choice was hopeless and the other would likely mean his death. Remembering Adrina's death, he shivered and a real heavy need to pee came over him.

"I will find Katie, but not just yet. We have work to do here." He knew the direction he had to go, because it was the one his father would have chosen. "Here's what we are going to do..." In a minute, he outlined his painfully simple plan of opening a gate onto the Void.

"But I'm not a gypsy!" his mother protested.

"And I'm..." Talitha paused in the middle of her outburst and shot a look at her mother and then at the priest, before continuing in a quieter voice that was practically a whisper, "And I'm not a virgin."

"And I'm not a hero," Will replied. "I'm scared to death. You guys don't know what Ba'al Zubel did to Adrina... it was horrible. But I'm going to risk it, because this has to be done."

Father Vogel, who had stoically listened to his part in the action without flinching, said, "I agree that it has to be done, but that doesn't change the fact that essential elements to opening a gate and summoning the demon seem to be missing here."

"Then we lose nothing," Will countered.

"I'm Italian, not a witch," Gayle insisted.

"Adrina hinted broadly that gypsies were nearer than I knew, I think she was worried that I would take offence if she came right out and said it. And she also said not to be fooled by a non-gypsy sounding name. And," Will looked next at his sister, "Adrina said when finding a virgin to find one with the purest soul and yours may be the purest there is, after all you stripped away all the evil in you to make...your other self."

Talitha had grown more pale as they had spoken, "Let's suppose that your conjecture concerning our ancestry is correct, and mom is able to open the gate. If the demon doesn't buy off on my being a virgin, you may doom her. You know about the connection. You know there will be a link between their souls. There is even a chance that the demon will posses mom. Are you willing to take that risk with what you know about... my physical history?"

"Yes, because I don't think it'll be a risk at all. The demon we're summoning is Ba'al Zubel and he hates you so much I'm sure he will accept you as an adequate offering." He said this as gently as he could, but Talitha still blanched.

"Ba'al? Does it have to be Ba'al?"

"I'm afraid the summoning spells are specific and this is the one that we got from Luke and he got it from Amy, who got it from Henny."

Vogel spoke up, "But why summon a demon at all? Why not just do that part of the spell that opens a gate?"

Talitha sighed before answering, "These spells come from demons who would gain nothing if any old gate was opened. I'm sure the spells are interwoven. Will, can you look at my neck? I'm feeling pretty weak."

The necrosis looked to be spreading and the wound itself had not closed and was oozing fluids that looked just like blood except that it was grey.

When he told her, she tried to put on a brave smile. "Pretty soon, a sacrifice is all that I'll be good for."

"You're not going to be sacrificed, that's not how it's going to work. When mom summons Ba'al, I'll challenge it. All I have to do is hold on for seconds, two or three at the most and while that's happening, Father Vogel will simply stab the blade into the opening and bam! Mom closes the gate and brings you with her. With Ba'al focused on me and then with the sword flying passed him, he'll be too preoccupied to worry about you two." He paused looking around at the three of them. They were a sad looking lot, even the priest who's lips were now drawn too tight to be anything else but a show of nerves.

"You forget, Will. The incantations are magically encrypted," Vogel replied.

Like an autumn tree in an early storm, whose limbs droop and fail under the weight of unexpected snow, Will sagged at the pronouncement. His plan, his only plan was all he had. There was nothing else rattling around in his brain in the way of an idea. That is, other than praying, which seemed his only option, but just then, he *knew*.

"Wait! You're wrong, Father. Luke did something to this incantation. I just had a vision: Luke was bent over the papers. He said *Ixino Ianai* and then there was this green light... I think it was a counter-spell or something, so that the gypsy from last night could read it." As he spoke, he hurriedly pulled out the coffee stained paper. "Mom, try it."

Gayle took the papers, looking timid and shy. She said the words in a whisper, " *Ixino Ianai* ."

Green light blazed briefly and then she stared at the papers in disbelief. "I can read this," she said in surprise.

"I'm really a gypsy?" Gayle asked, stunned.

Talitha held her hand. "If you're a gypsy, then I'm one too, mom."

Gayle gave her a little smile. "Ok, us gypsies have to stick together. What do I do?"

"Let me see," Talitha said, taking the papers. In minutes, she'd read over the incantation, frowning nonstop, as she did, "This shouldn't be so easy. These papers should be burned as soon as possible." No one disagreed. "I'm going to need a sharp knife and some blood, sorry Father, but yours would serve the purpose the best."

No one had a knife, but since glass had to be broken to gain access to the building, its shards were used instead; one shard for the priest's blood and another for the ceremony. Talitha went to work drawing the diagrams on the empty floor while her mother sat near, mumbling over the words to the spell, trying to wrap her tongue around the demonic language. It made Will physically sick to hear and he went to the car and sat with Lisa. With no one around, he began singing to the baby inside of her, hoping that she at least could hear him.

A few minutes later, Gayle came out, "We're ready."

Will's butterflies had been bad before, but now they kicked into high gear and he suddenly remembered how he had needed to pee. It would have to wait, his mom looked like she was about to vomit and he didn't want to delay the spell any more.

Still, he did pause to kiss his wife one last time and then hurried into the darkened building. The diagrams had been drawn very close to the front window of the building where the light from the nearly full moon and the street lamps gave them some visibility. Talitha lay in the middle of the diagram and her shaking hands she held close to her chest. His mother knelt beside her just outside of the drawing. She looked dead pale in her fright. Father Vogel stood to the side and in his hands he held the hell blade wrapped in a towel.

Will went to the circle opposite him. "Ok, Mom."

This was the extent of their preamble. The four of them looked back and forth at each other, but no one could find even the simplest words of encouragement and Gayle's lips seemed incapable of anything but quivering until she saw that the other three were staring at her, waiting.

She read from the paper in a stuttering voice, but all the same, the words were demonic in nature and Will felt them grating on his soul. It was as if sand had been poured into his chest and scritched annoyingly as he breathed. Quicker than expected Gayle finished and looked around, breathing rapidly, panting like some long forgotten hound.

"The blood! Cut your left hand and then cut Tal's and press your hands together. Hurry." Will ordered, remembering his dream from the day before. Had it only been the day before? This thought staggered him. So much had happened since then.

His mom acted as though her hand was without feeling. Very quickly and without the least grimace she slashed open her palm and then did the same for her daughter. Only then did she pause. Drawing in a deep breath, it looked as though she were about to speak, but instead she grabbed her daughter's hand and squeezed.

"Uhhh!" Talitha gasped, and then gritted her teeth, somehow able to cope with the pain that Will knew from his visions had to be extreme.

Bamn! The sound of metal on metal boomed throughout the building sending echoes chasing each other around the empty rooms. Will and Father Vogel both jumped at the noise and Talitha began to writhe in misery still holding on to her mother's hand. Gayle's eyes bugged and she looked about, unsure of what to do and Will was just about to reassure her, when a great rush of air whipped passed him in a sudden soundless fury. Black vapors began to churn six feet above his sister. They started small, twisting and boiling, but very quickly they grew into a great frothing cloud.

The gate was open!

Will clutched his chest with both hands as fear grew inside him, and then another metallic sound rang out. It smote the air, running along in hard fast waves like a heavy wind, sounding more like a death knell than anything else. This sound meant that the demon had accepted the offering of Talitha and was coming to claim the gate, but for the moment it felt to Will that the opening was still unattended.

Childish hope surged in him. Pushing aside the painful responsibility that he had taken on he cried, "Now Vogel! The sword!"

The room, in the space of seconds, had become fantastically cold and the priest didn't so much as dart forward, but lurched instead, honest fear touching his face for the first time. His eyes however, were determined and he yanked out the broken sword, when at that moment the demon, Ba'al Zubel arrived and sent his mind through the gate. The creature immediately discerned the priest in all his goodness and attacked. Father Vogel screamed and then began jittering in place as if he were being electrocuted; the sword dropped from his hands and clattered on the cement.

Twelve feet away, Will saw the sword bouncing on the floor and it seemed to be dancing on his heart. He knew a desperate need to make a dash for it and destroy it, and he even took a half step in its direction before he stopped, gripped by a chaos of uncertainty. On one hand, the poor priest was giving him precious seconds by enduring what looked like a horror of pain, but Will had been down that road before. He knew that if the demon went unchallenged, it would torture each of them in turn and he would get no closer to the sword than Ba'al would permit.

Yet Will paused in shock, in dread fear and fascination. Sudden lines, fine and red as if drawn from a pen, appeared on the priest's face. These split open and blood poured from the thin wounds, drenching the man. The lines then started to trace downwards running beneath the man's clothes and Vogel began tearing at his shirt, ripping it away.

It was then that another muffled scream caught Will's attention. It was his mother. Gayle hadn't let go of Talitha's hand and was now jerking about trying to free herself, her eyes were wild with panic.

"It's taking me too, Will! Oh God, help! Eeeiiieee!" The scream went right to Will's soul.

Everything had gone dreadfully wrong and all because Will had hoped for an easy victory. He should not have sent the priest at the gate; rather he should have waited for the demon and challenged him as he had planned. But he had known the pain involved and had so badly wanted to pass the cup from his lips that he had hesitated. And now his misery would be a hundred fold worse.

"Ba'al," his voice cracked. In his mind, he saw the image of Adrina's arms being rolled up and heard the terrible snapping of her bones. "Ba'al I challenge you." This was louder, but went ignored as the priest fell to floor and looked to be attacking himself. "Ba'al Zubel! Do you fear me? Are you afraid of Will Jern?"

This last could not be ignored and the demon turned on Will and their minds clashed.

It was not an epic battle of titanic forces, rather it was one man looking small in the presence of his foe, the dread Ba'al Zubel, ruler of the eternal Void.

The world and the room around Will went black and became at first intangible and then distant, as if it no longer mattered. The one thing that did was the demon. It had grown to magnificent proportions, a tremendous fiend with jet-black wings that stretched beyond into the darkness that surrounded them. Its greedy mouth was filled with long sharp, rapacious teeth and its hunger for Will's soul was undeniable.

Without a sound the thing pounced on the seemingly defenseless man, but Will was not quite so. In his heart, he felt the power of the love that his God had bestowed upon him. It was a white-hot fire compared to the darkness and when he opened his mouth to rebuke the demon, the Word of the Lord exploded from him in a blinding flash. It was almost like the light that had poured from him when he had been trapped by Ba'al Fie-ere in the Void, but whereas then he was only part of a vision, now he had an actual connection to his body and its warmth fed the energy of the Word.

The demon was lit by the power for a moment and then in a great deafening explosion was destroyed so thoroughly that nothing remained. Black wisps eddied throughout the air, yet strangely, the darkness continued. Will stepped back unnerved despite the ease of his victory and just then, a barking, hacking laugh came to him. It turned his insides cold.

"You are a fool and see not through the simplest illusion." These words did not come from a human mouth, but from something not at all natural. They hung in the darkness for only a second and were followed by the appearance of the demon once again. "You are nothing and Ba'al Zubel is all."

Too late, Will realized his mistake. The Word had left him—he had wasted its energies on an illusion! And without the power of the lord Will was nothing. He saw before him only despair and pain. There would be no challenging the mighty demon—there would be no buying time for the priest. There would be no victory. The despair and the fear were crushing.

"Run! You are afraid. You fear pain."

The demon, so dreadful, was right. Will wanted to run but there was nowhere to go. This wasn't the Void or the earth—this was different. He was part of the connection that had summoned Ba'al and there was nowhere to run. His fears escalated to such a point that he began to back away.

"This is how you fight the great Ba'al?" The demon's

voice betrayed its disappointment. "You are nothing and never defeated the great Ba'al. This you will learn." For the demon, their pathetic battle of wills was over. Ba'al bent over and swallowed Will Jern whole, taking his soul as captive and then the creature turned back to the portal.

Ba'al peered through the gate and saw the priest on his hands and knees, bleeding and moaning, it saw the bodies of Will and Talitha Jern lying full out on the concrete, unmoving. Finally, it took in Gayle Jern, who looked close to passing out, yet still clawed feebly at the hand of her daughter. The demon began sucking the life out of her and Will knew that the beast would leave her alive, but barely so, just enough to keep the gate open.

Will was utterly defeated. His will, his sense of being was only a vague memory. He saw what Ba'al wanted him to see and felt what Ba'al wanted him to feel. Right then Ba'al was happy to show him the souls of his mother and sister, Talitha. For now, the souls still resided in their respective bodies, but Will knew that Ba'al could take them at any time it pleased. The demon was connected to them, Will could feel it since in a way he was connected as well.

He could feel their life and knew a moment of jealousy, their bodies would live forever, while his had already stopped breathing and his heart was counting down its last beats. Ba'al turned away from the women and looked upon the priest, who keeled over immediately and began to twitch and kick.

Strangely, unlike the demon who was enjoying torturing the priest, Will didn't turn from the women. He had no will of his own, but he had desire and like a moth to flame, he was drawn involuntarily to the connection that he shared with Ba'al and his mother. She was alive. Very alive and warm. And alive with the Word of the Lord, the love of God. The power was in her, only she didn't seem to know it or recognize it, but Will did and he craved it and he reached out along the connection with a part of himself that wasn't in any way physical, but was all together spiritual. That part of him touched his mother's heart, releasing the word.

Love and light ignited the world of darkness in a blinding flash and now a scream of rage and pain erupted from Ba'al.

In an instant, Will blinked his eyes, amazed and overjoyed to find that the black world that he had shared with the demon was gone and that he was back in his body. He felt so good he wanted to dance and sing; only the nearness of the gate stopped him. Imbibed with sudden energy, Will leapt up and took stock of their situation. The gate still boiled away and the demon was just beyond it but it hesitated, perhaps still reeling from the shock of what had just happened. Father Vogel, a man of proven courage, but finite strength was just getting to his hands and knees, moaning and bleeding as he did and looked on the verge of collapse. Talitha lay unconscious, and next to her Gayle knelt, blearily staring about, massaging the hand that had only very recently grasped her daughters.

The broken and burned sword sat on the ground, looking ugly and forgotten. It was a bleak reminder that though Will yet lived, he had won nothing. Temptation pulled him to it; with Ba'al delaying his return to the gate this may be Will's best opportunity to destroy the hell blade. No one else seemed to have his energy or focus, but Will held himself in check. To go for the sword was the same mistake he'd made only a bare minute earlier.

"Ba'al Zubel!" This time his voice was a strong bellow and it was with a touch of sadness and a great deal of pride that he heard himself sounding like his father. "Ba'al face me, you coward." A second slipped away and then another and Will could only hope that more would slip by since Father Vogel could barely make it to his feet. "Ba'al!" he roared again.

The demon could not long ignore such a blatant challenge and it sent its mind through the gate and Will again felt his world go shadowy and black. He stared up into the dark, but the demon was nowhere to be seen.

"Ba'al?"

"You are nothing. You hide behind your mother. You are coward and weak."

Will almost jumped out of his skin, the voice, small compared to the powerful one that he had heard before, came from very near him and much lower than he expected. A grizzled creature of roughly eight foot in height stalked out of the gloom. It was thin, hard, and pitiless. Its figure looked to be made from sharp black quartz and had edges that were jaggedly cruel.

"You are small. You are weak. You are nothing." Ba'al continued on, coming closer as he spoke and Will took a step back with every word. "I have beaten you. You have never won against the great Ba'al."

The words suddenly struck Will as *affirmations* and he countered them, "I have won every time. I am not weak. I have grown stronger. It is you who are weaker than before." Despite his words, Will felt fearfully nervous and wished that the priest would hurry up and grab the sword. Foolishly, he cast a look back into his world and saw the priest moving as if wading upstream through a river of molasses. Time as always was against Will.

When he brought his distracted mind back to bear on the demon, he was shocked to see the creature flashing toward him and a split second later the demon had him by the throat. Its skin was jagged but slick like barbed and oiled marble and though Will beat on its arms it was like beating on the side of a mountain.

"You lose. You are weak. You are flesh." The demon grunted into Will's red straining face. He was starting to see flashes before his eyes and knew he was just about done and decided to change tactics. Instead of hammering on the creature's great arms, he exerted all his strength on a single one of the demon's thumbs and was able to pry it back enough to breath.

Will gulped in air and felt his energy renew, but instead of looking to attack the demon, or scramble away, he hugged the thing close. This wasn't a fight that he necessarily had to win, he just had to keep the demon occupied long enough for the priest to do his part. It wasn't easy however. The touch of the demon was dreadful. It was as if Ba'al was constructed from infinite layers of sin that had stratified over eons to create its form. Nothing Will had ever touched was more miserable.

The demon sensed the shift in its opponent's tactics and changed as well, it brought it arms together and squeezed. Air shot from Will's lungs. The demon squeezed harder. Ribs began to snap in his chest and horrifyingly Will felt something burst within him like a balloon filled with grease. He let out a garbled choking scream. The sound only lent more energy to the demon and it began to crush the life out of the man. Will didn't care as long as he held on long enough. The pressure of the demon forced his head back and he was able to watch as Father Vogel slowly raised up the hell blade. Unhurriedly, as if time had lost meaning and his death unimportant, Vogel seemed to pause with the blade held up high.

Despite the fantastic pain, a smile came to Will's lips, "You...lose."

Ba'al cranked his head around and Will was gratified to see something close to shock in its dead eyes, "No!" the beast cried out in his fell tongue and then it made to turn on the clergyman, but Will Jern hadn't lost the battle of wills yet, nor had he lost sight of his objective: delay. With renewed vigor at the proximity of his objective, he held onto Ba'al tooth and nail, until time finally drew against his opponent. Ba'al was too late.

The priest slammed the blade into the gate and literally all hell broke loose. It was as if two black holes had smashed into each other. Smoke and howling wind rent the air and the cold grew so intense that Will felt his arm's stiffening around the demon. What he took for the floor heaved and buckled, before suddenly turning fluid, becoming like a storm tossed ocean. The wild action under the two combatants, flung them apart and Will was down among the rearing shadows, but he feared for his mother and sister and was up again in a blink and threw himself on the demon's back.

Above, the room looked remarkably tranquil and he saw his mother right herself before reaching for her daughter's hand. The gate would be closed in moments.

The demon did not seem to realize. It threw Will to the rolling floor and raised his stone hard foot to crush the man.

"Look!" Will pointed and the demon turned to see Gayle closing her eyes and now they both knew that she was about to close the gate and end the connection. The floor bucked again abruptly, turning a cartwheel and suddenly Will was up standing over the prostrate demon. "I have won. Go back to your hell and know who it was that beat you...Will Jern."

The demon opened his mouth to speak, however Will demonstrated his supremacy by turning his back and commanding his spirit to return to his body.

The change was dramatic. He went from the tempest of a tornado to the open floor of an empty building in a heartbeat. Surprisingly his body still stood, just as he had left it and he wobbled slightly on his feet as his mind adjusted to the sudden calm.

After a second, the realization that they had won sunk into him and he made to shout for joy, but then he saw his mother kneeling over the still form of Talitha. "Mom?"

Gayle's tears were a warm rain on a cold body. "She wouldn't come back. I tried to bring her out, but she wouldn't come. She...she kept insisting that she was evil and not worthy of..." Gayle broke down and couldn't go on.

Despite the fact that he wasn't surprised by the news, Will felt like he had been kicked in the stomach. His legs went weak and he sat down hard. "I'll find her, don't worry. Just give me a few minutes." The strength that he had felt a few seconds earlier was gone completely and he started to get the shakes.

"Oh...oh my. This rather hurts," Father Vogel sat down next to Will grimacing and wincing. "I take it we won." The man was a disgusting bloody mess, however his wounds weren't gory, but razor thin and only a few bled still.

"Yeah...except that Tal refused to come back."

The priest nodded, commiserating, "I heard and I'm very sorry. When you go to the Void, will you need any help?"

Will was about to answer, when his mom jumped in. "You're not going." She held up a hand to silence his protest. "I...I can't risk it. Not again. You've done great, Will, but your luck is going to run out. And don't be mad, but there is no 'Good Talitha' anymore. She changed in the Void. When we were there watching what was happening, she transformed and seemed to go crazy. It was just how she was back in the hospital. I tried to bring her back around, and then...and then," Gayle paused as her chest hitched. "And then, she threw me down and she smiled this insane smile as she did, but just as the sword went into the gate, she became confused and then calm again and turned back to her normal self. She was sad and full of remorse for what she had done to me but she explained that she wasn't going to fight her evil side any longer. She told me that it had finally won and this was the last anyone would see of the 'good' Talitha."

"I don't believe that," Will said with quiet conviction.

"I didn't want to believe it either, but there was nothing good about her. She was evil to the core and so dangerous. And...and the demon Talitha has to be far worse."

Will felt a little put out over his mother's lack of faith in him. "I beat the demon before. I saved dad and escaped, didn't I?"

"Yes, you did great, but Talitha...the demon Talitha,

Ba'al Fie-ere. She has Katie and she knows you. She knows you'll be coming for her. Do you think she'll let you waltz in and take Katie? Do you think she isn't right now plotting to trap you in some fashion?"

He hadn't thought about any of that and it drained the impetus out of his zeal to find either of his sisters. "Then what do we do?" At that moment, he missed Talitha so terribly it hurt. She would've had an answer, she would know what to do.

Father Vogel spoke up in a solemn manner, "We put our faith in God."

Chapter 29

Katie

The jeep grew cold, only the girl was so keyed up that she didn't notice. She waited with her life on the line for Pedro to answer her, to come to a decision on whether or not he would save her and by extension perhaps save himself. Long seconds passed as the Mexican sat staring straight ahead and it was all the girl could do not to fidget or reach for her knife.

"Pedro, I think there's still time for you," Katie whispered. His head moved up and down in a tiny nod and for a one wild moment, jubilation rocketed through the girl's heart, but just then a knock sounded on the window next to her ear.

"Let's go, Katie."

The blonde girl started in fright and turned quick to see Amy standing next to the jeep. The witch shook her head smugly as if she had guessed all that had gone on between the two and wasn't worried in the least. She then opened the door and stood well back, like she suspected Katie of something. She had every reason to. If Amy had been any closer, Katie would have tried to gut her with the knife.

Katie paused. "Pedro?"

Amy laughed. "What? You think you can turn Pedro? His soul is every bit as black as mine. He is doomed to hell no question, but if he follows me, he'll at least have power. What can you offer him? Nothing! Sorry, but after all the sin that has stained his soul, Pedro is mine." Amy flourished the gun and stood further back. "It's time, Katie. No more dawdling, but before you get out, leave the knife on the floor."

"I...I..." Katie was practically speechless. How had she

known about the knife? Even then it sat hidden under two layers of clothes

"It's in your right sock, now take it out and drop it on the floor, or I shoot off your knee caps. You won't die but it'll hurt so bad that you will wish you had."

There was nothing for it. Katie reached down and took out the knife, but she didn't drop it. The girl brought it up for Pedro to see and when she flicked the well-oiled blade out with the easiest motion, his puff-adder eyes finally opened wide. They both knew she could have attempted to kill him at any time in the last few minutes.

"There is another option left to me, I could kill myself," Katie brought the razor sharp knife to her throat. She knew she wouldn't, there were still cards to play after all. Her brother could still rescue her, Pedro could still turn to her side, Amy could still mess up. But it was satisfying to pretend and watching Amy's eyes go very wide was worth the little charade.

"No... if you kill yourself, it's a one-way ticket to the Void and it won't save you from the demon. She'll be madder than ever and it'll be worse on you, I can guarantee that." Amy looked frantic and lowered the gun slightly in order to pacify her captive. "You don't want to do this, Katie. I mean you never know, right? Maybe your brother will show. He's quite the hero."

"Or maybe you'll mess this up, like your mom did." Katie liked the little bit of power she had. It helped calm her ragged nerves.

"Yeah, I could fuck up. It's true and then I'd be the one that the demon would be after," Amy agreed nodding her head emphatically.

With a sneer, Katie tossed the knife into the car. "You already messed up. You should've gone after another girl."

Where she had been a nervous wreck a second before, Amy's face lit in triumph. "Wrong, bitch. I haven't messed up at all. I've got this all under control. Your brother is currently driving hell bent for Phoenix. That's the wrong way, in case you didn't know, so I don't think he'll be saving you. As for me screwing this up? Fat chance! This spell is so easy, it's freaking scary. Anyone could do it—you could do it and you're a moron. And as for Pedro turning against me..."

With stunning indifference, Amy pointed the gun at the big Mexican who had just come around the jeep. His eyes grew wide for the second and last time as she pulled the trigger twice in quick succession. Pedro flopped over onto the ground, turning and twisting in agony, making a choking gurgling noise. Amy aimed the gun again, but Katie couldn't watch and turned away in horror. That third gunshot was violently loud and stayed with the young girl for a long time, pulsing and vibrating, running up and down her insides, turning her brain numb.

Even minutes later, after Amy had drawn her symbols with the Mexican's blood and pointed for Katie to lie still in the middle of them, she felt the sound of that final gun shot. It shook her soul. It made her weak. It robbed her of the will to resist and she laid there in dreadful fear, wondering if she had been wrong not to kill herself. But the sound of the gunshot was nothing compared to the words that Amy began chanting. These were not made for human mouths to utter, nor for human ears to hear.

Katie felt her soul rebelling against the sound. It grated horribly against nature and she wanted to scream and drown them out. This went on for the longest few minutes of her short life, but then abruptly, Amy stopped and as she did, she laid aside the gun. For just a fraction of a second Katie saw an opening to make a grab for it but just then, in Amy's hand, as if by magic, a silver knife materialized. It was a long curved dagger and when the witch brought it up, Katie felt her breath stop in her throat, but Amy only slashed her own palm open.

"Give me your hand." Amy commanded.

This was it.

Katie believed in heaven as fervently as she believed in hell, but all her young life, she had refused to put her faith totally in God's hands. *God helps those who help themselves*, her father was fond of saying, but just then his adage was no longer applicable. She had done everything she could think of to keep this exact moment from happening and still it had occurred. Now she would to turn to God in prayer and supplication. She would beg him for all the help he could give.

That was her intention anyway, but when Amy slit open her palm and grasped her hand so that their blood co-mingled and a connection was made, it was too late for prayer. The pain was so intense all thoughts of God or anything else for that matter flew from her mind.

Katie screamed as if her soul was being ripped from her body. It was a throat-tearing scream, but no human besides the witch was anywhere near enough to hear. And it was drowned out a moment later when the sound of a tremendous collision of metal boomed throughout the ancient barn; windows shattered and boards dropped from the ceiling. The ringing crash drove down deep into both Katie and Amy, like a summons.

Even as the last of the echoes drifted out into the barren desert, a new sound fell upon the stunned girl's ears. It was the sound of a great wind, and a rush of air swept the barn, causing it to sway alarmingly. More boards shook themselves free and more windows came crashing down. Above Katie's head, a cloud of black appeared and became the focal point of the wind; from all points the wind raced to it and the cloud sucked it in and grew at a greedy pace. Now Katie felt the avaricious pull of the wind come even into her own lungs, where there started a furious tugging at something that physically she had never felt before, but knew all the same.

Her soul began to draw from the shell of her body.

The pull was undeniable but so too was her valiant resistance, she fought with frantic desperation to hold on, yet still her soul drew out of her body, stretching out of her like diaphanous taffy. That gossamer part of her true self, governed by the hell words, began to form the gate. She became structure, warping nature to fit the needs of a command.

And the beast that dictated that command, lurked just beyond, its eagerness insuppressible, its hunger insatiable, its malice unbearable. The closeness of the fiend drove the girl near to madness and she tried to scream, but her hold on her body had become too tenuous to command. She could look down and see only the faintest sheer strands of her soul still clinging desperately, but one by one, they tore away.

Beyond, the portal was near complete.

"Yes! I have opened the gate, great Ba'al!" Amy Harris, witch of Ba'al Fie-ere screeched her victory and raised her arms in triumph, the shining metal of the knife still clutched in her hand. Her malevolent felicity ran through Katie, and became knowledge in the demon's wicked mind. Ba'al gloated in fiendish jubilation and its joy was a sickening horror. The young girl knew the feelings of both witch and demon—she had become part of a connection. She was linked to them and could sense their delight at the prospect of the gate being completed.

Their goal was seconds away from happening and Katie's mind was irresistibly drawn to watch as her soul was spun and woven into a bizarre kaleidoscope of repeating patterns centered around a circular area of utter blackness. On the whole, the construct had the semblance of a fantastically intricate spider's web. It was a wonder to behold, but all the same, it lacked perfection. Infinitesimal elements of the structure began to change, turning from a glowing milky white to a dull grey, and these would then crumble away to nothing.

When she saw that happening, it was Katie's turn to

gloat.

Only the purest souls can withstand the unrelenting decay of sin to form a permanent bridge between the world and the Void. The truth of the matter was that Katie's soul was not exactly pure. She had feared the coming of a day such as the one that she had just lived through, for eight long years. And she had prepared.

Katie was only fourteen years old, but she was no virgin.

Purposely she had sought out a boy from her neighborhood and with grim determination, rather than anything resembling romance, had compelled him to make love to her. It had not been difficult.

From that point on her soul had been just the slightest bit tainted—but it was enough. The Void was the ultimate corruptor and where there was a microscopic imperfection, it gnawed until the flaw grew. All along the edges where the gate came in contact with the Void, segments turned grey. This happened time and again, until larger sections detached and drifted into the ether before disappearing altogether. The gate was crumbling away.

The demon, sensing that its triumph was collapsing along with the gate made a wild rush to force itself through, but this only exacerbated the deterioration and sped its destruction. The gate could last only seconds longer.

Katie felt the onrushing demon and in a panic, realized that her body was exposed and empty, a perfect receptacle for the beast. If the demon beat her to it, not only would her body be possessed, her soul would be stranded in the Void. Terror filled desperation lent strength to a frenzy of clawing and scrambling and she forced her way back into her body. It was like being reborn. Katie came alive with a tingling sensation running along her skin and laid there among the blood runes and breathed the cold air and looked up through the gaping holes of the roof and saw the stars, and she rejoiced. If nothing else, she had denied the demon its gate and what's more, she had denied it her body.

"You bitch! Whore! Slut! Skank!"

Katie jumped in shock and also in fright. The voice was not that of Amy Harris. Rather it was very deep and horribly throaty, so that Katie feared that when she turned her head she would see some sort giant demonic toad.

But it was Amy, only not how she had been. It was Amy, possessed. The demon had Amy's body and wore her skin like an ill-fitting suit. Cracks and fissures, bubbling and oozing blood ran helter-skelter along her face and neck and all her exposed flesh. Her eyes had changed as well. They had gone almost completely white as if the sclera had absorbed all the color of the iris, and the pupils had transformed from their normal circular shape. They were now tall and slim and looked for all the world like a cat's eyes.

"You did this to me!" The demon croaked. The noise made Katie's throat tighten and she swallowed involuntarily. "You set me up! You knew this would happen, but did you think I would sit by and let you get away with it?" The possessed woman raised the knife with a smile. It was the most horrific smile ever. As the corner of her lips went up, her eyes seemed to roll on their sides and they went from looking like cat's eyes to like those of a goat. The effect was wholly unnatural and Katie began to back away, barely holding in a scream.

The movement made the nasty goat eyes come alive and the demon charged with inhuman speed. Katie leapt up to run, but just then, her eyes fell on the pistol that Amy had laid aside and in a flash she had it and spun, bringing it to bear.

The demon was right on top of her and before she could pull the trigger, the fiend slashed down with the knife, laying open her face in a long diagonal that went from her temple to her chin. With the demon's momentum unchecked, their bodies clashed together sending them into a mish mash of arms and legs. Pain screamed from her wound, but Katie gritted her teeth against it, fighting to clear the gun to get a shot in that would count, at the same time desperately holding back the knife. However, she was too weak and the demon sent a knee onto the arm that held the gun and pinned it to the cement. After this, it was nothing for the demon to tear its knife hand free and stab at Katie's face, looking to run the blade through the blue of her eye.

The girl twisted away and the cold edge of death sheared through hair and skin driving a long line of across the side of her head. It hurt terribly, but Katie, who had prepared for this moment for so long, ignored the pain and she ignored the fact that she was about to die and she ignored the knife as well. Her right hand held the gun and the wrist of that hand was still slightly mobile. She gave it an easy flick and the gun arced gently over her budding chest and landed neatly in her left hand. Just as the demon struck again, she fired the gun. And despite the fresh pain from cruel sharpness of the knife's edge, she fired again. And fired. And fired. And fired. And in her mind, she knew she was in race to see if she would run out of blood before she ran out of bullets.

Chapter 30

Will

A leaden depression settled over the little group.

Each was mentally exhausted and physically they exhibited the wounds and scars of their ordeal, yet bore them in silence. That is, save for the occasional groan or accidental gasp from Father Vogel.

His wounds weren't life threatening, but were egregiously painful and it was decided their first stop would be to the nearest emergency room to drop him off. Their next stop...unknown.

No one had any idea what to do or which way to turn and none could think beyond the necessity of helping the priest. Spiritually, Gayle was shattered. Her family, the most important thing to her had been destroyed over the last eight hours. Her husband was dead. Both of her daughters consigned to an eternity of hell, her daughter-in-law comatose and the fate of her only grandchild unknown.

Yet despite all of this, she was literally the only one capable of driving. Father Vogel seeped blood from every pore, and after four days of torture and hellish stress, Will staggered under the weight of an intense fatigue. He had barely the strength to lift the slim form of Talitha into the Jimmy and within minutes, as Gayle took a series of wrong turns, he slumped over onto the still breathing corpse of his sister and fell deep into a slumber.

Dreams came quick.

Most were black and cold and he knew that he was in the Void. The images there pained him physically and to escape them, he fled to the river. He knew the way and quickly the sand filled the spaces in between his toes and crunched softly as he walked. The river hadn't changed; it was placid and serene, edging by almost imperceptibly. Even the people seemed the same.

He saw the dishwashers and the ladies doing their laundry, and he even saw the fisherman casting his flies with an expert snap of his wrist. However, of Adrina, there was no sign and he didn't know whether to be glad for her or afraid. Still, he searched, going along the river for a long while, but of the gypsy there was no mention, no whisper, no knowledge.

Will did find a newcomer. She was the saddest thing and by the looks of it, she had only just discovered the horrors of the river. The girl stood with her toes in the water, staring and crying as the images unfolded before her. There seemed to be a great many.

He decided it would be best not to get too close and skirted wide around her, figuring that anyone with that much sin could only be trouble. However, her sadness was of such intensity that it was apparent even from behind; this was unusual for the river. The multitude of others along its banks only rarely saw their most horrible sins and so only rarely grew this sad. They, as a group, tried to reconcile their sins slowly, incrementally. This girl looked to be punishing herself with them.

This intrigued him and he cast a look back, not realizing what horror he would see accidentally in the river before her. It stopped him in his place. The water showed a young man, tall, muscular, and handsome with straight features and a strong jaw, he was being burned by a torch until his skin grew black and fell away.

The man screamed and then begged, crying pitifully and then screamed more. It was an obscenity, painful and terrible to see, especially for Will because he was watching his own torture. That was his face twisted ugly by pain and those were his fingers, burned down to nubs. A scream rose in his throat and he nearly turned away to run as far away as he could, but then he took in his torturer. Talitha Jern's image was plain on the water.

If anything, her misery was greater than his. Her tears were nonstop. Every scream of his, she matched and if he begged for her to stop, she begged louder for forgiveness. At intervals, she would have to stop, the torture being too much for her, but when she did, the demon, Ba'al Zubel would whip her or beat her until bloody and she would be forced to take up the torch once more.

Watching the beating she took, stayed the horror that Will felt and he was moved to pity. It broke his heart to see his sister, a girl he loved, being warped into something she wasn't. Painfully, Will realized he had a duty to perform, so he did not interfere with Talitha and stood behind and to the side and watched as torture after torture befell the illusion of himself. It was a horrid sick task and he stayed with it until the images began to repeat.

Only then did he step forward, he put his hands on her shoulders and turned her about and looked into her red and puffy eyes, "Talitha, I forgive you." She could say nothing at first. Her eyes were wide in shock, aghast that he had seen her most vile sins, nothing had been held back. Talitha tried to turn away, but by this river he was far stronger and easily and gently turned her face to his. "My darling sister, you cannot deny my forgiveness. I have seen it all and hold you blameless."

"No...these are just pictures on the water, they mean nothing. It was worse...far worse...and...and." She looked around as if she wished to run far away and there was deepest misery in her wild eyes. "And you begged me. You begged me and I wouldn't stop."

"I know, I saw and that's how you should've know that it wasn't actually me you were torturing. I would've begged you to keep going," Will replied, remembering how his own father had been angered over Will's refusal to whip him. "Every time you stopped and Ba'al hurt you...that was the only thing that truly hurt me."

Talitha listened for a moment frozen with her mouth open, but then began shaking her head. "No! I can't accept your forgiveness. I am beyond evil. I am nothing."

"I'm sorry, Tal, but you don't make the rules here. You can't deny my forgiveness."

A small flare of hope came into her eyes. It didn't last, she dashed it with painful reasoning. "Perhaps not, but there were others that I hurt, you weren't the only one."

"Yes and they were illusions as well. You tortured illusions only. Remember that."

"But it was all so real."

"I'm sure at the time it felt that way and even now it might, but you of all people know that the Void is all about deception. Look at the water now. Don't be afraid." He turned her around and faced her at the water, which had grown more still than ever and the images on it could have been real people. The water showed two people and one was easily recognizable as Will Jern, however the second person had no face. Her features were smoothed away, blank.

"My face?" Talitha reached up and touched her slim nose and traced her strong jaw and high cheekbones. Her reflection only ran its hand over the nothingness.

"That's you, Tal. You haven't forgiven yourself. You are denying your true self."

"But..."

Will became stern and rather fatherly. "No buts! The water shows that I've forgiven you. Now you have to accept it. See yourself the way I see you. Talitha Jern is a lovely, sweet, smart woman, who is beautiful, and not just on the outside, but on the inside too."

Now, her face materialized in the reflection and she gasped before falling to her knees crying and staring at herself in wonder. "Oh my Lord. Thank you, Will." He refused to reply to that, instead he smiled and watched his sister continue to touch the fine features of her face, eventually she shook her head as if seeing something new and laughed and cried at the same time. "I'm pretty."

"Finally you can admit the truth!" he said with a laugh of his own. Coming down to her level, he thought about squatting next to her, but changed his mind and plopped down letting his long legs stretch out. "After twenty-four years, finally. What's with pretty girls? I've never met one who will come right out and admit that they're pretty?"

She laughed at this and shrugged, but then a tinge of pink hit her cheeks. "Is mom angry? That I wouldn't come back with her?"

"Yeah, but I don't think it was so unexpected," Will's eyes narrowed. "Though it is a little unexpected to see you here. I thought you were supposed to be in the Void in the guise of your other self? I thought you would be all bad-ass, rampaging through hell looking to be named."

The pink of her cheeks blossomed into apple red, and she turned away. "That was the plan. I never thought that I could be forgiven for my sins so I decided to come into the Void as a conqueror, and not as a victim, but that didn't work out so well. Father Vogel was right. Without the demon in me, that evil personality which kept coming out was only fading synaptic paths, which, I'm sorry to say, I nursed and kept alive. But that wasn't the real me and when I came to the Void, I found I couldn't hurt anyone, which is very un-demon like behavior. So, I came here and tried to cross the river. Didn't get so far, did I?"

"You could go further now, there's nothing stopping you," Will suggested. In his heart, he selfishly wished that she'd not go. "Or... you could come back with me, it would make mom so happy."

Talitha sighed and shook her head. "As much as I want to, I can't go back. My body is dying. That hell blade was like pure venom, or poison. I could hold on for weeks or maybe a couple of months at the most, but eventually it'll kill me."

Will crinkled up his face into a semblance of a smile,

but his eyes were wet. "Oh, well there you go. Your choice is all set for you then. I know you'll be happy, I mean it is heaven. Who couldn't be happy there?"

"Maybe me. I don't want to go yet. I never really got a chance to live." She pulled herself up and walking away from the water, stared up into the hills. "You know what I really want? I want a do over. I want to be able to go back and do it right and have fun. I want to be... me. I never really finished finding out who I could be and what I could do."

"Why don't you ask God when you cross over? Babies are born all the time and one of them could be you, and there is no one who deserves another chance more."

Talitha shook her head and sighed. "I don't think there's any going back. And besides, I wouldn't be me without you." She came back to the beach, but didn't approach too close to the river as if she couldn't decide between the opposing forces of earth and water. For a while, she was silent and sad, and an awkwardness came between them, but then she perked up and Will could tell that she was trying to put on a happy face. "Speaking of babies, what kind of father will you be, do you think?"

The image of William Jern came to him and brought with it an equal mixture of sorrow and delight. "Like dad, I hope."

"If you are, then your baby will be very lucky." She gave him an odd shy smile. "You know, I sort of wish that I could go back as her, your little girl."

His mind strayed to an image of Lisa, lying in her long sleep and he ached deep inside. He was so afraid for her, but he didn't let it show on his face. "Why don't you? If we can wake Lisa up, I'm sure she'll be happy to have you."

"I can't, your baby's soul has been chosen already."

"It has? Oh, well there you go," he said again. The two smiled at each other and their previous happiness was tinged with melancholy. "I guess..."

A sudden thunderous shout seemed to shake the air.

WILL!

His name had been called out so loudly, with so much force that he jumped, startled and quite a bit frightened. "What was that?"

Talitha frowned. "What? What was what?"

"I just heard..."

HEY, WILL!

With eyes that had grown huge, he scanned the dull sky and the hills and all about them. "I just heard my name being called. It was so loud that you had to have heard..." he left off with the realization that he knew the voice. "It's mom, I can hear her voice. She's calling me."

Talitha smiled with thin tight lips and pain in her eyes. "I suppose that means you better go back. She probably needs you."

"But you need me too..."

"No, I'm dead, or practically so. It's people with life or... a chance at life who need you, Will." Before he could say anything else, she gave him a kiss on the cheek and then a little shove. "Go on...but you can visit me again, if you want to."

WAKE UP!

His head rang with the words, causing him to stagger. "I will, I'll come back."

Talitha smiled and then she began to fade very much how the Cheshire Cat had done, leaving her sad smile for last. All the lands of the river faded as well and in a moment, he came to, lying in the back seat of the Jimmy, slumped over the dying body of his sister. Confusion and exhaustion made him slow and dull witted, so that it was a few seconds before he realized someone was shaking him.

"Will! Hey, Will. Wake up."

"I'm awake," Will said sitting up and blinking like a wide-eyed toddler disturbed from a nap. "I'm up, what's wrong?"

Gayle was still in the process of pulling over while at

same time she leaned around from the driver's seat and shook him. "Listen."

There was nothing to hear. "What?" He was a little perturbed to have been woken from his dream of his sister. Or had it been real? One of his visions. Just then, he couldn't tell and he wasn't really in the mood to make the mental effort to try to figure it out. "I don't hear noth..."

Behind him, a small voice stopped his words. "Will?" It sounded like a child lost in the dark, one who was afraid to draw attention to herself and called out only in a tiny whisper, "Will?"

Frantically, Will tore off his seat belt and while his heart withheld its life giving beat and his lungs stayed in mid swell, he turned to look back. Lisa was lying in a ball with the dead body of his father curled protectively around her. Astonishingly she was awake. Her beautiful green eyes sparkled in the dim light looking more like emeralds than any emerald ever had.

"Will, is that you?" She peered up at him, her eyes struggling to make out his features behind all of the bruising.

Tears wanted to jump from his eyes and in vain, he tried to hold them back, but there was no stopping them, joy of that magnitude couldn't be contained. "Yes, I'm right here. I'm right here." By way of explanation for his face he added lamely, "I sort of got in a fight."

Her eyebrows came up slightly. There were a light gold in color and thin but perfectly formed in an elegant arch. "Oh." She didn't look capable of much more, overwhelming confusion appearing to be her chief emotion. Despite that fact being indisputable, in his excitement Will was unable to repress the multitude of questions that filled his mind.

"Are you all right?" he asked, as he looked her up and down, for some reason expecting to see the cause of her slumber. "What happened to you? Did it hurt? Do you think the baby is ok?" She was able to blink twice between each question and then nod vaguely to the last one. "Oh, that's great," he continued, enthusiasm had him bent over the back seat and he stroked the golden curls from her face. "How did you wake up?"

This brought her to her first moment of concentration and her mouth came open as she thought. "Your little sister did it. She was able to do something to...to Amy Harris, I think it was."

"Talitha? What did she do? Was she in the Void or in..."

"No not Talitha. It was Katie. And..." More confusion had her blinking slowly as her mind tried to focus after her long ordeal, "And she had a message or wanted me to tell you something. We had a connection for a little while."

The air was suddenly gone from Will's lungs and no longer could he feel his body. He was completely numb from the neck down. His mouth went dry as well and he was only just able to spit out, "Is Katie, ok?" Lisa shook her head and Will couldn't tell whether it meant that Katie wasn't ok or that Lisa was still bewildered. "Can you at least tell me what she said?" he tried.

"Katie wants to know if you can give her a ride home."

Epilogue

"You're having a contraction." Will said in a tired voice.

"Oh really? I didn't know," Lisa's face was very white and was lined with a grimace of pain. Her mass of blonde curls sat tied up in a great blob atop her head and she wore a garishly flowered gown, which was in need of changing, the flowers looking ready to wilt right off of it.

She breathed in and out quickly, but nothing like how they had been taught in their lamaz classes. Many hours ago, Will had given up trying to remind her of the proper technique, it only caused her to glare at him. The contraction was brief and when it was over, Lisa picked up the magazine that sat in her lap. The cover, a glossy picture of some young starlet shown out at the world, smiling because her life was perfect. Lisa gave it a dull look and dropped it again.

"Would you like some ice?" Will asked as the dutiful and doting husband.

"No thank you," she sighed, bored. "Remember back when we were excited to have this baby?"

Will couldn't think that far back. "No."

"Me too. Uhg! Who ever heard of labor lasting so stinking long? Twenty-eight hours...maybe she's stuck, got turned around or something."

"She's probably..." Will became temporarily immobilized by tremendous yawn, "...she's probably going for the world record."

Lisa gave him a half smile, the most effort she could make and looked around the room with eyes that were vibrant in color. They were bloodshot from lack of sleep and the green stood out, and as always, they were her best feature. "How long is the record?"

"Nineteen months, it was set by a Tibetan monk, who ate nothing but moss the whole time."

"I thought monks were all men."

Will nodded. "Yeah, they're weird in China." An exhausted silence followed this; their conversations were getting shorter as the hours progressed. After a time, he found himself watching the line of paper spilling from one of the machines. There was little else to do and after thirty seconds or so, the running blue line on the paper edged upwards. Next to him, Lisa gasped.

"You're having another contraction, dear," he said in a pleasant helpful conversational tone.

"Thank God you're here to tell me these things," Lisa replied in between gritted teeth.

Feeling useless, Will could only watch as his wife panted and then grimaced and then panted some more. Gradually she began to calm. "Was that a big one? Did she come out a little?" he asked and then tried to peek beneath the sweat-dampened sheet, but Lisa held it down.

"Stop being a naughty boy," she glared, yet wasn't at all angry. "Oh, my, I'm so tired. At this rate, I'm going to be too tired to push when it's time. The baby is going to have to crawl out."

"This is taking so long, she's probably going to be able to walk out." He gave her a smile and felt grit in his eyes. "Speaking of walking, do you mind if I..." He nodded at the door.

"Sure, go check on your sister, but if she has her baby first, I'm disowning the lot of you."

He left her with a kiss, and stepped out into the hallway, where soft pastels ruled. They were at the very end of the Labor and Delivery ward and the area had been purposely left secluded. Father Vogel, who was supposed to be surreptitiously regulating who had access to the rooms, was instead sleeping uncomfortably in a very stiff chair. Will couldn't blame him a bit.

Stepping as lightly as his big frame would permit, Will eased by the priest and slipped into his sister's room. "Hey, how're the contractions coming along?" he asked Katie. In spite of her fatigue, the blonde sat pertly on the side of the bed, she gave her brother a shrug.

"They're picking up steam, it'll be soon," Katie yawned and stretched. As she turned her neck at different angles to work out the kinks, a wide scar, low down on the left side became visible, Will turned away and looked at a picture of some unknown baby dressed as a bug. His little sister was self-conscious of her scars and didn't care for people staring and he was the worst when it came to that.

The scars always brought back images of her lying in a great pool of blood shoving her fingers into the wound to keep from bleeding out. With the death of Amy, all of her spells had come unraveled and he had *seen* his sister, she had needed far more than just a ride home and had been within an ace of needing a ride to the morgue instead.

Thankfully, the demon-possessed witch had attacked her with the fancy ceremonial dagger instead of a normal knife. On her third strike, she had sent the curved blade into Katie's neck with such force that it passed all the way through and snapped in half against the cement beneath. After that, the blonde had received only nasty defensive wounds on her right arm and had succeeded in placing a number of bullets through the demon's heart and lungs, as well as the coup de gras that went out the top of her head creating a horrid fountain of blood and brains.

Will blinked away the image. "Where's mom?"

"Just getting more coffee, only she's doing it at record speed. She's so funny. She acts like she's the first grandmother on earth and doesn't want to miss anything." Katie smiled her bi-polar smile and Will saw it; she had turned too late. Normally, she only presented her right side to people, especially when smiling. That side had a dimple. The other side, her left, had a long wicked scar that became especially pronounced and sinister when she smiled.

As always, Will pretended not to notice. "I don't blame her, she's had a rough time of it. So, how's the baby?"

"Kicking like crazy, she definitely wants out. Here, you want to feel?" Katie hopped down from the bed with the easy grace of youth. Will advanced, but was slow to touch, he gave Katie a sheepish look. She forgot herself again and smiled without hesitation or turning. "Just touch the outside of the sheet. That's what I do. All that other stuff, I don't even look at."

"That's probably best," Will touched the small swell of his sister's belly and as if the baby was waiting for just that, it jumped and kicked.

"See, just don't think about it and it's like a normal mom and baby," Katie said, going through a series of stretches. To Will, she looked to have grown another inch and stood tall and athletically slim.

The baby kicked again and he turned from his little sister and stared down at what was left of the body beneath the sheet—what once had been Talitha Jern. There wasn't much left to her now, the venom driven necrosis of the hell blade had taken her extremities and much of her skin. She no longer had a face and her organs were pared down to a minimum, and even these wouldn't last another day, but her womb was an untouchable vault. It was there that she was giving herself her second chance, her do over.

Bishop Keenan had wanted to call the virgin birth a miracle. When Will mentioned this to Talitha she had bored him silly with a long-winded lecture on the wonders inherent to binary fission, mitosis, and cellular division in general. Will hadn't bother to follow along. All he knew was that instead of one baby, he would be having two and he couldn't be happier. And besides, he didn't need a bishop to pronounce the upcoming birth miraculous.

Talitha had never considered herself blessed, yet to him, she was a straight up miracle. No one had ever gone through what she had and no one ever could, at least not with so much courage. Had it been him, Will would never have made the choice to come back for a second shot at life, not after all she had gone through. He would've dashed across that river at the first opportunity.

But not her. Two months before, just after she had told him of her decision to come back, he had asked her if she was certain that it was a good idea. They were standing by the river and she turned her heavy gaze upon him and she knew what he meant.

"Yes, it's imperative that I go back. Otherwise for me heaven at best would be just a refuge from the possibility of danger, and at worst, it would become a prison. Don't you see? I would be prisoner of heaven and the walls of that prison would be made up of all my fears. That's not what heaven is about. I can see that now."

She had a way with logic, but in his heart, he still worried for her. "There's so much that could go wrong...even in a normal life. You could get married too young or end up with the wrong man or no man at all. You could get in a car accident and be paralyzed—your driving is atrocious, and we both know it. You follow so closely that you could..."

She stayed his increasingly strident worries. "You sound like a dad. In point of fact you sound like someone who could be my dad. I'll need one, you know. I've decided to start completely over and I'll have no memory of any of this. I'll be a baby like any other."

"And you want me to be your father?"

"I know you love me. I know that you'll lay down your life for mine. I know you'll stay up worrying when I'm out late and I know you'll ground me when I do. And I know you'll be the first to tell me when I'm messing up." They grinned at each other over the truth of that. "And I know that I love you and respect you and I always thought that you'd be great dad to your baby. You could be a great dad to me too."

"Will I get to spank you?" he asked thinking to make a joke. "Wait...that's too weird. How bout we have Lisa be in charge of spankings? Deal?"

"Deal."
The End

*

Author's Note

Thank you for reading The Trilogy of the Void. My goal when writing these books was not only to thrill and entertain my readers, but also to explore the possible nature of hell and purgatory(heaven being somewhat self-explanatory, I saw no need to go down that road). I tried to portray the two alternatives to heaven from the point of having a fully good and just God, one who does not create evil but allows it to exist only as an unfortunate side effect of free will.

If you enjoyed this series may I suggest *A Perfect America* and *The Sacrificial Daughter*. Both of these are not only compelling stories, they are also vehicles for delving into philosophical paradigms that most of us take for granted.

Finally, on a self-serving note, the review is the most practical and inexpensive form of advertisement an independent author has available in order to get his work known. If you could put a kind review on Amazon and your Facebook page, I would greatly appreciate it.

Peter Meredith

Fictional works by Peter Meredith:

A Perfect America
The Sacrificial Daughter
The Horror of the Shade Trilogy of the Void 1
An Illusion of Hell Trilogy of the Void 2
Hell Blade Trilogy of the Void 3
The Punished
Sprite
The Feylands: A Hidden Lands Novel
The Sun King: A Hidden Lands Novel
The Sun Queen: A Hidden Lands Novel
The Apocalypse: The Undead World Novel 1
The Apocalypse Survivors: The Undead World Novel 2
The Apocalypse Outcasts: The Undead World Novel 3
The Apocalypse Fugitives: The Undead World Novel 4
Pen(Novella)
A Sliver of Perfection (Novella)
The Haunting At Red Feathers(Short Story)
The Haunting On Colonel's Row(Short Story)
The Drawer(Short Story)
The Eyes in the Storm(Short Story)

www.ingramcontent.com/pod-product-compliance
Lightning Source LLC
Chambersburg PA
CBHW071219250626
47163CB00001B/43

* 9 7 8 0 9 8 3 7 0 7 2 9 5 *